Sha
competition by describing her ideal date: being flown
to an exotic island by a gorgeous ~~~~ ~~~~ ~~ful man
Little did she realise that she'd just wande ~~~~ ~~
dream job! Today she writes for Mills & Boon, and
her books feature often stubborn but always to-die-for
heroes and the women who bring them to their knees.
She believes that the best books are those you never
want to end. Just like life…

Melanie Milburne read her first Mills & Boon novel
at the age of seventeen, in between studying for her
final exams. After completing a master's degree in
education she decided to write a novel, and thus her
career as a romance author was born. Melanie is an
ambassador for the Australian Childhood Foundation
and a keen dog-lover and trainer. She enjoys long
walks in the Tasmanian bush. In 2015 Melanie won
the HOLT Medallion, a prestigious award honouring
outstanding literary talent.

INNOCENT MAID FOR THE GREEK

SHARON KENDRICK

FORBIDDEN UNTIL THEIR SNOWBOUND NIGHT

MELANIE MILBURNE

MILLS & BOON

First published in Great Britain 2023
by Mills & Boon, an imprint of HarperCollins*Publishers* Ltd,
1 London Bridge Street, London, SE1 9GF

www.harpercollins.co.uk

HarperCollins*Publishers*
Macken House, 39/40 Mayor Street Upper,
Dublin 1, D01 C9W8, Ireland

Innocent Maid for the Greek © 2023 Sharon Kendrick

Forbidden Until Their Snowbound Night © 2023 Melanie Milburne

ISBN: 978-0-263-30660-6

01/23

MIX
Paper | Supporting
responsible forestry
FSC™ C007454

This book is produced from independently certified FSC™ paper
to ensure responsible forest management.
For more information visit: www.harpercollins.co.uk/green.

Printed and Bound in Spain using 100% Renewable Electricity
at CPI Black Print, Barcelona

INNOCENT MAID
FOR THE GREEK

SHARON KENDRICK

MILLS & BOON

For my darling friend Professor Richard Shannon, aka Dick (though I only ever knew him as Blaine, a name we concocted on our first meeting, on discovering we shared a birthday). We enjoyed many lunches over the years, meticulously splitting the bill (he did rather better out of it than I!). He tried to teach me historical facts which I promptly forgot (though never the origin of the colour magenta).

He is sorely missed, but always, always remembered.

CHAPTER ONE

SHE'D ONLY RECENTLY SHOWERED, but already another bead of sweat was sliding down between Mia's breasts.

If only it weren't so unbearably *hot*.

Fanning her hand in front of her face, she peered out of the window. The sky was heavy. Thick grey clouds were tinged with a sickly sulphuric yellow and she could hear the ominous growl of thunder in the distance. Definitely not the sort of weather you associated with an English spring day.

Sometimes she thought about Greece. The scent of lemon blossom and pine. Golden sun and the sea and sky so blue. But she never thought about it for long because why would you do something which actively caused you heartache?

A sudden knock on the door made her jump because she wasn't expecting anyone and that was deliberate. She kept her tiny one-room home as a haven—sometimes it even felt like an escape. Her job was sociable enough, but outside work and her animal volunteering she kept herself to herself. She knew people thought she was a loner. A bit of a frump, even. Let them. She did what she did because that was how she coped—with her life, with the past, and with the memories which stubbornly refused to leave the edges of her mind.

The knock sounded again and although it was tempting to ignore it, her conscience wouldn't let her. It might be an emergency involving one of the other hotel staff and she—sensible and reliable Mia, in her newly promoted position—would know exactly how to deal with it.

But her smile froze as she pulled open the door and saw who was standing there, dominating every atom of the space which surrounded him just as he'd always done, his powerful frame making the institutional background of the staff corridor look even more unexciting than usual.

His expensive grey suit did nothing to disguise the strength of the muscular body which rippled beneath. His face was all hard, slashing lines and high cheekbones. His skin had the burnished hue of deep gold, while his eyes gleamed like polished jet. It was easy to understand why people used to say he resembled an ancient Greek god, because he did.

Her husband.

How strange it was to acknowledge those words—because he was her husband in name only. Well, not even that—not any more—for she always used her maiden name. She wanted nothing of his.

Theodoros Aeton.

The man she had loved so badly, until he had

betrayed her and smashed her heart into tiny little pieces.

Clutching the doorhandle, she felt a wave of dizziness wash over her. And she felt other things, too. Unwanted emotions which had started bubbling up inside her, like random ingredients dropped into a witch's cauldron. Hurt and anger and resentment. And desire, of course. Always desire. She wasn't naïve enough to deny *that*.

It was a face she hadn't seen in six years. Not since the evening of their wedding when her world had imploded. She'd been wearing a slippery white gown, which had done her abundant curves no favours—but she had bowed to her mother's superior knowledge about all things fashionable.

Mia remembered the frilly blue garter and the white silk stockings which had been digging uncomfortably into her thighs, but she hadn't cared about the discomfort. She had just been eager for the moment when Theo would slowly remove them with his teeth, as he had promised he would do in a throaty murmur just the night before. Along with all the other things he had promised, too. In retrospect, his words had been nothing but manipulative, but at the time she had lapped them up like a thirsty kitten—naïve and oh, so gullible.

She wanted to shut the door on him, but that would be the behaviour of someone cowardly and immature. And she wasn't either of these things. Not any more. She'd grown up. She was making her own way in the world, without any help or assistance from anyone. Certainly not from Theo Aeton.

Even so, she wished she weren't wearing an old pair of jeans and a T-shirt which could have done with an iron. She wished she were ten pounds lighter. She wished all kinds of things, but since none of them were likely to materialise in the next few minutes, it was better she got this over and done with. And wasn't the reality that she'd been expecting some kind of contact from Theo for a long time, even if she hadn't allowed herself to think about it? Some sort of closure. A request for a long-overdue divorce most probably, in order to allow him to move on. And if the thought of that produced a twist of pain then *more fool her*.

His name sprang from her lips, sounding unfamiliar, yet somehow shockingly familiar. 'Theo!'

'Mia,' he responded, his husky Greek accent sliding over the syllables, which had the unfortunate effect of making her think about his tongue.

She tried to pull her incoherent thoughts into some sort of order but that was a big ask, when she couldn't seem to dislodge the memory of that tongue inside her mouth and on her neck and… With a supreme effort, she pulled herself together. 'Well, well, well. This is a surprise,' she said brightly. 'I must say you were the last person I expected to see when I knocked off work earlier today.'

'But here I am,' he prompted softly.

'Yes, here you are,' she echoed, her heart pounding wildly.

She peered at him more closely and suddenly she could see the change in him. He looked different. Almost...dangerous. His ravishingly handsome features seemed to have been coated in a layer of dark ice, which had the effect of making him seem cool. Formidable. Even *cruel*...

'Aren't you going to invite me in?' His voice was mocking. 'Or are you so blown away by seeing me again that you can't think straight?'

Irritated by his totally accurate assessment of her mood, Mia glared before opening the door a little wider, reluctance written in her every gesture. 'That's not how I would have described it, Theo, but since you've come all this way, I suppose you'd better come in.'

But quickly, she moved as far away as she could, not wanting to be close to him.

And you're a liar. You want to be close to him. You want him to pull you against that hard body and kiss all the breath out of your lungs. You want to remember how it feels to be in his arms. To remember how he made you feel as if *this* was the reason you were put here on this earth.

Stop it, she urged herself fiercely as she regarded him with a veneer of polite curiosity. 'Why didn't you give me some sort of warning you were coming, Theo? Why just turn up out of the blue?'

Shutting the door behind him, Theodoros Aeton took a moment before he answered, and not just because he was a man who always chose his words carefully. He was grappling with an uncharacteristic feeling of confusion. A sense of being taken off-guard because—infuriatingly—his reaction to her had taken him by surprise. He had expected to feel nothing when he saw her again. He had *wanted* to feel nothing—because a man who allowed himself to feel ran the risk of making himself vulnerable and hadn't he done that once before—with her?

His mouth twisted, because he *did* feel something. There was a residual anger, which mostly he kept buried away deep inside him, but there was bitterness, too. As bitter as the hyacinth bulbs which many of his native countrymen still ate, surprisingly for pleasure. Because this was the woman who had crushed his dreams. Whose words had reinforced what he'd always really known about himself and made him realise the only thing he could rely on was his innate streak of cynicism. It was that hard-wired cynicism he reached for now as he studied her, curious to see how much she had changed.

Physically, she didn't look so very different. Her shape was as voluptuous as ever, the curve of her hips and breasts still sending out a siren call to his senses. Small of stature, she was nothing like her lofty English supermodel mother—the thick chestnut hair was the only thing she seemed to have inherited from her. But her mother's hair had been sleek and coppery, and Mia's was a chaotic head of curls, currently scrunched up on top of her head with damp tendrils dangling down beside her flushed cheeks. Her proud features hinted at her Greek heritage—as did the jet-dark lashes which framed her slanting blue eyes and golden-olive skin. He didn't approve of her old jeans and crumpled T-shirt, but surely her lack of effort with her appearance implied she wasn't expecting someone else. Some faceless man he would have been forced to eject, by whatever means he considered appropriate. Theo's mouth hardened. He didn't know why that should give him a brief sense of pleasure, only that it did.

His gaze flickered around the cramped dimensions of the room. What *was* remarkably different were her circumstances. He glanced at the narrow bed, the utilitarian wardrobe and the small plywood locker which reminded him of a hospital. Who would ever have imagined that Mia would end up living in a cramped room which overlooked a fire escape?

'I gave you no prior warning because I have always enjoyed the element of surprise,' he said, with a hard smile—and that was the truth. Hadn't he wondered what her instinctive reaction on seeing him again would be? Had he imagined her features might soften with signs of longing, or regret? But there had been nothing like that. Just wariness and a thinly veiled hostility which—bizarrely—pleased him. It reinforced his certainty of how ill-judged their liaison had been and the sooner he was properly free of her, the better.

'Well, you've achieved what you came for. I am *very* surprised,' she said, before adding curiously, 'Tell me, how did you find me?'

The cheap T-shirt clung to her breasts, and Theo felt his throat grow dry as his attention was unwillingly caught by their generous thrust. Breasts which were taunting him, reminding him that he'd placed her on that damned pedestal, insisting on telling her they wouldn't have full sex until she was his wife. He felt a stab of irritation as he recalled his foolish idealism. Why hadn't he just taken her to bed when he'd had the chance? All those times she had pressed against him and whimpered with raw desire—why had he insisted on doing the *decent thing*? 'The acquisition of information is never difficult for a man like me,' he informed her coolly. 'I paid for someone to discover your whereabouts.'

'Gosh! A private investigator, no less!' Her eyebrows shot up and disappeared into the mass of coppery curls. 'Am I supposed to be impressed?'

He shrugged. 'Why not? You're only human,' he mocked, but then reminded himself of the reason behind his visit and his voice softened. 'You need to come back to Greece, Mia. Your grandfather is sick.'

He saw her lips crumple. Saw the darkness which invaded those wide blue eyes, which were the colour of the Aegean on a bright spring day.

'How sick?' she whispered.

'What do you want me to say? That a man of almost eighty is bouncing around like a boxer? You might know something of his state of health if only you had bothered to keep in touch with him!'

'It isn't as simple as that,' she protested. 'You must know that, Theo. He cut me out of his life and said he never wanted to see me again! And every time I've tried to contact him, I have been rebuffed.'

'He was a proud man. Running away on your wedding night caused a scandal in the local neighbourhood. And you know how he felt about scandals.'

She bit her lip. 'I don't want to talk about that night.'

'Well, that's good because neither do I.' Theo felt his jaw tighten and his muscles grow tense as he reminded himself he wasn't here because of the past, because that was over and done with. He was just doing a favour for an old man who didn't realise he needed one. A man to whom he owed everything. And if that meant having to see a woman whose memory he would rather have erased from his mind, then so be it. He could cope with that. With her. She was just somebody he used to know. 'You need to see him,' he reiterated. 'And soon.'

'Is he…dying?' The gaze she turned on him was so wretched that Theo could do nothing about the answering clench of his heart, and silently he cursed her for that, too.

'Yes, he is dying,' he said, his voice brittle. 'He is no longer the man he once was—with the heart of a lion and the body of an ox. Age has caught up on him, as it catches up on us all.' He saw the tell-tale glimmer of tears in her sea-blue eyes. 'You will be shocked when you see him again, Mia.'

She nodded. 'And did he…did he ask for me?'

There was a heartbeat of a pause before he answered, and Theo wondered how she would react if he told her the truth. But ultimately, she would thank him for his intervention because wasn't he giving her the chance to so something which had never been afforded to him? His mouth clenched. 'He needs to see you.' He glanced around the room. 'How quickly can you pack?'

His peremptory question reminded Mia how different their worlds were. They always had been—she just hadn't been able to see it at the time. Or maybe she hadn't wanted to. She had believed herself in love with him and, inevitably, that had distorted the way she'd viewed the world.

Since their split, she had stopped herself from stalking him on the Internet because that way lay madness, but she'd found a financial newspaper lying in one of the hotel bedrooms when she'd been cleaning it, and her attention had been captured by the brooding good looks of her estranged husband. Her eyes had quickly skimmed the text and she'd discovered how successful he was. A hedge-fund manager apparently—whatever *that* meant—though judging from his many assets she'd concluded that such a job was highly rewarded financially.

But even if she hadn't known how rich he was, she could tell just by looking at him. A sense of power radiated from him, in a way which was almost tangible. And hadn't he done it all off *her* back? She wondered if he felt a glimmer of shame for his actions, but she wasn't going to bring that up now. It would make it look as if she cared, and she didn't.

'I can't just get up and go to Greece,' she objected. 'I have a job. I work at the Granchester hotel.' She gestured around the small room. 'I live in their staff accommodation.'

'*Neh*, I know. My investigator didn't have to do very much to discover *that*.'

Mia wondered what else his investigator had uncovered. That she lived a simple, almost nun-like existence? That her horizons and ambitions were modest when compared to the high-octane world he undoubtedly inhabited? Had he been surprised when he'd discovered how humble her life had become—or just relieved that he hadn't been forced to endure their farce of a marriage?

She heard another growl of thunder and ran her finger along the neckline of her sticky T-shirt. 'Then you will also know that people rely on me—'

'I'm sure they do,' he interrupted silkily. 'But nobody is indispensable, Mia. Not even you. Tell the hotel you need compassionate leave.' He shrugged. 'If you think it's worth it.'

His words were a challenge and she thought how, in the past, she would have surrendered to his stronger will and been happy to do so—because Theo was a man who seemed to have all the answers, while she had doubted herself all the time. But she wasn't that person any more. She was no longer prepared to accept things on face value, or to always trust somebody else's judgement above her own.

She thought of her grandfather, whose home had always provided a bright oasis during the few weeks of the school holidays when she'd been permitted to visit him. The man she had adored, despite the vitriol poured into her ear about him by her mother. But he had cut her out of his life as ruthlessly as if she had been a tumour he wanted to excise. She had been disbelieving and hurt—yet part of her had wondered if maybe it was all for the best. At least she didn't have to go back to Greece and see him, and run the risk of bumping into the man she had married.

It had taken a long time for her to realise how much she had missed her grandfather and how much she regretted the rift which had formed between them. No matter what had happened she still loved him—didn't she? Because love, she had discovered, was a remarkably difficult thing to kill off. It clung to the human heart like a baby chimp to its mama. And hadn't one of the lasting regrets of her laughably brief marriage been the rupture in her relationship with him? If he was sick and asking for her, then she needed to go to him.

'Of course I'll come. I'll do whatever it takes,' she said. 'I'll speak to my line manager and arrange a leave of absence, and as soon as I can arrange a ticket, I'll fly out to Athens.'

'*Ochi.*' He flicked his fingers through the air as if disposing of a troublesome fly. 'You need not concern yourself with transport, Mia. My plane will be at your disposal.'

'Your *plane*?' All attempts at neutrality forgotten, Mia couldn't keep the disbelief from her voice, finding it hard to reconcile such an obvious symbol of wealth with a man who had first come to the attention of her grandfather when he'd been caught stealing eggs. But even as she said it, she met the glint of something cold and hard in the depths of his black eyes.

'It is something of a transformation, *neh*?' he suggested silkily. 'Or do you still think of me as a man who steals all that comes before him, *zouzouri mou*?'

'I don't think about you at all,' she said quickly, walking forward to open the window a little wider, as if that would have some kind of magical impact on the stifling atmosphere within the small room.

But the air remained as motionless as before—and all Mia could think of was the way he had tapped so accurately into her thoughts. Which was disturbing. It reminded her of how well Theodoros Aeton had once known her, because she had opened herself up to him in that dumb and trusting way. And she didn't want anyone *knowing* her or having the potential to hurt her. She had become used to her new life and single status. Sometimes it got lonely, but it never got painful. She'd found that animals could love you far better than humans ever could. And wasn't life easier that way? 'I would prefer to travel independently,' she said proudly.

His smile was hard. Almost…wolfish. And annoyingly, it made a ripple of awareness shimmer down the length of her sweat-sheened spine.

'I'm sure you would,' he said. 'But unless you have unlimited time at your disposal, I suggest you accept my offer of a flight and accommodation.'

'Accommodation?' She looked at him blankly.

'You mean, stay with…*you*? I think I'd rather stay with my grandfather.'

He shook his head. 'His house is no place for visitors,' he informed her obliquely. 'And I don't live so far from him.'

Mia swallowed. No, of course he didn't. The two men had often seemed joined at the hip. Sometimes she'd genuinely thought her grandfather preferred the young man he had mentored to his own flesh and blood—*her*. Or maybe that wasn't such a crazy idea. After all, Theo had been an unwanted orphan—a clean slate to write on—while she had always been weighted down by her tainted legacy. The daughter of the son who had disappointed him and the narcissistic woman he should never have married. That she had been an innocent child in a toxic marriage seemed to make no difference to her grandfather. It had taken Mia a long time to realise that she'd never been seen as a person in her own right—just someone who represented the sins of her parents.

But Theo's black gaze was lasering into her and she couldn't seem to shift the erotic images which were suddenly crowding into her head. 'You must be out of your mind,' she breathed, 'if you think I'd ever contemplate staying with *you*.'

'What's your objection? Surely you don't think I will try to persuade you to consummate our marriage, Mia?' His words were a taunt which matched the mirthless quality of his smile. 'I would have thought my track record on sexual restraint speaks for itself.'

Mia could feel the sudden pounding of her heart. 'How can you be so *hateful*?'

'Is it hateful to confront reality?' he challenged. 'I don't think so. And besides, your worries are unnecessary. I live on a property big enough to ensure we need never see one another, unless we choose to.'

'Which is never going to happen!'

His black eyes glittered. 'The alternative is that you find some overheated room in Athens and be forced to rely on taxis to ferry you to and from your grandfather's—a total waste of time and money, which you don't seem to have in any abundance. At least, judging by appearances.' His dark gaze raked around the cramped room as if to add veracity to his words, before shooting an impatient glance at the watch which gleamed gold against his hair-roughened wrist. 'So which is it to be, Mia? I am due at a meeting in precisely forty minutes and have neither the time nor the inclination to hang around here. You have my offer—take it or leave it.'

By the sides of her ancient jeans, Mia curled her fingers into fists, her short, neatly filed nails digging into the palms of her hands.

She ought to hate him. She *did* hate him.

If only her stupid body would stop reacting to him in this debilitating way. Her poor, starving body which had been promised so much pleasure by this man, only to have it snatched away at the eleventh hour.

Theo Aeton's virgin bride had remained a virgin and she'd convinced herself she didn't care.

But it seemed she had been wrong.

Because without doing anything, he had reignited the slow burn of desire, making her realise what she'd been missing during all these long, bleak years. Other men left her cold, but Theo had always been able to make her indecently hot. Was he aware that beneath her creased T-shirt her nipples were becoming hard? Quickly, she crossed her arms over her chest, as the pebbled nubs pressed painfully against the thin cotton. Surely she shouldn't even be *thinking* about such things, when her grandfather was so sick?

But although she was still a virgin, she recognised the importance of sex and, in many ways, the high price tag it carried. And she had few illusions left. In some social circles ancient values prevailed and marriage was still used as a bartering tool. Which was exactly what had happened to her. You could have a mobile phone and a car, you could wear a miniskirt with glittery trainers and walk into a restaurant on your own and nobody would bat an eyelid. But underneath that modern guise, her circumstances had been positively *medieval*. She had been sold by her grandfather to the man in front of her. Traded for a valuable piece of land. A ripe, innocent body exchanged for a metaphorical sack of gold. And nobody had told her about it until it was too late.

Yet things had changed. She was no longer the same naïve woman who had allowed raw teenage emotions to blind her to the truth. She was no longer grateful, or needy, or searching for love in all the wrong places. She would do what she needed to do.

The right thing. She wouldn't make a scene, or stubbornly insist on renting some scrubby place miles away from her grandfather's exclusive residence. She would act with pride and dignity as she accepted Theo's offer and visited her aged relative. But she would keep her distance from the man whose wedding ring she had flung deep into the waters of the Ionian sea and watched as it sank without trace. That was the most important thing of all. She must stay away from the Greek billionaire and all the temptation he represented.

'In that case, thank you. I'll speak to my supervisor as soon as you've gone.' Pointedly, she angled her gaze towards the door. 'And find out how soon I can leave.'

He pulled out a small business card and pen from his jacket and she watched as he scrawled something on the back of the card. And suddenly Mia found herself recalling that he hadn't even been able to write his own name until he was fourteen. Who could possibly reconcile that illiterate teenager with this towering man, in his handmade suit and the golden pen which moved so fluidly across the expensive piece of card?

'Let me know when you're able to travel. My office will make all the necessary arrangements. I'll see you on the plane. That's my private number,' he informed her abruptly, as if that were important.

She didn't know what made her say it. A fishing expedition, perhaps? An attempt to discover if there was anyone on the scene and prepare herself for the possibility of a lover's presence on his Greek estate? 'I suppose there are women who would pay a fortune to get their hands on this?'

There was a heartbeat of a pause. 'You'd be surprised,' he said silkily, 'how persistent women can be.'

And Mia knew she had nobody to blame but herself for the shaft of jealousy which stabbed through her.

What were you expecting him to say? That no woman has ever come close to you—the dumpy bride he couldn't even bear to have sex with?

She took the card from him. The brush of his fingers against her own was barely perceptible, yet it was like being touched with fire. Mia could feel the base of her stomach liquefying as memories came flooding back to haunt her with cruel and sensual clarity.

Theo, stripped to the waist and chopping logs, with sweat glittering on his skin like diamonds as he swung an axe through the air.

Theo's fingers straying beneath the lace of her bra, kneading the pliant flesh of her breasts until she was moaning with pleasure.

And Theo kissing her passionately in the moonlight, holding her tightly and telling her he would always respect her.

But those words had been worthless. Each one crumbling to dust as they fell from his lips.

She found out later there had been women before her. Women he had bedded with impunity, unlike her. It had been *her* he had tantalised and teased—leaving her so aching for him that she couldn't think straight. She'd realised afterwards that he must have done it to control her—to make her understand who was in charge. And it had worked, hadn't it? Oh, yes—it had worked, all right.

She needed to be careful.

More than careful.

So she gave the kind of smile she might have bestowed on a nervous new chambermaid on her first day at the Granchester hotel. Friendly yet impartial. As if her pulse weren't thudding erratically at her temple. As if her stomach weren't tying itself up in knots. 'I appreciate you coming here to tell me this—and for offering to help me—but I really need to get changed now.'

'You're going out?' he demanded.

'Yes.'

'With a man?'

Mia wondered how he would react if she confessed that the only person who was longing to see her was Rusty at the dog rescue centre—the ugly little mongrel with the over-long tail. 'That's really none of your business, is it?' she questioned politely.

'Better make sure you take an umbrella.' He directed a glance towards the window, his voice dipping with silky emphasis as he glittered his dark gaze back towards her. 'I'd hate to think of you getting *wet*.'

Mia flushed at the sexual implication, grateful when he turned away, hopefully without noticing her response. As the door closed behind him she could hear his footsteps retreating down the corridor, when suddenly the room was lit by a bright flash of lightning and the sound of thunder crashed through the air.

With sweat still trickling between her breasts, Mia stared out of the window as the long-awaited storm broke.

CHAPTER TWO

THEO TAPPED HIS fingers impatiently against the gleam of his desk as he stared out at the dark sapphire gleam of the Aegean Sea. But for once, he didn't register the dazzling view from the windows of his home office, or the glory of the private beach which lay beyond it. Uncharacteristically, he found himself unable to concentrate on the complex financial negotiations which usually consumed him and which had made him one of the most successful hedge-fund managers on the planet. All he could think about was Mia and the fact that she was due to arrive at any moment.

He wasn't interested in the voicemail message left by a foxy Swedish politician he'd met last month, who'd made it very clear he was her kind of man. Up until a couple of days ago, he had been intending to slot her into his diary—a long weekend in Stockholm or Paris, maybe—though the venue was irrelevant since he doubted they would leave the bedroom. But today such a liaison was the last thing on his mind.

Today, his heart was thudding, his body aching in a way which felt breathtakingly new, yet which haunted the periphery of his senses like the memory of something sweet and mostly forgotten. A pulse began to pound at his temple, because seeing his estranged wife in the flesh a couple of days ago had made him unable to think about anything but her.

His mouth hardened. He had been expecting his duty visit to Mia to give him a sense of closure. Having almost entirely eradicated her from his thoughts, he had imagined his desire for her would have withered when he saw her again, like unpicked grapes on the vine. He tightened his fists and his knuckles cracked, a ghostly white through the olive-darkness of his skin. Because this was a woman who represented his youthful folly and greatest mistake. Whose cruel words on their wedding night had been chosen in order to inflict as much pain as possible and had left a lasting scar upon his heart. He had found that hard to forgive—so it had been easier to forget.

But he had been shocked by the humble circumstances in which he had found her, briefly overwhelmed by a wash of guilt and the knowledge that he had the means to save her from such an existence. But these considerations had been swamped by the unwelcome discovery that his hunger for her hadn't abated, despite her unremarkable appearance. Had he hoped it would? Of course he had. But nobody had ever possessed the power to make him feel the way Mia did.

As if he could explode with lust at any second. As if he had lost temporary control of his senses.

He had left her tiny room, high on a cocktail of lust

and jealousy, for hadn't she implied she was meeting someone? Oblivious to the high-powered dealings of his subsequent meeting, he had found himself obsessing about how many men she might have taken to her bed since their split. He knew he was applying the double standards which many men like him were guilty of and, although he knew this was unreasonable intellectually, he found he didn't care. She had implied she was going on a date that day he'd seen her in London. He realised many women enjoyed casual hook-ups, didn't they? And while Theo knew it was old-fashioned to disapprove of such behaviour—he couldn't help himself.

It was the way he'd been brought up.

Or rather, the way he'd *dragged* himself up from the gutter into which he had been born.

Abandoned as a baby, he had been discovered squalling his lungs out in a cardboard box at the roughest end of Athens' main port, Piraeus, on the wettest night of the year. Soaked and starving. It was a wonder he had survived. But survive he had. His mouth hardened into a mirthless smile. Nobody could ever accuse him of a lack of tenacity, or defying the odds. A passing sailor had scooped him up and given him over to the care of a childless, middle-aged woman, who was desperately poor. She had named him Theo Aeton—meaning a gift of God who was as swift as an eagle. Or so she had hoped.

A roof—of sorts—had been provided in exchange for all the food he could bring in as soon as he was old enough to forage. He'd quickly learnt which restaurant bins provided the best bounty—and to get there before the feral cats did. He'd taught himself to fish, and to take tourists around parts of the city which did not feature in their glossy guide books. And even though they sometimes stupidly left their purses gaping open, he never stole their money, for that was a line he would not cross. Need, not greed, had always been his maxim.

Perhaps he would have continued with that hand-to-mouth existence if his 'mother' hadn't died very suddenly, just as most of the city was shutting down for Christmas. Experiencing a grief he hadn't been expecting, which culminated in an urgent need to get away from Athens, Theo had hitched a ride to the luxurious Saronikos gulf, gazing into the lit windows of the beachfront mansions, his stomach rumbling with hunger and his heart aching with envy.

If Mia's grandfather, Georgios Minotis, hadn't caught him stealing eggs, what would have become of him? But nobody had ever been able to answer the conundrum of *'what if?'*, had they?

All Theo knew was that he had faced down the millionaire's wrath with a defiance spurred on by his gnawing hunger. A job had been found for him on the vast estate. He had been put in the servants' quarters and done manual jobs around the place, but after a few months, Georgios had claimed to have seen something special in the boy. A quality he'd never found in his own son—a reckless gambler who had drunk himself to death when his daughter Mia was still a child.

That had been why he'd sent Theo away, to be educated at the finest schools in Europe. Exclusive establishments which initially taught the illiterate boy how to read and write and then, to learn. A thirst for knowledge had been born which had quickly become voracious. Theo's vacations had been spent at different summer schools, acquiring a host of language skills along the way. His winters had seen him skiing in select resorts, mastering first the black runs and then the most treacherous of off-piste skiing. He'd learnt how to ride. Which knife and fork to use at dinner and which fine wines should accompany it. He had learned how to pleasure himself, and the hordes of women eager to share his bed. He'd found himself a job in a bank in Paris and worked there diligently and then, when he was twenty-three years old, he had returned to Saronikos for the summer vacation, at the invitation of his mentor.

And had met the seventeen-year-old Mia.

He had been blown away by her. That voluptuous beauty. The brightness of those blue eyes. She had been holding a wounded puppy, an expression of fierce intent on her face as she'd nursed the mess of his tiny muzzle, for the creature had been injured and blinded in one eye. As she'd lifted her head and their gazes had met, his universe had seemed to shift and realign as he'd recognised something in her which had resonated inside him. Something which had reached out to him. An inner loneliness and a sense of being an outsider. Or at least, that was what he'd allowed himself to believe. His mouth twisted. What a deluded fool he had been. It had been sexual chemistry, pure and simple, given an extra edge by the stark differences in their circumstances. They should have quietly consummated their relationship—the rich girl getting her fulfilment from her experienced *bit of rough*—then gone their separate ways.

But something had held him back and stopped him from satisfying the urgent needs of his body—and hers. An idealism he had not felt before, or since, and which he had been reluctant to put a name to. He had asked her to marry him and when she had accepted, her grandfather had behaved like a man who had just won the jackpot.

So lost was he in his uncomfortable memories that it took a moment for Theo to acknowledge the light tap on his door, which opened on receipt of his terse command, to reveal his housekeeper, Sofia.

'The helicopter is preparing to land, Kyrios Aeton,' she informed him quietly. 'Your guest will be here shortly.'

He could see the curiosity in her lined eyes, because he didn't *usually* request prior warning before a visitor's arrival, nor insist on going to greet them himself. In fact, quite the contrary. Invitations to his private residence were considered such an honour that often guests would be taken to one of the property's many rooms, given a cool drink and asked to enjoy the spectacular view while he finished whatever he was doing, which they seemed happy enough to do. But he did not enlighten the matronly woman who had worked for him for the past five years about the significance of this particular guest. Instead he rose to his feet.

'Efharisto,' he said gruffly, making his way along the cool marble corridors to the main entrance hall and stepping outside into the warmth of the Greek day. But for once he was oblivious to the potent scent of lemon blossom or the sound of birdsong as he made his way towards the helicopter pad. Instead his eyes were fixed mesmerically on the shiny black craft as it hovered above the pad like a giant insect, before touching down.

The helicopter door opened and there she was with the sun streaming down on her like a spotlight and bathing her in rich gold, her chestnut hair blowing wildly in the upwind. A vision. A pocket-sized goddess—all curves and curls. He ran forward, holding out his hand to assist her, but she shook her head and dismounted the footplates herself, clinging onto the billowing skirt of her dress with one hand, as if her life depended on it.

'This way,' he shouted, above the sound of the engine, and she nodded as they made their way towards the house.

Sofia must have left the front door open, but Mia stood in front of it without moving—as if the hounds of hell were contained within its white portals. Theo glanced down at her and as she met his gaze her expression was one he didn't recognise—for it was wary and fierce. And he could do nothing about the sudden tightening of his body as his gaze drank her in. Today she wasn't wearing a pair of old jeans and a T-shirt which had badly needed ironing, but had replaced them with a pretty dress which emphasised her voluptuous shape. Her full lips bore the soft sheen of pink lipstick and Theo felt a sudden rush of heat, as desire began to beat its way insistently through his veins.

'Mia,' he said, unable to prevent the husky timbre of his voice.

Mia felt her throat dry. Don't say my name that way, she wanted to plead. And don't look at me like that, either. Because that sultry tone and molten gaze didn't mean anything. They never had. They were just weapons in his armoury of seduction and he used them well. Theo had always been a master at making her feel what he'd wanted her to feel. He had used her. Big time. And she should forget that at her peril.

'I don't know why you're looking so surprised,' she said, hitching the strap of her shoulder bag and fixing him with a cool smile. 'You were the one who sent your plane for me and then a helicopter to pick me up from the airfield, which I thought was slightly over the top. Surely you hadn't forgotten I was coming, Theo? Although...'

'Mmm?' he prompted, his ebony gaze fixed to her mouth as her words tailed off. 'Although what?'

Mia hesitated, but her determination to remain immune to him was proving near impossible. It was hard to concentrate when he'd left the top two buttons of his shirt undone like that. Had he done that deliberately? Exposed an enticing glimpse of olive skin, which gleamed like oiled silk, inviting the touch of her suddenly restless fingers? It was a terrible distraction and so was the way he was looking at her. But you could hardly ask a man to avert his gaze because you didn't like the way it made you *feel*, could you? It had taken all her resolve to agree to stay in his house and it wasn't going to do her frazzled nerves any good if she went to pieces every time she was close to him.

Her tongue flicked out to moisten a mouth which had grown uncomfortably dry. 'I was expecting you to be on the flight with me from England,' she croaked. 'At least, that's what you said to me in London.'

'I know I did.' He shrugged. 'But something came up.'

She almost said, *And you didn't bother to tell me?* before reminding herself that she, of all people, had no right to sound like a nagging wife.

'I had to fly to Paris last night on business and it made sense to come straight on here this morning.' His gaze was mocking. 'And I thought you'd be pleased at the thought of travelling alone.'

'Obviously.' Mia certainly wasn't going to admit that when he hadn't shown up, she had experienced something which had felt weirdly like *disappointment*. It was one thing to convince herself that she hadn't wanted to endure three and a half hours of Theo's company during a claustrophobic flight to Athens. Quite another to have that option removed without her knowledge, leaving her feeling distinctly wrong-footed when the stewardess had sashayed into the plane's plush interior to inform her that her boss wouldn't be coming after all.

'Where is he?' The words had shot from Mia's mouth before she could stop them and she'd been unable to miss the woman's look of surprise— presumably at her daring to ask such a direct question. She wondered how much more surprised the stewardess would be to discover that Mia was actually the legal *wife* of the boss!

But nobody knew—a decision they both seemed to have arrived at, without prior consultation. She had never once used his name and had noticed there was no mention of her in his biography. It was weird, really—how easily you could be airbrushed from someone's life. Had it been easy for him to forget the plump teenage bride who had provided him with a prestigious piece of the Greek coastline?

Was that the reason why she had dressed for the journey with the kind of care she hadn't taken for ages, because he'd caught her looking so scruffy when he'd turned up the other day? Admittedly, her navy and white dress was a little snug around the hips, and her espadrilles could have done with a new set of ribbons, but her hair was freshly washed and the red-brown curls were bouncing around her shoulders. She'd even applied a little make-up and dabbed on a slick of lipstick. And then, when she'd learned about his no-show, she had felt like a little girl who had dressed up for a party and got the date wrong. As if she'd tried too hard.

But there was nothing wrong with taking a little trouble with her appearance, she reasoned. It was what most women did every day of their lives. Usually, she dressed casually during her down-time, because the dogs at the rescue centre left her covered in hair, but that didn't rule out an occasional change. It certainly didn't mean that she was trying to ensnare Theo Aeton, or make herself more attractive to him. Of course it didn't.

She forced herself to remember the reason she was here. The *only* reason.

'How is my grandfather?' she questioned.

'I spoke to his nurse this morning. He's stable. I'm planning to go and see him this afternoon—'

'Can I come with you?' she said quickly.

'That's something we need to discuss. But not on the doorstep. Do you want to come inside, Mia?' he questioned, pulling the door open a little wider. 'Or just stand there, looking decorative?'

Decorative? Mia frowned at his choice of word. Was that a good or a bad thing? She wasn't sure. It made her think of a Christmas tree. She glanced back in the direction of the helicopter pad. 'My luggage—'

'Someone will take care of that and bring it to your room.'

'How comfortable you sound, with all your servants,' she observed wryly.

'Hopefully the people who work for me are just as comfortable. I try never to forget I was once a servant myself.' His mouth twisted into a mocking smile. 'As people like you were so keen to remind me.'

My, how the tables had turned, Mia thought as she stepped over the threshold and looked around the entrance hall, trying to take in the opulence of her surroundings. Their roles had been completely reversed, she realised. He had a mansion, while she lived in a poky rented room. He was rich and she was poor and it was...well, it was more than a little disconcerting.

She had been gobsmacked as the helicopter had skirted a private beach, then hovered over massive, flower-filled grounds containing a huge blue swimming pool, shaped like a T. Her lips had curved with slight derision when she'd seen *that*. They had flown over a modern house—a vast steel and glass construction bathed in different shades of blue as it reflected the sky and sea. And Mia had realised with a sense of disbelief that this was Theo's property. Or rather, Theo's estate, with its olive and lemon groves, which were obviously commercially farmed. He owned the lot.

And all because of her.

All because of her.

Her inheritance had provided this for him. The land he had acquired when he'd signed the wedding certificate must have financed it all. No wonder he could afford to look smug. But no way was she going to be bitter, because there was no point. She had turned her back on the old life. She didn't need vast wealth. She'd seen the unhappiness and discontentedness it could bring and was happier with her modest goals. She certainly wasn't going to start doing checks and balances, or comparing her lifestyle to that of the towering billionaire in front of her.

She didn't even want to think about Theo, in those dark trousers which moulded his powerful thighs and a silk shirt the pale, creamy colour of raspberry yoghurt, which hinted distractingly at the rocky torso beneath. So she smiled politely, just as she might have done if she were being shown around a stately home in England, searching for something appropriate to say. 'Mmm… Very impressive,' she said. 'The modern architecture works really well against this landscape.'

His eyes narrowed, as if her cool deliberation had come as something of a surprise. 'Let me show you the rest.'

She shook her head. 'No, honestly, that won't be necessary, Theo. There must be someone else you can ask. I'm sure there are much more important calls on your time than having to act as an unofficial guide to me.'

'Possibly, but I prefer never to delegate tasks which could be potentially troublesome. And unless your Greek has improved dramatically and as nobody speaks English as fluently as I do,' he added, his eyes glittering with unholy humour, 'it seems you're stuck with me.'

'Is your swimming pool really shaped like the initial of your name?' she questioned archly, intending to goad him. 'I couldn't believe it when I saw a giant T. The ego has landed! Are there monograms on your towels, or woven into the rugs?'

But he didn't take the bait, his lazy shrug indicating he was unmoved by her sarcasm. 'My architect persuaded me it would be a good idea. The vertical part of the T is a lane pool designed for swimming lengths, which I do every morning, and the horizontal bar is the infinity part, which overlooks the sea. It's a practical design rather than being done for reasons of status,' he concluded drily before beckoning her. 'Come.'

Slightly irritated by his imperious command and her mind now stuck in an annoying groove of imagining Theo swimming, Mia was left with little option but to follow him, trying to take it all in as he showed her around the sprawling villa. The huge rooms. The white walls. The bold oil paintings which added bright pops of colour. Butter-soft leather sofas occupied light-filled spaces and there were several glass tables on which stood exquisite pieces of blue china. Yet as she looked around, she found herself thinking this was no place for a child. Was that intentional? She wondered what would happen if—when—he met a woman he might want to make babies with and the thought upset her more than it should have done.

She still didn't know if there was anyone in his life. Maybe she should ask him for a divorce—wasn't it time one of them did that? That would be the most diplomatic way of finding out about his personal circumstances and might spur her into taking action to formally end their sexless union. She swallowed. Unless she was intending to continue in this strange marital limbo of theirs for ever.

In an attempt to lose her uncomfortable preoccupation, Mia turned her attention to the gardens, which they had just entered via a vine-covered veranda. The sunlit grounds were very beautiful and, despite her barbed comments, the swimming pool was even more impressive when seen from the ground. The glassy blue water shimmered invitingly as Mia tried to remember the last time she'd swum anywhere which wasn't an echoey public bath which smelt strongly of chlorine.

'It looks fabulous,' she said.

Theo inclined his black head. 'Use it whenever you want.'

'Thanks.'

He introduced her to a cook who was doing something complicated with filo pastry in the kitchen and to Sofia, his housekeeper, saying something in Greek too rapid for Mia to understand—she caught the word for lemon, but her grasp of the language had always been superficial and her mother had actively discouraged her from speaking it.

But once they had mounted the wide marble staircase and found themselves alone on the first floor of the enormous villa, Mia turned to him curiously, hating the way her gaze was drawn so irrevocably to the sculpted lines of his lips. Hating even more her sudden burning wish to have those lips kiss her again. She hesitated. 'What did you tell Sofia?'

He knitted his dark brows together. 'I said we might drink some lemon *pressé* on one of the terraces once I'd shown you around.'

'No, not then,' she said, more crossly than she had intended. 'I mean, what have you told her about me?'

Theo felt a beat of irritation, turning away from the question in her blue eyes, and continued to walk along the upper level of the house. He heard her follow, her footsteps light on the silken rug, but his pace didn't slacken until he reached a suite which had been chosen deliberately because it was the furthest from his own. His mouth hardened. He didn't want her accusing him of using proximity to his advantage. More importantly, he didn't want to put any temptation in his way.

Throwing open the door of the airy chamber, he walked inside. 'This is yours.'

'Does she know? Sofia, I mean,' she persisted, paying absolutely no attention to her surroundings. 'Who around here is aware that I'm your wife, Theo?'

He turned around to meet a stubborn expression he didn't recognise, forcing him to acknowledge she had changed. They had both changed, he realised. 'Very few people know.' His mouth twisted. 'A failed marriage isn't something I tend to boast about. I prefer to focus on my successes, not my failures.'

'What about my grandfather's staff?'

'There is nobody left there who knows you.'

'Nobody at all?' she questioned, with a frown. 'Not even Elena, or Christos?'

'They have all gone,' he said coolly. 'His life is very different now, Mia. When he first became ill, he withdrew from everything he knew. In many ways he adopted the life of a hermit. Against my advice, he dismissed all his permanent employees and now a skeleton of temporary staff keep him and the place ticking over—just about.' His gaze became narrowed. 'My own staff have been acquired within the last five years, and, to all intents and purposes, regard me as a single man.'

There was a pause. 'And do you behave like a single man, Theo?' she said quietly.

It was a question he hadn't been expecting and Theo felt himself tense. A pulse began to beat at his temple, and somewhere else, too. He was hard now, just as he'd been hard when he'd seen her in London. He shifted his weight. 'Are you asking me whether I've had sex with other women since we've been apart, Mia?' he queried huskily. 'Because, to echo your own words, that's really none of your business.'

'Of course I'm not,' she answered hastily. 'I just wanted to know…'

As her words tailed off Theo thought of all the questions she could have asked him. Things like: had he ever really loved her, or had he just done it for the money? Or, even more crucially, had he ever regretted never having consummated their relationship? Which, of course, he had, more times than he cared to remember. Questions she'd never asked at the time but which he had little appetite to answer now, because surely they were as inconsequential as the leaves which fell from the autumn trees before drying to dust on the ground.

As was she.

But suddenly she didn't seem so inconsequential. Not when she was here, in his house, and his long-repressed fantasy of having her alone in a bedroom was actually being realised. The breath had caught in his throat and suddenly he was having to steel himself against the powerful impact she was having on his senses.

His throat dried as his hungry gaze drank her in. Those big blue eyes and the coppery tangle of her curls. And her body. How could he have forgotten that voluptuous body, which he had denied himself for reasons which now seemed like insanity?

He could see the sudden tremble of her lips and read the desire which was darkening her eyes. A desire as heavy as the atmosphere just before the storm which had broken when he'd left her room in London, leaving his shirt and jacket saturated with rain and clinging to his chest.

He could hear the thunder of his heart and he was so caught up with the idea of having sex with her that his words became a taunt, intended more as a provocation than because he was particularly interested in hearing the answer.

'What do you want to know, Mia?' he demanded softly. 'Ask me anything you want and I'll tell you.'

She tilted her chin, but not—as he had hoped—as a silent invitation to kiss her. No, her mouth had tightened, not softened, and her bald words shattered the sensual bubble which had surrounded him.

'Why have you never asked me for a divorce?'

His lips hardened into a cynical smile. Why did she think? That he was a sentimentalist, who believed in the sanctity of marriage above all else? Or that he was holding out hope that she might return to him, so that they could start a family of their own?

'Interesting you should say that,' he mused, dampening down the tumult of his thoughts and replacing them with the cool logic which had given him such a formidable reputation in the boardroom. 'When I've been thinking exactly the same thing. Because you are the one who has everything to gain from a legal termination of our marriage, Mia.' He paused. 'So why have *you* never asked for a divorce?'

CHAPTER THREE

MIA GAVE A click of irritation as Theo's lips twisted into a hard smile, because he *always* did this. She had asked him a question and he had turned it back on her. He used language not as a form of communication but as a barrier—and a weapon. And he did it in five different languages! He was too clever for his own good, she thought resentfully.

Yet hadn't that always been one of the things she had so admired about him—the way he'd embraced learning so eagerly, even though he had started so much later than anyone else? He had behaved as if education was a privilege and an honour, not a right or a burden. He had seemed to know everything, while she had known nothing—or so it had seemed at the time.

Meeting the dark gleam of his eyes, she attempted to answer his question without giving too much away. Because somehow that was important. As if revealing how badly he had hurt her would make her feel vulnerable, all over again.

'There was no reason for me to seek a divorce,' she explained.

'Really?' He raised his brows. 'Even though your life is far more humble than your beginnings must have prepared you for? The man you married is now a billionaire, Mia—'

'Would you like a quick round of applause?'

'Which means any judge would award you the kind of settlement which would keep you more than comfortable for the rest of your life,' he continued, unperturbed, though he gave a flicker of a smile as his gaze travelled over her flushed face. 'You wouldn't have to work in a hotel and live in a room not much bigger than a cloakroom.'

'You think that money is the answer to everything?' she demanded. 'Is that the god you worship?' She turned away to look out of the window—not because she wanted to appreciate the sapphire slash of the sea, or the creamy froth of the distant citrus orchard, but because she didn't want him to see the prick of tears in her eyes. How annoying that he could cut right through her defences, almost without trying. Quickly, she blinked them away, waiting until she had composed herself, before turning to face him again. 'I suppose you must do, since you were prepared to marry me in order to get your hands on the stuff!'

But he didn't rise to the insult.

'How easy it is for people to be dismissive of the power of money, when they've been cushioned by wealth all their lives,' he offered coolly.

She was conscious of his gaze raking over her unruly curls. 'I didn't have wealth,' she defended hotly. 'Not really. You met me on one of my annual visits to see my grandfather—you had no idea what my life was like back in England.'

There was a pause. 'So why don't you tell me what it was like?'

The question took her by surprise, because it sounded as if he really wanted to know. As if he were genuinely interested in her background, in a way he'd never been before. Why had that been? How could they have agreed to marry when they'd known so little about each other?

Because they'd both been on a high—too preoccupied with the fluctuation of youthful hormones and the lure of the sex he seemed intent on denying her.

Facts had taken second place to feelings and she had been completely captivated by those. Mia tried to cast her mind back to a young woman blinded by need and romantic illusion—and that person was someone she could barely recognise.

'Yes, we lived in a big house but it had hardly any furniture in it,' she said slowly. 'Because my father gambled away most of his inheritance and after he died, my mother frittered away what little was left. So my grandfather paid my school fees and arranged for grocery deliveries to be made. He provided all the basics, but nothing more.' She shrugged. 'And my mother resented him because she wanted more. It's why she used to let me come over and stay with him during the summer holidays, even though she hated him. She thought I might be able to soften him up. Her dream was that I would return to England with a fistful of euros. But that never happened.'

'Your grandfather has many assets,' he observed thoughtfully. 'But cash has never been one of them. Most of his wealth is tied up in the land.'

'As I was soon to discover for myself,' she said, the sharp reminder of his betrayal making her forget her determination not to be bitter.

'Mia—'

'No!' she interjected, with a fierce shake of her head. 'You asked me a question and you need to hear my answer without any attempts to absolve yourself.'

'Absolve myself?' he echoed.

'That's what I said!' But defiance was a new-found weapon in her armoury and it took a little getting used to, and Mia found herself sinking onto a leather seat, her legs feeling strangely wobbly 'I met you that summer when I was seventeen and I'd…'

'What?' he prompted softly as her words tailed off.

She thought about sugar-coating it. About making it sound as if it had meant nothing. But that would be a lie told to salvage her own ego. And hadn't she lost enough already because of her failed marriage? Surely the truth shouldn't be another casualty.

'I'd never felt like that about anyone before,' she admitted. 'Perhaps because I'd never really had the chance to meet any men. Despite my mother having been a model, I'd led quite a sheltered life and went to an all-girls school.' She pulled a face. 'And, like I said, there was never enough cash to splash on school trips or new clothes, so I was always the odd one out.' There had been another reason for her almost hermit-like lifestyle, which had little to do with poverty. Because the willowy ex-supermodel who had given birth to Mia could never quite get her head around having produced such an ugly duckling of a child. The little girl who had been intended as an accompaniment to complement her mother's remarkable beauty had been hidden away at home—while all methods intended to improve her appearance had been doomed to disappoint.

If she tried—which these days she never did—she could still hear her mother's tinkling English accent as she'd trilled out her various observations.

Surely you're not going to eat *that*? No wonder you're so chubby, darling!

If you don't move a bit more, Mia, then you'll *never* get rid of that spare tyre!

'I know you married me to get the land, Theo. I know that,' Mia reiterated. 'And it sort of makes sense now. I couldn't understand at the time why someone like you…who could have had anyone…should have wanted…me,' she finished, trying very hard not to gulp.

He stared at her and the silence which followed seemed to go on for a very long time. 'Your mother told you that, did she?'

Swallowing down the lump in her throat, Mia nodded as the hateful words came spiralling back down the years.

Surely you don't think a man like Theodoros Aeton would marry a little fatty like you, if he weren't being paid?

'She told me when I was changing for the evening party.' Mia hadn't thought it possible to hurt that much. To feel as if a knife had ripped open her chest and a ragged-nailed hand had reached inside the gaping cavity to tear her heart out. She'd been standing in front of a full-length mirror at the time, in her too-tight white wedding dress. She had felt like a white, bloated maggot and she had looked like it, too.

'And you believed her?' Theo demanded.

'Why wouldn't I? She told me you'd struck a deal with my grandfather.'

His gaze was very steady, but there was a glint of something hard and bitter in the depths of those black eyes. 'But you didn't stop to find out my side of the story, did you, Mia? That didn't occur to you?'

Mia chewed on her lip. Of course she hadn't. How could she explain how naïve she'd felt when the facts had fallen into place and she'd finally understood why the most devastatingly gorgeous man she'd ever laid eyes on had asked her to be his wife? If he'd explained from the outset that he was courting her because it was financially advantageous for him to do so, then maybe she could have accepted it. She had adored him so much that she thought she would have accepted whatever scraps he deigned to throw her. But he hadn't. He had spun his silken words like a spider spinning a golden web and she had become enmeshed in them. So she had melted when he'd husked into her ear that he'd never desired a woman as much as her. He hadn't mentioned love, but that hadn't seemed to matter. Because she'd believed in her love for *him*, imagining she had enough for both of them and it was strong enough to withstand anything fate had in store for them. But she had fallen at the first hurdle, because betrayal and deceit were powerful weapons when you held them up against something as fragile as love.

'Why bother,' she questioned, her words tinged with acid, 'when it was true?'

Theo felt the erratic pound of his heart as impatience vied with an anger which had suddenly become red-raw. Surely she should know that life was never that cut and dried. But facts were facts and he couldn't change them now. On one level he had been aware that she had idolised him more than was healthy, but she had been so sweet about it that he had accepted it. He hadn't wanted to crush her dreams, because in a way he had been caught up in them himself—for the first and last time in his life.

And she had been vulnerable. Like a small shoot pushing its way up towards the light, she had needed careful nurturing. It had been the only time Theo had ever met a woman who had been totally without agenda. She had been warm and giving. Her ripe innocence had been her both her strength and her shield and, from the start, he had felt an overpowering protectiveness towards her. His simplistic view of what constituted a 'good' woman had been personified in the curly-headed virgin who had responded so passionately to his kisses.

And so he had waited—even though it had half killed him to do so. His determination not to possess her fully until she was his wife had driven him. It had been yet one more achievement to add to his list.

'I agreed to what was, in effect, a dowry,' he said slowly, 'because I knew that unless I did so, your grandfather would refuse to let me have your hand in marriage.'

'Oh, how very admirable!' Those Aegean eyes sparked blue fire at him. 'So you did it out of the goodness of your heart?'

'Think about it,' he came back at her. 'I was a modestly paid bank worker at the time—certainly not able to keep you in the manner in which you deserved to be kept!'

'I am not an animal, I don't need to be *kept*,' she retorted, her voice shaking. 'I didn't need his land. I didn't want it!'

'And neither did I,' Theo ground out, the words rushing from his lips like a swollen river breaking through the banks and suddenly he realised how long he had repressed this. All this time he had lived with the knowledge that she'd thought so little of him and it seemed she still did. He felt the fierce fire of injustice and allowed the cold swamp of anger to blot it out. 'Don't you know why he did it, Mia? Why he made me that offer?'

Silently, Mia shook her head, taken aback by the sudden bitterness in his voice.

'Because he thought if he gifted you the land, then your mother would manipulate you and wrangle it away from you.' His gaze bored into her like a dark laser. 'And subsequently sell some of the most valuable coastal real estate in Greece to some disreputable property developer, who would fill the place with high-rise hotels and turn this haven of a place into a tacky holiday destination. Can you imagine what that would have been like? All this beauty which surrounds us vanquished, and in its place all-day breakfasts and happy hours.'

Her breath was coming thick and fast and as Mia stared at him uncomprehendingly, the world as she knew it was suddenly upended. 'Why didn't you tell me this before?'

'Because I was waiting for our wedding night, when we would finally be alone. As your husband, I was planning to sign it all over to you. Every. Damned. Acre. But you didn't stop to ask, did you?' His mouth twisted into a bitter line. 'You just assumed I was bad and greedy and manipulative. It was as though you'd been waiting for something like this to happen. Something to condemn me in your eyes.'

And to her shame, Mia couldn't deny his words. She *had* been in a state of disbelief. She hadn't believed it possible that a person could make her feel as good as Theo did and of *course* she had suspected his motives from time to time. Her mother's carping criticisms had worn her down over the years, like the drip-drip of water against the walls of a cave. She'd accepted all those negative assessments about her appearance because, deep down, she'd known they were true. She *was* dumpy and dull. She *was* a very average pupil at school. She had been angry with Theo for having deceived her, but even angrier with herself for allowing herself to be such a pathetically easy target. And that anger and hurt had fuelled the words she had flung at him.

'Do you remember what you said to me that night?' he questioned coldly, again tapping uncomfortably into her thoughts.

She bit her lip so hard she could taste the metallic slick of blood. Of course she could remember. No matter how hard she'd tried to forget, fragments of those accusations had remained in the recesses of her mind—branded like fire onto her memory. She had hissed at him like a cornered possum. Told him he had let himself down and shown his true colours. That his gutter mentality had come to the fore and thank goodness she had found out in time. And she hadn't stopped there. She'd been high on fear and rage and hurt, and the words had continued to come rushing out in a vitriolic spill. Words she hadn't really understood but which she realised afterwards must have been spoken by her mother and she must have subconsciously soaked them all up, like a sponge. She had accused him of being a fortune-hunter. A thief. And a gigolo. It had been that single word which had caused the final rupture before she had run off into the night. She had seen him recoil, and his mouth flatten with a look she'd never seen before, but once the anger had fled from his black eyes, he had recovered his composure with remarkable speed.

'Hardly a gigolo, *zouzouri mou*,' he had drawled, somehow managing to make the formerly tender endearment into a vicious insult. 'I didn't actually have *sex* with you in exchange for the land—no matter how many times you begged me to.'

Something had twisted and died inside her—was it her hopes and her dreams, or just the realisation that she had been punching above her weight all along?

Mia had fled from the room. Even now the memory of his response made her want to run away again. She would have given anything to have escaped Theo's modern mansion and the teeming painful memories and the penetrating gleam of his black eyes. But where would she go? She had accepted his hospitality in order to see her dying grandfather. She mustn't let his words get to her. He shouldn't still have that power over her.

She turned from his dark gaze to stare out of the window again, oblivious to the bluebell tint of the sky. 'I should have stayed right here and faced the music,' she said, and couldn't stop herself from wondering if the outcome would have been different if she had done. Would she have remained as his wife if she had been honest with him? His *real* wife? Would they have created the family she'd longed for, the family she'd never really had? A dark wave of longing washed over her and she had to swallow down the lump in her throat before she could continue. 'But I was young,' she husked.

'We were both young,' he said, his voice gravel-hard. 'Tell me what you did next.'

'I went back to England,' she said slowly. 'And realised there was no way I could carry on living with my mother. Anyway, she'd met a rich American by then. A sugar daddy. Her words, not mine.' She gave a short laugh. 'So she went to Florida to live with him, hoping he would marry her, though he never has.'

'And you? What did you do, Mia?'

She shrugged. 'I needed independence and to find my own way in the world, but of course I had no money.'

'Not quite so straightforward without the cushion of cash, is it, *zouzouri mou*?' His lips curved. 'Weren't you tempted to come back, to ask for some proceeds from the estate? Or to demand that I sell up the land and give you the proceeds?'

'With my tail between my legs? *Begging* you?' she questioned proudly. 'Never in a million years! I'd had it with that kind of life, Theo, so I decided to do what most people in that position do. I started looking for a job and, since I didn't have very much in the way of qualifications, I found one as a maid.'

'A maid?' he echoed.

The disbelief in his voice was unmistakable and it riled her, because hadn't she encountered this kind of prejudice time and time again? 'It's a very worthwhile job,' she defended staunchly. 'Creating order out of chaos and enhancing people's enjoyment of their stay. Nobody's ever going to object if someone else is making their bed for them, are they? I mean, there are a lot of…um…' she pulled a face '…unsavoury things which people leave in their rooms, but mostly—I liked it.'

'So you left me standing at the altar in order to become a maid?' He gave a cynical laugh. 'I suppose I should be offended, but instead I find it rather...*amusing*. Tell me—does your grandfather know about the unexpected career you have chosen?'

'He wouldn't take my phone calls, and he never answered any of my letters, so I don't know if he read them. I suppose I must just be grateful that he wants to see me now.'

His expression suddenly became closed and he crossed the room to open the French doors, which led out onto a large and leafy terrace. And although Mia told herself she was grateful he'd put some distance between them, the change of perspective was making her aware of things she'd been trying very hard not to focus on before.

Emphasised by the bright sunlight streaming in from behind him, his body was outlined with heart-stopping definition. Through the fine material of his silk shirt the musculature of his broad-shouldered back was plainly visible. Against her will, her gaze travelled over the powerful shafts of his long legs and the ebony gleam of his thick hair. As she watched him, she could feel a silken flicker begin to pulse deep inside her. Her heart was jumping all over the place and her cheeks felt hot and flushed. Mia told herself she should be over him by now—so why was her stubborn body refusing to listen? As he turned round, did he catch her practically drooling over him? Was that why his eyes glinted with dark fire?

Suddenly, she was pathetically grateful to hear a tap on the door. 'Who's that?' she questioned hoarsely.

Theo tensed, not wanting to be disturbed and

sorely tempted to demand that the caller go away. *'Ela,'* he said tersely and the door opened to admit Dimitra, his maid, the daughter of his gardener. She was new to the job and very nervous as she deposited Mia's suitcase in the centre of the room, before scuttling out again. Almost immediately, Sofia appeared, carrying a jug of lemon *pressé* and two frosted glasses on a tray, which she placed on a table beside the window, correctly interpreting his almost imperceptible shake of the head, before slipping quietly from the room.

And then he and Mia were alone again—facing each other like strangers and acting as if there weren't a huge bed within tumbling distance. Theo stared at the woman he had married—at the curves of her firm flesh, which were drenched with golden sunlight—and felt the beat of something he didn't recognise. Was it frustration? 'You will have something to drink?' he questioned, finding himself in the unfamiliar position of waiting on someone.

She nodded. 'Sure.'

Ice cubes chinking, he carried the cordial across the room to her, watching her mouth pursing as she sucked a long draft of *pressé* through the glass straw, leaving her lips gleaming and wet. She wasn't being deliberately provocative—at least he didn't think she was—but there was something about her fresh beauty which made watching her feel like a necessity rather than a choice. As she took another gulp, her head was bent, showcasing those snaky spirals of copper which had always given her that faintly wanton appearance—which was ironic, given that she had been so innocent. Six years on, she was unlikely to have remained a virgin and the thought of her being with other men was unendurable. He tensed as a fierce pain twisted darkly at his heart.

As she raised her eyes and caught him watching her, something in the air seemed to shift and change. Something raw and powerful which, when Theo thought about it afterwards, had seemed inevitable from the moment she had set foot inside his house.

He moved towards her and, taking the half-drunk glass from her unprotesting fingers, heard her sharp intake of breath. Her eyes were unblinking and her lips tremulous as he stared at her for a very long time, as if mulling over his options—and hers—before pulling her into his arms.

And she let him. Actually, that was a lie. She didn't just *let* him—she melted into his waiting embrace as if she was powerless to stop herself. As if she had been waiting for this to happen for as long as he had.

How long was that?

Since he'd walked into that cramped and muggy room in London and found her looking hot and crumpled, with sweat gleaming like polish on her clammy skin? Or when she'd arrived here this afternoon with that summery dress swirling around the undulation of her hips and her curls glinting like bright fire in the sunlight. His lips flattened. Or maybe this was the same seed of hunger which had been planted a long time ago. Planted and then left to wither and die.

But it hadn't died. It must have been growing

stealthily inside him all this time and now it was all-consuming. It was heating his blood and making his senses raw. It was hardening his groin. Unbearably.

He moved his face closer to hers and saw her eyes grow dark—two pools of fathomless ebony fixed on his. Her lips were parted and even though those plump, pink cushions had always tantalised him, he did not kiss her immediately, even though invitation was screaming from every pore of her body. He allowed himself a heartbeat longer, seeing the sudden confusion on her face. A wave of something like satisfaction washed over him as he welcomed the familiar mantle of power—of being the one in the driving seat. Thank God for his legendary control, he thought grimly. That steely control which he had never needed more than he did right now.

'You want this?' he said, his question almost careless.

Those Aegean eyes narrowed and she seemed to hesitate before she nodded—as if she wanted to demonstrate that she had power, too. But he saw the capitulation in her eyes the moment it happened—and the hunger, too. The sharp, intense hunger which easily matched his own.

'Yes,' she answered, almost angrily. *'Yes.'*

CHAPTER FOUR

THERE WAS NO finesse in Theo's kiss. No build-up, or teasing, or provocation. His lips were urgent and hungry and although Mia instantly responded to the hot, hard pressure of his lips, she couldn't stem the frantic questions which rushed into her mind.

Why was she letting this happen?

Why?

But it was a long time since she had kissed anyone and it seemed that sexual frustration was a powerful driver. Much too powerful to resist—and she had never had much luck resisting Theo anyway. With a little moan she opened her lips, kissing him back with clumsy need but also with a kind of despair. Because she didn't *want* to feel like this. As if he were consuming her and dominating every single one of her senses, until all she could think about was him and only him. She didn't want to make those swooning little sounds as he flicked his tongue inside her mouth, as if he *owned* it or something. Or squirm with frustration as her breasts met the rocky resistance of his chest. And she definitely didn't want to part her legs to allow one powerful leg to slide between her trembling thighs.

But she did all those things. She did them with a fervour which shocked her, no matter how loudly her conscience was clamouring in her ears. Already she felt out of control, while Theo seemed in total command of himself. He whispered his fingertips all the way down her back and then tangled them proprietorially in her hair, cupping the back of her head with his hand so that he could increase the pressure on her mouth.

How could a kiss be so incredible, she wondered dazedly, and how long did it last? She couldn't tell. Not when time seemed to be playing tricks on her. Suddenly she didn't *care* about the lack of romance and affection. It didn't seem to matter, because a kiss could make past and present merge into one blissful whole and make you feel happy again, couldn't it? It could make you remember what it felt like to be alive and in love. Was that why she pressed her breasts so brazenly against him? And why his palms cupped her buttocks to bring her up against the cradle of his pelvis, so that she could feel the unashamed outline of his arousal.

'Oh, God,' she breathed in wonder as he circled his hips against hers very deliberately.

'I want you,' he said, with cool calculation as he drew away from her. 'Can you feel how much?'

His words should have shocked her, but they did no such thing. They thrilled her. They made her want more. 'You kn-know I can,' she answered brokenly. 'Y-you're so big. So h-hard.'

Was it her stumbled response which made him shudder like that?

'Mia,' he said, breaking the kiss to suck in a great gulp of breath, as if to replenish his oxygen-starved lungs. *'Evge...!'*

That Greek exclamation she knew—an expression of praise she'd heard him use in the past—but the other words which were falling from his lips were a mystery. Not just because of her lack of fluency but because his rough tone was making them almost incomprehensible. Was he flattering her, or damning her? It sounded like a mixture of both.

But she didn't care. How could she care about anything other than this...? *This.* The thumb which was grazing over her cotton-covered nipple was unsteady and the groan he gave as he buried his mouth in her hair made him sound as if he had temporarily lost control.

So what if he had?

Hadn't she?

Wasn't this the best thing that had happened to her in six long years?

His mouth was on her jaw.

And then drifting downwards.

She could feel the warmth of his breath against her skin. He was whispering kisses down her neck, until he reached the scalloped edge of her sundress. Holding her breath with anticipation, Mia could feel her swollen breasts pushing towards his lips, bullet-like nipples sending out a silent scream for him to bare them, or touch them, or do *something* rather than leave her aching like this.

Did he realise how wet she was? Was that why he began to ruck up her skirt with a low laugh of triumph? That should have been enough to make her stop, but her starved senses were refusing to let her. She could feel his hand tiptoeing up over her leg and the goose-bumping of tender skin as he edged towards the juncture of her thighs. And now came the light graze of his finger—negligent, almost careless—as it skated over the engorged mound of her panties.

Mia gasped, her eyelids fluttering to a close because his finger was moving against the silk-covered bud with exquisite accuracy and the scent of her arousal was filling the air with musky perfume. She was parting her thighs, eager for him to push aside the damp fabric and caress her heated flesh. Or maybe to tug the unwanted panties down and let them flutter to her ankles like a white silk flag of surrender. Already, she was close. So close. And Mia knew if she didn't call a halt to this, something was going to happen.

She froze. Not just *something*. Any minute now and she would be gasping out a helpless orgasm, administered by a cold-blooded man who had made no secret of his contempt for her. What would *that* do for her feelings of self-worth? She wasn't a teenager any more, whose sexual response was being governed by a man who liked to control. *She* was the one in charge of her own body and she couldn't let this happen.

She didn't say a word. She didn't have to. He must

have correctly interpreted her wishes because he let his hand fall, before quickly walking away from her as if her touch had begun to contaminate him. His shoulders were hunched, his ragged breathing the only sound breaking the fraught silence. Her heart thundering, Mia surveyed the forbidding set of his body as she tried to rationalise what had happened, feeling as if some sort of explanation was required. As if she needed to say something which would rid her of the stupid certainty that she had just passed up on a piece of paradise. A few words which might help claw back what little remained of her dignity.

'We…we shouldn't have done that.'

'*Parakalo,*' he said coolly, holding up the palm of his hand, like a city policeman stopping the traffic.

'Please, what?' she questioned, because this word she *did* understand.

His black eyes were so cold as they flickered over her face that she wondered if this could really be the same man who had just been kissing her so passionately.

'Spare me the morality lecture, Mia,' he continued. 'You wanted it. I wanted it. It was a mistake. So what?'

She bristled at the way he said it—as if it had been an insignificant event, best forgotten—but at least it sent out a warning that she couldn't afford to be vulnerable around him. Clearing her throat, she attempted to replicate his own cool tone. 'I didn't come here to reignite our physical relationship.'

'I believe you. Believe me, it wasn't what I intended either.' He lowered his voice. 'But the fact that we still want each other throws up something of a dilemma.'

'What sort of dilemma?' she echoed cautiously.

'I suppose the question is, what are we going to do about the insane chemistry which still exists between us?'

Theo's gaze was steady as he registered her look of shock, aware that his words were brutal—but why bother playing games? Why pretend everything was civilised when, beneath the surface, it was anything but? That white-hot desire still burned beneath the surface. It was burning now, despite the coolness of his words. It was making him harder than he could ever remember. How did she *do* that? Was it just the frustration of never having had her, which made him want her so much?

'Because it's a lasting regret of mine,' he continued slowly. 'That I was never *properly* intimate with you.'

'Intimate?' Her shock had given way to surprise and her voice had become very brittle. 'Surely that's nothing but a fancy way of describing sex?'

With a nod of his head, he acknowledged a frankness she would never have used in the past and the baldness of her question should have reassured him she was no longer thinking along foolish fairy-tale lines of love, and romance. But it did no such thing. It didn't reassure him. It made his body tighten and a flare of jealousy begin to ignite. Because underneath it all, Theo was still an old-fashioned man. Especially with her. For this was the woman onto whose finger he had once slid a golden ring, intended to bind them together for life. Where was that ring now? he wondered caustically.

'Perhaps you would prefer me to skip the euphemisms and talk dirty to you,' he suggested silkily. 'Is that what you like these days, Mia? Is that what *turns you on*?'

She tilted her chin—perhaps to conceal the blush he was finding intensely appealing—but all that resulted was that her chestnut ringlets cascaded around her shoulders, and Theo was momentarily transfixed by her voluptuous beauty. Her eyes flashed blue fire and for a moment he thought she was going to rise to his challenge and tell him exactly what she *did* say to the men who had shared her bed. And wouldn't that kill his hunger for her more effectively than anything else, if he imagined her being possessed by another man?

But she said no such thing and he was relieved to have been spared that mental torture.

'How dated your views sound, Theo,' she chided softly. 'What I do in or out of bed is nobody's business but my own. Just like your private life is nothing to do with me. We're divorced in all but name. We've both moved on.'

Had he? Sometimes he wondered. But his track record was irrelevant. There was only one thing which seemed relevant now. His objectives had changed, he realised. They had been changing since he'd sought her out in London. Suddenly it was no longer enough to facilitate a meeting with her grandfather, in order to pay back some of the debt he owed the old man. He had told Mia their kiss had been a mistake, but what if he had been wrong? What if he had been blinding himself to the truth all this time? What if sex with the woman who had deserted him would be less of a complication, and more of a closure?

Because wasn't the reality that Mia had been like a subtle thorn embedded in his flesh all this time? The thorn had burrowed deep enough for him to imagine that it had been absorbed into his body. Determined not to think about her, for the most part he had succeeded—and to the outside world his life was one of supreme accomplishment, on just about every level. No party was ever complete without Theo Aeton on the guest list, with the most glamorous woman in the room hanging eagerly onto his arm. No opening night as special as when the newspapers carried an image of his carved and unsmiling features.

But Mia had always been a shadow lingering on the edges of his heart. She had always represented something unfinished—and for a man whose beginnings had been so messy, that had not sat easily with him. Now he had seen her again. He had touched her and tasted her. Against his will, the fire in his body had been reignited and this time he wanted it to burn out. He wanted more than a kiss and a few frantic stolen caresses. A pulse thudded erratically at his temple. He wanted what should have been his on their wedding night.

Mia.

In his bed.

And him, deep inside her. Doing it to her, over and over again.

Back then she had been a virgin and he would have been the first.

He should have been the first.

But that didn't matter. This wasn't about ego or pride, or his stupidity in putting her on that damned pedestal and essentially placing her out of reach. It was much more fundamental than that. He wanted to have sex with her. To finish off what he had started and erase her from his memory once and for all.

He looked across the room to where she stood, his diminutive copper-headed wife who was surveying him with such belligerent eyes. Yet the desire which shimmered through her delicious body was as palpable as the sunlight which dappled the leaves of the trees outside. It was written in the darkening of her eyes and the trembling of her lips. In the diamond-hard points of her nipples, which were pushing against the cotton of her dress and silently begging for his touch.

Yes, she desired him. Of course she did. He had been desired by women since he'd been barely out of puberty. He gave a bitter smile. How many times had he been told he was irresistible? Or that he resembled a god with his mane of black hair, his glittering ebony eyes and muscle-packed body? But the deep cynicism which ran through Theo's veins made him suspect that his billionaire status might have a lot to do with his allure. Didn't the appeal of diamonds and a bloated bank account exert its own powerful pull on the opposite sex?

Yet Mia had wanted him when he was...

A pulse began to hammer at his temple. Not exactly poor, no—but certainly on a salary which seemed like a drop in the ocean compared to the vast reserves he had now. And wasn't he forgetting something? Yes, she might have professed to have loved him, but those had been meaningless words. How could you tell someone you loved them yet believe they were stealing from you? His throat tightened.

Her words meant nothing.

Love meant nothing.

She had walked away at the first opportunity. His own mother had dumped him, hadn't she? Dumped him and left him to die beside the hulking great ships in the stormy port. Women were capable of cruelty on a grand scale and he should never forget that.

He lifted up his drink, his dust-dry mouth grateful for that first quenching slug of *pressé*, and he put the empty glass down to survey her.

'You say we've moved on but we haven't really, have we, Mia?' he mused. 'Not when we are still man and wife.'

'Only on paper,' she objected.

'But that piece of paper ties us together— legally at least. And perhaps we need to do something about that.'

A frown pleated her brow. 'Get a...divorce, you mean?'

'Isn't that what couples usually do when a marriage comes to an end—or fails to start, as in our case? I thought you were curious to know why I'd never demanded one before.'

'I was, but if you remember you didn't answer my question.'

He wanted to hurt her then. To hurt her as she had hurt him. To make her jealous and realise what she'd been missing. What she was still missing. 'Some versions of my biography refer to a brief, early marriage and the assumption is usually made that the marriage was dissolved.' He smiled. 'And for a long time, I regarded having a secret wife as a kind of insurance policy. On one level I enjoyed keeping the information to myself. Knowing that no woman had ever become close enough to me to find out. And of course, it prevented me from ever doing anything as stupid as getting married again.' He gave the ghost of a smile. 'But I am no longer that man and I have no great need to protect myself.'

'You mean...' Her voice faltered. 'You've found someone you want to marry? Someone else?'

He saw the distress she was trying to hide—and he let her endure it for a moment longer before he answered, because he wanted to hurt her as she had hurt him.

'I never say never, but that's unlikely to happen. For me, it's more a question of tying up all the loose ends and simplifying my life. There is nothing to stop us from agreeing a settlement and you could walk away from this marriage as a wealthy woman.'

He shrugged. 'Naturally, I would be prepared to be more than…*generous*.'

But he saw no obvious reaction of pleasure or greed. He watched her eyes narrow—as if the idea of walking away with a massive settlement was a burden rather than a liberation.

'If only you knew how patronising you sound!' she declared. 'It makes me realise what a lucky escape I had. I don't *need* your *generosity*—I've managed very well without it so far!'

Her feisty attitude made her even more desirable. The flash of fire which lit up her blue eyes was very beguiling, as was the sudden pout of anger which made him want to crush her soft lips beneath his own. If it had been any other woman than Mia, this conversation would have ended one way only—with them in bed. But it *was* Mia, which made it complicated.

'You think so?' he queried. 'That's surely a matter for debate. You can't tell me you're happy working as a maid and living in cramped accommodation in the city? I always thought you were a country girl, at heart.'

She opened her mouth as if to respond, then seemed to think better of it, drawing her shoulders back in a gesture of kittenish pride. 'When I want any career advice from you, I'll be sure to let you know.'

In spite of himself, he smiled. 'As you wish,' he said softly. 'Now, why don't you settle in while I'm working? Use the pool if you want. There's a library if you want to read. And later, I'll take you to see your grandfather.'

He glanced down at her suitcase, which stood in the middle of the floor, and thought how out of place the battered piece of luggage looked in the pristine surroundings. His mouth hardened. He would facilitate a reconciliation between her and her grandfather, and afterwards, he and Mia could meet with his lawyer and agree a divorce. Then, and only then—when the connection between them had been legally severed—might he consider having sex with her.

He gave a flicker of a smile. When he stopped to think about it, it might be a fitting kind of farewell.

CHAPTER FIVE

AFTER THEO HAD GONE, Mia realised she was shaking. Actually *shaking*. Was that down to the sensual encounter she'd ended so abruptly, or the difficult conversation which had followed on from that? She fished around in her handbag for her hairbrush. It didn't matter. None of that mattered.

She went into the en-suite bathroom adjoining her bedroom—which was even bigger than the bathroom in the Presidential Suite of the Granchester hotel, which was saying something. All gleaming marble and silvery fittings, it contained a bath the size of a small swimming pool, a rainfall shower—and as many luxurious scented creams and gels as you'd find in an upmarket department store.

But all this unashamed opulence left Mia cold as she washed her hands and splashed water onto her face, though it had little effect on the vivid flush of her complexion. All she could think about was Theo and what he'd done when he'd pulled her into his arms and started to kiss her. Or rather, what he *hadn't* done. Because she'd been up for it, hadn't she? Deep down, she had been longing for him to sweep her into his arms and carry her over to that huge bed and do what she had been aching for him to do for so long now.

Why *hadn't* he?

That was her secret, shameful fantasy. Why hadn't she just encouraged him and gone for it? she thought crossly. Surely it would have freed them both from this niggling frustration which seemed to have been reactivated without either of them wanting it to.

She stared into the mirror, at the natural blue shade of her eyes, which was almost obscured by the blackness of her pupils. Her mind was buzzing as she dried her fingers on a fluffy towel and began to indulge in forbidden thoughts. What would sex with Theo be like? she wondered. What if, after all these years of longing and regret, it turned out to be a big fat disappointment? Would that be ironic, or disappointing? Liberating, even? She sighed. No. She mustn't lose sight of reality. How could sex with Theo Aeton be anything other than blissful?

But that wasn't why she was here. She was here to build bridges and be a dutiful granddaughter to a man who needed her and who now, it seemed, was regretting having rejected her.

Quickly, she unpacked the contents of her suitcase, thinking how forlorn her cheap clothes looked hanging in a tiny segment of the bank of fitted wardrobes. She finished off her lemon drink and tried to read a book about canine infectious diseases, but the words were nothing but a blur on the page because

Theo's darkly golden looks kept flitting distractingly into her mind.

Putting the book down, she glanced at her watch. There were still a couple of hours to go until they left to see Pappous and if she had to stay in this room much longer, she'd go nuts. She found the swimming costume she'd brought and hauled it on over her protesting curves, before pulling on an all-concealing wrap. Mia wasn't as insecure about her body as she used to be and the world was a lot more accepting of different shapes these days, but even so, she still didn't relish looking at herself in a full-length mirror.

Slipping through the marble corridors, she made her way to the pool, where the cool water felt like liquid silk gliding over her heated flesh as she slipped beneath the surface. Purposefully, she swam length after length until she was pleasantly tired and finished up in the infinity section, where she floated on her back and tried to enjoy the bright Greek sunshine and the tantalising scent of lemon and pine which drifted through the air.

After a while she headed back to her room, dived into the rainfall shower and, after a bit of indecision about which of her three dresses she should wear, presented herself downstairs at the appointed hour, to find Theo waiting for her.

His powerful figure dominated the airy entrance hall and her already thudding heart missed a beat. His eyes were shielded by a pair of dark glasses which made him resemble an enigmatic movie star and he was wearing a cool grey suit which emphasised his towering height. Silently, Mia acknowledged the sting of her breasts. He looked tantalising yet somehow unapproachable—and everyone knew that things which were out of reach were always more alluring than things which were there for the taking. At least, that's what she tried to tell herself.

And anyway, Theo's allure was not her primary concern—and neither was the smoulder of heat which had begun to whisper over her skin. A very important meeting lay ahead and she could tell from the clamminess of her palms just how nervous she really was.

'Ready?' he questioned.

'I'm scared,' she admitted.

'Don't be.' The curve of his lips was almost kind. 'You're his favourite granddaughter.'

'I'm his only granddaughter,' she retorted as she stepped into the afternoon sunshine to see a gleaming black car sitting outside. 'Where's the chauffeur?' she questioned, peering inside.

'No chauffeur. I'm driving.'

'Really?'

'Does that bother you?'

'Why should it?' she answered insouciantly, sliding into the passenger seat and smoothing down the skirt of her cotton dress. 'You may have many faults, Theo—but as I recall, poor driving wasn't one of them.'

Theo bit back a smile as he removed his jacket before getting behind the wheel, aware of the subtle scent of shampoo and soap which was radiating from his passenger and somehow the innocent freshness of those combined fragrances seemed disproportionately evocative. It made him feel uncomfortable. It reminded him of the man he had once been, and the man he was today. But that earlier version of himself had been a fool. He had mistaken desire for emotion. He had been taken hostage by his own feelings and had vowed never to let that happen again.

For a while he said nothing as he drove towards the old man's house, but when he could resist no longer, he shot her a glance, noting the tense way she was sitting. 'How was your afternoon?'

'It was all right. I went swimming.'

'I saw.'

She turned her head, with a cascade of bright curls. 'You were watching me?'

'Didn't you catch the glint of my binoculars in the sunshine?'

'You *are* kidding?'

He heard the squeak of horror in her voice and a smile played at the edges of his lips. 'Don't worry, Mia. I've never had to resort to voyeurism,' he informed her drily. 'I happened to look out of the window and saw you dive in.'

'It was an awful dive.'

'It could have been better,' he agreed. 'You should have kept your head down.'

'I wasn't actually asking for your advice.'

Theo decreased his speed and turned off down a smaller road leading towards the sea, his hands gripping the wheel tightly. He was behaving as if her technique had been his key consideration, when that had been the last thing on his mind. He had seen her splash into the water and had quickly moved away from the window because gazing at his half-naked wife had been doing dangerous things to his blood pressure.

But he hadn't been able to get the image of a swim-suit-clad Mia out of his head. It had made his body clench with hunger as he had stared blankly at his computer screen, the complicated sequence of numbers making little sense. The only thing he could see was a green swimsuit clinging to the curves of her body and dark red spirals of her hair contrasting against the glimmering blue of the water. It had taken every ounce of his resolve to resist the temptation to set aside his work and go and join her in the pool.

'We're here,' he said as they drove in through the big wooden gates of her grandfather's estate.

'I can see that for myself. I have been here before, Theo. Remember?'

Her words were spiky, but couldn't disguise the unmistakable nervousness underpinning them, and although vulnerability was a characteristic he tended to avoid, for once Theo was curious. As they reached the front of the house, he cut the engine and turned to look at her, observing the strained set of her profile as she gazed straight ahead. 'How does it feel, being back here?'

He expected her to cut off his question with an impatient aside or to tell him that was also none of his business. But to his surprise, she didn't. She spoke as if he weren't there. As if she had forgotten who he was, or where she was. 'How do you think it feels? It's…painful. It brings back memories I'd rather not have. It still hurts that he rejected me for all those years and made me vow never to set foot on his land again.' She bit her lip. 'But things change. I'm happy he's asked to see me again. If he hadn't… Well, I don't think I would ever have returned, to be honest.'

Theo felt the stab of something uncomfortable as he got out of the car, intending to open her door but Mia had already jumped out. She was standing in the sunshine, looking up at the big white house with a wistful expression on her face, the flower-sprigged dress making her look so unbelievably pretty that for a moment he couldn't drag his eyes away.

He had always come and gone as he pleased on the sprawling property and today that suited his purpose. It meant he could avoid bumping into any of the servants, because he was in no mood for conversation. He could see Mia's gaze darting here and there—as if registering what was the same and what was different. And her sudden look of sadness produced in him a powerful stir of guilt.

'Would you like to walk around first?' he questioned abruptly. 'Maybe acclimatise yourself with the place before you go in?'

She nodded. 'Yes. I'd like that.'

In contemplative silence, Mia fell into step beside him as they began to walk through the extensive grounds, along shaded paths lined with large pots of neglected plants and unpruned orange trees. She started wondering if Theo was thinking along the same lines as her. Was he looking at the outdated rectangular swimming pool and remembering the way the two of them had dived and raced like fishes, their laughter pealing through the sultry heat of the Greek air? But now the pool looked forgotten, with fallen leaves floating forlornly on the surface.

'Does nobody come here any more?' she asked suddenly.

Theo shook his dark head. 'Only me,' he said.

Mia felt a stab of guilt. Theo wasn't even a blood relation. She was, yet she'd stayed away all these years. She felt as if she'd had a raw deal with her family—as if she'd been short-changed on just about every level—and her grandfather's snub had been the final nail in the coffin. But maybe she hadn't been looking at the bigger picture.

Had she allowed her pride and hurt to keep her away from a place which had felt like the closest thing she'd ever had to home? She had been scared her grandfather might reject her, yes—but she had been just as scared of bumping into Theo. Had she subconsciously realised that his effect on her would be as powerful as it had always been, no matter how many years had passed—and wasn't there something awfully sad about that? It was a myth that she had distanced herself from her husband and he no longer had any influence on her life. Behind the scenes it seemed he had never really stopped influencing her.

'I'd like to go and see Pappous now,' she said.

He nodded and they reversed their steps through the unkempt gardens to make their way towards the house, until they came to a halt in front of some shut-tered doors on the ground floor.

'Are you ready?' he questioned, pushing open one of the doors. 'You'd better prepare yourself, Mia,' he added softly. 'He isn't the man he once was.'

There was a moment of hesitation, before she nod-ded. 'I'm ready.'

No sound came from within and the silence felt immense as they stepped into the dimly lit room, where the air was cool and air-conditioned. A nurse dressed all in white sat motionless beside the bed and, catching sight of Theo, she nodded and rose noise-lessly from her chair, before slipping from the room.

With a fierce knotting of her heart, Mia looked around, her gaze taking in all the paraphernalia of end-of-life care. The neatly lined bottles of tablets. The sterile dressing pack. A jug of water covered with an embroidered cloth and the glass beside it, the liquid untouched. The figure in the bed was covered with a sheet and completely inert but even from here she could see how much his once mighty frame had diminished. She gave a little snuffle. She wondered if it was that which made Theo reach out to touch her elbow. It was the lightest contact imaginable—yet wasn't it crazy how that simple gesture could feel so warm and comforting? As if he were her rock and she could lean on him. Was her grandfather sleeping? she wondered. Or was it wishful thinking which made her imagine a faint flickering movement of his eyelids?

But before she had a chance to investigate a bundle of brown and white fur came hurtling across the room towards her, yapping and jumping up excitedly, its paws scrabbling wildly at Mia's dress as the animal began to yelp with joy and confusion.

'Tycheros!' Mia whispered in disbelief, stroking his head and blinking back her tears as she crouched down and stared into the face of the dog she had rescued as a puppy. Instantly, the animal rolled onto its back, paws in the air as it bared its pink belly in a gesture of total trust and submission. 'Oh, Tycheros,' she said again, her voice catching as she whispered half to herself, 'I never thought I'd see you again.'

'Mia?' An unsteady rasp rattled from the direction of the bed and there was a sudden rustling of the sheet. 'Mia? Is that you?'

She could see now that her grandfather's ancient eyes were definitely glittering but Tycheros was still barking and it sounded unrealistically loud in the subdued atmosphere of the sickroom. Mia tried to quieten him with a cautionary forefinger but the dog Theo had christened Lucky continued to jump up with whines of delight, its tail waving back and forth like the windscreen wiper on a car. 'Will you take him outside?' she asked Theo firmly and as he led the dog away, she walked slowly towards the bed. '*Ochi*, Pappous. It's me. It's Mia. Oh, Pappous!'

With great difficulty—and waving away her offer of help—the figure in the bed wriggled up to get a better look and it took all the fortitude she possessed not to recoil in shock when she saw the pain-filled face of her grandfather. Because Theo had been right—it *was* a shock to see him like this.

Georgios Minotis had always been so robust and strong—a powerhouse of a man who had seemed to defy the years. Last time she'd seen him he had been full of life and vigour. But now? She blinked. Now he was nothing but a husk—a mere shadow of his former self. The salty spring of tears gathered in her eyes as she thought of all the time she had wasted. All those years they would never get back. Why hadn't she just taken the initiative and come here before? Swallowed her stupid pride before he did, and made amends?

'I should have known it,' Georgios snapped, his hooded gaze flickering towards the window where Tycheros was now pursuing a stick which Theo had presumably hurled towards the far end of the garden. 'Damned animal growls at anyone else. Even Theo.'

'Oh, Pappous,' Mia whispered, preparing to go over and hug him tightly, with all the love which was bubbling up inside her, even as she acknowledged that illness seemed to have done little to subdue his famously cranky nature.

But there was no answering softness in the faded black eyes as they turned to scrutinise her. They were filled with an emotion Mia didn't recognise. Or maybe she just couldn't bear to.

'What the hell are *you* doing here?' he demanded.

She tried to tell herself that sickness made people volatile and not to react to the hostility which was etched on his face, but it was difficult not to be hurt by his callous greeting. 'I'm here to see you, Pappous,' she offered cautiously.

'Why? Who let you in? Who brought you here?'

Mia hadn't even noticed him return from the garden but Theo must have been standing in the shadows at the edge of the room. He stepped forward, his powerful body seeming to fill the place with purpose.

'I did,' he said. 'I brought her.'

'Why the hell did you do that?' Spidery venom distorted the old man's voice and the lines on his ravaged face became even more pronounced. 'I told you I never wanted to see her again.'

'Because I thought you should see her,' said Theo calmly. 'That it would be good for you.'

'What right do you have to know what is *good* for me?' The old man's gaze raked over Mia, his voice quavering as he sneered. 'What do you want? My money? Has your mother sent you to claw back what you can from a dying man?'

'No,' said Mia, the hurt she felt at being spoken to that way now morphing into a slow and simmering anger. Briefly, she glared at Theo, before once more meeting her grandfather's eyes. 'My mother lives in Florida now. I may not see her very often but she certainly doesn't want your money. Your tainted money!' she added, wondering if she had imagined the brief nod of acknowledgement from her grandfather, as if he were only capable of dealing with people who dared stand up to him.

Had she been naïve enough to think he'd changed? That he had undergone a sudden transformation which had freed him from the shackles of his mistrustful mind, which made him unable to look at anyone without suspecting they were after his money?

Well, she wasn't going to stay here and listen to it. She had escaped from the cesspit of this toxic world and she had no intention of jumping straight back into it.

She was about to head back towards the garden when Theo stayed her with the faintest shake of his head before beginning to speak, the resonance of his words whispering over her skin like velvet, as he captured her in his night-dark gaze. 'You might change your mind about that, Georgios. When you hear what we're about to tell you.'

Mia's anger was superseded by confusion as she looked from Theo to her grandfather. *We?* What was he talking about? Why was he making it sound as if they were a unit? A couple— instead of two people on the brink of divorce. And why *had* he brought her here when clearly she wasn't wanted? He must have known that. Maybe he hadn't thought or cared that this kind of reception could hurt. Or maybe he thought she deserved to be hurt.

But she could see that her grandfather's face had changed. The hostility had vanished and he was looking at the two of them with interest. As if the world had very few surprises left for him and he was curious to hear what Theo had to say. Come to think of it, she was pretty curious herself.

And then everything began to change in a way she could never have imagined. Theo's arm was snaking around her waist with a familiarity which felt sublimely comfortable as well as very sexy. Suddenly their bodies were touching, and she cursed the appreciative shiver she gave as her fleshy hip collided with the bony jut of his.

'Can't you guess?' he said softly. 'We're back together. Mia and Theo. Husband and wife.'

He dropped a soft kiss on top of Mia's head and she cursed him for that too because, despite all her best intentions, it was making her long for things she had no right to long for.

It was all an act, she reminded herself bitterly.

Nothing but an act. Just as it always had been.

She knew she ought to tear herself away, but Mia didn't move. She told herself it was because any protest she made would appear callous—especially when her grandfather's wide smile seemed to have taken ten years off him. As she registered the delight which had transformed the old man into a closer approximation of the person he had once been, she felt trapped and compromised—but, in a strange way, willingly so. A feeling which was intensified by Tycheros, who must have slunk back into the room unnoticed and was quietly licking her hand. That crazy feeling of coming home assaulted her yet again, and the weakening effect of Theo's touch was making her powerless to resist.

'You are intending to make this marriage work?' the old man verified querulously.

'We certainly are,' affirmed Theo, a silky emphasis in his voice as he stroked his thumb over the base of her spine.

Mia looked up into his face to silently warn him to stop all this playacting, but his black eyes were glittering with something she didn't recognise. As he tilted her chin and bent his head towards her, she realised with a mixture of horror and delight that Theo Aeton was about to kiss her.

It was a show put on solely for the benefit of a captive audience. And even though his lips conveyed no other emotion than the hard stamp of possession, it didn't stop Mia from closing her eyes and kissing him back.

CHAPTER SIX

'I CAN'T *BELIEVE* you just did that!' Mia howled, as the car purred back through the gates of her grandfather's estate. Furiously, she turned to stare at Theo's profile, irritated beyond measure that the accusations she'd been hurling at him since they'd left the house didn't seem to be hitting home, because his features remained as implacable as ever, his gaze fixed responsibly on the road in front of him. 'Or maybe I can believe it. You've got form for being sneaky and underhand, haven't you, Theo?'

'Will you please calm down?'

'No, I will not. Don't keep telling me to calm down, as if you're working on some telephone helpline.'

'I realise you're angry.'

'Too damned right, I'm angry.' Mia bit into a lip which, infuriatingly, kept wobbling. 'In fact, I can never remember feeling this furious.'

Or betrayed. That was the worst bit. Once again, Theo had betrayed her by doing something which impacted deeply on her life, without any prior consultation. Yes, he might have brought delight to a dying man—but he had done so by placing her in an invidious position. And she couldn't see how she was going to get out of it.

Yet hadn't she betrayed *herself*—and in front of them all? Theo, her grandfather, and the one-eyed dog she'd found bleeding on the roadside all those years ago and which Theo had christened Lucky— saying how lucky the animal had been to have been rescued by her.

Mia huffed out another angry breath. When her estranged husband had pulled her into his arms and branded her lips with a fiery kiss intended for show hadn't she responded as if he had just made the most romantic gesture in the world? She had practically swooned as his mouth had covered hers and she'd kissed him back with a hunger which had been building inside her all day. She'd heard the grunt of approval her grandfather had given—as if they had just demonstrated to his satisfaction that a reconciliation was definitely on the cards. They had pulled apart and for a moment she had just stood there, grinning stupidly, her face flushed with pleasure as Theo's fingers curved possessively around her hip.

Had she learned *nothing*? Was she still that same woman so desperate for this man that she would accept whatever scraps he deigned to throw her way?

'When you touched my arm when we first went in, was that touching little squeeze of comfort just for show too?' she demanded. 'Did you do it because you knew my grandfather was watching and would falsely interpret it as a sign of true affection?'

He flicked her a brief look. 'You really think I'm that calculating?'

'I don't think it, Theo. I know it.'

His eyes returned to the road ahead. 'Very well, Mia. Think the worst about me, if you must. You think I care?'

His arrogant query only increased her fury but Mia didn't say another word for the rest of the drive home. She thought it unwise to give vent to her rage while he was driving and Theo seemed content to let her fume in silence. When he stopped the car in front of the house she went straight out into the garden to try to cool off, strangely confident he would follow her—which he did. And though she didn't *want* to feel a spear of sexual excitement, she wasn't going to deny the thrill it gave her to know that this devastatingly handsome man was pursuing her through the grounds of his property. Was that because, for the first time in their relationship, she felt as if *she* was the one with the power?

Her mind had been whirling with possibilities about where to have this very necessary confrontation. She didn't want to go to the bedroom and she certainly wasn't going to talk to him in the house, with Sofia and his maid hovering in the background. She didn't want to be overheard, or disturbed.

Her footsteps were fast and so was the beat of her heart, but it was difficult to maintain a high level of outrage when everything looked so beautiful in the honeyed light of the setting sun. The approach of evening had made the perfume of the flowers even more pronounced, and the wide ribbon of sea looked as if it had been highlighted with strokes of glittering bronze. A sudden sense of melancholy cloaked her, as she acknowledged the beauty all around her. Why couldn't she just sit down and enjoy the glory of her surroundings, as she used to do in the old days when she used to come to Greece during her summer holidays? Because everything had changed, that was why. For a start, she wasn't on holiday. She was here on sufferance and Theo had lied to her. Those were the facts. Stark and unpalatable, but true. Again, she felt the wash of anger, but Mia waited until they were alone in a courtyard garden she'd noticed on her way back from the pool, as she steadied her breath for long enough to ensure that her words were coherent.

'Why did you spring that on me, Theo?' she demanded. 'My grandfather didn't even know I was coming, did he? I couldn't believe it when I walked in and saw the shock and, yes, the horror on his face. I felt like I'd ambushed him, or something. Which I suppose, in a way, I had.' She shook her head and felt the tickle of wayward curls brushing against her warm skin. 'He hadn't expressed any desire for some sort of reconciliation with me, had he? There was to be no touching deathbed conversion.'

There was silence.

'Have you finished?' he questioned quietly.

'No, I haven't finished! I haven't even started, to be honest, except you probably wouldn't recognise honesty if it came up and hit you in the face.' She sucked in a shaky breath and suddenly she was afraid of doing something irreversible—like bursting into tears of disappointment and making him realise he still had the power to hurt her. Even now. 'You told me a big fat lie, Theo,' she whispered. 'You brought me out here under false pretences and what I want to know is…why? I mean, what's in it for you?'

'You think that's my only motivation?' His eyes narrowed. 'Self-interest?'

'I do, yes. Leopards don't change their spots.'

Oddly frustrated by her negative assessment of him, Theo turned to look at a statue of a woman, into whose marble basket one of the gardeners must have placed a bright, pink bloom which was glowing in the fading light. Suddenly, a bird flew on top of the statue's head and began to sing its heart out, and as the sweet notes penetrated his consciousness he felt as if he had just woken up from a long sleep.

When was the last time he had been in this part of the garden? he wondered, enjoying the violet and rose light which illuminated his surroundings and which made him feel as if he were standing in the middle of an oil painting. He frowned. He never really came here to enjoy the beauty or stop to reflect, did he? Just as he never used his pool for anything other than relentless, early-morning exercise. He had always been so driven. So determined never to take his foot off the accelerator. He had never really learned how to relax, or to enjoy the moment. He wondered what had made him think of that now.

Dragging his thoughts away from unwelcome reflection, he stared into the accusatory glitter of Mia's blue eyes. 'You want to hear my side of the story?'

She pursed her lips together before nodding, pushing away the tangle of her copper curls. 'It would be a start,' she conceded grudgingly.

He wished she wouldn't do that with her lips because it made it difficult not to start thinking about kissing her again. Theo cleared his throat. 'Let's start with the land. I have no self-interest—certainly not of the monetary kind. I never have. The piece of coastline your father gifted to me on our wedding day is in your name. I signed it over to you the day after your somewhat...' his mouth twisted mockingly '... abrupt departure.'

'You mean...' She stared at him. 'It's been mine all the time?'

'Yes.'

'But you didn't bother telling me?'

'Why should I?' He gave a sardonic laugh. 'You expected me to go chasing after you, did you, Mia? Pleading with you for your forgiveness? I thought you would return and when you didn't...' He shrugged, making out he hadn't cared, when at the time he had. More than he'd thought possible. Yet her sustained absence had worked in his favour, or so he'd thought. He'd convinced himself she was nothing but a child—too scared to come back and face the music—and that he'd had a lucky escape. He felt as if her response had given him permission to go out and behave as he wanted to behave. Which he had done.

'I felt pretty sure you wouldn't come back if you

thought the old man was going to reject you,' he continued, fixing her with a piercing look. 'Am I right?'

'I suppose so,' she said reluctantly.

'And yes, your grandfather can be an annoying and cantankerous old man,' he said slowly. 'But I have never forgotten the way he helped me, when I had nothing. I wanted to help him, and the bottom line is that he always wanted us to stay together, as man and wife. For some reason, he imagined we shared something which could work.' He held his hand up, his lips hardening into a stony slash. 'It's okay. You don't have to tell me you don't share his opinion—I can read it on your face. For what it's worth, I happen to agree with you.'

'You do?' she questioned.

'Of course I do. Our marriage was a mistake. It should never have happened. You were too young and I was determined to do the right thing, because I knew how much it would hurt him if I simply had an affair with you. So I asked you to marry me.'

'Right,' she said, trying to tell herself that here at least she could silently commend him for his honesty, but stupidly enough—it hurt. 'That's the reason you wanted me to be your wife? You didn't want to take my virginity without putting a ring on my finger, just to please your great mentor?'

'What's the point in raking over all that now?' he questioned impatiently. 'The past is just the past and the point is that he's dying, Mia. We can both see that. And his greatest wish was—is—for us to stay married.' He paused, his eyes narrowing as he met the stubborn expression on her face. 'Couldn't we give him what he wants—if only for a short while?'

'What good will that do?' she answered sulkily.

'We could make an old man happy enough to reconcile with the granddaughter he loves and free you both from the chains of bitterness,' he said roughly. 'Don't you want that to happen? Or will you go away from here with his angry words ringing in your ears, and live to regret the fact that he died without the two of you having made up?'

'Don't you dare play with my emotions!' she howled.

'I'm not playing with your emotions. I'm trying to use my own experience to prevent you from doing something which can never be undone.'

'What experience?' she questioned, her blue eyes suddenly growing hooded.

Theo delayed answering because this was a subject he never addressed. Not with her. Not with anyone. Why probe a sore which would be better left to heal on its own? Or shine a light on the shadows of his past and make him aware of just how grim that past had been?

But perhaps some sort of explanation was necessary—more as a bargaining tool than for any real desire for her to learn more about him, because it was too late for that now. Already she knew more than most people, yet she still thought the worst of him in any situation. But she didn't know this bit. Nobody did. He had seen to that. Early on in his career, he had taken control of all available information about himself and deliberately sanitised his background. He had shaved away the facts until they were nothing but dull bullet points. Little of his life before Georgios Minotis had adopted him was known, except perhaps to this woman with the wary blue eyes.

'My mother dumped me as a baby,' he said harshly.

'Yes.' Her voice had softened now with husky affirmation. 'I know that, Theo.'

And she had never talked about it, he realised suddenly. She might have used her knowledge as a weapon against him when she'd discovered that her grandfather had given him the land. Yet, despite her pain, she hadn't brought those juicy facts into the public arena and capitalised on what she knew—she had stayed loyal to him. Other women in her situation might have been tempted to sell their story, but Mia hadn't chosen that route. She had preferred to live in humble obscurity in London, rather than rake in the money she could have earned from some down-market tabloid with an appetite for the secret lives of billionaires.

His jaw clenched, because this wasn't supposed to be about concentrating on her good traits. It was all about winning her over to his idea. His mouth hardened. 'Over the years, I've read enough literature to understand that such an abandonment can have a profound effect on the psyche of the child—'

'How forensic you sound,' she breathed.

He slanted her a cool and questioning look. Would she have preferred to see him go to pieces? To demonstrate the kind of frailties which might make him appear weak? Then she would be waiting a long time, he concluded grimly. He thought back to when she had run away and the bitter tang of emptiness he had experienced as a result. He had hated feeling that way—that sense of emotional dependence he'd never fallen victim to before or since. Was that why he had decided to discover more about his roots— as a way of distracting himself? As a way of getting Mia Minotis off his mind?

'After the debacle of our wedding, I decided to seek out my mother,' he told her. 'To discover what circumstances had forced her to take such a desperate step.' He could feel the rough catch at the back of his throat and wondered how, even after all this time, it still had the power to affect him. 'I thought she must have been destitute. That perhaps she still was, and that maybe I ought to help her, as I had become a wealthy man. And don't they say that altruism always makes a person feel better about themselves?' he enquired mockingly.

'I guess they do,' came her response, toneless enough to barely register in his troubled thoughts.

'But it seemed any altruism on my part was unnecessary,' he continued, and a pulse began to thud angrily at his temple. 'I discovered that my mother had married, and married well. She was an extremely wealthy woman herself, though childless. Maybe she never liked children.' His lips curved with derision. 'Why else would she have chosen to abandon a helpless infant in a torrential dockside gutter, where they were most likely never to have been discovered?'

There was silence for a moment as she absorbed this. 'Oh, Theo,' she said at last, but must have noticed his gaze warning her against sympathy, for she quickly changed tack. 'You must have been so angry.'

He nodded. Angry, yes—but surprised, too. And the biggest surprise had been in finding out how much it had hurt. Like every child, Theo had painted vivid pictures in his imagination. He had imagined his mother as young and frightened and abandoned. A distraught woman at the end of her tether, who could see no way out other than to abandon her beloved child. What he had not expected was to find a face-lifted socialite, sipping cocktails on a vulgar yacht. With a little digging, he had discovered there had been a period of absence in the recorded story of her life. A year's absence, to be precise. Long enough for her to have a secret baby and then to leave it on the ground, like a piece of rubbish.

'So what did you do?' she probed, her blue eyes wide and troubled. 'Did you get in touch with her?'

'Of course I didn't,' he negated. 'Why would I? The thought of even being in the same room as her made my flesh crawl. So I left her to her privileged life and carried on with my own.' He sucked in a deep breath and slowly let it out. 'Until one day I received word that she had died and I...'

'What, Theo?' she prompted as his words tailed off. 'How did that make you feel?'

This was the kind of intrusive query women often liked to make, but when Mia asked it—with her voice so soft and concerned—Theo found himself answering, almost without meaning to. But he didn't give her the uncensored version, because that would be a confidence too far. He didn't tell her that he'd wanted to throw his head back and howl with rage and bewilderment.

'I found myself regretting not asking her why she'd done it,' he admitted. 'Why she had made such a cruel and potentially dangerous decision. And I realised that now I would never get the chance. Because death really is final, Mia.' His gaze bored into her. 'Intellectually, it's something we all know—but somehow we never really believe it's true. I think you'll regret not making up with the old man, no matter how much you try to convince yourself otherwise.'

The concern had left her eyes and in its place was the blue spark of mutiny. 'And presumably you've told me all this to guilt-trip me into agreeing to your ridiculous scheme?'

'Is it really such a ridiculous scheme?' he questioned curiously.

'You know it is.'

'Why? I think we could convince the world we're a reconciled couple, don't you? You don't seem to have any problems responding to me as a loving wife might do,' he continued, and now his mind was filled with a whisper of erotic possibility. 'Not earlier and not at your grandfather's, when I kissed you,' he concluded huskily.

'I expect most women react like that when you kiss them?'

'And if they do?' he drawled.

He saw her wince.

'It doesn't matter,' she said quickly, the flush in her cheeks intensifying. 'So it won't actually mean anything—this marriage of ours?'

'How *can* it mean anything? It will be a fake marriage. A marriage of convenience. And would it really be so different from a million others?'

She pushed a bright curl away from where it had strayed to the edge of her mouth. 'What others?'

Theo could feel the sudden powering of his heart because all he could think about was covering that mouth with his. Or feeling her lips at his groin, circling the stiff shaft which was currently throbbing with frustration and need. 'I'm talking about unhappy couples, and unhappy marriages. I know plenty of those, don't you, Mia? I have no illusions about the institution of marriage. But all the people who are unhappy don't automatically separate. Some of them stay together for years. Some for all of their lives. They hide their pain and their boredom and their infidelities behind different masks.' He ground out a bitter laugh. 'So why don't we find our own masks to wear? Why don't we remind the world that we are man and wife, for your grandfather's sake?' His ebony eyes glittered. 'It's not for ever. At most, a few months. And afterwards, we can divorce.'

'Are you...serious?'

'Why wouldn't I be?'

'There's my job, for a start. I arranged three weeks' leave of absence—this could be a much longer arrangement.'

He shrugged. 'You're a maid, and maids are easily replaceable.'

'Not good ones,' she argued hotly. 'And besides, I got promoted. I became a housekeeper, and then a supervisor, which is what I'm doing at the moment, though not for much longer.'

His eyes narrowed. 'Why, what else are you planning?'

Mia twiddled a coppery curl with her finger as she gazed up into his face, because suddenly it became important for her to make him understand that she hadn't just stayed static since they'd been apart. That the person he'd judged her to be wasn't the person she really was.

'I realised I didn't want to stay working in a city hotel,' she said, her attention momentarily caught by a pale moth fluttering frantically in the dying light of the day. 'You probably don't remember, but my dream had always been to work with animals.'

'The first time I met you, you were holding Tycheros,' he said slowly.

Mia blinked. 'You remember that?'

'How could I forget?' A look of something vaguely uncomfortable passed across his features. 'You were covered in his blood from where that bastard had taken out his eye with an air gun, but you didn't flinch. I'd never seen a woman behave like that before.' He shook his head. 'With such courage and such fortitude.'

Something about his approval made her go all mushy inside and her needy response angered her.

Mia forced herself to concentrate on the facts because even *feeling* this vulnerable was dangerous, let alone showing it. It suited her much better to think he'd married her to get his hands on the land—only now she'd discovered that he hadn't done that either.

'I've been saving up to go to school to be a veterinary nurse,' she continued. 'I've got a place which starts in September and in the meantime I help at the dog rescue centre in my spare time. So I can't just come and live here indefinitely in what sounds like a horrendous situation. *Pretending to be your wife!*' She shook her head. 'I've forged a new life for myself and it's one I'm proud of.'

But his expression remained implacable.

'You've seen how sick he is,' he said. 'The doctors told me it would be a matter of weeks. It's now April, and your college place doesn't start until September.' He paused. 'What if we see how things go? I can always get my team to help the Granchester find a replacement for you, if needed, so you're not leaving them in the lurch. Couldn't you do it? For him?'

Mia hesitated. The obvious answer was no, especially when she considered the pain she could inflict on herself by agreeing to such a crazy masquerade. She wanted to ask whether he'd thought about *her* feelings—or did he just consider them necessary collateral? But if she admitted her worries and her fears wouldn't that make her appear weak? As if she hadn't moved on at all, when clearly he had.

Because earlier today Mia had broken her self-imposed rule of not probing into Theo's life. When she'd got back from her swim and had been killing time, she had given into temptation and looked him up on the Internet. Not the business side of his life, which extolled all his achievements as well as his many virtues, but the other side of his life.

His personal side.

And his vices.

It had been something she had long suspected but finding out for certain had been a chilling wake-up call. Because while Mia had spent the last six years untouched by another man's hand, it seemed Theo had been behaving very differently. With masochistic intent, she had studied the images which had flashed up on her computer while her heart had beaten painfully fast. She'd wanted to shut the screen down but there had been a terrible, irresistible compulsion to keep scrolling down over the photos. And there they were. Paparazzi shots of him with models and actresses. Heiresses and athletes. All of them beautiful. All of them gazing up at him as if they couldn't believe their luck.

Blondes.

Brunettes.

Though interestingly, no redheads.

Why had it hurt so much after all this time to realise he must have had lovers? When she stopped to think about it—why wouldn't he? Unless she was daft enough to think that a rampantly alpha man like Theo would have behaved like a saint after his chubby bride had rejected him.

She had lulled herself into believing that she'd

moved on with her promotion and her plans for the future. She'd convinced herself that she didn't care what Theo did or didn't do with his life. But she hadn't moved on at all. Emotionally she had remained stuck in the past—and how was that going to change unless she did something about it? Mia shuddered as she caught a glimpse of the future which could be hers if she stayed locked in this weird kind of limbo. Never having a proper relationship because she never let any man close enough to kiss her—let alone have sex with her.

And she knew why.

Theo Aeton had proved an impossible act to follow, because their relationship had never been allowed to play itself out in a normal way. They were married but they'd never had sex. Their entire association had been underpinned by a deep sense of frustration and a lack of fulfilment. She had yearned for him during their engagement and the bitter truth was that she had yearned for him ever since. Hadn't his harshly beautiful face haunted her dreams when she was least expecting it— usually when she'd been asked on a date by another man? It was as if her subconscious were determined to remind her that she was setting herself up for an evening of disappointment—which inevitably always came true. It was as if her husband had stamped his presence indelibly on her unconscious mind—and now she was worried she would never be free of his memory.

Unless…

Tilting her chin to survey him with a calmness

she was far from feeling, she managed to keep her voice steady. 'What kind of marriage did you have in mind, Theo?'

His expression was inexorable. 'There is only one kind I will consider. A proper marriage.'

And in spite of everything, Mia's heart leapt. She looked at him with breathless hope. Did that mean... Was he actually suggesting they start over? Forget the past and do it properly this time? She swallowed. 'A real marriage?' she echoed, wanting—no, needing—clarification.

'Neh.' His black eyes glittered. 'A marriage with sex. Enough sex so that I'll be able to get you out of my head, once and for all.'

The younger Mia would have wept to have heard such a pitiless declaration, but she was older now. Maybe not much wiser, but certainly her vision was no longer distorted by rose-tinted spectacles. Because what if Theo's vision was the right one? She wanted him and he still wanted her, didn't he? That much was plain. A starving person satisfied their hunger by feeding it, didn't they? So it followed that consummating their relationship, instead of *dreaming* about consummating it, would set her free.

Because she needed that. She really did. She needed to be free of him. And this time she would be no pushover. This time she would be his equal.

She held his gaze for a long moment—long enough to see a flicker of doubt enter his eyes—and then she smiled. 'Okay,' she said at last. 'I'll do it.'

He reached out to cup her face in the palm of his

hand, his thumb tracing a slow line around the trembling outline of her lips. And that touch was like magic. Like wildfire. She could feel the instant tug of heat and the slug of her pulse. The molten sweetness at her thighs. Did he realise that already she was wet with need? She ached for him. She wanted him to take her now—with an urgency which might quieten some of this heated agitation. But somehow common sense prevailed and she shook her head, even though she could feel the shiver of her body's indignant objection. 'No,' she said and then, with a little more fervour, 'No.'

He stared at her with undisguised disbelief. 'You've changed your mind?'

'No, I haven't changed my mind, but I'm not doing it here,' she said, pointing to the fiery ball of the sun which was about to disappear into the sea in a blaze of gold and violet. 'I've waited six long years to have sex with you, Theo Aeton, and it's still light.'

'What's that got to do with anything?' he growled.

'We could be seen,' she said in a low voice. 'And I don't want one of your staff finding us.'

'Nobody will see us. The only other person who comes in here is my gardener—who will have knocked off work a couple of hours ago.'

'I'm not remotely interested in hearing the details of your staff rota!' she hissed. 'I'm just telling you that I have no intention of making out in the open air and being discovered.'

'Not a natural risk-taker, then, Mia?' he probed mockingly.

Momentarily wrong-footed, because his question implied a lot more experience than he was about to discover she had, Mia sought refuge in evasion. 'I couldn't possibly say,' she said carelessly.

He scowled at this, raking his long fingers back through the dark mane of his hair. 'Then we'd better go inside and find ourselves a bedroom,' he said roughly. 'Now.'

CHAPTER SEVEN

'CONSIDERING YOU'VE WAITED *"six long years"* for this,' quoted Theo softly as he began to unbutton his shirt, 'you don't look particularly excited.'

Mia opened her mouth to deny his accusation, but how could she when he'd touched on a raw nerve? Though it wasn't a lack of excitement she was feeling. It was a sheer, primitive terror which seemed to have engulfed everything else. Because her scheme appeared to have backfired on her. She had resisted his kiss in the garden, primly insisting on going inside the house to have sex as if she made those kinds of decisions every minute of the day.

She'd been afraid of losing her virginity in a rapid and undignified way, by allowing herself to get carried away. What if she'd ended up leaning against some marble statue, or lying on an uncomfortable garden lounger which might leave unattractive basket-weave patterns on her bottom? She hadn't said a word of this to Theo, of course, citing the fear of discovery as her reason for stalling. She licked her lips. The trouble was that now Theo obviously thought she was experienced, while nothing could be further from the truth.

He had shut the door of his bedroom quietly behind them and, after sliding the final shirt button from its confinement, was surveying her with a slow scrutiny which was making her heart race.

'I suggest we strip off and get straight into bed,' he said.

'S-strip off?' she verified cautiously.

'I don't know how much longer I can bear to prolong the anticipation,' he confessed, his voice low and velvety. 'Once I start kissing you again, I don't know if I can trust myself not to rip that damned dress from your body. Which would be a shame.' His gaze flickered over her cotton-covered curves. 'Because it's such a pretty dress.'

'Okay,' Mia agreed with a nod of her head, aware of the curls tickling her bare shoulders. She kicked off her sandals. 'Why not?'

She swallowed as his shirt fluttered to the ground and he smiled as he met her widening eyes—as if her rapt voyeurism was perfectly normal. Was this what he usually did when he took a woman to bed? she wondered. Did he stand there removing his clothes with that look of lazy provocation glinting from his eyes, while she was expected to do the same?

Yet in a setting which must have seen far more experienced sexual participants than her, she remained as nervous as hell—and her environment wasn't helping. It was a room which was a testament to masculinity and power. There was no softness here. The soaring dimensions and matchless view over the sapphire sea hinted at the wealth of its owner—as did the bold oil paintings, the glass sculpture of a woman, and a seat beneath an arc-shaped lamp, which Mia imagined would feel like sitting on a moonbeam.

Fearfully, she stared across the vast room to the equally vast bed. Its smooth, unruffled surface made her think of it as an arena where, instead of ponies trotting around performing to music, countless women must have flaunted their magnificent bodies and demonstrated the sophisticated sexual tricks they'd picked up along the way. Wasn't he going to be awfully disappointed when he found out the truth about her? That she knew absolutely zero about sex.

But it was too late to back out now—and the truth was she didn't want to.

She jerked her hand round to the upper part of her back, wishing she'd attended more of those yoga classes which would have given her a bit of added flexibility as she struggled to locate the tip of the zip.

'Here, let me,' said Theo, his silken chest gleaming as he walked towards her.

'Honestly, I can manage on my own,' she squeaked, her face getting hotter as she tilted her head back to make it easier. Because she didn't want him touching her when she felt so disadvantaged and out of place. When the balance of sexual experience felt so heavily weighted in his favour. She needed to calm herself down. To steady her breathing and remind herself that this was what she really wanted—which it was—and everything would be fine.

Theo frowned as he undid the belt of his trousers and slid the zip down over his aching shaft, unable to shake off the feeling that this wasn't quite what he had been expecting. What *had* he been expecting? He had no idea—because he'd never thought it would happen and, in many ways, Mia was still an unknown quantity. He had let her closer than he'd ever let any other woman—before or since—yet he hadn't seen her for over half a decade. Which made her...unique. And, because he was a man who had experienced just about every permutation of seduction in the book, wasn't the novelty value of this encounter making his heart feel as if it wanted to explode?

He had thought she might flirt a bit more, or play games. Tease him and provoke him with her sexual power—for she must be in no doubt about how much he wanted her. But she seemed almost *nervous* and, though he knew he could dissolve those nerves with one long kiss, she was making him curious enough to want to observe her behaviour rather than seek to change it.

At least she had managed to unzip her dress at last, her cheeks growing even more heated in the process. His breath caught in his throat as the flower-sprigged garment slid to the floor and he was confronted with the vision of Mia standing before him wearing nothing but her bra and pants. He ran his gaze over her generous curves with a mixture of awe and lust. How could he have forgotten how utterly magnificent she was? An abundance of creamy flesh was spilling over the top of a lace-edged bra which barely constrained her delicious breasts. A pair of surprisingly sensible panties adorned the luscious hips—but it was amazing how a garment which had clearly been chosen to support rather than enhance should manage to achieve both so effortlessly. He liked the faint curve of her belly and the soft lines of her arms.

'Don't look at me like that,' she beseeched and then seemed shocked at having spoken out loud.

'Like what?'

'Like...'

'Come on, Mia,' he reprimanded silkily as she stemmed her words by biting down hard on her lip. 'Surely you and I go back far enough to enjoy the luxury of speaking the truth in the bedroom. What's wrong with the way I was looking at you?' He paused, and even though a shaft of jealousy sliced through his body like a hot blade, he forced himself to ask the question. 'Surely men must have looked that way at you before?'

Her expression of intense concentration was followed by one of wobbling uncertainty, and if Theo had been a gambling man he might have wagered a bet on her blurting out that this was a bad idea and then rushing from the room. His brow furrowed as he wondered if he would attempt to stop her, despite how much he was aching for her. He wasn't sure. Because wouldn't part of him have agreed that this was a very bad idea?

'I'm a virgin!' she burst out.

Theo froze.

'Please tell me I'm hearing things,' he said quietly.

'You're not. I'm a virgin. I've never… I've never had sex with anyone before. Obviously,' she said, with a shrugging attempt at humour which didn't quite come off.

Theo could feel the sudden pounding of his heart as his gaze bored into her, unable to shake off a surreal sense of disbelief. 'Why the hell didn't you tell me this before?'

'*When*, Theo? It's not the sort of subject you can casually introduce into the conversation, is it? Should I have announced it when I arrived? Or on the way to see my grandfather? Perhaps I could have slipped it in when we were enjoying a glass of lemon cordial, though obviously I would have needed to have waited until Sofia had left the room since I'm not sure how good her English is.'

Theo felt the boil of rage and frustration and the equally annoying sensation of being wrong-footed—and in the bedroom of all places. Why the hell hadn't he guessed, when the clues had been there for him to see all along? Didn't that explain the subliminal aura of innocence which always seemed to surround her—even after all this time? Or the sense of wonder she'd displayed when he'd kissed her earlier today, as if no man had ever kissed her like that before? He frowned. Had that really only happened a few hours ago?

'You should have told me,' he said flatly as he bent down to pick up his discarded shirt. 'Call me selfish, but I would have preferred not to have started all this, then been forced to stop.'

'Stop?' She was blinking at him. 'Who's talking about stopping?'

'I am!' He hauled the shirt on over his shoulders, needing to get out of that room as quickly as possible, unwilling to watch her put her dress back on and struggle with the damned zip and wriggle that delicious body until he was in danger of losing his mind. His throat constricted. 'Obviously, this changes everything,' he said tightly.

'Why?' she demanded. 'I mean, why does it have to?'

'I'm not having sex with a virgin,' he snapped.

She was shaking her head, the glossy spill of copper curls tumbling down over her shoulders, and he wondered if she had any idea how lovely she looked right then. No, he thought. One thing Mia could never be accused of was vanity. Hadn't her narcissistic mother cruelly punctured her self-confidence once too often, leaving her with none? Wasn't it time that he told her just how beautiful she really was?

'I still don't understand,' she whispered. 'You want sex with me and I definitely want sex with you. A piece of paper says we're legally married—so what's the problem? Please explain it to me.'

He chose his words carefully. 'The fact that you haven't been intimate with anyone else is significant.'

'How?'

He shrugged. 'It suggests you still care for me and will read too much into it,' he continued repressively. 'And I really don't want that to happen.'

Mia stared back, her heart slamming hard against

her ribcage as she took in what he'd just said. 'Of all the arrogant things you've ever said to me, Theo Aeton—and there have been plenty of those,' she breathed, 'that one really tops the lot.'

'Is it arrogant to articulate my reservations?' he demanded. 'I thought we were being honest with each other.'

He used words very cleverly, Mia thought with reluctant admiration. Was her innocence too heavy a burden for a man like him to take on and was he going to rethink this whole marriage-with-sex idea?

And if he did, what then? Would they be expected to flit around the place pretending to everyone they were man and wife, and all the while existing in the same kind of state of frustrated celibacy they'd endured before? Was she going to allow that to happen for a second time?

No, she was not.

It dawned on her that she was standing there in nothing but a pair of pants and a bra, and that although Theo was clipping out logical reasons about why they *shouldn't* be having sex his eyes kept straying reluctantly to her cleavage. And didn't that make her feel good about herself for the first time in years? Or should that be bad? She wasn't sure.

She licked her lips and saw him watching *that* too, like a dog sitting patiently underneath the dining table, knowing that, a few feet away, a juicy piece of meat was being consumed. In the garden she had thought about her sexual power—which had now joined the list of stuff which was important to her, like self-worth and making her own way in the world.

And she realised that if she allowed Theo to dictate what happened next she would find herself back at square one. She would change back into someone docile and accepting—a person who allowed herself to be moved around like an object, rather than reaching out and taking what she really wanted. Which was him. It had always been him.

Her heart was beating very fast as she began to walk across the room and any shyness she might have felt at being half-naked was quickly melted by the hungry burn of his eyes. He said nothing as she approached and still nothing as she hooked her arms around his neck, brushing her lips against his.

'I won't read anything into it,' she said. 'This won't mean anything. I promise.'

He seemed to hold himself rigid and tense and for a moment she wondered if he was going to push her away, but then he gave a growl of what sounded like desire, underpinned with something she didn't dare focus on, in case it was resignation—or regret.

Or could it be submission?

Because now there was no slow striptease, or lazy and provocative smile from the man she had married. All that tight self-control had left his face. His expression dark with intent, he picked her up as lightly as if she were a sack of feathers rather than a stocky little maid, and carried her over to the bed.

He laid her down, his eyes not leaving her face as he tore off the unbuttoned shirt and it drifted to the floor out of sight. Her gaze followed the movement of his hand to the zip of his trousers, but she was determined not to betray any trace of shyness as he carefully eased it down.

And wasn't the truth that she *didn't* feel shy? Not a bit. They had indulged in plenty of foreplay in the shadowed and secret corners of her grandfather's estate, but they'd never got this far before. They'd never even entered any of the bedrooms—control freak Theo would never have allowed it.

But here they were. *Here they were.* And after so many stop-starts, Mia was determined to enjoy every second of it. As he kicked off his trousers and slid his shorts down to expose the massive shaft of his erection, she couldn't help thinking how *right* it all felt. Was it crazy of her to be happy she'd never done this with anyone else—and happy she had saved this part of herself for him? Of course it was. She wasn't supposed to be reading anything into it. Certainly not sentimental stuff like that.

He was naked at last and, greedily, she ran her gaze over his incredible body. Honed muscle rippled beneath the olive-gold silk of his skin. The broad bank of his shoulders tapered down to a hard chest and narrow hips. His legs were long and athletic, his thighs powerful and strong. He was beautiful, she thought yearningly. There was no other way to describe him. And she had waited a long, long time for this moment.

The mattress dipped as he joined her on the bed and as she felt the hard brush of his leg against hers she felt the first faint shimmering of apprehension.

She was scared of disappointing him. Scared of disappointing herself. Did he realise that? Was that why his black eyes became smoky and hooded as he bent his head towards her?

His kiss was everything she needed. Beneath his seeking lips Mia eagerly opened up as his mouth drugged her into an instant state of compliance. She ran her fingertips over his arms, his shoulders, and the tight silken curve of his buttocks—as if she needed to touch him all over to make sure he was for real.

And he was.

So *very* real.

His hands were moving over her too and he clicked out a sound of rueful impatience as he encountered the lingerie she was still wearing. His fingers found the catch of her bra, which he released easily, so that her breasts came tumbling out into his hands and Mia gasped as he cupped them. His fingers were tracing circles over her nipples and every nerve-ending was firing into exquisite life. She squirmed with excitement beneath his questing touch and he drew his mouth away from hers.

'Always so responsive,' he murmured, looking down into her face. 'Every. Single. Time.'

Mia opened her mouth to say something—though she wasn't quite sure what her answer might be—but by then he had started sliding her pants down over her thighs and words became impossible. And suddenly she didn't care that she'd always thought her legs a bit like a rugby player's—because Theo was murmuring appreciatively as he kneaded his fingers over her skin, telling her she was beautiful. And right then, she *felt* beautiful as his fingers found her aching bud and began to stroke her with a delicacy of touch which was driving her crazy with equal amounts of pleasure and frustration. Could he tell how much she wanted him? Was that why he gave a low laugh as he delved deep into her honeyed heat, using the lubrication to slide slickly over her quivering flesh again, until she was writhing with unashamed need.

'Theo,' she breathed, because almost immediately she found herself on the brink of an orgasm, as she had been so many times before. 'Oh, God, Theo.'

But he withdrew his hand and pulled away, the faint shake of his head sending arrows of disappointment shooting up her spine.

'No. Not like this,' he informed her sternly. 'This time we do it properly.'

Or improperly, thought Mia dreamily, vaguely aware of him reaching for what was obviously a condom as she heard the tearing of foil. Did he always have one to hand? she wondered jealously. Through half-closed eyes she watched as he slid the protection on and she had to suppress the stupid thought that if they'd stayed married they might have had a little baby by now. Or a small child, even.

But then he was kissing her again and all those pointless thoughts dissolved. Everything was forgotten as her world became centred in this bed and what Theo was doing to her. His big hands had begun to explore her body, as if he were reacquainting himself with every centimetre of her flesh. His rapt thoroughness thrilled her, even if he seemed curiously detached at times. A rush of liquid warmth flooded through her and he gave another murmur of appreciation as his fingers relocated its source. He licked her breasts, her belly and her thighs, though his mouth stayed poised above her aching bud and she could have screamed out loud with frustration.

Was his effortless self-control threatening to desert him? she wondered. Was that why he gave that almost angry little growl as he moved over her, the warmth and weight of his body making her feel deliciously fragile, for the first time in her life?

'Do you know how long I've waited for this?' he ground out harshly.

And now Mia could see that his self-control wasn't effortless at all. Judging by the tension which made his face look like dark marble, he only just seemed to be holding onto it by a thread. His eyes didn't leave her face as he positioned himself over her, but as she felt the broad tip of his hardness nudging against her molten heat, Mia quickly shut her eyes. Because what if all her love and longing came back the moment he entered her?

And then he did. Filling her with that first long, slow thrust. The pain was swift—forgotten almost as quickly as it had happened. Had she cried out? Was that why he stopped, his words an urgent imperative?

'Open your eyes, Mia.'

Tentatively, she obeyed, her lashes fluttering open to meet the gleaming black searchlight of his.

'Does it hurt?'

She shook her head. 'It did. A bit. But not now. Not any more.'

He swallowed. 'Does this?'

Soft heat began to filter through her veins as he began to move with infinite precision inside her. 'Oh, no,' she whispered, with breathless delight. 'That definitely doesn't hurt.'

His fingers tangled in her hair as kissed her and began to take up a rhythm, slowly at first, until her body had relaxed enough to accommodate him. On a purely anatomical level, it was astonishing that he was able to fit so comfortably inside her. And then she was done with analysing. Done with everything apart from what was happening to her. She was doing things she hadn't realised she knew how to do. Lifting her legs, she hooked her thighs around his back and he gave a low laugh of pleasure as he cupped her buttocks with the palms of his hands, and increased his speed. She gasped as he drove deeper inside her and he bent his head so that his warm breath fanned her lips.

'You like it like this?'

'Isn't it obvious?' she gasped. 'Do you like it too, Theo?'

'Isn't it obvious?' he ground out mockingly.

But when it happened it shocked her—because surely one orgasm was the same as any other, and Theo had made her come plenty of times in the past. But as her body contracted around his and he made a sudden choking moan which sounded almost...helpless... Mia realised she had been wrong.

Because this was different. *This* was intimacy. This man. Inside her. Her heart beating against his. Their flesh joined. Literally. The slowing pump of his seed. Just the thought of it blew her away. Made her grow soft with yearning.

But that way of thinking was spiked with danger and right now she didn't want anything spiky in her life—not when she could feel a delicious languor creeping over her. She felt sleepy and thoroughly satisfied. So she laid her head against Theo's chest and listened to the muffled thunder of his heart, and in that moment Mia felt something very close to contentment.

Theo lay with his eyes wide open as Mia slept against him, her head resting on his heart. He could feel the steady rhythm of her warm breath and feel the tickle of her hair, which curled like fiery snakes against the darkness of his chest.

He was tempted to stroke her magnificent breasts again but, despite the proximity of a peaking nipple, he resisted the temptation, grateful for this brief respite. Relieved to have been left alone with his thoughts, even though they were making him uncomfortable. He stared up at the ceiling, at the motionless blade of the fan which reminded him of the helicopter which had brought her here today. He thought how remarkable it was that, in a few short hours, the world as he knew it had changed.

His body was sated. He could never remember feeling so empty yet so satisfied, all at once. As if he had just devoured a delicious meal yet already his appetite was sharp and hungry for more. His body had begun to stir, the warmth of the naked woman in his arms making him grow harder with every second that passed.

His mouth was dry and he swallowed, but that did nothing to alleviate the dustiness of his throat. He could have reached out to pick up a glass of water from the bedside table but he didn't want to move. He needed to get his head straight before she woke and to put everything in perspective.

He sighed. He'd spent a long time wondering what sex with Mia would feel like and although everyone knew comparisons were odious, it was human nature to make them. And now he had made the unwelcome discovery that nobody compared to her. Because the sex had been…

Ever the perfectionist, he searched around for the right word. Sublime. *Neh.* He suppressed a bitter laugh. The best sex of his life. *And he didn't want it to be.* Hadn't he been hoping it would have been something of an anti-climax, especially when he'd discovered that she had remained a virgin? Hadn't he wanted it to be clumsy and forgettable?

But there had been no awkwardness or embarrassment, despite her inexperience. He could never remember kissing a woman as deeply as he had kissed Mia. Could never remember coming so hard, or for so long, of feeling as if she'd ripped out a fundamental part of him and exposed it to the light. His mouth hardened, as the desire to touch her again overwhelmed him and this time he did not resist. He ran his fingertips over her spine and as she murmured something incomprehensible against his chest, he started to play with her nipple, which obligingly sprang into life.

It was no big deal.

Of *course* it was going to feel amazing. Everyone knew there was nothing as effective as delayed gratification. Didn't he enjoy his own hard-earned wealth more than those of his contemporaries who had inherited theirs, because he'd known real hunger and real poverty? And so it was with Mia. He'd waited a long time for this. Again, he frowned. Of course he hadn't actually *waited*—for that would imply something had been missing from his life. Or that he'd intended for this to happen—which, of course, he hadn't. It had happened by chance—it wasn't some far-fetched concept of destiny, because there was no such thing. Just as there was no such thing as love, or happy families, or a whole list of meaningless things which people wasted precious time trying to attain. What the hell was a *soulmate* anyway? he thought contemptuously.

A sense of resolution crept over him. All he needed to do was to have as much sex with her as possible, before she flew back to her very different life in England. His lips hardened. A glut of intimacy would make their entrance into society as newly-weds that bit more convincing and it would also give this *thing* a chance to burn itself out.

And he wanted it to burn out.

He needed it to burn out.

He wanted her out of his head, once and for all.

Slipping his other hand between her thighs, he edged his thumb upwards to slide over her swollen bud and she wriggled her hips appreciatively.

'Theo,' she whispered, her breath growing more rapid as, delicately, he began to strum lightly against her satin heat.

'What?' he whispered as the smell of her sex filtered into the air and he breathed it in, like oxygen.

'I don't know,' she said drowsily. 'Just Theo.'

'Do you want me?'

Still she didn't open her eyes, but she opened her thighs. 'What do you think?'

But Theo didn't want to think. Not any more. He didn't want to do anything except be inside her. Deep and hard. Hot steel against cool silk. He wanted to make her scream, over and over. He wanted to imprint himself on her body so indelibly that any man who came after him would be incapable of giving her this much pleasure. But as he sheathed himself with another condom, he found himself consumed by a sensation he didn't recognise. A sensation which was powerful and all-consuming, which demanded definition.

It was delayed gratification, he reminded himself as he eased himself into her tight wetness.

Nothing more complicated than that.

CHAPTER EIGHT

MIA OPENED HER EYES. Outside the enormous and unfamiliar window the sky was as bright as a field of
cornflowers, and in the distance she could see the
sapphire sea glinting in the morning sunshine. Still
drowsy, she looked around. She was lying on a huge
bed, completely naked and completely alone. Spot-
ting the ruffled sheet, which must have fallen to the
ground, she reached down and hauled it up over her
aching breasts, using her free hand to push back the
tangle of curls which was flopping wildly over her
face.

Like an animal in the undergrowth, she grew very
still, listening intently for sounds—the whoosh of a
shower, perhaps, or the brushing of teeth. But there
was no sight or sound of the man who had spent the
night giving her the kind of pleasure she'd only ever
dreamed about. She plumped up the soft pillows and
leaned back against them. They'd had sex so many
times, she'd lost actual count. At one point—it must
have been past midnight because none of the servants were in the house—Theo had gone down to the

kitchen to forage for food because the grumbling of her stomach had made her realise she hadn't eaten a thing all day.

She had fallen on the Greek salad and delicious bread, the garlicky hummus and succulent slices of melon, and washed them down with some more of the lemon drink they'd had earlier. She remembered Theo watching her with a look of wry amusement on his face, telling her that it was rare to see a woman enjoying her food so much. She wasn't sure if she liked the sound of *that*. And when they'd had their fill, he had lifted a spoon to trickle some thick dark honey into her belly button and then spent a frustrating age licking it out, so that by the time his sticky tongue had flickered between her thighs, Mia had orgasmed almost immediately.

Anxiously, she glanced down at the sheet, looking for any tell-tale signs of their sexual antics—as a maid she was used to rapidly assessing the state of bedlinen—but thankfully there was no leftover honey to make the servants gossip.

She blanched. The servants! What would they say when they discovered—as they invariably would if they were doing their jobs properly—that her bed hadn't been slept in? Should she creep in there now and ruffle it up, the way they did in films?

Slumping back against the soft pillows, Mia expelled a huge sigh. None of this was supposed to have happened, and part of her despaired at how easily Theo had managed to manipulate her. For a start he had extracted her agreement that they would masquerade as a married couple, in order to please a dying man. How insane was that? And then he had seduced her. No. That would imply that what had happened had been one-sided, or that he'd had to persuade her, when the truth was that she had grabbed at the experience eagerly.

Had she really taken off her clothes in front of him, stubbornly refusing his help with her zip? Yes, she had. Had she really—this had been much later in the night, of course—taken him in her mouth and heard him moan with pleasure as she had swallowed the salty essence of him? Yes, that too. Again, Mia sighed. He had left her physically satisfied, but he'd left her feeling emotionally vulnerable too. Why else was she lying alone in this great big bed, feeling as if he had ripped away a layer of her skin, leaving her longing for the sort of things which were never going to happen? Come to think of it—where *was* he?

As if on cue, the door opened and Theo walked in, dressed in dark trousers and another pale silk shirt. His black hair looked damp and his skin gleamed like burnished gold. He looked full of energy and vigour, but his ebony eyes were cool and unfathomable.

'Good morning.'

His voice was cool, too, as if nothing out of the usual had occurred last night, and Mia's mushrooming vulnerability only increased, which probably explained why she didn't return his civilised greeting and came out with a blunt and needy question instead. 'Where have you been?'

He raised his eyebrows. 'I went for a swim.'

'A *swim*?' she questioned.

'*Fisika*,' he agreed equably. 'I always swim in the mornings. I think I already told you that? Then I came up here to shower and dress and you were still asleep and you looked…' A pulse briefly flickered at his temple. 'You looked so peaceful that I decided to go downstairs and do some work.' His smile was brief. 'I always find I'm more productive when the world is quiet.'

And he'd seen no reason to break his wretched routine? Mia wondered. No, of course he hadn't. Because this was nothing new to him. Certainly nothing like the earth-shattering experience it had been for her. She was just another woman in his bed—who knew nothing about post-sex morning etiquette. Which was why he had absented himself. He had probably been sending out a very deliberate message and helpfully reminding her that this wasn't a *real* relationship. So stop behaving like a wimp and show him your strength.

'I'm just wondering what happens now,' she said. 'In terms of…?'

Holding the sheet firmly against her aching breasts, she stared at him and all her determination to stay strong began to falter.

In terms of are you even going to bother kissing me, or does that only happen as a precursor to sex?

'I'm naked in your bed, Theo.' Mia paused, enjoying the sudden flash of fire in his eyes, which was the only chink in the cool mask he'd worn since entering the bedroom. Pushing her curls away from her face, she saw the flash in his eyes intensify. 'So naturally I'm wondering if anyone is around to see me going back to my own room, which is some distance away. Sofia, or Dimitra, for example.'

'And if they do see?'

'You must admit, it would be slightly awkward.'

'I agree, it might have been.' He paused, his jaw firming. 'Had I not gathered all the servants together after my swim and informed them of your true identity.'

Did he mean to make it sound as if she'd been taking part in a police line-up? Mia blinked. 'You've told them I'm your wife?'

'I did. We aren't intending to keep it secret, are we? My new maid actually giggled and, when I asked her why, told me she'd already guessed— apparently, she's friendly with someone who used to work for your grandfather back in the day.'

'Oh.' Mia stared at him blankly and the strangest thought stole into her head. That here she wasn't alone and anonymous. Here people actually knew her—or knew of her. That feeling of being rootless and disconnected briefly evaporated and she felt a brief burst of connection.

'So why don't you borrow my robe and get ready?' he continued, his velvety voice disrupting her introspection. 'After breakfast we'll go and see your grandfather to reinforce our *togetherness*. Strike while the iron is hot, as my English teacher used to say.' His eyes glittered. 'How does that sound?'

It sounded like a timetable. It sounded like Theo

taking control just the way he always used to, but in this instance she was happy to let him. She needed to get her head straight and to work out the best strategy, going forward. Because obviously they were both coming at this marriage of convenience from different places. She had hoped for a kiss, or an echo of the enchantment they'd shared during the night.

But he had been...

She sighed.

He wasn't being unkind, no, but certainly nobody could mistake his matter-of-fact attitude for romance. And the only reason that might upset her was if she cared about him, and she didn't. She mustn't. That was the only thing she needed to remember. Because if she allowed herself to care for him, she was going to get hurt all over again.

'Great idea!' she said brightly, climbing out of bed to make her way across the room, glad her back was to him so he couldn't see her look of discomfiture, because she was acutely aware of her wobbly bottom.

Alone in the bathroom she was shocked by the face which stared back at her from the mirror. Those wide, dark eyes and kiss-bruised lips which indicated just how thoroughly she had been ravished—not to mention the wild disarray of her hair. She took a moment to untangle her curls and brush her teeth, finding a bathrobe and knotting it tightly around her waist before returning to the bedroom, hoping Theo might have gone downstairs and spared them another awkward encounter.

But he hadn't gone anywhere. He was standing exactly where she had left him—as motionless as the glass statue on the other side of the room. The only thing which moved were his eyes and they flickered as they glanced at the robe which covered her—way too big and flapping around her ankles—as if drawing attention to how much taller and bigger he was.

'Mia,' he said, his voice suddenly growing rough.

'I'm off to my room to have a shower,' she informed him as she passed him by, but he stalled her by catching hold of her wrist and encircling it within his own big hand. It was loose enough for her to break free, so why didn't she? Why was she revelling in the warm brush of his skin against hers, which was making her heart race as if she'd been sprinting for the bus?

'I don't think you want to go anywhere,' he contradicted silkily.

'Theo!' But the word was more of an incitement than a protest. She really had to stop saying his name like that because it was giving him the wrong idea. Or should that be the right idea? She swallowed, her eyes fluttering to an infuriatingly close as he bent his lips to her neck.

'Theo, what?' he murmured, the feel of his mouth against her skin inciting her even more.

'I th-thought…' she stumbled, before her sentence faded away.

'Mmm?' His tone was careless as he untied the oversized bathrobe and Mia's knees threatened to buckle as he began to play with her breasts. 'What did you think, my beauty?'

But it was impossible for her to remember. Her brain had turned to mush and so had her body, especially as he was manoeuvring her over towards the bed and, oh, she wanted that. She wanted that *so much*. His lips had now moved to her mouth, that first taste causing him to pause.

'Did you use my toothbrush?' he questioned huskily.

Mia's eyelids snapped open and the sight of the raw desire on his face at last gave her the courage of her own convictions. 'Why shouldn't I?' she declared, ribaldly repeating what she'd heard some of the bolder chambermaids say at work. 'We've shared more than a bit of saliva during the night, surely.'

His corresponding laugh was low as he unzipped his trousers and let them fall, before sitting on the end of the bed and pulling her towards him. Mia moaned. She was wet for him. So hungry that she could barely wait until he had stroked on a condom. And then she was straddling him, gasping as he pulled her down onto the velvet-steel of his erection. And he was groaning as she tilted her hips and shifted her weight towards him, feeling him going deeper and deeper, until they were both choking out their pleasure at exactly the same time, and he muffled the sound of their cries with the hard press of his lips.

Her head lay heavy on his shoulder and reluctantly Theo loosened his hands from around her waist, though he could have stayed like that all morning, with the soft fan of her breath against his skin.

'I suppose I'd better go and get dressed,' she said

drowsily, lifting her tousled head to survey him with sleepy eyes. 'See you at breakfast.' She yawned. 'Didn't Sofia say something about it being served out on the terrace?'

'That's right.' And even though his instinct was to peel her grapes and slowly pass them from his mouth into her own, he quashed it. 'You'll find everything you need.'

'But you'll be there?'

'No. I had some breakfast after my swim,' he added, feeling her soft body grow tense against his.

'Oh.'

'Come and find me afterwards,' he said, hardening his heart to the note of disappointment in her voice. 'I'll be working in my office. One of the staff will show you the way if you can't remember how to get there.'

'I'm sure I can manage to find my way around a private house—no matter how grand,' she retorted. 'After working in a two-hundred-and-fifty-room hotel.'

Despite her bravado, Theo couldn't miss the brief shadow of hurt on her lips, but although he told himself he didn't care, that wasn't strictly true. She was starting to *get* to him and he didn't want that. He felt like a piece of soft clay in her hands, which she had begun moulding without first asking his permission. That was the reason why he had distanced himself from her this morning, after the intensity of the night they had shared. Those deliciously erotic hours in the moonlight, when it had been all too easy to forget how badly she had hurt him.

Ignoring the siren call of her body, he had left before she was awake, taking himself off to the pool to conduct a more punishing than usual early morning swim. After getting showered and dressed, he had walked in here intending to resist her, but resistance had been futile. One look at her and he had been lost. Despite his best intentions, he had lowered her onto his aching shaft, physical pleasure obliterating any concerns about his uncharacteristic lack of resolve.

Still, he thought, as he took his second shower of the morning—why not just go with the flow? He had spent far too much time already resisting Mia. Why not take as much as she was willing to give and reciprocate? Because, when the chips were down, was she really any different from any other woman? How could she be? With repeated exposure, her undeniable allure was bound to evaporate. He would become bored by her—it was as inevitable as the passage from night into day. His jaw firmed. And the sooner that happened, the better.

But when she appeared at the door of his home office an hour later, growing bored of her seemed too big a stretch of the imagination. Beneath his breath, Theo cursed, his immediate stirring of lust reinforcing how completely she had captivated him. How had she managed to maintain that air of shining sweetness, despite the decadent night they'd just enjoyed? Her copper curls were tamed into glossy ringlets, her cheeks flushed with roses and she was wearing another of those simple cotton dresses—this one awash with tiny bluebirds rather than flowers. She looked fresh and wholesome and, despite her undeniable effect on his senses, thoroughly out of place in the pared-down luxury of this house.

'I phoned Pappous's house,' she announced. 'And apparently he had the best night's sleep he's had in a long time.' Her voice grew soft. 'The nurse said how much better he looked this morning.'

Theo put his pen down. 'I'm pleased. And yesterday, he saw you.' He raised his brows. 'The two facts can't be unrelated.'

'I wouldn't dream of making that connection,' she responded quietly. 'But like you, I'm pleased.'

Shutting down his computer, he leaned back in his chair to study her. 'You know, before we go and see him, we need to arrange a shopping expedition.'

Her eyes narrowed with suspicion. 'What sort of shopping did you have in mind?'

'Things to wear, mainly.'

'For me?'

'Of course.' His gaze flickered to the same cheap espadrilles she'd been wearing yesterday and even though the ribbons tied around her slim ankles were undeniably cute, they were also undeniably frayed. 'And shoes, of course.'

'What's wrong with the ones I'm wearing?'

'There's nothing wrong with them, Mia.' There was a pause. 'But you're supposed to be my wife.'

'And you don't think I look the part?'

He raised his brows. 'Do you?'

She tilted her chin in a defiant gesture and once again, Theo felt his throat dry.

'You're saying you want me in silks and satins because my very ordinary cotton dress lets you down, is that it?' she demanded.

He shook his head. 'I think you look lovely as you are,' he said suddenly, and the brief delight which replaced her mulishness inexplicably stabbed at his heart. 'But you're dressed like a maid rather than as the wife of a billionaire, and not only will it make our supposed marriage unconvincing, you'll also run the risk of feeling out of place when I take you out.'

'And we can't have that, can we?' she said waspishly. 'Very well, Theo. Do your worst. Fix me up with some personal shopper or whatever it is you rich people do—though I warn you I don't have the kind of figure for clingy silk dresses, so I'll probably look even more out of place.'

'I'm not proposing dressing you up like a doll,' he said coolly. 'Just buying you something new, which looks like it hasn't happened in quite a while.'

'I've been saving up for my veterinary course, which I'm funding myself,' she said. 'And I don't need more than an abbreviated wardrobe.'

'Clothes which are scanty?' he hazarded, with the quick beat of expectation.

'Don't be facetious, Theo. I just don't want to buy a lot of *stuff*,' she elaborated. 'The bare minimum, in fact. I won't be…' Her rosy face crumpled, as if suddenly remembering the grim purpose behind her visit. 'Because Pappous is very sick, so I'm probably not going to be here for long, am I?'

'No,' he said, his voice heavy. He broke off, as his maid appeared in the doorway. 'Yes, Dimitra, what is it?'

'Would you like some more coffee, Kyria Aeton?' she questioned shyly, in her cautious English.

'No more coffee for me, thank you, Dimitra,' Mia said, with a soft smile. 'My breakfast was delicious and the flowers you put on the table are very pretty. Thank you so much.'

'Parakalo,' said Dimitra shyly, and her beaming smile as she scuttled from the room was something Theo had never witnessed before. Suddenly he imagined a very different kind of life, with a full-time woman in it who made the servants smile.

What was the matter with him? His career was on yet another upward trajectory. As one of the wealthiest men in Greece, he was highly respected by his peers, by politicians—even by various minor royal families to whom he had given financial advice over the years. His diary was full to bursting with invitations to the kinds of parties which, as a boy, would have seemed like an impossible dream to him. Next week he had been asked to give the keynote speech at a world-leading conference in Nice. His formidable reputation went before him and there was little in the world of venture capitalism he did not excel at.

His body grew tense.

Yet suddenly, all he could think about was Mia.

CHAPTER NINE

THE SHOP THEO took her to didn't look much like a shop and when Mia said as much, he laughed. With its gleaming frontage and sophisticated window displays, she thought the grand neo-classical building seemed more like a temple. Housed in the very centre of Athens, it wasn't far from Syntagma Square and the imposing parliament building which dominated it.

But despite her pleasure at being back in the hustle and bustle of the historic city, Mia found herself shivering as she stepped inside the air-conditioned interior of the department store, recognising it as the natural habitat of the very wealthy. How her mother would have loved it! It was filled with the same kind of women who had their nails regularly painted in the Granchester spa, with their tiny waists and skinny bodies which owed their sinewy muscularity to obsessive gym sessions and sustained denial of food.

Was she imagining every female customer and assistant turning to gaze at the man who towered by her side? No, she was not. Of course they were looking at him. It was as much as she could do not to stare at him herself, he looked so utterly delectable in the handmade charcoal suit, which drew attention to the muscular power of the body beneath. He had chosen not to drive today and the chauffeur-driven car which had brought them here only served to reinforce just how powerful and wealthy he was.

She was introduced to a terrifyingly sleek personal shopper and they were taken into a beautiful wood-lined room, lit by vast chandeliers and decorated with vases of blood-red peonies, which the shopper informed them came from Mount Parnassus.

'I'm terrified they won't have anything in my size,' Mia hissed to Theo, as all her old body insecurities came flooding back.

'We have plenty,' said the shopper, with a reassuring smile. 'Just wait and see.'

'You speak perfect English,' said Mia, going a little red.

'I would have great difficulty doing my job if I didn't,' said the woman gently.

As a runner was dispatched to bring back armfuls of clothes, Mia thought what a waste it was that she'd never studied the Greek language properly, in order to make herself understood in a land she had always loved. And yes, her mother had discouraged her—but she could have ignored her advice, couldn't she? Jasmine Minotis might have been a bad mother on many levels, but she was hardly going to punish her only child for *learning*, was she?

In front of an enormous mirror which ran the risk of cruelly highlighting every bump and blemish, Mia slithered into a day dress of filmy silk chiffon. Part of the problem had been with *her*, she realised. Everyone in her life—her grandfather, her mother and then Theo himself—had treated her as if she were a mindless object who could be moved around at will.

But she had allowed them to do that, hadn't she?

Even now, wasn't she allowing Theo to splash the cash and treat her as his puppet?

She sighed. No. She was discovering that there was always a different way of looking at things. Her grandfather was a crashing snob—he always had been—and she had seen the flicker of disapproval in his eyes yesterday, when he'd seen what she was wearing. Was it such a big ask to wear the sort of outfit which would make him happy?

When she looked into the mirror, she was slightly taken aback by what she could see. She had imagined the fancy fabrics the shopper had guided her towards would do little for her voluptuous shape, but it seemed she had been wrong. Cleverly, the woman had selected a more upmarket version of her existing wardrobe for her approval. The delicate material was exquisitely cut—especially on the bust and hips. It enhanced her body in a way which flattered and the dark green suede shoes she chose made her stand differently. Walk differently. Suddenly, she was filled with a new-found sense of confidence and self-belief.

'How's this?' she questioned, pulling back the red velvet curtain before swishing into the room, and when Theo looked up from his laptop, Mia felt a sudden tightening of her heart as she saw his unguarded expression. Had she imagined the brief spear of pensiveness which had replaced the habitual flintiness of his black eyes? Didn't he used to look at her that way in the past?

But just as quickly his gaze became shuttered, his slow speculative smile indicating that there was nothing other than sex on his mind.

Of course it was.

Exactly the same thing as was on hers, she told herself fiercely.

Soon a small collection of purchases began to pile up. More dresses. A couple of swirly skirts and gossamer-fine blouses. A denim jacket. Sandals and shoes. But no trousers.

'I don't want to see you in trousers,' Theo growled. 'It is a crime to cover up legs like yours.'

And even though Mia knew this was an outrageous thing for him to say, she couldn't deny the thrill it gave her—particularly when she saw the shopper's expression of dreamy appreciation. But didn't plenty of women fantasise about masterful men who expressed distinctly unfashionable sentiments? She swallowed. Guilty, as charged.

Keeping on her favourite of the dresses—and the green suede shoes—she returned to the outer sanctum, where Theo was tapping out a message on his phone.

'Could you have the car drop me off after you go to the office?' she asked him.

'Or I could delay going into the office.' He slid the phone in his pocket and glanced at his watch. 'And we could have some lunch. There's a very good restaurant on the sixth floor.'

'Is this all part of the PR campaign?' she suggested wryly as they took the elevator up to the top floor. 'Showing off your "wife" in all her new finery?'

'Or could it possibly be because I thought you might be hungry?'

She tilted her head to one side. 'You associate me with appetite, do you, Theo?'

'I do,' he concurred, dark eyes glinting. 'All the appetites.'

'Oh. Are you flirting with me, by any chance?'

'I am,' he answered throatily.

But even as Theo acknowledged her quick smile of pleasure, loud warning bells were beginning to sound in his head. Because nothing was turning out as he had anticipated. He had long forgotten any ideas about punishing her for her desertion, but in place of revenge had come a relationship which confounded him. They were angry with each other for a lot of the time, yet she had given her virginity to him and blown his mind in the process.

Were they enemies with benefits? Was that an accurate description?

He gave a ghost of a smile as they were shown to a prime table in the window of the restaurant, where he ordered for both of them, at Mia's behest. While they waited for their meals to arrive, two glasses of pink champagne were delivered to the table and Theo stared at the fizzing flutes in bemusement. 'I didn't order these.'

'No, sir,' said the beautiful young waitress. 'But Kyrios Pavlidis has just telephoned. He heard you were here and wanted to extend his congratulations to you and your wife.'

'Efharisto,' said Theo, and the waitress smiled back before turning to deal with another customer.

'Who is she talking about?' questioned Mia, running her finger along the twisted stem of the glass.

'Vangelis Pavlidis. He owns the store and many more like it.' He gave a short laugh. 'Word certainly gets around quickly that I'm out on the town with my wife.'

'I thought that was the whole point,' she observed crisply. 'New clothes and a very public lunch will give credence to our fake marriage, which will ultimately make my grandfather happy. It's a win-win. Isn't that so, Theo?' But her voice grew softer as she clinked her glass against his and took a sip of champagne, miming startlement as some bubbles dissolved against her nose. 'What time are we planning to see him?'

There was a pause as a click of warning shuttered into Theo's mind. He thought about the woman who had reared him and used him as a meal ticket. When he hadn't been foraging on her behalf, he had been instructed to stay out of the way as much as possible while she entertained her increasingly rowdy and casual boyfriends. He never remembered her cuddling him, or being kind to him, and it took a long time for him to stop hoping she would instead of accepting the grim reality. But that had been his life and he needed to accept it—not behave like a cuckoo in the nest, trying to muscle in on Mia's life. '*We* aren't planning anything,' he said suddenly.

'But you said—'

'That we'd both go, *neh*. But I've changed my mind. I'll go later, on my own. It's better that way.' He steeled himself against the confusion in her eyes. 'It's you he wants to see,' he said roughly. 'Not me.'

She put her glass down with a bump, so that more pink bubbles fizzed to the top of the glass. 'But he'll want to see you, too! You're like family, Theo. You know you are.'

'No,' he negated harshly. 'That's where you are wrong. I have a particular relationship with him, that's all. I'm more like an employee.'

'No—'

'*Yes,*' he interrupted firmly. 'He enjoys my success and I have served as his conduit into the world of business, particularly after he retired. But it hasn't all been plain sailing. As you know, he can be an extremely difficult man, with traits I am prepared to tolerate because I have grown fond of him over the years and because his generosity is a debt which can never properly be repaid.' Theo felt the sudden race of his heart. 'But he is not my family, Mia—and he never will be. I don't *do* family. Don't you understand what I'm saying to you? I don't know how to do family. And neither do I want to.'

Mia bit her lip for the vitriol of his words was hard to hear—not just because of the anger but because of the underlying pain which had distorted his voice. She wanted to reach across the table and lay her hand over his but his body language was so forbidding that she didn't dare. And wasn't it weird how tension could kill off your appetite?

Their salads arrived and she stared uninterestedly at the glistening red tomato, white feta and gleaming black olives, before raising her eyes to his.

'Are you hungry?' she said.

There was a pause before his dark gaze was briefly directed towards the plate. 'Not for this, no.'

His words were razor-edged silk and his black eyes were glinting with something raw and hot, which Mia recognised instantly. Desire. It was pulsating through the air between them like honey and making her achingly aware of her body beneath the filmy dress. Suddenly Mia started teasing him. Encouraging him. Wanting him. She wanted him so much. 'What are you hungry for, then?' she murmured.

He didn't answer. He was calling for the bill. And besides, Mia didn't need an answer. Not a verbal one, anyway. Everything she wanted to know she could read in his tense, hard features. They got into the car but he didn't talk to her, or hug her or kiss her. Instead he slid his fingertips beneath the filmy layers of her brand-new dress and played with her aching bud until she was closing her eyes and murmuring a plea which sounded like his name, as he continued with his light and teasing rhythm. She gasped, her fingernails digging into the soft leather of the car seat, but just as she was about to come, he withdrew his hand,

and her eyes snapped open to gaze in dazed disbelief as he shook his head.

'Not here,' he said softly.

'Wh-why not?'

'I would prefer to wait until we are in the bedroom.'

Mia stared at him in confusion. 'So is this about you losing control, or taking it?'

He looked at her consideringly. 'Does it really matter?'

Mia tensed, reminding herself that this was only supposed to be a temporary relationship so, no, it shouldn't matter. Yet somehow it did. It reminded her that Theo was calling all the shots, just as he'd always done.

She realised she was in danger. Of thinking and behaving like a *real* wife and she needed to stop all that right now. The most sensible and dignified reaction would be to tell him to go to hell when they got back to his estate and take herself off somewhere on her own. But her gnawing sexual hunger overrode every other consideration. To hell with dignity, she thought distractedly as the blood pounded hotly in her veins. To hell with everything. Her heart was racing as they mounted the stairs towards his suite, but neither of them said a word. The door sounded loud as he kicked it shut behind them, but once they were enclosed in the private world of his bedroom, Theo didn't move from the spot. His black gaze was flickering over her like dark fire, making her tremble wherever it lingered and burned.

'Take off your clothes,' he instructed softly.

This was nothing to do with control and every-thing to do with power, she recognised. His, versus hers. Was that because he had allowed her to see a glimpse of unfamiliar vulnerability when he'd talked about family earlier? Was it that which had resulted in this heartless but very sexy battle of mental dom-ination?

She wondered what he would say if she refused—if she told him she'd changed her mind—but deep down she suspected he would simply shrug. Maybe tell her he really didn't have time for lunchtime sex anyway, and he'd see her later. And Mia thought she would die if that happened. She was so hot—so *eager* for him to touch her—that she did exactly as he asked.

She thought how much things had changed since yesterday, when he had taken her virginity with one delicious thrust and she'd been stricken with nerves. Yet today she no longer felt like a novice in his pres-ence and today, she didn't struggle with her zip. It slid down with fluid ease and her dress fell to the floor with a whisper. She heard his ragged breath, as if finding himself suddenly short of oxygen, and as she glanced up to see the frustration on his face she assumed an expression of mock innocence.

'Oh. Didn't you realise I was buying new lingerie as well?' she questioned, cupping her breasts with her palms, the movement pushing them forward to em-phasise the deep plunge of her cleavage against soft apricot lace. 'The shopper insisted the new clothes would look much better with the correct foundations underneath and I think she was right, don't you? Although I don't know whether these panties actually qualify as *foundation*, do you?' She did a little twirl, anxious for him to see her matching thong. 'Theo? Theo! What do you think you're doing?'

'You know damned well what I'm doing,' he roared as he picked her up in his arms and carried her over to the bed, before laying her down in the centre of it with hands which were distinctly unsteady.

And things seemed to have changed for him too, Mia realised. Maybe it was because she *was* no longer his virginal wife. Did he consider her his sexual equal now? Was it that which was making him treat her with such…? Mia gasped. Was there such a thing as tender roughness? Oh, God. There must be. She sucked in a breath as he squeezed her breast. How else would you describe it? She fell back against the soft pillows and, when she saw him undoing his belt, instinctively closed her eyes to increase the sensory experience and block out the tumult of her thoughts.

She heard the rasp of his zip and the tearing of foil as he pushed his trousers down to his ankles. Somehow she knew this was going to be quick and urgent, and she was right. He didn't even bother to remove her panties, her exultant little shout encouraging him to shove aside the moist panel and plunge straight into her waiting heat.

She moaned with pleasure at the sheer *intensity* of it. 'Oh, Theo,' she breathed and then, more brokenly as he moved inside her, 'Th-Theo.'

His eyes were dark, almost…*wounded*, she thought

distractedly as he stared into her eyes before bending his face to hers, and his kiss seemed unbearably sweet and unbearably sad, all at the same time. He pushed deeper and filled her. His hands were in her hair, he was groaning and so was she. She felt the building of expectation. Of layer upon layer of pleasure, taking her higher and higher—until it was too much to bear any longer, and as she felt herself contracting around his rocky and pulsating shaft she called out his name.

At last, their bodies spent, he pulled her against him and she nestled into his hard warmth, her finger sliding over his silk shirt as she breathed in his heady masculine scent. She thought he must be sleeping, when suddenly he spoke, his words muffled by the thickness of her curls.

'Do you want to come to Nice with me next week?'

Fractionally, she pulled away to meet the dark gleam of his eyes. 'Why would I want to do that?'

'Because you're my wife and that's the kind of thing wives do?'

'Isn't that taking method acting a bit too far?'

The trace of a smile played at the edges of his lips. 'How about me wanting to see you lying in a tiny bikini by the edge of an extravagant swimming pool?'

'I don't wear tiny bikinis,' she said repressively.

'You should, especially since you look so good in a tiny thong.' His finger slid over the curve of her hip. 'I'm speaking at a conference and it's a great city. Ever been there?'

His question punctured her bubble. Would his lip curve with scorn if she told him the only time she'd ever been to France had been on a day-trip to Calais, organised by boss of the Granchester, who paid for his employees to have a fun day out every Christmas?

But Mia wasn't trying to score points, or to contrast their very different lifestyles. She was masquerading as his wife to please her grandfather. The tricky part was discovering how much she liked being with the man she had married, despite his mercurial nature.

'Sure, why not?' she agreed coolly, as if her heart weren't thumping with dread at the thought of how much she was going to miss him and she wondered why, of all the men she could have fallen for, it had to be him.

It had only ever been him.

She swallowed. Sometimes powerful emotions and feelings came out of nowhere but you didn't have to let them take you prisoner, did you? Because she was strong. *Remember that*, she told herself fiercely. *You've changed.*

She tried to rationalise why going to Nice would be a sensible move.

'I guess it will make our reconciliation look all the more convincing if we can't bear to be apart,' she hazarded.

'I guess it will,' he agreed, lying back against the pillows, his arms cushioning his dark head.

Mia jumped out of bed and headed for the bathroom, aware of his gaze on her. But to her delight, she didn't feel a bit shy about her semi-clothed state or that very urgent bout of lovemaking. In fact, it was easy to exult in Theo's very obvious approval. Perhaps he was teaching her to love *herself*—even if he didn't love *her*. Wouldn't that be something positive she could take away from all this?

There was no sign of him when she emerged from the bathroom, her appearance suitably repaired, and she was driven to see her grandfather who, as the nurse had promised, was noticeably brighter than yesterday.

'You're out of bed, Pappous,' Mia said, trying to iron the emotional wobble from her voice. 'This… this is fantastic. *You* look fantastic.'

'*Neh*. I am like Lazarus,' the old man proclaimed, with a touch of his old arrogance. 'I have risen from the dead!' With a mischievous look, he complimented her on her new dress and asked if she wanted to drink some *soumada*. But Mia didn't want their precious time to be interrupted and so she shook her head and sat down beside him. For a moment there was silence, until at last they began to talk.

They discussed things which had always been taboo before and for Mia it was painful to listen to at times. He talked about her father. About the adorable little boy who had grown up to be so troubled. He talked of his guilt at never being able to help his son conquer his demons. He told her he was sorry to have cut her out of his life so ruthlessly, but that he'd been hurt, and bewildered because he thought she and Theo made a perfect couple.

'I still do,' he added gruffly. 'He is a good man, Mia.'

But she quickly changed the subject and, although

she felt a little ashamed at the way they were deceiving him by pretending to be reconciled, didn't his evident contentment make it worth it? Instead she remarked on how well Tycheros was looking. And the dog, which lay close by her feet whenever possible, lifted his head on hearing his name, and licked at her hand.

The day before she left for Nice, Mia felt a sense of resolution. She kissed her grandfather goodbye and whispered that Theo would call in to see him after work and as she saw the old man's nod of approval, she was aware that she sounded like a real wife. She probably looked like one, too, with a stupid smile plastered all over her lips as she remembered that tonight she and Theo were planning to dine beneath the stars, and afterwards he would take her upstairs and they would reach for those very stars which blazed down with unpolluted white fire.

She reached down to tickle Tycheros's ears, when her warm feeling of satisfaction was punctured by another nagging splinter of doubt. For the first time since she'd arrived in Greece, Mia was beginning to get worried, because nothing was turning out as she'd thought it would.

Quite apart from the fact that she'd never been intending to have sex with Theo, this trip and this *marriage* were supposed to be time-limited—her brief tenure defined by her grandfather's precarious state of health. There had been a beginning and there was supposed to be an end—except the end was no longer in sight. A miracle seemed to have happened and the old man had recovered much of his former vigour. And while that brought Mia great joy, it also brought her pain. And fear.

She wanted Georgios to live for as long as possible—of course she did—but she couldn't remain here indefinitely, pretending to be Theo's wife and allowing her emotions to be compromised with every second that passed. Because he was invading her thoughts and occupying her mind. Her heart and her body were full of him.

She walked through the overgrown rose bower towards the waiting car, clenching her hands into tight little fists, as the reality of her situation was revealed to her—like a thick layer of dust being removed from a mirror.

Because suddenly Mia realised that she had walked into a trap of her own making. Proximity had a power all of its own and so did passion. And if she didn't start protecting herself, she could get badly hurt.

CHAPTER TEN

'WHAT WE NEED to ask ourselves is...' Theo paused, his delivery crisp and precise as he looked around the gilded room, at all the privileged faces who were watching him so raptly '...do we really want our children and our grandchildren accusing us of being the generation who knew the cost of everything, and the value of nothing?'

A split second of silence greeted his closing words, before the jammed room started applauding. People were on their feet. Beneath the stained glass of the domed ceiling, shouts of *'Bravo!'* and *'Encore!'* were echoing. A beautiful brunette he half recognised was blowing him a kiss. Theo's gaze scanned the room for Mia, alighting at last on her diminutive form standing at the back of the room, beneath the portrait of an early French king. He thought she looked a little... *anxious* and he frowned. What was making the little maid appear so uncomfortable?

He really needed to stop thinking about her that way, he told himself fiercely, focussing instead on her resilience, her independence and pride. And, of course, the enduringly soft and kittenish appeal which lay beneath her feisty new exterior. A softness which invoked in him a powerful protectiveness— a response he kept telling himself was inappropriate under the circumstances. Because Mia didn't need his protection. She had made her feelings very clear during their two-day stay at Nice's most magnificent hotel, which overlooked the famous Promenade des Anglais.

She had been...

What?

His brows knitted together, because it was difficult to put his finger on. She had charmed everyone she'd met and shown a very real appreciation of their five-star hotel—despite mentioning something about the alignment of cushions, which he gathered had not met with her approval. Their lovemaking had been as exquisite as always. So what was it?

He frowned.

Something he hadn't expected.

Ever since they had arrived, she had been behaving with a certain detachment towards him, which was usually *his* thing. She had been watchful and wary. She had seemed...distant. And while none of those things should matter to him, he was finding that they did. His eyes narrowed as he crossed the room, fielding the many pats on the back he received as he made his way towards her.

He noticed several women watching his progress, yet not one of them had a fraction of the appeal of the petite redhead in the floaty dress. Her fiery curls

were piled haphazardly on top of her head, several
tumbled strands giving her a delicious just-got-out-
of-bed look. Which to some extent was accurate. Not
in the least tempted by the many enticements this famous seaside town had to offer, they had spent the
majority of their time in bed.

His throat constricted. He had tasted her, sucked
her, drunk her and eaten her. She was like a non-stop
feast he couldn't seem to stop devouring because he
couldn't get enough of her. How had she managed to
do it—this innocent and unpretentious young woman?
To have woven such a spell of enchantment, that at
times he couldn't think straight?

'Mia,' he said as he reached her. 'How do you think
my speech went?'

'Well, obviously, your peers loved it.' A little self-
consciously, she adjusted the strap of her sundress.
'I've never heard applause like that, outside of a con-
cert. Mind you, I don't think I've ever listened to a
forty-minute talk on venture capitalism before.'

He made an impatient clicking gesture with his
fingers. 'And?'

Mia chose her words carefully. She'd been doing
a lot of that since they'd got here—walking over verbal eggshells, so to speak. Since she'd been in Nice it
had seemed vital that she distance herself from him
as much as possible. Not in an obvious way. In bed,
she was no different—her sexual response to him as
ecstatic and enthusiastic as it had always been. But
she was trying hard to focus on all the reasons why
Theo was not a good long-term bet—the biggest one

being that their marriage was nothing but a farce, a temporary union which would be dissolved as soon as her grandfather died.

Because it was funny how being in a different location made you look at things in a different way. She looked around, listening to the rising buzz as the sophisticated audience chattered among themselves in the dome-ceilinged room. She wasn't like these people. She'd observed their reactions when she had been introduced as Theo's wife. The quick double-take before looking her up and down as if they might have missed something, first time round. As if wondering why the man who could have anyone had settled for someone like her.

Why had he brought her here? He certainly hadn't needed to. As far as she could make out, there were hardly any other wives or partners at the convention.

But that wasn't a question to ask him now, in this public arena—not when he was regarding her thoughtfully, his jet-dark eyes narrowed, as if he had picked up on the unease which had been growing for days now. She thought about the concluding words of his speech and a terrible sense of inevitability began to ripple up inside her as she acknowledged why she had found them so disturbing. Because things were coming to a head, weren't they? That was what happened in life. Nothing ever stayed the same.

'You were brilliant,' she said. 'You know you were.'

He smiled. A tight, hard smile which pierced

through her emotional armour without any obvious effort on his part.

They returned to their lavish suite, with its wall of windows overlooking Nice's glittering coast. When they had arrived it had felt a bit like a honeymoon destination, because it was quite obviously the finest accommodation in the upmarket establishment. But now, the magnificent view of the Promenade des Anglais left Mia cold, as did the golden glimmer of the walls and the amazing artwork, which must have been worth a fortune. She might as well have been in a railway waiting room for all the notice she took of her surroundings.

While Theo put in a call to his office, she went into the bathroom, her heart thumping as she gazed into the mirror, knowing she couldn't keep on blotting out questions which needed to be asked, just because she was afraid of what the answers might be.

So was she going to ask him? Or was she just going to keep burying her head in the sand?

She found him outside on the vast expanse of terrace, gazing out at the turquoise glitter of the sunlit sea. He had removed his jacket and was leaning on the wrought-iron railings, looking utterly magnificent against the iconic backdrop. The rich sunlight highlighted the ebony darkness of his hair and illuminated the powerful body she knew so well. She stood very still for a moment, committing the delicious image to memory, but he must have heard her for he turned. His shuttered expression was unreadable, his hard face shadowed.

'You look troubled,' he observed slowly.

'I suppose I am,' she answered, slightly surprised by his question because wasn't that a bit *probing* for Theo?

'And why's that?'

'Think about it.' She lifted up her hands in exasperation. 'Most people might say that *pretending* to be married is stressful enough, but there are plenty of other things which have the ability to keep me awake in the middle of the night.' She paused, the tip of her tongue travelling over her bottom lip. 'Which I don't suppose you'll want to discuss. I thought your speech was brilliant, by the way.'

His intelligent black eyes gleamed, as if he was perfectly aware that she was stalling. 'So you said.'

'You ended it by talking about children.' She swallowed. 'And grandchildren.'

His expression was still closed and shuttered. 'I did. What of it?'

'You created a very powerful image with your words.'

'That's the secret of giving a talk which doesn't make people want to fall asleep.' Above the obsidian glitter of his eyes, his dark brows rose. 'But I suspect my use of powerful imagery isn't what's troubling you.'

'No.' Just *say* it. 'Do you want children of your own, Theo? Was that what made you address it?'

He shook his head. 'No.'

'And have you ever…have you ever wanted them?'

There was silence. 'You mean, with you?'

Mia's heart was beating so loud she was surprised he couldn't hear it. Surely the whole hotel could hear it. She nodded.

'Yes, I wanted a family,' he said at last. Raking his fingers back through the liquorice thickness of his hair, he expelled a long and ragged breath. 'A real family, like I'd never known. A happy family. When I still believed such a thing could exist.' He gave a bitter laugh. 'I wanted everything with you, Mia. Or at least, I thought I did.'

'Everything?' she verified breathlessly, even though her heart was breaking to hear him refer to it in the past tense.

'Of course.' His mouth twisted into a bitter smile. 'Because I was young and idealistic and you exemplified everything I'd never known in a woman before. You entranced me. Fascinated me. I was bowled over by your innocence and compassion and the way you never judged me, when I had been judged for all of my life. And you adored me.' A smile tinged with regret played at the edges of his lips. 'You left me in no doubt about that. You didn't hold back from telling me you loved me because you were waiting for me to say it first. You didn't try to manipulate my emotions. You were everything I thought a woman should be.' He paused. 'A black and white drawing on a piece of canvas,' he finished quietly. 'Which I coloured in to fit my own specifications.'

'I'm afraid that kind of imagery is beyond me,' she breathed. 'I don't understand.'

'No. I didn't understand it myself for a long time.'

Theo turned to look out at the sea, as if he might find the answer somewhere within the glittering dance of the waves, but he saw nothing other than swimmers splashing around in the shallows. And when he faced her again he could see that Mia's face had grown pale and her eyes were dark and huge, as if she already knew she wasn't going to like what he was about to say. But she had asked him, hadn't she? And since she had asked, she should listen to his answers. It might hurt her—and maybe it would hurt him, too—but it might enable them both to move on.

'I idealised you,' he said slowly. 'I made you into the woman I wanted you to be. That's why I insisted you came to our marriage as a virgin—not because your grandfather would be angry—'

'Well, he would.'

'*Neh, neh*, I know that,' he said impatiently. 'But my main motivator was that a virginal bride fitted my view of perfect womanhood. I looked on it as an old-fashioned arranged marriage. That's why I never told you I loved you, even though I knew how much you wanted me to,' he continued, and now his words became heavy. 'Because I didn't.'

'You…didn't?' she choked out, though the expression in her eyes suggested he was only confirming what she already knew.

'No. But don't take it personally. I'm not capable of loving anyone, Mia, and since you were nothing but a figment of my imagination how could I possibly love someone who didn't really exist?'

He could see her throat working.

'But you didn't really exist either, did you, Theo?' she whispered. 'You married me because you claim to have wanted a happy family, but you weren't prepared to contribute anything to get it, were you?'

'I was earning—'

'I'm not talking about *money*! Everything with you comes back to the money, doesn't it?' she yelled. 'I'm talking about emotion! All the emotion you held back, like a miser hoarding his gold.' She sucked in a ragged breath. 'How can you possibly bring children into this world if you aren't prepared to show them love?'

'Maybe because I didn't know how?'

'But you're an intelligent man. You could have learnt.'

'You really believe that, do you?' he questioned mockingly. 'That love is something you can be taught—like maths, or tennis?'

'That's what I had to do. To teach myself,' she said simply. 'Because I never got any at home, either.'

And suddenly Theo was reminded of the first time he'd seen her. How, behind her tenderness towards the wounded puppy, he had detected a deep sense of hurt in her eyes. A sense of being alone, which he had identified with. He had wanted to reach out and tell her that, but something had stopped him. It was stopping him now and it always would. Because he couldn't give her what she needed. And she couldn't give him what he wanted. He didn't want her world of messy emotion, and pain.

'What's done is done,' he said, with brutal finality. 'And there's no point in raking over it.'

'I agree. Which is why we really can't continue with this farce of a marriage. I can't stay here like this—playing this fictitious role as your wife, which is going to get more complicated the longer it goes on. I need to go back to my real life. I feel...' She dragged in a breath. 'I feel so happy to have seen Pappous and I'm very grateful that you made me come here. The fact that my visit has coincided with, or caused him to enjoy, better health is, of course—wonderful. But now it's starting to scare me.'

Theo frowned. 'Why?'

'Can't you work it out for yourself? Because we've deceived him.' She bit her lip and he could see the shimmer of tears in her eyes. 'How is he going to react when he finds out what we've done? He'll probably be hurt and angry. Dear God—the shock could kill him.'

He shook his head. 'Your grandfather is made of stronger stuff than that,' he negated.

'You hope.'

Theo allowed his mind to assimilate all the facts, as if this were nothing but a question of logistics, and the sweet tremble of her lips undoubtedly influenced his next question. 'You wouldn't consider staying on—at least until your course starts in September? Like I said, I could easily have my office arrange for someone to cover your housekeeping role.'

'You mean...carry on?' She stared at him. 'Like this?'

'Is "this" really so bad, then, Mia?' he mocked softly. 'Good sex. Good company. I could live with that for a while longer. Couldn't you?'

She was shaking her head, the glossy curls glowing like a sunset. 'You just don't get it, do you, Theo?' she breathed.

Should he ask her to elaborate? Behind the set line of his lips, he gritted his teeth. No. He didn't want her to highlight their differences or present him with a catalogue of complaints about his behaviour. He just wanted this conversation to end, and for that they needed to decide what to tell Georgios when they got back to Greece. The truth, probably. No more lies. The important thing was that the old man had healed the rift with his granddaughter and nothing else really mattered. Mia would go and he might miss her, but it would only be for a while. He'd had sex with her now. She was no longer a mystery. And she knew now that he had never loved her.

Her phone began to ring and shattered the silence, but she ignored it.

Almost immediately, his own began to clamour.

'I'd better...' he said.

Her face was filled with scorn. 'Of course.'

But this wasn't the welcome interruption of work. He knew it was bad news the moment he accepted the call. A number and a voice he didn't recognise, filled with the careful compassion of someone doling out professional sympathy. He listened for a while in a state of unnatural calm and when he had terminated the call, he looked into Mia's sea-blue eyes, trying to find the right words.

'You'd better sit down,' he said heavily.

'I don't want to sit down. Tell me, Theo. Just tell me.'

And even though her pale cheeks made him suspect she had already guessed, he nodded. 'I'm afraid it's your grandfather,' he said, swallowing down the sudden lump which had constricted his throat. 'He died a few minutes ago.'

He wanted to take her in his arms and comfort her, but deep down he knew he didn't have the right, not after everything he'd said.

And touching her was always fraught with complications.

CHAPTER ELEVEN

THEO BARELY SAID a word to her, throughout the journey to Greece. Not on the plane, nor in the waiting car which took them straight to the funeral parlour. He had sat gazing out of the window, seemingly lost in thought. His face, Mia thought, looked as if it had been carved from some dark and unforgiving piece of granite. His features were bleak and stony, his body language forbidding. Was this his way of dealing with the grief of Georgios' passing? Had it made him close in on himself even more? Unable to offer her even the most rudimentary element of comfort?

She had not shared his bed. She had not shared so much as a kiss or a hug, since news had reached them in the south of France, right after their uncomfortable showdown which had left her in no doubt about how little she really meant to him. Perhaps with her grandfather gone, he no longer saw the need to maintain any kind of masquerade. And didn't that make sense, on so many levels? The need for pretence was gone.

But she took her lead from him, clinging onto her composure and not giving into tears—not once. Not because she was afraid of showing her grief in front of the man who was still technically her husband, but because she was afraid that once she started crying, she might never stop.

Wearing the black dress and shoes which had been hastily purchased from the hotel boutique in Nice, Mia prepared to say her final farewell to her *pappous*.

'Do you want me to come in with you?' Theo asked.

Of course she did. She'd never even seen a dead person before. She wanted him to stand by her side and squeeze her hand. And afterwards hold her tight and dry her tears, and offer her the condolence she so badly needed.

But she didn't articulate her wishes because she was afraid of sending out the wrong message. To Theo, yes—but, more importantly, to herself. That might imply she was expecting him to behave like a real husband, or that she had started to rely on him, and was looking to him for support. And why get used to something which was only going to be snatched from you?

'No. You go in after me,' she said. 'I'll be fine.'

At least Theo took over all the funeral arrangements—booking the church, contacting friends, and putting notices in the paper—and Mia was grateful for his cool efficiency. The church was full, bright with the light of the candles which every mourner held. In a daze, Mia greeted them all—some she knew, though many she didn't. She recognised most of the nurses and thanked them for their care, and the first crack in her carefully constructed composure came when she was hugged by Georgios's old house-keeper, Elena. And that was when she had crumbled. Clinging to the matronly woman who had known her since she was young, she had sobbed her heart out.

The rest of the wake passed in a blur and Mia was dry-eyed by the time she slid into the passenger seat beside Theo and he drove her back to his house. But when she stood in a hallway in the light of the setting sun, she suddenly felt as if she'd lost her way—like someone stumbling around a maze in the dark. She found herself looking around, as if she had never been here before—as if she didn't recognise any of it. Was it really here that she had given her virginity to this man and stupidly reactivated all those deeply buried feelings for him?

'Come outside and sit down,' said Theo, still with that cool and remote manner which was making him seem like a stranger.

'I'd better go and pack,' she said stiffly, her fingers curling round her black patent clutch bag.

He frowned. 'You don't need to do that now, do you?'

'Well, actually, I do, if I'm leaving tomorrow.'

'This is news to me.'

'I wasn't aware that I had to run my travel arrangements past you first.'

'I'll need to arrange for my plane to be ready.' He studied her consideringly. 'Don't you want to stay for the reading of the will?'

A flicker of anger stirred to life inside her and

in that moment Mia could have slammed her fists against his chest. Even the most insensitive person might have faked a little surprise at her abrupt departure, or fabricated a trace of disappointment, but not Theo. It was still about the money for him, she thought bitterly. 'I don't care about the damned will, Theo. I just want to get back.'

Something else which had been nagging at her suddenly occurred to her. 'What about Tycheros? Who's going to look after him now that Pappous has gone?'

'Don't worry. I'll make sure he goes to a good home.'

'A *good home*?' she echoed. 'With people we don't even know? Why can't you take him? There's plenty of space here for him to run around.'

'Because my lifestyle is incompatible with having a dog, Mia. I travel a lot of the time and wouldn't be here for him.' His mouth hardened. 'And I don't want the tie of having to look after an animal.'

Mia flinched at his words. He had all those staff but he didn't want a tie and he couldn't provide a home, not even for a dog as beloved as Tycheros.

'I want him to come to England to live with me,' she said suddenly. 'Will you help me do that?'

He loosened his black tie, his chiselled features sombre. 'So who's going to look after him while you're out all day studying? You need to think about whether that's what you really want.'

'Don't you dare patronise me!' She glared at him. 'I'll sort something out!'

His eyes had narrowed into jet-hard shards. 'You're looking very pale, Mia,' he said. 'This isn't a conversation we should be having now and you're not packing anything tonight. What you need is a drink.'

It was Theo taking control again. Theo being strong and masterful—and if she hadn't been so bone-tired, Mia might have challenged him. But the thought of going upstairs to remove her shabby suitcase from the luxurious wardrobe wasn't an enticing one, so she let him lead her out to the veranda.

The air was warm and thick with the scent of jasmine and the crystal glass into which he poured the brandy was as heavy as lead. She almost choked as the strong spirit burned its way down her throat, but at least the drink dissolved some of the tension which had been tightly coiled inside her all day. Or maybe it was just a sense of relief that her grandfather was at peace at last, which began to loosen some of her inhibitions.

This was her last night, she realised.

Her last night in Greece.

Her last night with Theo.

Tomorrow she would go back to her world, and he to his. She wondered how difficult it was going to be to forget him this time around. She wondered whether he would even give her a second thought.

Easing her feet out of her shoes, she glanced across the table at him. He had removed his black tie completely now, and although he had poured himself a glass of brandy, she noticed he hadn't touched any. His features were granite hard, his dark eyes unreadable. He looked so *unknowable*, she thought. And so remote. Just as he'd always been. As if what had happened between them hadn't made a dent in his iron-hard exterior. Had it?

'Before I go, can I ask you something, Theo?'

'What?'

Her voice was quiet. 'Have you cried yet?'

His eyes narrowed with a dangerous glitter, but his voice was deadly calm. 'Excuse me?'

'Don't do that haughty thing, Theo,' she said softly. 'After tomorrow, you'll never see me again so why can't we talk about it? My grandfather meant a lot to you and grief is supposed to be cathartic, isn't it? So...' She put her brandy down. 'Have you cried yet?' she persisted.

'Honestly?' He gave a short laugh. 'I have never cried.'

'What, *never*?'

'Never, ever, at least that I can remember.' The look he shot her was tinged with cold defiance. 'Satisfied?'

'Not in the least.' She studied him curiously. 'So, why not? Because you're a man and big men don't cry?'

He made an impatient sound with his tongue and for a moment she thought he was going to avoid the question, when suddenly he spoke.

'Because abandoned orphans have to fight to stay tough,' he informed her, his voice like gravel. 'And crying doesn't help you survive. Being rejected is bad enough but compound it with tears and you make yourself completely unlovable.'

It was the most candid admission he'd ever made and something about the raw and painful delivery of his words made Mia want to weep. But she didn't offer him the sympathy she suspected he would misinterpret as pity. Was *that* the reason why he didn't do love? she wondered. Because deep down he considered himself unlovable, even after all this time? Unwilling to give up, she tried a different tack. 'You're going to miss my grandfather,' she said.

He nodded, as if relieved by the sudden change of subject. 'I certainly won't miss his contrary nature or argumentativeness,' he said drily. 'But yes, I will miss the old rascal. He was...'

'What?' she prompted as he lapsed into silence.

'Nothing,' he said. 'It doesn't matter.'

She thought it did, but she let that one go. Her elbows on the table, Mia clasped her fingers together and rested her chin on them, her gaze very direct. 'Do you know the first thing he said to me, every time I went to visit him?'

'Since I've never been gifted with clairvoyancy, obviously I don't,' he drawled sarcastically. 'Is it relevant?'

'I think it is.' Her voice softened. 'Each time, without fail, he would look over my shoulder, and say, "Where's Theo?"'

'So?' he demanded brusquely. 'What of it? He probably wanted me to query something on his bank statement.'

'No, it wasn't that.' She drew in a deep breath. 'What I said the other day was true, Theo. You really were like a son to him—'

'Enough!' He sliced through her words like a guillotine. 'I am *not* going to sit here and listen to this sentimental hogwash.'

'Well, I think you *should*!' she returned. 'Unless, of course, you're too scared to hear what I've got to say.'

The silence which followed became so loaded with tension that Mia felt she could have reached out and cut it with a knife. His black eyes were blazing now—their dangerous warning unable to conceal the smoky flicker of lust. For a moment she thought he was going to come round to her side of the table, and pull her into his arms, and didn't her heart thump with painful longing as she found herself wishing he would? Wouldn't his angry kiss blot out all her pain and confusion—so that maybe she could reach out to him when he was soft and sated and more open to persuasion?

But he didn't.

His black gaze iced into her. 'Too scared?' he echoed furiously.

'What else am I supposed to think?' she demanded. 'You say you don't do family because you've never known one yourself. But that's not really true, is it, Theo? Because all that time, you had a relationship with Georgios which was better and deeper than many father-son relationships.'

'Enough, Mia,' he repeated warningly.

But Mia couldn't stop. She felt like a shaken bottle whose top had been wrenched off and all the words were spilling out—words she should have said to him a long time ago. 'You were more of a son to him than my own father was—you know that. He was proud of you, Theo. So very proud. Why else did he invest in your education and place so much hope in you? He relished all your achievements. Every one. And yes, sometimes he drove you mad with his cantankerous nature, but that wasn't enough to drive you away, was it? You were the one constant in his life,' she breathed. 'You say you don't do family, but he *was* your family. And you were his.'

'Mia—'

She thought he was about to berate her again but she was wrong. He was still shaking his head, but tears had begun to slide down his hard cheeks—rivulets of gold in the setting sun. He bent his head and buried his face in his hands, his big body convulsing with silent sobs. For a long time, Mia sat there, rooted to the spot, keeping a silent vigil over the weeping man she had never been able to stop loving. And when at last his shoulders had grown still, she pushed his untouched glass of brandy towards him and he lifted it up to quaff it back, in a single draught.

Still she said nothing, despite the bright glitter of his eyes which burned into her like black fire. She felt as if she were walking on a tightrope—one false move and it would all be over. Perhaps it already was. Because Theo was the personification of a proud, alpha man and she wasn't sure how this would sit with his image of himself. Would he resent her for bearing witness to his heartache and his pain? Would he regard his meltdown as an expression of acceptance, or weakness?

After a while, bright stars began to pepper the Saronikos sky and he seemed to stir himself, like a giant wakening from a long sleep.

'Are you okay?' she whispered, her words barely louder than the whirring call of the cicadas which surrounded them. 'Do you want to talk about it?'

A pulse worked steadily at Theo's temple as he thought about the candour of her question, and how impossible it was to answer with any degree of accuracy. He felt drained. Exhausted. As if he had just climbed to the top of a hill in the heat of the midday sun, the stones beneath his feet tearing his flesh to pieces. He was still trying to process some of the things she'd said, but although he had no trouble rationalising complex numbers, he didn't have the ability to do the same thing when it came to his feelings. He had no template for dealing with emotion. All he knew was that right now he felt empty.

In the starlight, only the oval of her face and the brightness of her hair were visible, her black funeral dress absorbed by the darkness. Her eyes were huge and her lips were soft, and a shuddered sigh left his lungs. She was a siren to his senses and, oh, how he wanted to take her in his arms and lose himself in her delicious heat. How easy it would be to alleviate the pain he felt with that.

He swallowed.

Easy, yes.

But simple?

No. Nothing was ever simple where Mia was concerned.

A pulse began to work at his temple. Just before her grandfather's death, she'd told him she wanted to go back to England, to carry on with her life, and she'd pretty much repeated that tonight. Why wouldn't she be eager to get away from a hastily conceived fake marriage which had served its purpose?

'I'm all done with talking,' he said flatly. He felt like a ghost, as if he had no real substance, and he rose to his feet and stared down into the upturned oval of her face. 'Would you mind very much if I called it a night? If you want dinner I can ask Dimitra—'

'It's all right, Theo. I'm perfectly capable of finding myself some hummus and pitta bread in the kitchen, if I get hungry.'

Her words were more than a little angry and more than a little hurt. As if he had disappointed her. As if she had been expecting something more. Some radical change of heart, perhaps? But Theo knew that this was the only thing he could do, for how could he promise something he might not be able to deliver, and disappoint her all over again? No. He must behave honourably and the best way to achieve that would be to sever his ties with her. For she was beautiful and kind, and he was damaged.

The scent of the jasmine which filled the air was beguiling his senses. He wanted to stay here. To whisper his fingertips over the silk tangle of her hair and then to bend his lips to hers. He wanted to stroke the soft satin of her skin and lose himself in it. But even as desire began to ripple through his body, Theo's hard-wired survival techniques kicked right back in. He needed to stay away from her and he should start the process immediately.

'I'll see you in the morning,' he said tonelessly.

Mia stood there mutely and watched him go, glad he wasn't witnessing the totally predictable tears which had sprung to the backs of her eyes.

Earlier, she'd thought she didn't have the appetite for packing but she had been wrong because Theo's cold words had tipped her right over the edge. She went upstairs and tugged out her battered old suitcase, careful to take only the clothes she had brought with her, staring balefully at the outfits and shoes which Theo had bought her. Let him keep his fancy clothes, she thought. She wasn't going to need them any more.

Her restless night was also predictable and she didn't see him in the morning either. But that was a deliberate move on her part. She waited until he had started his early morning swim before ringing for a taxi to take her to the airport, where she found a budget airline desk, because anything would be better than catching *his* plane. She might not be in megabucks Theo's class, but she certainly had enough money to buy herself an economy ticket back to London.

Afraid of her hasty departure being discovered by her husband, she didn't dare risk saying goodbye to Sofia and Dimitra, but she left them both an ap-

preciative note of thanks. And although there were
seven missed calls from him while she was waiting
for her flight—before she finally took the courage to
block his number—for Theo she left no note at all.
Because what could she say?

I hate you.

I love you.

It was one of those strange things about human
nature that both those things could be true at exactly
the same time.

CHAPTER TWELVE

'YOU'RE TO GO up to the Presidential Suite right away, Mia.'

Mia stared at her line manager in dismay, wondering why she had gone to all the trouble of seeking her out in the staff canteen at this time of day, especially as she was officially off duty. Kirstie McLellan might be excellent at her job, but sometimes she forgot people were human. Or that they got hungry.

She glanced down at her toasted teacake. 'Erm, have I got time to eat this?'

'Not really. You'll have plenty of time for snacking later,' said Kirstie smoothly.

'But it's my—'

'There's a top-secret VIP guest expected within the hour,' Kirstie explained, seemingly unabashed by Mia's objections, or the rapidly cooling bun. 'And Mr Constantinides's office has just sent an urgent message down. Red carpet alert! We need to ensure that everything is as it should be, so I'd like you to give the entire suite the benefit of your expert eye.'

'Okay,' agreed Mia, trying to ignore the loud rumble of her stomach. It was ironic really, because she'd barely been able to eat a thing since she'd arrived back in England last week and had only just started to get her appetite back. All she wanted right now was to fill her face with some comfort food, in the wan hope that it might help alleviate some of the numbness which had refused to leave her, ever since she'd left Greece, and Theo. It was either that or going to her room to bury herself underneath the duvet and howl her heart out.

But she had her professional reputation to think of and the hotel had always been so kind and accommodating towards her, giving her the leave of absence she'd needed to visit her grandfather, which had been less than two weeks in the end. She could always add it to her overtime. And besides, nobody ever said no to Zac Constantinides, the big boss. With one last, longing look at her plate she took the staff lift to the top floor of the Granchester where, after checking the corridor outside for any dust or spillages—none found—Mia quietly let herself into the yawning expanse of the Presidential Suite.

The compact kitchen was gleaming, there was vintage champagne on ice and a mass of perfumed pink roses dazzled at the centre of the shiny dining table. So far, so good. It must be someone very important for the big boss to take a personal interest, she thought as she surveyed the pristine surface of the bed in the master bedroom and gave one of the velvet cushions an unnecessary tug.

She was just walking into the main reception room,

with its famous view over London's Hyde Park, when Mia got the distinct sense that she wasn't alone. A sense which was confirmed when she saw the powerful body silhouetted against the huge windows.

She narrowed her eyes as a sharp arrow pierced her heart.

It couldn't be.

But it was.

Darkly beautiful and statue-still, Theo Aeton was standing and surveying her with an expression she couldn't work out—but what else was new?

How cruel life could be sometimes, she thought bitterly. Wasn't it enough that she was constantly haunted by him in her dreams? Surely she hadn't started to conjure him up in her daily life, too? She closed her eyes, but when she opened them again, he was still there. So he wasn't a hallucination at all, but real. Gloriously and vibrantly real.

The sharp arrow imbedded itself more deeply into her heart, penetrating through the terrible numbness which had descended on her like a grey cloud these past few days.

'No,' she said, her voice a reedy whisper, hating the instant prickle to her breasts as she looked at him.

He nodded, his hair gleaming like rich tar against the pale English light. 'Yes.'

She sought words to say. Something which wouldn't condemn her. She didn't want to tell him how much she missed him. Or beg him to hold her, or kiss her, or stroke his fingers through her curls, no matter how much she wanted him to do all those things, and more. She needed him to leave her alone to lick her wounds and recover, just as Tycheros had done in those early days when she'd found him.

'Go away,' she said huskily. 'Haven't we said everything that needs to be said?' But then she remembered how dismissive he had been with her on their last evening together and she screwed up her face into a belligerent scowl. 'And what are you even doing here, in my hotel?'

'I figured that booking out the suite was the most effective way of seeing you,' he said. 'Seeing as how you've blocked my number and won't answer any of my emails.'

'You could have always ambushed my room again!' she declared sarcastically. 'Don't tell me— you and Zac Constantinides are in some secret billionaires' club, where rich men are prepared to do each other *favours*, should the need arise?'

'Something like that.'

'That's outrageous,' she said automatically.

'I'm afraid that's how life works.'

'Your life, maybe. Not mine.' But she was feeling surprisingly calm, considering that her heart was banging like a drum beneath her pink polyester uniform. Had he told Zac she was his wife? She wondered frantically if that particular snippet of gossip would spread through the hotel like wildfire. Well, she wasn't going to be his wife for much longer, came her next grim thought. 'Is this about the divorce?'

'No, Mia. It's not about the divorce.'

'What, then? Hurry up, will you? I'm officially off duty and you're eating into my free time.'

Theo tensed as he met the flash of her blue eyes, which told him as clearly as her words just how angry she was. Had he thought she'd be so delighted to see him again that she would fling herself into his arms, without him having to redeem himself? That she would let him tumble her down on the bed and they could kiss and make up in the most delicious way possible?

Of course.

But nothing in life worth having ever came without a fight—he of all people should have known that. For the first time it occurred to him that she really might not want him any more—and could he blame her, were that to be the case? He had pushed her away so many times. He had erected barriers to stop her getting close and had resisted all her efforts to knock them down. Yet somehow she had managed to melt the icy carapace which surrounded his heart, where everybody else had failed.

He had underestimated her so many times and in so many ways and, suddenly, he recognised that this might be too little, too late.

Did he have a single chance left, or had he blown it?

He thought of all the different words he could use which might bring her round to his way of thinking, though in his heart he knew there was only one thing which might startle her enough to listen to him. He could tell her that he missed her, which was true, or he could use the words he'd never said before. Was that what made his delivery uncharacteristically halting?

'Mia, I…'

She looked at him impatiently, her brows raised.

'I love you,' he said suddenly.

The sudden pallor of her face was the only indication she'd registered the significance of his statement, but her expression remained fierce and defiant and he swallowed. She really was going to make him fight for this.

'Is that why you pushed me away after my grandfather died?' she demanded. 'And why you acted so cold and remote? Is that the behaviour of a man in love? I don't think so. If you've come here because you want to have sex with me, then why not just come right out and say it? But please don't dress it up in pretty words you don't mean as a way of winning me over.'

Her taunt was provocative, but Theo stuck to all the things he knew he had to tell her. 'I have loved you for a very long time,' he said.

'Really? You've got a funny way of showing it.' But she screwed her face up suspiciously. 'How long?'

'Ever since I asked you to marry me, all those years ago.'

'No!' She shook her head and several coppery spirals broke free from her updo. 'Don't you *dare* lie to me—'

'These aren't lies, Mia,' he interjected softly. 'Why would I come all this way to lie to you? Of course I loved you. Why else would I have married you? Tying myself down with a wife at the age of twenty-three was the last thing on my agenda. I had everything I needed. I was on the road to financial success. I was able to have any woman I wanted and, no…' Anticipating another objection, he sighed. 'That wasn't intended to be an arrogant boast. I'm just trying to tell you the way it was. I didn't want anything more from your grandfather because he had already given me enough, but I most certainly wanted you. Hell, yes.' He paused, searching for something in her eyes, but they were still veiled and wary. 'I really, *really* wanted you. I'd never felt that way about a woman before.'

'Go on,' she said, though her tone was slightly softer now.

'I can see now that my determination to make us wait until we were married must have felt as though I were disempowering you. That I was guilty of taking away *your* choice.'

'Because you did. You treated me like a child, Theo.'

'Maybe I did. But you were only eighteen and I was very conscious of that.'

'That's no excuse. We didn't communicate properly,' she added fiercely. 'If you and Pappous had trusted me enough, you would have realised I would never have allowed my mother to take my inheritance away from me—especially not a piece of land which I loved so much.'

'Can you be so sure of that?' he questioned softly. 'She still had a big influence in your life. You believed her when she told me I was stealing from you.'

'I know.' She sighed. 'I should have stood up to her.

In fact, I should have stood up to you all. But those days are long gone. It's all in the past now.' She was biting her lip. 'And I still don't understand why you're here. What do you want, Theo?' she whispered. 'What do you actually *want*?'

He thought how speaking to a group of the world's most powerful financiers in a glitzy hotel in the south of France was a walk in the park compared to laying his feelings on the line to his wife. But what choice did he have, if he wanted to grasp the personal happiness which had eluded him all his life?

'You made me confront my grief about your grandfather,' he said unevenly. 'And to realise that, yes, he *was* my family. And once I had acknowledged that, I accepted it was but a small leap of faith to realise that I *could* make my own family work.' He paused, suddenly aware of the raw emotion in his words and his words were husky. 'But there's only one woman I want to have a family with and that woman is you. It's always been you. Nobody else but you.'

Still she said nothing. She really *was* making him fight. He drew in a shaky breath. 'I want to spend the rest of my life showing you how much I love you, Mia,' he said. 'I want you to forgive me for closing my heart to you, and to tell you that I will try hard never to do that again.'

'How hard?' she interjected suspiciously.

'Very hard.' He smiled. 'I want to have babies with you and make a family. A real family. And I know your dream is to be a veterinary nurse, so I'm not sure how that would work, but maybe that's something we could look into. Now, I don't know if some or any of that appeals to you, but I need to hear your thoughts.' His throat constricted as he considered the possibility that she might refuse him and he wondered how he might bear it if she did. 'So, what do you say?'

What did she say?

Mia thought about it for a moment. Given their tumultuous history, wouldn't some women have held out for more? Hadn't she heard someone at work talking about making her man *grovel*? Well, maybe that was okay for some people, but not her. It smacked too much of manipulation and that was just not her thing. Because she had adored this man from the moment she'd met him and had never stopped adoring him, no matter how hard she'd tried. Her clever, charismatic, mercurial and always surprising Theo. The man who had been so short of real love despite all his stellar achievements.

She thought of the journey they'd travelled to get to this place and nobody could deny what a difficult and meandering path it had been—but none of life's paths were ever completely straightforward, were they?

What did she say?

There was really only one thing he needed to hear. Eternal words which encompassed just about everything.

'I love you, Theo,' she said.

EPILOGUE

'YOU LOOK...'

'Tired?' Mia prompted as Theo's words trailed off.

'Different,' he said thoughtfully.

She finished removing her blouse and dropped it in the laundry basket before putting her arms around his neck. 'How?'

'I don't know.' His eyes narrowed. 'You look particularly beautiful this evening.'

'Theo, I don't.'

'Mia, you *do*.'

'How can I when I've been helping at the rescue centre all afternoon and the air-conditioning broke down?' She wriggled her shoulders and gave a satisfied sigh. 'And all I want to do now is to have a long, cool shower.'

'Mmm... What a good idea,' he murmured, unclipping her bra with consummate ease and bending his mouth to hook it around one rocky nipple. 'I just might join you.'

She giggled as they wriggled out of their clothes and turned on the powerful jets, her laughter quickly turning into gasps of pleasure as she wrapped her legs around Theo's back and he thrust inside her, the tiles deliciously cool against her back. Ecstatically her fingers dug into his wet flesh as he took up a hard and exquisite rhythm which made her gasp with pleasure. He knew her so well yet every time he made love to her, it felt as incredible as the first time. Soon she was shuddering out his name, revelling in his own urgent moan, which was drowned out by the gushing torrents of water.

Afterwards they dried off and wrapped themselves in light silk robes to wander out onto the bedroom terrace, where they sat on the swing seat in the soft heat of the early evening and gazed out at the gold-edged and glittering sea.

'Would you like something to drink?' he murmured against her damp curls.

But Mia leaned her head back against his arm and shook her head. 'Not yet,' she said drowsily. 'I just want to sit here and count my blessings.'

And there were so many.

Following Theo's declaration of love, Mia had left the Granchester hotel—the farewell party they threw for her was still being talked about weeks later—and had moved permanently to Greece, where she'd started learning the language in earnest.

After renewing their wedding vows in the same small church where they'd married the first time, Mia had laid her posy of pure white lily-of-the-valley on the grave of her beloved grandfather and said a silent prayer for him.

She had advised the veterinary nursing college that she'd have to let her place go—she was going to be busy enough learning Greek and setting up their new animal rescue centre. And being Theo's wife, of course. Because Theo *was* her life, as she was his. They enjoyed friends and concerts, eating out and reading. All the usual stuff. But her relationship with her husband underpinned her happiness.

A contented Tycheros now lived with them and Mia had been angling for a puppy to keep him company, and although Theo wasn't *quite* convinced, she was confident he'd come around to her way of thinking. He usually did. Her grandfather had left his entire estate to her, which she had ploughed into the rescue centre, where she volunteered as much as she could. Of course, that would all soon change because she wouldn't have quite so much time on her hands.

With the swing-seat rocking softly, she turned to look at the man beside her—at the dark chiselled profile which looked much softer these days—and her heart turned over with love and longing.

Sensing her gaze on him, he glanced down, his lazy smile indulgent. 'What?' he questioned.

'I love you,' she said.

'And…' His eyes narrowed perceptively. 'I sense there's an "and" coming.'

'I'm pregnant, Theo,' she whispered, her voice breaking a little. 'I'm having your baby.'

A split second of incredulity was followed by a look in his eyes which Mia couldn't properly describe, though later she tried her best, when they were lying in bed in the bright moonlight. She told him she had seen his hope and excitement—along with a tiny dash of natural fear. All the stuff which happened to every prospective parent.

As she gazed out at the metallic sea in front of them, Mia gave a sigh of blissful contentment…

Because most of all she had seen his love.

* * * * *

FORBIDDEN UNTIL THEIR SNOWBOUND NIGHT

MELANIE MILBURNE

MILLS & BOON

To Louis Jacques, my beautiful toy poodle puppy.

You are only a baby but you have already brought so much laughter and joy to us.

You are a mischievous pocket rocket who is unstoppable and completely and utterly adorable.

xxxx

CHAPTER ONE

AERIN SAW HIM before he saw her. Drake Cawthorn was standing on the corner of the street opposite her, checking something on his phone while he waited for the 'walk' signal at the busy London intersection near his office. She took a moment to study him in secret and a little frisson danced down her spine. Drake was head and shoulders over everyone else in the crowd, with hair as black and sleek as a raven's wing and a strong nose that looked like it might once have been broken. He was wearing a dark blue suit teamed with a crisp white business shirt that emphasised his olive-toned skin. His tie was a checked blue, but it was loosened at his neck, as if he had tugged at it impatiently at one point during the day and not bothered to readjust it. He would have ticked number one on her soulmate checklist for 'tall dark and handsome' perfectly if it weren't for his bent nose and the jagged scar that interrupted his left eyebrow.

The pedestrian signal beeped and Drake lifted his head from his phone and his eyes met Aerin's. Even though she was several metres away, as soon as that bottomless dark brown gaze meshed with hers it was like being struck by a bolt of lightning.

Every. Single. Time.

Which was why she didn't cross paths with him unless there was absolutely no choice. He was the celebrity lawyer who specialised in iron-clad prenuptial agreements she and her wedding business partners recommended to clients from time to time. But Aerin wasn't standing outside his suite of rooms hoping to see him about a business matter—she preferred to email or send a text to inform him of a client's wish to see him. This visit was personal. Embarrassingly, skin-crawlingly personal. Aerin hadn't seen him face to face in months, and normally, she liked it that way. She had turned keeping her distance from him into quite a consummate skill. She found his arrant masculinity a little too…unsettling. His hardwired cynicism too jarring to a hopeless romantic as herself. And his sardonic smile and those dark chocolate eyes a little too mocking.

Drake strode across the intersection in long easy strides, carving his way through the bustle of people until he came to her side of the street. Her feet were suddenly glued to the footpath, her heart doing a complicated gymnastics routine in her chest and her cheeks feeling hot enough to buckle the bitumen.

'Hi there, Goldilocks. Were you on your way to see me?' His tone was as gently teasing as his smile.

Aerin could hardly deny it was him she had come to see when she was standing outside his office building, but she would have dearly liked to. She had done a walk-by or two to summon up the courage to see him, oscillating whether she should go ahead or melt back in the crowd before she made a complete and utter fool of herself. But she only had five days to find a stand-in date for her high school reunion. If she didn't find a date to accompany her she would have to suffer the embarrassment of being the last of her school friends to find a partner.

Every year that passed, she was becoming more and more of a pariah to her friends. The only singleton. The only virgin. The pitying looks from her school friends were worse each year, she was sure she wasn't imagining it. The covert whispers, the speculation about her single status, the pointed questions and glances at her ringless left hand, when each of her friends had such gorgeous sparklers winking on their ring fingers you could practically see them from outer space. It was making her wonder if her dream of finding her own Mr Perfect was a little…well, out of touch with reality. It was quite hard to meet people these days and she wasn't going to download the social media app unless things got desperate. Well, even more desperate than they already were with her nearly thirty and never been kissed.

But she *believed* in true love.

It was her goal, her lifelong hope.

Her Mr Perfect Soulmate had to be out there. All she had to do was find him.

Aerin gave Drake a mock glower. 'I wish you'd stop calling me that.'

His wide grin made his eyes dance and fine lines

crinkle at the corners. 'I've been calling you that since you had braces on your teeth and pimples on your chin. I must say, you've improved greatly with age.'

As her older brother's friend from university, Drake had been a regular visitor to her family home in years past. For years he had simply been Tom's friend, Drake Cawthorn, barely worthy of her notice. But once she hit late puberty, she became increasingly aware of him as any young woman did over a handsome and charming man. Fortunately, she had never embarrassed herself by communicating any interest in him. Not that a worldly playboy like him would ever be interested in someone as homespun and conservative as her.

'Please don't remind me I'm turning thirty in January.'

Drake widened his eyes as if in stunned surprise. 'No way. Got anything planned? A big party to celebrate?'

Aerin could feel a blush stealing over her cheeks hot enough to contribute to global warming. What was there to celebrate about turning thirty when she didn't have a partner, had never had a partner and had not even been kissed? Argh. Her dream of finding Mr Perfect before she turned the big Three O was becoming a nightmare and her biological clock was ticking loud enough to wake up an entire cemetery of bodies. She shifted her gaze from his and gave a dismissive shrug. 'I'm not sure. Maybe.'

He jerked his head in the direction of his suite of

rooms. 'Did you want to see me about a client? I've got just under an hour before I'm due in court.'

Aerin shifted her weight from foot to foot and re-adjusted her tote-bag strap over her left shoulder, conscious of his steady gaze. 'Erm... I don't want to bother you when you're busy...'

'I've always got time for you. Besides, you send a lot of business my way.' His eyes twinkled again, and he added, 'I heard your other business partner, Harper, got herself engaged to Jack Livingstone. Are they going to come and see me about a prenup?'

'Not that I know of.'

'Pity. With Jack's sort of wealth, it could be a messy divorce without one.'

Aerin gave a stiff smile to cover her annoyance at his cynicism. 'I don't think they're ever going to divorce. They're too much in love and besides, they have baby Marli to consider.'

Drake shrugged one impossibly broad shoulder. 'Everyone is in love until they aren't.'

'Have you ever been in love?' The question popped out of her mouth before she could slam the emergency brakes on her tongue.

'No. How about you?'

Her cheeks warmed up again and she couldn't hold his gaze. A relationships cynic like Drake would mock her quest to find the love of her life. But it was no secret she was waiting not just for Mr Right but Mr Perfect. 'No, but I'd like to one day.'

There was a short but weighted silence, even the

sounds of rushing pedestrians and busy traffic seeming to fade into the background.

'What did you want to see me about?' Drake asked, looking down at her with a small frown between his eyebrows.

Aerin chewed at one side of her lower lip. 'It doesn't matter.' She began to step away, but he reached out and placed his broad-spanned and tanned hand on her forearm. Her cashmere coat wasn't enough of a barrier to block the electric heat of his touch. She could not think of a time when he had ever touched her before—or at least not since he had teasingly ruffled her hair when she was a kid. Her gaze connected to his and another fizz of awareness shot through her.

His hand fell away from her arm as if he too had felt the same current of energy, his frown deepening above his dark brown eyes. 'Is everything all right?' His voice was pitched low, a deep rough burr of sound that sent another delicate shiver along her spine.

Aerin swallowed thickly and gave him a strained smile. 'Can we take this somewhere a little more private?'

'Sure.'

He led the way to the front of his office building and Aerin followed, wondering if she was being a fool for even contemplating asking him to be a stand-in date for her reunion. But who else could she ask? She didn't want to take a stranger or someone off a dating app. She needed someone who could act convincingly as her love interest for the weekend meet-up in Scotland. Drake was the most experienced man she knew and, even better, he had known her for years. He was perfect…well, not exactly perfect according to her soulmate checklist but good enough to get her over the line. She could not suffer the embarrassment of being the only single person at her school reunion weekend—their last reunion before one of the girls emigrated to Australia with her husband. If Aerin didn't show up, they would assume it was because of her feelings about still being alone. She had to go and she had to take a stand-in partner. That was the plan.

'My office is on the top floor,' Drake said, walking past the four lifts situated on one side of the marble-floored foyer.

Aerin gave him a sideways glance of horror. 'You're not expecting me to walk up fifty flights of stairs?'

His mouth tilted in one of his wry smiles that never failed to make her stomach flip-flop. 'I have my own private lift back here.' He shouldered open a door and indicated for her to come through while he held it open for her. She moved past him in the doorway, catching an alluring waft of his lemon-and-lime-based aftershave on her way past his tall and lean athletic frame. The door closed behind him with a solid thump, and he led her to a lift marked Private. Drake took out a security tag from his trouser pocket and used it against the sensor and the doors swished open. He held one muscular arm against the lift door and said, 'After you.'

Aerin stepped inside the lift and he followed her in, the doors closing on a whisper behind him. The sensation of being enclosed in a small space alone with Drake Cawthorn sent her heart rate soaring. The lift was mirrored on three sides, and she caught a glimpse of her flushed features and inwardly cringed. Why did she always have to act like an awkward teenage girl around him? Was it because he was the epitome of sophisticated man about town? A self-made billionaire playboy who had women from all over the globe flocking after him? She was a successful businesswoman, not a gauche teenager.

Well…a single-and-hating-it successful businesswoman. She loved the success, not the singledom.

There was a pinging sound when the lift arrived at Drake's floor. 'This way,' he said, and she followed him down a wide plushily carpeted corridor, past a reception area where a middle-aged woman was typing on a computer. Aerin was fairly certain it was the same woman she had spoken to on a couple of occasions when she'd called to book an appointment for clients.

'Hold my calls, please, Cathleen,' Drake said.

Cathleen's smile of greeting was friendly towards her but Aerin wasn't sure if it was one of recognition or not. 'Will do.'

Drake led Aerin to a door marked with his name on a simple plaque. He opened the door and gave a brief on-off smile to indicate for her to go in. She stepped over the threshold and glanced around at the neat but understated décor. Drake's qualifications were framed on one wall to the left of his large wooden desk. She suspected they were only there to display to his clients he was more than qualified to act for them rather than out of any sense of pride in his own achievements. She knew that Drake had graduated with First Class Honours and taken out the university prize, but she had heard that from her brother, not Drake. There was a selection of artwork on the other walls—nothing too over the top but tasteful landscapes in an old-world style—and the windows afforded a spectacular view over the River Thames and Tower Bridge.

'Take a seat. Can I get Cathleen to bring you a coffee or tea?' Drake asked, shrugging off his coat and hanging it inside a cupboard near his desk.

'No, thanks. I had one not long ago.' Actually, she'd had three, which was probably why her pulse was racing so fast. Caffeine courage instead of Dutch courage was never a good idea. Her heart was palpitating from the stimulant…or was it because the thought of asking Drake Cawthorn this favour was sending her heart rhythm way out of whack?

Aerin sat, knowing he was too polite to take his own seat until she had taken hers. She placed her tote bag on her lap and laid her hands on top to keep it from slipping to the floor.

Drake sat in his office chair and rolled it closer to his desk, his forearms resting on the polished surface, his fingers loosely interlaced. Aerin's gaze drifted to those long, tanned fingers and she wondered what it would feel like to have them glide along her skin. She tried to disguise a little shiver, tried but failed. Why was she suddenly thinking about his hands touching her? He was not the type of man she could ever build a future with. He was too worldly, too cynical.

'Are you cold? I can turn up the heating if you like.'

'No, I'm fine…' She licked her lips and forced a smile, conscious of the glowing warmth in her cheeks and the nerves eating at the lining of her stomach like piranha teeth. 'I have a…a favour to ask.'

He lifted his scar-interrupted eyebrow in an arc, his sharply intelligent gaze unwavering on hers. 'Go on.'

Aerin gripped her tote bag a little more firmly. Her heart beat out a syncopated rhythm in her chest. *Boom-pitty-boom…pitty-pitty-boom-boom.*

'I have a high school reunion this weekend. It's a drinks and dinner catch-up in a remote village an hour out of Edinburgh, close to our old boarding school, and I… I have no one to take me.'

Drake lifted his arms off his desk and leaned back in his chair, his expression unreadable. 'Why can't you go on your own?'

Another wave of heat exploded in her cheeks. 'For the last twelve years I've met up with my school friends once a year just before Christmas and I've always gone alone. It wasn't so bad in the early years because some of the girls were single or between partners. But I'm now the only one without a partner. I can't face yet another year without producing a date. It's so mortifying to be the last singleton. I'll never hear the end of it. They teased me so much last time I thought I would die of embarrassment.'

'Then why go if they're only going to give you a hard time?'

Aerin absently fiddled with the silver buckle on her tote bag. His gaze flicked to her busy fingers and she forced herself to stop their restive movements. She got the sense he was reading her, analysing her, observing every nuance of her expression and it made her feel exposed and terribly unsophisticated. He was only seven years older than her but in terms of experience it was more like a century. An aeon.

'We have a perfect track record of meeting up. Twelve years and not one of us has failed to show up. I don't want to be the one to break it. But if I were not to show up, everyone is going to assume I'm embarrassed about still being single, so I have to show up with someone—I can't win either way. I was talking to Harper and she suggested I ask you, since you've known me a long time. It's either that or hire a male escort.'

Drake shot out of his chair, his features set in frowning lines. 'You will *not* do that.' The stern note of authority in his tone would have annoyed her on any other occasion but for some strange reason, this time, it did not.

She looked up at him hopefully. 'So, does that mean you'll be my date for the night?'

Drake ran a hand over his face and then loosened his tie even further. His frown was more of a scowl and his mouth was set in a firm line. 'I thought you said it was a weekend thing?'

'It is but I would only need you to be there for the

drinks and dinner thing on the Friday night. I'll tell them you had to fly back for work or something.'

He continued to hold her gaze with unwavering intensity. 'So, what's the story you're going to spin to them about our...relationship?'

'I'll tell them we've fallen madly in love and—'

He held up his right hand like a stop sign and his features screwed up in distaste. 'Whoa there, Goldilocks. No offence but I'm not the type of guy to fall head over heels in love. Why can't we say we're having a fling?'

Aerin shifted her lips from side to side. 'Because I'm not the type of girl to have a fling.'

'You must have had plenty of flings, you're almost thirty.'

There was a silence so intense Aerin could hear the creak of her chair when she shifted position. She slowly lifted her gaze to his and saw the dawning shock and surprise.

'Are you telling me you're a *virgin*?'

The word seemed to bounce off the four walls of the room. Did he have to make it sound so...so shocking? Plenty of people were celibate for various reasons. Aerin let her bag slip to the floor as she stood. 'I know it's a little unusual but that's why I need a date this weekend. I've been teased about my virginal status for years.'

'Is there some reason you haven't...?'

'Done the deed?' Aerin sighed. 'Yes. I'm waiting for my soulmate to show up. I don't want to waste myself on someone who doesn't get the importance of what this means to me. I want everything about my first time to be perfect.'

Drake walked over to the windows of his office, and, placing his hands on his lean hips, looked out at the view below. She hadn't noticed before how broad his back and shoulders were from behind. They tapered down to trim hips and a taut bottom and long lean legs. Her mind began to undress him and her heart rate picked up again. She could imagine he would look wonderfully sexy in nothing but his olive-toned skin. What would it feel like to run her hands over his naked flesh? She was shocked at her wayward thoughts, wondering why they were entering her mind now. She was only interested in him as a stand-in date, not as a real date.

It was a moment or two before Drake turned around to look at her, his hands going back down by his sides. The afternoon sun coming in from behind him cast his features into shadow, giving him an even more rakish look.

'Look, I'm flattered you asked me, but—'

'Please don't say no, Drake. I'm desperate. I can't go alone, not this year because it's the last year we will all be together because one of the girls is moving to Australia with her husband.' Aerin didn't care that she was at the begging stage. 'We don't have to mention it to anyone. Even Tom doesn't have to know or my parents. In fact, it's probably best if they don't hear about it.'

Drake moved back behind his desk but didn't sit in his chair. He stood grasping the back of it instead, his fingers white-knuckled against the leather. 'Will the press be there?'

'No, it's a private event.'

'But no doubt you and your friends will post photos on social media.'

Aerin tried not to think of how many followers some of her so-called influencer friends had. At last count it was in the hundreds of thousands. 'I'll tell them not to post any photos of us. I'll tell them we're keeping our relationship a secret from my family for a little while longer. I'm sure they'll go along with it. They know how full-on my dad can be.'

Drake let out a long sigh and removed his hands from the back of his chair. 'I'm not sure I'm the right guy for the job.' He shook his head as if he still couldn't believe she had asked him. 'It's got all sorts of wrong about it.'

Disappointment swept through her and she caught her lip between her teeth. 'It's just one night. You don't have to do anything but pretend to be my partner. I'm not asking you to actually *be* my partner.'

'I'm not planning on being anyone's partner.'

Drake resumed his seat but didn't roll the chair close to the desk, sitting with one leg casually crossed over his other knee, the fingers of his right hand lightly drumming against his thigh. His eyes didn't leave hers and she fought against the desire to squirm in her seat. He had his lawyer face on, the stillness of his features revealing nothing of the razor-sharp inner workings of his mind.

'Because you're afraid to love someone in case they hurt you?' she ventured.

His fingers stopped drumming against his leg and there was a sudden movement in the back of his gaze—a movement as quick as a camera shutter click. But then his lips twisted in a sardonic smile. 'People can hurt you whether you love them or not.'

'I guess...'

He uncrossed his leg and rolled the chair back to the desk. 'Okay. I'll do it. But only because I don't want you to get in over your head with someone who might do the wrong thing by you.'

Aerin breathed out a gusty sigh of relief. 'Oh, thank you so much. I was working myself into such a state at the thought of hiring someone or taking a stranger and having to share a room with them.'

There was a long beat of silence.

'Will you be comfortable sharing a room with me?' His tone was mildly teasing, the glint in his eyes even more so.

Aerin tried to ignore the tiny feather-duster flutter along the floor of her belly. Tried to ignore the sudden leap of her pulse and the hitch of her breath in her throat. 'I'm sure you'll be a perfect gentleman.'

His scarred eyebrow came up again in a cynical arc. 'Me? Perfect?' He gave a deep chuckle of wry amusement and added, 'I hardly think so.' His hooded gaze dipped to her mouth for an infinitesimal moment, the atmosphere in the office charged with a nerve-tingling energy. His gaze came back to hers, and she let out a breath she had forgotten she was holding. That was surely why she was a little light-headed, right? Not just because he looked at her with those intensely dark eyes.

'I—I'd better get going…' Aerin scooped up her bag off the floor and slung its strap over her shoulder. 'I'll book the flights and get back to you with the details. The dress for the dinner is formal. I know that seems a little over the top, but we've always done it that way.' She turned for the door, more flustered than she cared to admit in his alluring presence. She had never been alone with him for such a long period before. How was she going to manage the weekend?

'Aerin.' His deep voice stopped her in her tracks. He had called her Goldilocks for years; she couldn't remember the last time she had heard her name on his lips.

She turned to look at him, clutching her tote bag close to her side. 'Yes?'

His dark eyes held hers for a heart-stopping moment, his expression unusually sombre. 'You'll be safe with me. You have my word.'

'Thank you.' She gave him a quick smile and turned again for the door.

'Another thing—I'll book the flights.'

'But I don't expect you to pay—'

'It's not a problem.'

Aerin knew it would be pointless arguing with him. 'Okay, that's kind of you, thank you.'

'Wait. I'll come down with you.' He picked up a folder of papers off his desk and slid them into a leather briefcase, then closed the lid and locked it. He took his jacket out of the cupboard and shrugged himself back into it. Then he lifted his hand to his tie and tightened it back in place close to his neck. The actions were things she had seen her brother and father do hundreds if not thousands of times and yet, when Drake did them, there was something so...so arrantly masculine and so darn sexy about it.

They travelled down in the private lift in a silence that throbbed with something Aerin had not been aware of before. She cast covert glances at him, but his features were set in inscrutable lines. The lift doors whooshed open on the ground floor and she stepped out. She was aware of his tall frame only a step or two behind her, aware of the citrus scent of his aftershave, and aware of her body's secret reaction to him.

Aerin turned to say goodbye. 'Thank you again. I hope you didn't have anything important planned for this weekend?'

His smile was lopsided and didn't reach his eyes. 'Nothing I couldn't cancel at short notice.'

'Erm... I didn't think to ask but are you currently seeing anyone? I mean, that could make things rather awkward, and I would hate to complicate things for—'

'No.' His answer was unmistakably definitive.

'Oh, I thought you nearly always had someone on the go.'

'Not this close to Christmas.'

Aerin frowned. 'But Christmas is a month away. I thought you changed partners just about every week.'

A shutter came down over his face. 'I've got to rush. I have a mediation meeting at court in ten minutes. See you Friday.' He turned to leave.

'Drake?'

He stopped moving to look down at her. 'Yes?'

Aerin gave him a tremulous smile. 'You won't suddenly change your mind and leave me to face the violins alone?'

He gave a quizzical frown. 'The violins?'

'It's a saying Harper used. It refers to the pity symphony I get every year from my school friends for still being single.'

His frown faded and his mouth tilted in a half-smile. 'I won't change my mind.'

Change his mind? That was exactly what Drake knew he should do and yet he couldn't bring himself to let Aerin down. But what the freaking hell was he doing agreeing to partner his best friend's kid sister to a reunion in Scotland? A weekend pretending to be someone he was not. He was not Prince Charming or Mr Perfect or Mr Right or Mr Soulmate. But how could he let innocent and naïve Aerin take anyone else? She was as trusting and idealistic as he was cynical and jaded. Her confession about still being a virgin had shocked him to the backbone and beyond. He knew she was conservative but not to the point that she had left it so long to experience sex.

Of course he had to agree to take her to the re-

union. What other option was there? How could he
be sure some other less principled guy wouldn't jump
at the chance to take her virginity as some sort of
prize? The most Drake had ever done with her was
ruffle her golden hair as a kid. But placing his hand
on her arm earlier had sounded a warning in his
body. A warning that she was not a gangly teenager any more. She was an adult woman with gentle
feminine curves and a soft pillowy mouth he could
barely take his eyes off. A mouth he could not stop
thinking about tasting to see if it was as sweet and
delicious as it looked.

He had never really noticed her before other than
as his friend's younger sister. But sitting opposite
her in his office, watching her drum up the courage to ask him to help her, had shifted something
in their relationship. A subtle shift that made him
aware of her in ways he had not been before—or at
least not consciously. Aerin was not supermodel-gor-
geous, but she had a girl-next-door natural beauty that
was equally breath-snatching. Her golden hair was
straight and fell past her shoulders to the middle of
her back in a silken skein. Her body was as slim and
finely boned as a ballerina's, her eyes a smoky grey-
blue. Her ski-slope nose was—unlike his—perfectly
aligned above a full-lipped Cupid's bow mouth. A
mouth that promised sweetness and sensuality in its
plump curves. A mouth that was forbidden territory
for someone like him.

He could look but not touch and not taste. That
would be crossing a line he had sworn he would never

cross. He wasn't interested in complicating his life with a young woman who had fairy dust in her eyes. Aerin was after perfection in a partner, she believed in for ever love and had waited this long to find it. Thirty years old and still a virgin? How could that be possible in this day and age?

He had lost his virginity the month after losing his family. Back then, sex had been a mind-numbing escape from pain and in a way it still was. He never allowed himself to get close to anyone other than physically. His relationships were transactional and brief. No promises, no strings, no emotions other than lust, which wasn't an emotion in his opinion but a physical drive. He dealt with it efficiently and, of course, respectfully and always consensually but that was as far as it ever went. He had sworn off ever falling in love and did everything in his power to keep the armour around his heart in place. Armour so thick and strong and such a part of him now, he was barely aware of it being there.

But sweet untouched and innocent Aerin with her heart-shaped face and kissable mouth was a threat because he already had a relationship with her of sorts. A hard to define relationship but it was long-lasting, and he didn't want to compromise it or his relationship with her brother, Tom, and his parents, who he also considered friends. Too many people would get hurt if he didn't keep the boundary lines in place. And the last thing he wanted was to hurt anyone, especially people he cared about. He had paid a high price for relaxing his guard when he was fifteen.

He would *not* do it again.

Aerin Drysdale was off limits to him in every way. Too sweet, too innocent, too good for a man who had such dark secrets in his past.

CHAPTER TWO

AERIN HAD A work meeting the following day with her business partners, Ruby and Harper. Ruby was only just back from a brief honeymoon having got married to Lucas Rothwell a couple of weeks ago. And Harper had recently become engaged to Jack Livingstone, the father of her surprise baby, Marli. Witnessing her friends' blissful happiness only made Aerin's single status all the more painful. Day in day out, she was surrounded by happy couples; her parents were as in love after thirty-seven years of marriage as they were when they first got together. Her brother Tom and his wife, Saskia, had been married six years and, although they were struggling with some fertility issues, she knew they were a match made in heaven and would stay together for ever.

Aerin believed in true love and desperately wanted it for herself. She had planned her future since she was a little kid. She was meant to be married with two kids by now. No way did she ever think she would still be a virgin so close to turning thirty but there hadn't been anyone she was even mildly attracted to...until now.

But she *wasn't* going to think about Drake Cawthorn as a potential partner. He was a stand-in date, that was all.

'So, did you ask him?' Harper asked with a teasing waggle of her eyebrows.

'Ask who?' Ruby said, having a turn at cuddling baby Marli, who was soundly asleep.

'I told Aerin to ask Drake Cawthorn to be her stand-in date for her reunion weekend,' Harper explained to Ruby, then, turning back to Aerin, asked, 'So, did you ask him?'

'I did.'

'And?' Both Harper and Ruby said in unison and with almost identical expectant expressions.

Aerin leaned forward to put her electronic planner on the table in front of her. 'It took some work, but he finally agreed.'

'Oh, wow,' Ruby said, eyes gleaming with excitement. 'This could be the start of something.'

Aerin rolled her eyes in an expressive manner. 'I don't think so. Drake might be handsome in a rugged way, but he doesn't tick any of my other boxes.' There was a part of her that was starting to wonder if there was anyone out there who could tick all her boxes, but she didn't want to admit it to her friends. She barely wanted to admit it to herself. She had clung to the hope of finding a perfect partner so ardently and passionately for so long, it would make her look foolish to back down now. Surely the right man was out there for her? How could she lose faith now?

'How well do you know him?' Ruby asked. 'I knew Lucas since I was a child and yet I didn't truly get to know him until he whisked me away to his private Greek island.' She gave a blissful sigh as if just thinking about that trip brought back a host of wonderful memories.

'I know him well enough to know he's not the settling down type,' Aerin said. 'My brother had enough of a job convincing him to be his best man. Weddings bring him out in a rash.'

'I guess handling all those messy divorces would make anyone in his line of work pretty cynical about relationships,' Harper said. 'Oh, well, at least you don't have to suffer the pitying looks from your school friends now. An experienced man like him is sure to do a good job of pretending to be your love interest.'

'But how are you going to convince your friends he's the real deal?' Ruby asked. 'I mean, are you going to kiss and hold hands and stuff and act all lovey-dovey?'

Aerin could feel her cheeks heating up enough to warm the room. The entire planet. 'We haven't actually discussed that angle yet. I guess we'll sort that out on the flight to Edinburgh.'

'And will you be sharing a room?' Harper asked with another waggle of her eyebrows.

'We'll have to otherwise no one is going to be convinced we're together,' Aerin said.

'I guess you could say you're waiting until you get married,' Ruby offered.

Harper gave a wry laugh. 'We're talking about Drake Cawthorn here. Who's going to believe a worldly playboy like him would wait to sleep with his intended bride? Or even that he'd propose marriage to someone in the first place?'

'Good point,' Ruby said. 'But miracles do happen. Look at us two. I didn't dare hope I could be as happy as this. Lucas is everything I could have wished for in a husband.'

'Jack is too,' Harper said with a dreamy sigh. 'We want the same for you, Aerin. It would be so wonderful to see you settled with the man of your dreams.'

Aerin wanted it too, so badly it was an ache in her heart. But Drake Cawthorn was hardly the man of her dreams. He was the complete opposite of what she wanted. She wanted someone loving and romantic, someone who believed in marriage and commitment and for ever love. Not a hardened cynic who thought marriages should only be conducted between two people with a get-out clause in place.

Drake handed his middle-aged secretary, Cathleen, some files to put away on the way out of his office on Friday after lunch.

'You're leaving early,' Cathleen said, looking up from her computer. 'Have you got something special planned for the weekend?'

'No.' He wasn't comfortable lying to his secretary, nor was he comfortable calling a weekend away in

Scotland with Aerin Drysdale a special event. Even though it was. Big time. He had never been alone with her before, or at least not for that length of time. But he was confident he could keep the boundaries in place. He had drawn a line in his head and he was not stepping over it. He couldn't.

Cathleen cocked her head at him, her whisky-brown eyes curious. 'This early mark hasn't got anything to do with Aerin Drysdale's visit the other day, has it?'

Drake's eyebrows snapped together. 'You recognised her?'

Cathleen smiled. 'But of course. She planned my niece's wedding last year. She did an amazing job of it too. Gillian hardly had to do a thing but show up on time at the church. I hadn't met Aerin in person, but I recognised her from Gillian's photos. I've spoken to her on the phone a couple of times when she's booked an appointment for a client with you. She's beautiful in a rather understated way, isn't she?'

He gave a non-committal grunt. 'Passable, I suppose.'

The last thing he wanted to think about was how naturally beautiful Aerin Drysdale was. He had no interest in compromising his relationship with her older brother by having a dalliance with her. It was an unspoken bro code, and he was going to do everything in his power to hold to it. Besides, he didn't do virgins or get involved with women who wanted the fairy tale.

Cathleen's eyes danced and her smile widened.

'You've known her a long time, right? Weren't you best man at her brother's wedding a few years ago?'

'That was the first and last time I'll be standing at an altar,' Drake said with heavy conviction. 'You and I both know how often supposedly happy couples end up here a few years later hating their exes and wanting out one way or the other.'

Cathleen's shoulders went down on a sigh. 'But some couples do make it and that's what everyone wants really, isn't it? To love and be loved for the rest of their life.'

Drake had witnessed 'love' in various guises as a child. Obsessive love. Possessive love. Abusive love. Love that taunted and tortured and destroyed those to whom it was directed. But there was no way he would ever reveal the dark shadows of his childhood to his secretary or anyone else for that matter. Even his closest friend, Tom Drysdale, didn't know the ugly truth about his background. He didn't want to fall passionately in love as his parents had. He resisted it, rejected it, spurned it as if it were a deadly disease.

For in his family of origin, that was exactly what it had turned out to be—deadly.

Aerin had arranged via text message to meet Drake at the airport, but he texted back that he would pick her up himself at her flat. He had never been to her home before, only to her family's residence in Buckinghamshire. She sent him her address and waited for him to arrive with her stomach twitching with sudden nerves.

She was effectively lying to her school friends about her 'relationship' with Drake. She wasn't the most convincing liar on the planet but what else could she do now? She had already told them she was bringing her new partner. The excitement her announcement elicited on the group chat was off the charts. The fact that she had insisted on them keeping it a secret had only fuelled their interest and delight. It was too late to back out now, she had to go through with it no matter what. But every time she thought of Drake her body shivered and her heart raced. Had she made a mistake in asking him rather than a stranger?

Aerin paced the sitting room floor as the time for Drake to arrive approached, her hands twisting in front of her body.

You are spending the weekend with Drake Cawthorn.

Her pulse began to pick up its pace, her palms moistening in panic. What if she wasn't able to pull off the charade? What if she ended up being exposed as a liar and a fraud?

There was a soft knock on the door and she opened it with an overly bright smile on her face. But it wasn't Drake standing there but her elderly Scottish neighbour, Mr McPhee, who lived opposite. His equally elderly dog, Mutley, was at his feet, wagging his shaggy tail from side to side and looked up at her through rheumy eyes not unlike his owner's. Mutley had probably been adorably cute in puppyhood but as a senior he had developed some bald patches on his rough coat. He was of indiscriminate breeding and short and stout with stumpy legs and with a black patch over one eye like a pirate. One of his ears pointed up, the other folded down and his jaw was out of line, the bottom overshot like a drawer that hadn't been closed properly. Oh, and he had terrible breath and farted. A lot.

'Oh, hello, Mr McPhee. Hi, Mutley. I'm just heading out for the weekend. Did you want me for something?'

'Sorry to bother you, lass, but do you have a wee cup of sugar? I seem to have run out.' Mr McPhee's expression was sheepish and Aerin knew from experience he didn't need the sugar as much as he needed human contact. Widowed eight years ago, he was close to ninety and had no relatives living nearby, or at least, none who visited regularly. He often popped over for a cup of tea and a chat and she enjoyed his company for he reminded her of her maternal grandfather, who was also a proud Scot.

'Of course. Do you want to come in while I get it? I have some of those treats Mutley likes so much.'

'I don't want to take up your time. Where are you off to for the weekend?'

'Erm… Scotland, actually.'

Mr McPhee shuffled into her flat with Mutley waddling beside him. 'Och, now then, that will be good for you, although November's not the best time. Cold and grey and wet. You might even get a flurry of snow. It wouldn't be the first time.'

'I know but it's a high school reunion, so we'll be inside most of the time.' Aerin bent down to give

Mutley a doggy treat, and then went to her small pantry for the sugar.

There was another knock on the door, firmer this time and her heart gave a skip. 'Erm, will you excuse me for a moment? That's my lift here to collect me.'

Aerin went to the front door and opened it to find Drake standing there dressed casually for travelling in jeans and a roll-neck cashmere sweater and a black, butter-soft leather jacket. She gave him a nervous smile. 'I'm just helping my neighbour with something. I won't be long.'

Just then, Mr McPhee shuffled out of the kitchen with Mutley close behind, the dog's long claws clickclacking on the polished floorboards until he got to the carpet runner. 'Is this your beau, lass? About time, I say.' Mr McPhee thrust out his hand to Drake. 'Hamish McPhee.'

Drake grasped the older man's hand. 'Drake Cawthorn. Pleased to meet you, Mr McPhee.'

Aerin was conscious of the heat pooling in her cheeks, which did not bode well for the weekend charade. Or global warming. She would have to get used to people calling Drake her beau or boyfriend or... or lover. Gulp.

Mutley sniffed Drake's leather shoes and looked up at him and gave a croaky bark, his tail wagging. At first, Aerin thought Drake was going to ignore the dog but after a moment, he bent down and gave Mutley a gentle scratch behind the ears. Something passed over Drake's features—a flattening of his mouth, a tightening of his jaw, a rapid blink of his eyes. Then he straightened and glanced at her. 'There's no rush if you want to chat to Mr McPhee. I'll take your luggage down to the car.'

'Och, no, I'm going home anyway for it's time for this wee chap's supper,' Mr McPhee said, whistling to Mutley to follow him. 'Have a grand time, you two. I wish I was your age again. It's times like these I miss my Maisie. But we had sixty-one years together, so I should be grateful, eh?'

'That's a lovely attitude to have, Mr McPhee,' Aerin said. 'But it must still be terribly hard for you.'

'Aye, lass, it is, but that's what you sign up for when you love someone. If you're lucky you grow old together but then one day they're no longer with you and all you have are the memories.'

'It was nice to meet you, Mr McPhee,' Drake said, and extended his hand again.

The old man shook it warmly. 'Take good care of her, eh? She's one in a million.'

'I will.'

A short time later, Aerin was sitting in Drake's show-room-perfect sports car, her luggage stowed in the boot along with his.

'Mr McPhee is rather a sweetheart,' she said to fill the silence. 'I hope it didn't embarrass you when he mistook you for my...erm...'

Drake sent her a sideways glance, his dark eyes glinting. 'Lover?'

Another wave of heat flooded her cheeks. 'I actually told him you were my lift to the airport, but he jumped to conclusions.'

'Why haven't you dated anyone?'

Aerin looked at her hands rather than meet his gaze. 'I don't want to make a mistake. Choosing your life partner is such an important decision. Your entire life can be shifted way off course if you get it wrong. I want to get it right the first time. I don't want to have a trail of broken relationships behind me. I've had good role-modelling from my parents and grandparents of how a well-functioning relationship works, so I don't want to waste time on dating men who don't come close to my dream partner, my perfect soulmate.'

Drake started the engine with a throaty rumble and put the car in gear. 'Is there such a thing?' he asked with a note of cynicism in his tone.

'A perfect soulmate? Of course there is. Look at my parents. They're still madly in love all these years down the track. And then there's Tom. He and Saskia are so perfect for each other in every way.'

A frown brought his dark brows closer together. 'You think so?'

Aerin glanced at him with a frown. 'Of course I do. I know things are a little tough on them now after Saskia's last miscarriage but Tom adores her and she adores him.'

He didn't respond other than give a non-committal grunt.

There was a lengthy silence broken only by the

swish of the tyres on the wet roads on the way to the airport.

'Drake? There's something we need to discuss before we get to the reunion.' Aerin took a deep breath and continued, 'If we're going to convince everyone we're a couple, we have to act like we're in love.'

'How do you know a couple is in love? What signs do you look for?'

Aerin immediately pictured Ruby and Lucas and Harper and Jack in her mind. 'Well, they usually touch each other a lot, hold hands or have their arms around each other.'

'So, you'd be okay with me doing that with you?'

'I guess…' Aerin shivered at the thought of his muscled arms around her. He had a tall and rangy build with muscles taut and toned by endurance exercise. What would it feel like to have those arms gather her close? To have her chest pressed against the rock wall of his? To be so physically close she would feel the hard contours of his body against her softer ones? She had never been that close to a man.

'What about kissing?'

Her heart skipped a beat. 'What about it?'

'Is that something you'd expect an in-love couple to do?'

Aerin licked her suddenly dry lips. 'Yes, but not all couples are comfortable with public displays of affection.'

'So, no passionate kissing in public, then.'

Aerin twisted her hands together in her lap, suddenly imagining Drake's firm lips pressed to hers.

What would he taste like? What would it feel like to have his mouth against hers in a passionate kiss? She had never been game enough to allow anyone to kiss her. She had always wanted her first kiss to be perfect, but she had spent so much time planning it, it hadn't happened.

'I guess a peck on the cheek or a brief kiss on the lips might be okay…'

'Anything else I should do to be convincing?'

'Well, one thing I've noticed about men who are in love with their partners and vice versa is a certain look they have in their eyes, kind of soft and tender and dewy.'

Drake screwed up his face in a grimace. 'That's probably outside my acting capabilities, I'm afraid. I'm not the soppy type.'

'Yet another fail on my checklist,' Aerin said not quite under her breath.

She felt rather than saw his glance. 'Tell me about this checklist of yours. I probably should know what's on it if I'm supposed to be pretending to be the man who's actually managed to tick every box. How many are there?'

'Eight.'

He whistled through his teeth. 'I'm starting to see why you've got to almost thirty without finding a partner.'

Aerin flashed him an irritated look. 'Personally, I think there would be a lot less divorces if men and women did think a little more deeply about what they want in a life partner. It would save a lot of heartache in the end.'

'I'm sure it would.' Something about his tone brought her gaze back to his but his expression was unreadable. 'What's number one on your list?' he said after a moment's silence.

'I'm only going to tell you if you promise not to mock me.'

'Okay, I promise not to mock you.'

She studied his inscrutable features for a beat or two. 'I know it's a bit clichéd, but I want a man who is tall and dark and handsome.'

'Why not a blond or red-haired man?'

'I can't explain it other than I've always seen my-self with someone with dark hair.'

'And number two?'

'Well, this is one you certainly don't meet. I want a man who believes in love and is a romantic at heart.'

Drake's top lip curled. 'Three?'

She took a breath and let it out in a steady stream. 'He has to be open and not ashamed of showing his feelings.'

He gave a low grunt that could have been agree-ment or scorn or maybe a bit of both. 'Some men show their feelings too much. They have little or no emotional regulation. And their partners pay the price for it.'

'I guess you see a lot of that in your line of work. People behaving badly.'

'There's a saying amongst lawyers—we see bad people behaving badly and good people behaving badly.' He shifted the gears going around a corner and continued, 'What's number four?'

'He needs to be close to his family.'

Another gear change, this time a little more forceful. 'In proximity or emotionally?'

'Emotionally, of course.'

'Number five?'

'He has to want to have kids.'

Drake whistled through his teeth. 'You're right, I don't tick any boxes on your list.'

'You don't want kids? Ever?'

'No.'

'Because?'

He flicked her a brief glance. 'Kids get hurt when parents break up.'

'Not all parents break up.'

'Close to half do.'

'Yours didn't. They were still together when they had the accident, weren't they?'

Drake's jaw hardened and his grip on the gear stick tightened. 'What's your number six?'

Aerin was not so easily put off by his attempt to steer the conversation away from his background. It intrigued her why he was so reluctant to talk about it—or did that have something to do with having lost his family so young? But wouldn't he want to keep their memory alive by talking about them?

She realised she knew very little about his background other than the occasional snippets of information she had gleaned from her brother. But even Tom hadn't been all that forthcoming, and she hadn't wanted to appear *too* interested. All she knew was that his parents and younger sister had died in an accident when he was fifteen and he had been raised by relatives. It kind of explained his aura of self-sufficiency and hard-wired cynicism. He had loved and lost and had since learned not to rely on anyone but himself. 'Weren't your parents happy?'

There was a long drawn-out pause before he spoke. 'No.' His tone had a flat, almost deadened note to it.

'Does it upset you to talk about your family?'

He let out a stiff curse word. 'What do you think?'

Aerin gave a soft sigh. 'I think it must be very hard to lose your entire family when you were so young. But how else will you remember them if you don't talk about them? Or is it just too painful?'

'It's…' his jaw worked for a moment and then he continued '…complicated and painful and I'd rather not talk about it.' He rearranged his shadowed features into a more relaxed pose as if he'd flicked a switch in his brain. End of subject. 'So, what's number six on your list?'

'My future partner has a dog or cat, or at least would like to have one.'

'Another tick against me.' Amusement coloured his tone but it wasn't reflected in his expression.

'But you like animals, right? You bent down to scratch Mr McPhee's dog, Mutley.'

Drake gave a dismissive shrug. 'I like animals and I like kids, but it doesn't mean I want them. What are we up to now? Number seven?'

'I want my partner to be musical or creative in some way.'

'I can play chopsticks and I draw a mean stick figure.'

Aerin fought back a smile. 'Be serious. Can you write poetry?'

'Not my forte, I'm afraid. So, what's number eight?'

'He has to love Christmas.'

There was another beat or two of silence.

'Let me guess,' Aerin said, looking at him again. 'You don't like the festive season. 'You've never once accepted my parents' and Tom's invitation to join us for Christmas.'

Drake had now parked the car and turned off the engine before he answered. 'Christmas isn't a time of joy for me.'

'Is that when you lost your family? At Christmas?'

'Christmas Eve.'

'Oh, Drake, I'm so sorry. That must have been so awful for you. I mean, to lose them at any time of year would be devastating but just before Christmas… it's such a family time.' How on earth had he coped with such a loss? Her heart ached at the thought of him all those years ago, suffering such sadness and trauma when he was only a teenager. No wonder he was so reluctant to talk about his family. It would be reopening a wound that hadn't quite healed…maybe it never would.

Drake glanced at the clock on the dashboard and

then unclipped his seat belt. 'We need to get a move on. We can't have you missing your reunion, can we?'

Drake hadn't spoken to anyone of his family in years, not even his aunt who had looked after him until he was eighteen. Talking about them reminded him of his failure to protect his mother and sister. He carried the burden of guilt like a heavy yoke around his neck. A yoke that scratched and itched and rubbed his conscience raw. In hindsight, there had been clues about his father's criminal intentions, clues Drake had ignored because he had been lulled into a false sense of peace. His father was good at that—getting everyone, including Drake, to believe the storm was over and would not be returning. That *this* time, everything would change. That his father would change. But his father had not changed, he had planned and plotted a devastating assault on the people he claimed to love most in the world. An assault Drake had missed by mere chance. A twist of fate that left him the last one standing with a burden of survivor guilt that was impossible to shake off.

There was a time when Christmas had been his favourite time of year. Not just for the anticipation of presents but he liked the tradition itself. The gathering of family, the celebration of being together, the nice food his mother so lovingly prepared. Now, he couldn't stand the sights and sounds and smell of Christmas. He wished he never had to see another Christmas tree with presents nestled around it for it reminded him of his family's tree with presents that had never been opened.

But somehow, Aerin with her gentle voice had coaxed out of him information he had shared with no one, not even her brother, Tom. He would have to remain vigilant around her this weekend for she had a way of getting under his guard. The proof of that was in the very fact she had got him to agree to the charade in the first place. He should not have agreed but if he hadn't taken her, someone who was less trustworthy might have and then he would have even more guilt to lug around.

A few minutes later, they had cleared security and then Drake led Aerin to a private boarding gate. 'I took the liberty of booking a private flight.'

Aerin stopped dead in her tracks to look up at him. 'But why? I mean, that would have cost a fortune and I don't mind travelling on a commercial flight.'

'If I was the type of guy to fall madly in love with someone, I'd want to spoil them, especially since I can afford it.'

Aerin cocked her head at him. 'Are you *sure* you're not a romantic at heart?'

Drake gave a deep rumble of laughter. 'Not a chance, Goldilocks. Now come on, your winged carriage awaits.'

CHAPTER THREE

AERIN TRIED NOT to look too impressed with the luxury of the private jet but since it was her first time in one, it was hard not to be a little wide-eyed and open-mouthed. The jet was decked out with two large cream-coloured leather seats in the front section with thick ankle-swallowing soft carpet on the floor. The next section had larger sofas running along each side of the jet with a large central coffee table, no doubt for conducting meetings or conferences in mid-air. There was a king-sized bedroom at the back end with its own bathroom, two other bathrooms situated at the front and rear of the aircraft.

There was a single flight attendant, a smartly dressed young man who issued them with drinks once they had taken their seats.

'Champagne for you, Ms Drysdale,' Henry said. 'And iced water with a slice of lemon for Mr Cawthorn.'

'Oh, lovely, thank you,' Aerin said, taking the tall slim flute of fizzing bubbles off the silver tray.

Drake took his glass of water with a tight smile

and the young man melted away and disappeared behind a sliding door that cordoned off the galley from
the cabin.

Aerin swivelled in her seat to glance at him.
'You're not a fan of champagne?'

He put his glass of water on the table in front of
their seats. 'I'm not a fan of alcohol, full stop.' He
flashed her a wry smile and leaned back in his seat.
'Is that another point against me on your Mr Perfect
checklist?'

'Not at all, it's just I didn't know that about you,
that you don't drink, I mean.' She was surprised she
hadn't noticed until now since he had been to her family's home on various social occasions. But given she
mostly had tried to avoid him, it was no wonder she
hadn't noticed whether he consumed alcohol or not.

'There's a lot you don't know about me.' His tone
was mild and yet a fleeting shadow in his expression
sent a tremor of disquiet through her.

'If we're going to be convincing this weekend,
you'd better start filling me in a bit,' Aerin said. 'Why
don't you drink?'

'It's a choice I made a long time ago.'

'Because of your family's accident? Was it a drunk
driver or—?'

'No, they weren't killed by a drunk driver.' His jaw
clenched for a moment and his eyes became hard, as
if some memory from his past was stirring up emotions he didn't want to revisit. 'I drank when I was a
lot younger but I never liked the taste. I only did it to

be cool, to fit in, so I eventually made the decision
to be a teetotaller.'

'My business partner Harper is a teetotaller too,'
Aerin said. 'She had an alcoholic mother, so didn't
want to risk it in case there was any genetic tendency
for alcoholism. It was just as well since she had a
cryptic pregnancy with Marli.' She waited a beat before adding, 'Were you close to your family?'

He picked up his glass of water and blotted some
of the condensation away with the pad of his thumb.
A brooding frown carved into his forehead and his
mouth was set in a grim line. 'My mother and sister,
yes, my father less so as time went on.'

'Why was that?'

He put the glass back down on the table in front
of him and leaned back in his seat, his frown still
in place. 'He wasn't the sort of man you could get
close to.'

'Like you, you mean?'

Drake went completely still as if he had been snap-
frozen. His expression was guarded, the drawbridge
up on his emotions, but she could sense she had hit
on a raw nerve with her comment.

'I'm sorry,' Aerin said into the silence. 'I didn't
mean to upset you or anything…'

'You didn't upset me.' His relaxed tone didn't
match the tension she could sense still lurking in his
body.

'I'm guessing you don't like being compared to
your father.'

'You're guessing right.'

Aerin wondered what made Drake so uncomfortable about being compared to his father. Not all sons had good relationships with their dads, even Tom had hit a rough patch in his teens with their dad. Their power struggle had gone on for a year or two until it eventually resolved as Tom had matured a bit more and their dad had loosened up.

But had Drake's father's untimely death meant he had never been able to enjoy getting closer to him? She could only imagine the guilt he would feel at never being able to fix things with his father. Many psychologists spoke of the father wound in modern men. Was Drake one of those men who carried deep emotional wounds from a distant, uninvolved father?

Aerin was wary of asking too many more deeply personal questions. She wanted their weekend together to work well in order to achieve her goal of satisfying her school friends that she had finally found a partner. But she also wanted the weekend to be positive for Drake, not an ordeal he had to endure.

On the other hand, there were things she needed to know about him in order for their charade to succeed this weekend. And there was a part of her that *wanted* to know more. She found him increasingly intriguing, like a complicated puzzle she was keen to solve. Her work required her to pay attention to every detail, from the tiniest to the largest and everything in between. Her powers of observation stood her in good stead for event planning but also gave her a talent for seeing and sensing things other people did not.

And she was seeing and sensing things about Drake Cawthorn that demanded further investigation.

'I'm sorry for asking you so many questions but I need to know a little bit about you otherwise it will look strange to my friends. I'm a details person—I've always been like that. They would expect me to know everything there is to know about you.'

One side of his mouth came up in a cynical slant. 'Is that even possible? To know everything about a person? You can't. You can only know what they're willing to tell you. After that it's all guesswork.'

'Who did you go to live with after the accident? Your grandparents?'

'No, both my parents were estranged from their parents. I went to live with my aunt, my mother's older sister.'

'It must have been such a terrible time for you,' Aerin said. 'Were you badly injured in the accident?'

'I wasn't injured at all because I wasn't there.' There was a strange quality to his tone, a flat emptiness that seemed to echo with self-recrimination.

Her gaze went to the jagged scar on his left eyebrow. 'Oh? I thought that's where you must've got that scar and your crooked nose.'

Drake stroked one of his fingers across his scarred eyebrow. 'No, I got both of those in a fight when I was a teenager.' His expression still had a grim set to it as if he wasn't proud of that time in his life.

'You weren't in the car? I didn't realise that.' Aerin could only imagine the survivor guilt he must have felt, or still be feeling. If he had been in the car, he might not be alive today. The thought of him not existing made something deep in her chest ache. He had been a part of her life for so long she could not imagine life without him.

'No, I wasn't with them that day.' His voice still had that strange quality to it, an echo of regret, deep sadness and something else she couldn't put her finger on. She noticed his hands were clenched into fists against his strongly muscled thighs as if he was working hard to contain the emotions their conversation had stirred.

The pilot spoke at that moment through the intercom to inform them about the flight conditions and time of arrival. Aerin listened with one ear but she was still mulling over the things Drake had told her. She had always thought he had been in the car with his family—that was certainly the impression her brother had given her. She could only imagine the shock Drake would have experienced when informed of his parents' and sister's deaths. And how the sudden changes brought about by such a tragedy could impact a boy of fifteen.

The pilot stopped speaking and the jet began to taxi down the runway.

Aerin placed one of her hands over Drake's tightly fisted one resting on his thigh. 'I'm sorry if I stirred up sad memories for you by asking you so many questions.'

Drake looked at her hand on top of his for a beat or two. Then he placed his other hand over the top of hers and gently closed his fingers around hers. He turned his head and gave a crooked smile but there were shadows in his eyes that plucked at her heart-strings.

'It's okay, it was a long time ago and I've moved on.' His voice had a gravelly edge that hinted at the depth of emotion he was keeping contained.

Aerin's gaze drifted to his mouth and something flipped over in her stomach. His top lip was sensually contoured and his philtrum ridge between his nose and top lip was so well defined it could have been carved by a master sculptor. His lower lip was fuller than the top one and there was a shallow cleft in his chin partially hidden by his generously sprinkled dark stubble. She had a sudden urge to touch his regrowth with her fingers to experience its roughness against her softer skin. His broad-spanned hand was still anchoring her smaller one and the warmth of him seeped through her flesh like radiation. The heat travelled through her body, igniting a smouldering fire in her core.

His gaze drifted to her mouth, lingered there for a heart-stopping moment before returning to her gaze. His eyes moved between each of hers as if searching for something. Aerin suddenly realised she had never been this close to a man before. Close enough to see the individual pinpricks of stubble on his lean jaw. Close enough to see the flare of his ink-black pupils in the deep dark pools of his irises. Close enough to feel the soft waft of his warm breath against her face.

Aerin gave an audible swallow and sent the tip of her tongue across her lips. He followed the movement with his gaze, then one of his hands came up to the side of her face, cupping her cheek with a touch so gentle she shivered in reaction. His hooded gaze was focussed on her mouth, the ever so slight uptick in his breathing rate sending hers up as well.

'Are you going to…to kiss me?' Her voice came out breathless and a little rusty. *Please, please kiss me.* But of course she was too shy to say it out loud. She was too shocked that she actually *wanted* him to kiss her. It was a driving force building in her body, a wave of need she had never experienced before. A magnetic pull towards his mouth as if he had some sort of sensual power over her, drawing her inexorably closer. She had never wanted anyone to kiss her before now. And while Drake wasn't anywhere near her Mr Perfect, right then, all she could think about was feeling his firm lips against hers.

One side of his mouth tilted wryly. 'That would be flirting with danger, don't you think?'

She blinked and snatched in a much-needed breath. 'W-why is that?'

His hand cradling her cheek shifted to her chin, lifting it so her gaze was fixed on his. 'Because that wasn't part of the deal.'

The deal was a hands-off one but she suddenly realised how much she wanted him to kiss her. It was an urge, a desire she had never felt like this before. His mouth was a magnet drawing her like an iron filing. She wanted to feel those firm lips against hers, she wanted to experience her very first kiss from him. 'The deal?'

'We're not being observed right now.'

All the more reason she wanted him to kiss her. She didn't want her very first kiss to be watched by other people. She wanted it to be private and special and how could it be more special than with Drake? Someone she knew and trusted would not do the wrong thing by her. 'But I need to practise for when we are being observed.' She moistened her lips again and added, 'I've never actually been kissed before so what if I get it wrong?'

He released a puff of air through his wide nostrils, a heavy frown pulling at his forehead. 'Seriously? You've never been kissed?' The shock in his tone made her feel even more of a pariah than she already did.

Aerin pulled her hand out of his, and, checking the seat-belt light was off first, unclipped her seat belt and rose from the seat to put some distance between them. 'Go on, laugh at me. Mock me for being such a…a misfit.'

He unclipped his own belt and came over to her and took her hand again and stroked his thumb along the back of it. 'Hey, look at me.'

She met his concerned gaze and bit her lower lip. 'I know to someone like you who changes partners every week or two, I must seem like I've been dropped in from another century.'

Drake glanced at her mouth again and his other thumb began a slow stroke of her chin. His touch was gentle and yet electrifying, sending tingling sensations through her body. 'I'm a little gobsmacked you haven't been kissed before now, because I'm sure every man you've ever met has wanted to.'

'Including you?'

His mouth slanted in a smile. 'Are you flirting with me, Goldilocks?'

'I think I might be.' Aerin couldn't stop staring at his mouth. The sensual contours of it fascinated her. It was easily the most beautiful male mouth she had ever seen. She had seen his mouth so many times in the past, but it had never held the fascination it held for her now...or maybe it had but she had pretended not to notice. But now it was as if a switch had been turned on inside her brain and she couldn't turn it off.

She *wanted* to be kissed by him.

Desire had flicked into life inside her body as if a match had been struck against the dry tinder of her unmet needs. There was a flame building, spreading, heat lashing out in hungry tongues of fire, burning, burning, burning, wanting, wanting, wanting. Sending incendiary heat to every part of her body.

Drake lifted his hand to her hair and threaded his fingers through it, sending shivers skittering across her scalp and down her spine. His eyes were so dark she couldn't make out his pupils, his warm breath mingling intimately with hers. She got the sense he was at war with himself. One part of him tempted to kiss her, the other part holding back. And wasn't that true of her too? She had waited for so many years to experience the perfect kiss. Would it be a mistake to kiss Drake knowing he was nowhere near her Mr

Perfect? But how could she resist him? He was the first man she had ever wanted to kiss.

He lowered his hand from her hair and captured one of hers. Aerin was conscious of every point of contact of his hand against hers, the slow stroke of his thumb on the back of her hand, his long fingers cupped around hers. She could smell the citrus notes of his aftershave with the understory of bergamot and wood, an intoxicating fragrance that stirred her senses into overdrive. Her gaze drifted to his mouth and her breath caught in her throat. Her eyes came back to his and something in the atmosphere changed. A tensing of the air, a crackling of electricity like the sudden surge of a high-voltage current.

Drake's eyes locked on hers. 'Once I kiss you, I can't un-kiss you. It will change our relationship, charade or no charade.'

Aerin swallowed again, heady anticipation building in every cell of her body. 'How will it change our relationship? It's just a kiss between…friends, isn't it?'

'Friends pretending to be lovers.'

Was he a friend? It wasn't easy to describe their relationship. She had never thought of him as a friend even though he had been in her life for so many years. Friends were people you loved and spent time with if and when you could, they were people you had things in common with and you were there for them and vice versa. Drake Cawthorn didn't quite fit that description and yet…and yet, he had come to her rescue this weekend.

'I've never really thought of you as a friend,' Aerin confessed. 'You're my brother's friend who I refer clients to for legal representation.'

His look was sardonic. 'Then why did you ask me to step in this weekend?'

She rolled her lips together. Why had she? 'I'm not sure… When Harper first suggested asking you, I was totally against the idea. In fact, I was horrified. But then I found myself near your office building the other day and I started to think about it a bit more. It made more and more sense to ask you rather than to ask a stranger. And…' she gave him a sheepish glance '… I was running out of time.'

Drake took one of her hands and brought it to within a couple of millimetres of his lips. 'Desperation makes all of us do things we later regret.' He moved his lips in a barely touching caress against her fingertips, sending a host of shivers cascading down her spine.

Aerin could feel her heart pounding as if it were going to crash through her chest wall. She was standing so close to him she could feel his body heat. She could feel the magnetic pull of him drawing her closer and closer and closer. She was mesmerised by his unwavering gaze, that bottomless brown gaze than saw so much but revealed so little. He lowered her hand from his lips and tugged her ever so gently towards him. She came in contact with the hard wall of his chest and the cradle of his hips, and a shock wave of lust rocked through her.

His mouth came down, down, down until it was

almost touching hers. 'Are you sure about this?' he asked in a deep rough-around-the-edges voice.

'I'm sure.' And she was, totally sure that it was his mouth she wanted to be the first to kiss her. It didn't make sense in some ways and yet in others it did. He wasn't soulmate material, he didn't tick any of the boxes on her checklist but, at that moment, all she wanted was the firm press of his lips on hers. She wanted it like a forbidden drug—a drug that might not be good for her in the long run but, oh, how much did she crave it right now.

Drake's mouth came down and pressed against hers in a light-as-air kiss. It was a soft, momentary touchdown and yet it sent a tremor of greedy want through her body. He pressed his lips back down on hers, moving them against her mouth in a gentle massaging movement that set her pulse racing. She murmured her approval against his lips, instinctively leaning into him in an effort to get closer.

His arms came around her, drawing her against his body, one hand at the small of her back, the other cradling the side of her face. He stroked his tongue along the seam of her mouth and she opened to him, welcoming him in with another breathless sigh of pleasure. He tasted clean and fresh and exotic at the same time, his tongue commanding as it called hers into sensual play. She touched her tongue against his and a lightning-fast bolt of heat went straight to her core. He deepened the kiss, angling his head to gain better access, his hand on the small of her back pressing her even closer to the hardened ridge of his stirring male flesh. A thrill went through her to think she had turned him on, that it wasn't just her attracted to him but a mutual thing that flared between them.

Aerin slid her hands up his chest and then around his neck, her fingers playing with his hair where it brushed his collar. He made a guttural sound and kissed her harder, more urgently, his tongue duelling with hers in an erotic battle that stirred her senses into a madcap frenzy. His breathing rate escalated along with hers, the explosive heat of his kiss making her dizzy with need.

Drake finally lifted his mouth off hers and looked down at her with a slightly dazed look in his eyes. But then he rapid-blinked and adopted his customary sardonic smile. 'How did I measure up?'

She looked at him blankly. 'Measure up?'

'You've waited a long time to be kissed. Did my performance meet your high expectations?'

Aerin was a little stung by his choice of words. Here she was thinking he was as swept away by their kiss as she was and yet it had been nothing more than a performance on his part? She stepped away from him and went back to her seat, clipping her seat belt on with a definitive snap. 'It was...okay, I guess.'

There was a beat or two of silence.

Drake resumed his seat beside her and took one of her hands in his. 'Hey, that was a little insensitive of me. I'm sorry.' He stroked his fingers across the back of her hand in a touch so light it was almost ticklish. 'The thing is...' he hesitated for another beat, his gaze meeting hers '... I was enjoying it a little too much.'

'You were?'

His expression was rueful. 'You couldn't tell?'

Aerin could feel warmth spreading over her cheeks and another even warmer sensation flowing to her core. 'I'm glad the kiss wasn't a one-way affair.'

His mouth tilted in a smile. 'It certainly wasn't.'

Aerin lifted her hand and traced over the jagged scar on his left eyebrow, then she stroked the same finger down the crooked slope of his nose. 'Did it hurt?' Her voice came out soft and a little breathless, for touching him sent a wave of longing through her that shocked her in its intensity.

'Like hell.'

She stroked his nose again. 'You didn't consider having surgery to straighten it?'

'No.'

'How did the other guy fare?'

Drake's mouth twisted and he took her hand again, his thumb resuming its gentle stroking on the back of her hand. 'I was seriously outclassed. He was bigger, meaner, stronger and fought dirty. I didn't stand a chance.'

Aerin frowned at the thought of such an ugly fight. 'You were lucky you weren't killed.'

Something flashed in his gaze and his mouth twisted even further. 'Yes, I was. Very lucky.'

CHAPTER FOUR

DRAKE WAS GLAD the flight was a short one because sitting so close to Aerin after kissing her had stirred his senses into overdrive. Hot flickers of lust still tingled through his body and all he could think of was kissing her again. He relived every moment of her lips beneath his, the softness of her, the sweetness, the exotic taste that set fire to his blood.

You're the first man to kiss her...

He tried not to think too deeply about that but how could he not? Aerin had waited until now to be kissed—by him. Why? Because he was familiar to her and not a total stranger? Because she felt the current of sensual energy that had first pulsed between them in his office the other day? But getting too close and personal was not good for either of them. This weekend was a charade, not a fling in the real sense. He could not allow himself to get close to her or anyone. But somehow she had teased out of him more about himself than he had told anyone—even the counsellor he was forced to see when he was a teenager.

Drake was all too aware of the danger of catching feelings, which was why he only ever dated women for short periods. And while a weekend hanging out with Aerin was hardly a long time, it was still full of emotional potholes. He already had a relationship of sorts with her, which had been strictly platonic until the moment his mouth touched hers.

Something had changed in that moment. A change he'd felt ripple through his entire body as if it were being reprogrammed. It might have been Aerin's first kiss but in a strange way it had felt like that for him too. The soft shy press of her lips against his had sent fireworks through his blood. The sweet and yet exciting taste of her igniting a ferocious desire in him like an addict reacting to a forbidden drug. One taste had made him greedy for more.

But he was *not* going to have more.

Drake was a man who knew how to control himself. He had worked long and hard at regulating his emotions, having seen first-hand how dangerous it was when others chose not to. He bore the physical scars of showdowns with his father as a young teenager. His feeble attempts to protect his mother and sister had done nothing in the end, only left him with scars and deep emotional wounds and a nagging sense of failure. He had failed to protect his mother and sister. He had loved and yet lost them.

He would *not* love again.

'You're finally here!' Bella, one of Aerin's school friends, greeted them in the foyer of the stately home they had hired for the weekend. 'And you must be Drake. I can't tell you how excited we all are to finally meet you.'

Aerin was conscious of the warm band of Drake's arm around her waist. And conscious of the speculative and excited gazes of her friends. Bella, Julia, Suzy and Chantal were each arm in arm with their own partners and it only reinforced her conviction that using Drake as a stand-in date was the right thing to do. She could not have borne the weekend sans partner. Her friends were all so happy in their relationships and as this was their last reunion before Julia moved to Australia, it was even more important everything was perfect. But…there was a big part of her that felt uneasy about the game she was playing. The kiss between her and Drake on the private jet he had arranged had stirred sensations in her that troubled her. Not because the kiss wasn't perfect—it was, in every way. But he wasn't after the things she was after and this thing between them was only a charade.

Aerin painted a blissfully happy smile on her face—not all that hard to do after that kiss. Her lips had only just stopped tingling, but the rest of her body had not. It was quietly thrumming away as if a potent drug had been injected into her veins. Drake's slightest touch sent her senses spinning and standing so close to him made her ache to get even closer.

'Thank you,' Drake said in his deep baritone. 'It's great to meet you all too.'

After all the hugs and air kisses and handshakes and introductions were out of the way, Aerin went with Drake to their room in order to get ready for dinner.

'Here we go,' Drake said, opening the door to their suite, which was quite a way from the other guests. 'The Blue Room.'

Aerin stepped over the threshold and turned in a circle to take in the décor and priceless-looking antiques, including a four-poster bed. 'It's like stepping back in time, isn't it?'

A frown was pulling at Drake's forehead. 'Did you happen to notice a sofa anywhere?'

Aerin glanced around the room but apart from a couple of spindly chairs, a writing desk and a love-seat there was no sofa. 'Maybe there's another room through here...' She opened the door but it proved to be the en suite. 'Oh, that's the bathroom.'

'We have a problem.'

'We do? I mean, of course we do.' Aerin's cheeks flared with heat hot enough to warm the room.

His eyes meshed with hers for a heart-stopping moment. 'I'll sleep on the floor.'

'That won't be very comfortable for you. I don't mind if you share the bed, I mean, not in that way, I meant you on one side, me on the other.'

One side of his mouth lifted in a half-smile that did serious damage to her already skyrocketing pulse rate. 'Can I trust you to keep your hands to yourself?'

Aerin gave him a mock gimlet glare. 'I didn't force myself on you. You kissed me quite willingly, if I recall.'

His eyes darkened. 'I did indeed.'

Aerin let out a wobbly breath and shifted her gaze from his and went to open her overnight bag. 'We have half an hour before dinner.'

'I'll go for a quick walk to give you some privacy.'

Aerin pulled out her navy-blue velvet evening dress and shook out the creases, glancing at him again. 'But won't the others think that's a bit strange? It's dark outside anyway. Besides, I can get changed in the bathroom.'

'Aerin.' The sombre note was back in his voice. 'You're safe with me, no matter what.'

'I know that. It's why I asked you to be here this weekend instead of someone I don't know and trust.'

His smile was wry. 'You trust me even after that kiss?'

Her gaze drifted to his mouth and her heart jumped in her chest like a startled frog. 'Yes, I trust you.' She licked her suddenly dry lips and hugged her dress close to her chest. 'I'm not so sure I trust myself, though.'

His kiss had made her hungry for more. How was she going to resist him? Why *should* she resist him? The sensuality he awakened in her was empowering. It made her realise how much she had been missing out on in being so cautious about dating. This was her chance to experiment a little. He wasn't Mr Perfect, but it didn't mean she couldn't enjoy a short dalliance with him. Or was she rationalising too much? Talking herself into a fling with him because she knew he would give her nothing but a fling?

Drake was standing within touching distance of

her but she had no idea which of them had moved or if both of them had. He sent one of his hands down the length of her arm in a lazy caress and even through the layers of her clothes her body leapt and tingled at his touch. 'The kissing and touching can't go any further than this weekend.' His fingers had got to the bare skin of her hand in a light as air touch that sent a shiver down her spine.

'I know.'

His eyes searched hers for a pulsing moment. 'I'm not what you're looking for.'

'I know.' Did he have to keep reminding her? He didn't tick any of her boxes and yet...and yet... that kiss. *Gulp.* She couldn't get it out of her mind. Couldn't wait to feel his lips on hers again.

His gaze lowered to her mouth and lingered there for a beat or two. Then he drew in a deep breath and released it in a jagged stream and finally brought his eyes back to hers. Dark, intense, determined and yet a shadow of something else lurking there. 'How long will it take you to get ready?'

'Five, ten minutes?'

'Take your time. I'll catch up on a couple of emails. Pretend I'm not here.'

Yeah, right, like that was going to be easy to do.

Aerin draped her dress over one arm and, snatching up her make-up kit with her other hand, disappeared into the bathroom.

Drake pinged back a couple of short emails, but his mind was well and truly in the bathroom with Aerin. He pictured her changing out of her travel clothes and into that stunning blue velvet dress she'd brought with her. She would look elegant dressed in a bin liner, but that midnight shade of blue was a perfect foil for her grey-blue eyes and creamy complexion.

He tossed his phone to one side and quickly changed into the tux he'd brought with him. He was about to tie his bow tie when Aerin came out of the bathroom. His hands fell away from his neck and his breath stalled in his chest. She had bundled her long hair into a makeshift bun at the back of her head that highlighted the elegant length of her neck. Some dangling sapphire and diamond earrings glittered from her delicate earlobes. Her make-up was subtle and yet made the most of her features—the smoky eye make-up, the shiny lip-gloss, the blush and highlighter on her aristocratic cheekbones turning her into a princess fit for a ball.

Her dress was even more stunning on her than he had imagined. The off-the-shoulder style clung to her slim frame in all the right places—places he wanted to touch and caress. Places he had forbidden himself to touch and caress. Places he knew would take every ounce of willpower and then some *not* to touch and caress. *Sheesh.* Why did he agree to this? It was madness to think kissing her wouldn't change anything. Of course it changed everything. He could not get her mouth out of his mind, her taste off his tongue and his desire, meanwhile, was still thrumming like a background beat in his blood.

'You look…amazing…' As a high-powered lawyer,

it was rare for him to be lost for words but right then Drake could barely get a full sentence out.

Aerin gave a tentative smile, her cheeks going a delightful shade of pink. She swished from side to side and the skirt of the dress swirled like a blue wave around her. 'Do you think so? I wasn't sure about the off-the-shoulder style. I normally don't show this much flesh.'

'You look stunning.' He was having trouble keeping his eyes away from her small but perfect cleavage.

'Could you help me put this on?' She opened her palm to reveal a fine gold chain with a sapphire and diamond pendant on it. 'The fastening is too fiddly for me to put on by myself.'

Drake took the pendant from her hand. 'Turn around.' He came up close behind her and looped the chain around her neck. Her flowery perfume teased his nostrils and dazzled his senses, the fragrance redolent of a summer garden. He wanted to bury his head beside her neck and breathe more of her in. He frowned in concentration as he worked to fasten the catch, but the chain and its clasp were tiny and it didn't help that his hands weren't as steady as he would have liked. And nor was his heart rate. Damn it.

'It's a tricky fastening,' Aerin said in a husky tone.

'I think I need to get my eyes checked. There, that's it.' He stepped back and she turned around to face him. The pendant glinted from just above her cleavage.

'Thanks.' Her hand went to the pendant and shifted

it back and forth along its chain. 'My grandmother gave it to me for my last birthday, along with the earrings.'

'They're very beautiful. And so are you.'

Her blush deepened and her hand fell away from the pendant. 'Thank you.' She glanced at his as yet untied bow tie. 'Do you need some help with that?'

Drake didn't but he couldn't resist the opportunity for her to touch him, even if it was simply to do up his bow tie. 'Go for it. I'm too much of a snob to buy one of those clip-on ones.'

Aerin stepped closer and he breathed in another heady draught of her fragrance. He would never be able to look at a rose or a sweet pea again without thinking of her. She took the ends of his bow tie and deftly knotted it around his neck. The movement of her fingers so close to his neck sent shivers rolling down his spine. He could not stop thinking of those soft little hands moving on other parts of his body. A low rumble of lust moved through his blood like a distant earthquake, sending shock waves and tremors through his entire body. How was he supposed to keep his hands off her when all he wanted was to draw her close and kiss that delectable mouth? To crush her slim frame to his hard one and feel every feminine curve stir his body into fervent heat?

Once she had completed tying the bow tie, she patted his chest with one of her hands. 'There you go.'

Drake caught her hand before she could step back, holding it against the *tump-tump-tump* of his heart. His eyes held hers in a silent lock, her pupils instantly flaring like pools of ink. The point of her tongue slipped out to sweep over her lips, and a rocket blast of lust slammed him in the groin.

Drake drew in a shuddering breath. 'I told myself I wasn't going to do this again.'

Her look was innocent and yet her words were breathlessly delivered. 'Do what?'

He gave a rueful smile. 'You know what.'

'You want to kiss me again?'

He brushed an imaginary hair away from her forehead. 'Don't sound so surprised, Goldilocks. I can't get our first kiss out of my mind.'

'It was my first kiss, not yours. You've probably kissed hundreds of women.'

'No one like you.' Drake lifted her hand to his mouth and kissed the backs of her bent knuckles, his eyes holding hers.

She shivered and moved a little closer as if unable to withstand the magnetic pull of attraction, the same magnetic pull he was feeling towards her. 'Why no one like me? Am I so different from everyone you normally date?'

'Different in too many ways to list.' Drake let go of her hand and gave a crooked smile. 'Now, we'd better get to the dinner before they think we've been waylaid up here doing something else.'

A vivid blush swept across her cheeks and she turned away to check her reflection in the mirror, catching his gaze for a brief moment before repositioning the pendant around her neck.

'I feel bad about lying to my friends. I know I

should've just been honest and told them I haven't found the love of my life yet but I don't want our last reunion to be all about me and my high expectations and so far unfulfilled dreams.' She let out a long sigh and added, 'I wish I didn't have to stay the whole weekend. I'm not good at acting, or lying for that matter, which in our case amounts to the same thing. I'm worried I'm going to make a fool of myself in front of them all.'

Drake came over to her to stand behind her, meeting her eyes in the mirror once more. He placed his hands on her bare shoulders and tried to ignore the rush of heat burning in his groin. 'We don't have to stay the whole weekend. We can stay for the dinner and overnight and then leave first thing. We can tell them we're heading someplace else for a bit of couple time.' Even as he was saying the words, a red flag was waving in his head. But he found he wanted to be alone with her, not surrounded by her friends and their partners, but just to be with her.

Her grey-blue eyes widened. 'You'd be okay with that? I mean, heading somewhere else tomorrow?'

'Sure. It will take the pressure off us both, pretending all the time to be something we're not.' He should *not* be okay with it. He should be telling her no, no, no, we shouldn't be alone together. Not totally alone. But somehow he couldn't find the words to say it. The desire to do the opposite was taking command of the control centre of his brain. His brain that was normally so rational and logical and risk averse and here he was suggesting a secret getaway.

Just the two of them.

And if that wasn't a risk, he didn't know what the hell was.

But wasn't pretending to be lovers in the company of others worse? At least if they were alone the pressure would be off. They could just hang out as friends and enjoy each other's company without worrying about giving off the wrong vibe or something. Besides, the more he acted like a lover around her, the more he wanted to *be* her lover. He was wary of allowing the charade to go too far, to drift from an act into reality. He was aware of how slim the divide was between pretending to feel passion to actually feeling it. And he did feel it. He had not stopped feeling it from the moment she'd turned up outside his office that day. The trick for him was how to turn it off before someone got hurt.

Aerin turned to face him and he had to force his hands away from her shoulders, when all he wanted was to bring her closer. He opened and closed his fingers to try and stop them from tingling from touching her silken skin. But touching her had sent his blood on a low simmer and he knew it wouldn't take much for a flame to leap into life.

'Drake, you've been so good about this situation. It's a perfect solution now that I think of it. It will reduce the risk of one of the girls taking photos that end up on social media. We can explain we want some time alone before we make any announcement about our relationship to our friends and family.'

Drake was glad she couldn't read his mind at that

point. He was still wondering how he was going to get through the night in this room with her. He prided himself on his self-control, but she was a temptation he had not been prepared for.

And he was *always* someone who was prepared.

But this time…not so much.

CHAPTER FIVE

AERIN ENJOYED THE dinner dance much more than she had in years gone past. It was lovely being part of a couple, even though she and Drake, strictly speaking, were not a couple. They were acting. But every now and then he would glance her way and smile and her heart would lift like a helium balloon in her chest. Everyone was in a joyous mood and the chatter around the table as dinner was served was lively and convivial. Drake occasionally contributed in his charming and relaxed way, but for the most part he quietly observed the others without revealing too much about himself.

Chantal leaned close at one point to talk to Aerin, while her partner Taddeo chatted to Drake about a business investment he had planned in the IT sector.

'Aerin, I'm so thrilled you and Drake got together,' Chantal said. 'How long have you been seeing each other? What does your brother think? Tom must be feeling pretty chuffed about you two hitting it off at last. And your parents. You've always had such high standards when it came to men. I thought you didn't even like Drake. You used to turn your nose up whenever his name was mentioned in the past.'

Aerin decided it was best to stay as close to the truth as possible because Chantal, as a long-term school friend, knew a lot more about her than a casual acquaintance, even though they were not as close as Aerin was to Harper and Ruby. 'It's too early to say where our relationship is going but that's why we're keeping it quiet for now.'

'Well, I think he's gorgeous,' Chantal said. 'And the way he looks at you just about melts my heart.' She gave a dreamy sigh and added, 'God, I love seeing a man fall and fall hard.'

Mmm… Well, it did seem Drake was doing an award-winning performance of playing the besotted man in love. Aerin only hoped she was doing an equally stellar job. She cast her gaze in Drake's direction and smiled and he smiled back and gave a cheeky wink that sent a hot wave of colour through her cheeks, not to mention her lower body.

But how much on her part was acting?

Aerin was starting to see him in a new light. The more time she spent with him, the more she realised how she had misjudged him in the past. His cynicism hid a sensitivity he didn't want anyone to see. His determination not to fall in love hinted at a man who was shy of commitment because he wanted to avoid the pain of a break-up. It didn't mean he couldn't love but rather he chose not to.

Finally, the dinner was over and the dancing began. And instead of being a wallflower as she had been every year in the past, this time she was in Drake's arms being spun around the floor as if they were the star performers at a dance academy.

'I didn't know you could dance so well,' Aerin said, somewhat breathlessly as they did a fast-paced circuit of the floor, somehow, rather miraculously, she thought, avoiding colliding into all the other couples.

'Look who's talking.' Drake drew her even closer to the hard frame of his body, his pelvis flush against hers. Hot tingles shot down her spine and her heart rate picked up, which had nothing to do with the energetic dancing. Being close to him stirred sensations in her she had never felt before. It was as if he lit a fire in her blood, a fire that smouldered and simmered and flickered with hot flames of lust. A lust she didn't know how to control. It had never been part of her plan to have a fling with someone. She wanted to fall in love with the love of her life. Flings were temporary and casual, and nothing about how she envisaged her life going forward was temporary or casual. She wanted for-ever love. Total commitment, till death do us part love. But being with Drake made her question the strict code she had lived by. Maybe it was time for her to loosen up a bit. To explore the chemistry that had fired between them.

Aerin laughed. 'You're way too generous in your praise. I stepped on your toes at least three times back there.'

He grinned down at her. 'I didn't notice.'

The air was suddenly charged with a current of electricity that seemed to pulse between their locked

gazes. *Fizzzt. Fizzzt. Fizzzt.* A current Aerin could
feel in her body from her head to her toe and to each
of her fingertips.

Aerin was aware of the broad span of Drake's hand
resting on the small of her back, the heat like a brand
searing her flesh, warming her blood to boiling. A
low deep throb drummed in her body, a call of nature so primitive and primal it was overwhelming.

Drake's eyes darkened to obsidian and he bent his
head lower, so his mouth was within touching distance
of hers. He hovered there for an infinitesimal moment,
which only ratcheted up her need to feel his lips on hers.

'Kiss me…' Her words came out on a barely audible whisper that, given the loud music playing, he
couldn't possibly have heard with any clarity. But
then his mouth came down and set hers alight as if
he sensed her need for him.

Drake's lips closed over hers in a light press of flesh
on flesh that sent a rocket blast through her blood. One
of his hands came up to cradle the side of her face, the
other remained in the small of her back, holding her
to the burgeoning heat of his hardening male body.
A blooming spreading heat that ignited her feminine
flesh like a match on tinder, flames of need racing out
of control to every erogenous zone in her body.

Drake finally lifted his mouth off hers and gazed
down at her with a lopsided smile and glittering eyes.
His hand still cradling the side of her face, his thumb
stroking her cheek in a gentle caress that made her
spine turn to liquid. 'Would it upset everyone if we
left tonight instead of in the morning? I know a place

only an hour or so away but it's completely private and that way you can have your own room.'

Aerin knew she shouldn't be feeling such a deep pang of disappointment about him insisting on her having her own room. For close to thirty years she had never shared a room with anyone other than the occasional sleepover with a girlfriend or two. But at the heart of his suggestion was his concern for her comfort and that meant a lot to her. 'But what will we tell them? I mean, about why we're not staying here?'

'I'll tell them I've planned a romantic getaway for the two of us. A remote cottage near a loch and no neighbours for miles around.'

Aerin tilted her head on one side, studying him as if he were a complicated puzzle. 'It does indeed sound very romantic. But aren't you worried they might think you're taking me away to propose to me or something?'

Drake shrugged one broad shoulder. 'We both know that's not going to happen.'

Yes, well, she didn't want him to propose since he didn't tick any of her boxes but did he have to be so adamantly blunt about it? Aerin painted a smile on her face. 'Do you know CPR?'

'Yep, why?'

'Because if by some miracle you did get down on bended knee, I would have a heart attack on the spot.'

Drake smiled with his mouth but not with his eyes. 'If by some miracle you said yes, I would too.'

As it turned out, no one was all that surprised by Drake's plan to whisk Aerin away for the rest of the weekend. The girls and their partners farewelled them as if they were indeed leaving for their honeymoon, with whoops and cheers and waves.

Drake drove through the moonlit night, glancing at her from time to time. 'Why don't you lay your head back and have a sleep? It'll be an hour before we get there.'

Aerin tried but failed to disguise a yawn, quickly covering her mouth with her hand. 'Sorry. I am a bit knackered. I don't think I've danced that much in years, actually ever.'

'Acting, too, can make you pretty tired.'

Aerin chewed his statement over for a beat or two. Had he found it trying to pretend all evening he was in love with her in front of her school friends and their partners? Had he hated every minute of it? If so, he had hidden it well. 'Yes, it can. Was it awful for you to pretend to be in love with me for the evening? Chantal was convinced you were head over heels for me.'

It was too dark inside the car for her to see his features clearly, but she caught a glint of something in his eyes reflected off the moonlight. 'People see what they want to see, especially when they've had plenty of alcohol.'

'Yes, well, there was a lot of champagne consumed.' She disguised another yawn and added sleepily, 'I might just close my eyes for a bit. Wake me if you want me to take over the wheel at some point.'

'I'm not used to letting anyone drive me. Call me a control freak but that's just the way I live my life.'

Aerin was tired but not so tired she couldn't hear

the note of determination in his voice. She turned her head where it was resting against the headrest to glance at him again. 'Because of the accident?'

There was a long silence. A silence that contained a strange energy, as if a ghost had suddenly joined them in the car. A shiver ran over Aerin's skin and she pulled her evening wrap closer around her shoulders.

'It wasn't an accident.' Drake's voice was heavy, weighed down with something she had not heard in it before.

Aerin sat up straighter in her seat, her earlier tiredness falling away leaving her open-eyed and fully alert. 'What do you mean?'

His mouth was twisted in a grimace. 'My mother and sister didn't die in a car crash.'

She swallowed tightly. 'How did they die?' Her voice came out in a shocked whisper.

Drake shifted the car's gears to take a sweeping bend that climbed further into the hills of the countryside. He drove competently and yet there was an underlying anger in his movements, an anger she could sense he fought hard to control. 'They were murdered.'

The words dropped into the car like a pulled grenade. Words Aerin had not expected. Words that were so shocking, so brutally shocking she couldn't process them in her brain. It was like being stunned by a physical blow to the head. Her brain was spinning without traction, none of her thoughts finding a foothold. Drake's family had been murdered? How had he lived with such dreadful pain? A car crash would have been tragic enough, but to have your entire family murdered by someone was just beyond bearing. How could anyone recover from such dreadful grief? Could you ever recover?

But then something did take hold in her brain as she recalled his statement: *'My mother and sister didn't die in a car crash.'* What about his father? Nothing was making sense. Everything she had been told about his family over the years—the little she had been told—was not true.

'I'm sorry,' Drake said after a long moment, his voice rough and heavy with regret, perhaps, she thought, even a little self-loathing. 'I shouldn't have told you.'

Aerin swept her tongue over her parchment-dry lips, her hands not quite steady in her lap. 'What about your father? You said your mother and sister were…murdered…' Even saying the word was horrifying to her. Of course one read about murders in the news every day but when you actually met someone who had lost someone they loved in such a despicable way, it made one realise the tragic enormity of such a loss.

'Please,' Drake said. 'Forget I said anything. It's not something I want to talk about. Ever. With anyone.'

'Does Tom know?'

'No.'

Another beat or two of silence passed. Aerin imagined she could hear her own heartbeat thumping in her chest like a drum. She could certainly feel the pulse of her blood hammering in her veins.

'Why not? I mean, why didn't you tell Tom? You've been friends for years.'

'Because I chose not to tell anyone about what happened that day.'

And yet he had told her. Not all of it but enough for her to ache to know more.

Aerin ran one of her hands through her hair, part of her up-do tumbling from its restraining clip. It was only as she put her hand back in her lap that she saw it was shaking. 'Oh, Drake, I don't know what to say. I want you to tell me everything, but I understand how awfully painful that must be for you. I can't get my head around what you've told me so far. I don't know how you've managed to cope with such a terrible situation. God, you were only fifteen…'

Drake changed gears to drive up a long, wooded driveway that led to a cottage on the top of a hill. The cottage was bathed in moonlight, the loch below it past the dark looming shadows of the woods picture-postcard perfect. A light breeze crinkled the surface of the water like a bolt of silver silk.

Drake's forehead was as crinkled as the loch, his eyes focussed on the driveway, his hands clenched on the steering wheel. His jaw locked. He brought the car to a stop in front of the stone cottage that was larger than it first appeared. He turned off the engine and released a long breath and turned to look at her in the moonlit darkness.

'Thank you.'

'For what?'

'For not hounding me for more information,' Drake said.

Aerin moistened her lips again. If only he knew how much she wanted to. But she was not a pushy person by nature and understood people had to be ready to reveal things. They had to develop a level of trust. They had to feel ready to share such sadness with a safe person. A trustworthy and safe person. But it saddened her to think not her even her brother, Tom, knew the full story. What did that say about her brother? Or was it that Drake didn't allow himself to trust anyone? That he didn't feel safe with anyone? 'I guess if you really wanted to tell someone, anyone, you would have done it by now.'

Drake reached out his hand and picked up one of her loosened strands of hair that had fallen from its up-do. 'You've let your hair down.' There was a wry quality to his tone and a twist to his mouth that made him all the more attractive. So attractive, she mentally ticked number one of her soulmate checklist: *tall, dark and handsome.*

Aerin couldn't keep her gaze from drifting to his mouth. She sucked in a shuddery breath and was suddenly conscious of the close confines of the car. She could smell the citrussy tang of his aftershave—a smell that was so tantalising to her senses she could feel herself melting. She could smell the warm minty freshness of his breath. Could feel the thrum of desire beating between her legs and wondered if he was feeling the same.

His eyes darkened to pitch and his head came down, his mouth covering hers in a brief kiss that was gossamer-soft. But as he lifted away, his lips clung to hers as a silky cobweb did to a dry surface. He gave a muttered groan that sounded like a curse and covered her mouth once more. Aerin breathlessly submitted to the commanding stroke of his tongue, her lips parting on a sigh, her heart thumping with delight, her arms snaking around his neck, her fingers playing with the thick strands of his closely cropped hair.

The kiss went on and on, sending shivers of reaction down her spine. Something about the darkness outside tinged with silvery moonlight gave it a magical quality, as if Aerin had stepped into a fairy tale. She was swept up in the moment, enjoying the roughness of his skin against her face, enjoying the more and more urgent sound of his breathing, the strengthening of his hold, as if he never wanted to let her go.

Drake's hands came up to cradle both sides of her face in a touch so gentle it made her heart squeeze. He angled his head to deepen the kiss, another deep, rough groan sounding in his throat. Aerin responded by meeting his tongue with hers, playfully dancing and duelling until her blood was simmering with need.

He pulled away to gaze down at her in the semi-darkness. 'I didn't bring you all the way up here to seduce you.' Another wry twist to his lips and he added, 'But kissing you is becoming a bit of an addiction, I'm afraid.'

Aerin traced her fingertip around the contour of

his mouth with a feather-light touch. 'I guess there are worse addictions, right?' She tried to keep her tone playful but all she could think about was wanting his mouth back on hers.

'Yes.' Drake put her from him and opened the car door and a blast of chilly air entered the car.

But even so, Aerin still burned for him deep in her feminine core. His passionate kiss had stirred her senses to life and she realised she wanted more than his kisses. Much more. But how could she ask him to be her lover when he wasn't interested in settling down in the future? Wouldn't that be compromising on everything she had written on her checklist? Her plan for her life. She wasn't the type of person to have flings and that was all it could ever be between them because that was the only type of relationship he ever had. Wasn't it naïve of her to think he might change for her?

Within a few minutes, they were inside the quaint two-storey cottage. Drake carried in their bags and placed them in each of the two bedrooms, while Aerin set to making a warm drink in the kitchen. She heard the movement of Drake's firm tread upstairs and her mind wandered... The cottage was a lovely place to spend time with a lover. So cosy, so private, so intimate. He had seemed to organise the booking of it with incredible speed. Had he brought someone else here in the past? Or did he or a friend own it? Had he brought her here because he could not bear the thought of spending the night in the same room as her back at the reunion hotel?

Aerin heard him come back down the stairs and then enter the sitting room. She had noticed a fire had been laid in the hearth on her quick tour around when they'd first arrived. She carried two drinks on a tray and entered the sitting room, where Drake was kneeling on one knee in front of the fireplace, frowning at the now flickering flames.

He glanced over his shoulder as she came in, his frown relaxing on his forehead, but she could still see a shadow of it in his dark eyes. 'Thanks for making the drinks. I've put you in the room overlooking the forest. It's the only bedroom with a lock on the door. I'm further down the hall.'

Aerin set the tray down on the table situated a metre or so in front of the fireplace, near the twin sofas. 'You think I don't trust you?' If only he knew it was herself she didn't trust. He had awakened needs in her she hadn't known she possessed, or at least not to that intensity. His kisses had stirred her into blazing heat like the fire he had just lit in the fireplace.

Drake straightened from in front of the hearth and then took one of the mugs from the tray on the coffee table, his expression inscrutable. 'I've been around people most of my life who say one thing and do the complete opposite. I want you to feel one hundred per cent safe with me.'

She took her own mug and sat cross-legged on one of the sofas. 'I do, Drake.' Her voice came out softer and huskier than she'd planned. She toyed with the handle of her mug and then added, 'Have you brought a lover here in the past? You managed to book it at short notice, so I thought maybe you either owned it or were familiar with it from previous visits.'

One side of his mouth tilted wryly. 'I do own it but I haven't brought anyone here before. I've only had it a few months.' He put his mug on the mantelpiece and added, 'It's one of several secluded properties I've bought for a women's shelter charity I set up a few years ago.'

Aerin cradled her mug between her hands, unable to take her eyes off his face that was so enhanced by the flickering flames of the fire behind him. He looked like a hero out of a Jane Austen or Charlotte Brontë novel—inscrutable, darkly handsome and intriguing. 'So, it's used as a shelter for women and children who need to escape their violent partners? But it's so incredibly isolated. Wouldn't that be scary for a woman in fear of her life?'

'It's not as isolated as you might think. The local police are on speed dial on the security pad over there.' He pointed to the security system panel she had noticed in every room but not taken too much notice of before. 'They would be here within minutes if needed. But this cottage is more of a holiday retreat for families who need healing time after the threat has been taken care of.'

'You mean once the perpetrator is in custody?'

'Yes.'

There was a long silence with only the sound of the flames flickering in the fireplace and the wind whistling outside.

Drake had turned back to stare at the fire and it gave Aerin a chance to study him again. He was frowning but in a brooding sort of way, as if some memories were troubling him. Memories triggered by their conversations in the car earlier and now. But how could she press him for more details of his background without appearing insensitive? He had told her repeatedly he didn't want to discuss his past.

Aerin leaned forward to put her mug down on the coffee table. 'Drake... I think it's amazing how much you help people. I had no idea you'd set up such a wonderful charity. I have to admit, I found your choice of legal speciality in prenuptial agreements a bit off-putting, a little cynical on your part. But I guess you've seen first-hand how difficult it is for women who have been financially disadvantaged in a divorce or break-up.'

Drake moved away from the fire as if the heat was getting too much for him. Even she could feel the warmth from her position on the sofa—waves of warmth that gave the room a safe and cosy feel. He sat on the sofa opposite hers, his expression still set along grave and serious lines.

'It's incredibly difficult for women and even some men to lose control of their financial affairs. Divorces are messy at the best of times...they don't have to be, but when there's money and assets to divvy up it can be shocking what lengths people will go to. That's why a prenuptial agreement can make things so much more straightforward.'

'But when people fall in love they believe the best

of the other person. It can sound so unromantic, even distrustful, to ask for a prenup. It's like saying, *I love you but this is just in case you or I fall out of love some time in the future.*' Aerin screwed up her lips in a self-deprecating smile. 'Sorry, I must sound so naïve and trusting and hopelessly romantic.'

Drake gave a lopsided smile that sent her heart aflutter. 'Promise me you'll sign a prenup when you do find your Mr Perfect. I'll do it pro bono for you.'

Aerin's own smile faded and she uncrossed her legs and sighed. 'I'm starting to wonder if such a person exists. I mean, I've always had such high standards about everything. I never do anything by halves. I'm all in or not in at all, which is why I've got to the age of almost thirty and never had sex.'

That one word dropping into the silence sent a wave of heat through her body and a strange energy into the atmosphere, like an audience taking a collective breath, waiting for something important to happen…

'Aerin.' There was a stern quality to his voice. And then he let out a long sigh and sent one of his hands through his hair in an agitated manner. His eyes met hers across the distance between the sofas. His gaze glittered darkly, his brows close together, his lips set in a firm line. But then she noticed a pulse beating in his neck and his jaw working like a miniature hammer was tapping beneath his skin. 'We're both tired and need to go to bed, before we step across a boundary neither of us will view the same way in the morning.'

'I wasn't going to ask you to sleep with me.' Or *was* she? Aerin hardly knew what was going to come out of her mouth next. When she was alone with Drake Cawthorn, her body and her brain misfired, making her want things she hadn't thought she would want under such circumstances. Like more of his touch, his deeply passionate kisses, the stroke and glide of his tongue against hers. The heat that roared between their bodies, the surprisingly erotic heat that threatened to overrule her carefully constructed plan for her life. Her Mr Perfect checklist said nothing about having a short-term fling with a man who had openly declared falling in love was not in his game plan. Ever.

Aerin rose from the sofa and began to clear away the mugs.

'Leave it. I'll tidy up. You go on upstairs. I'll see you in the morning.'

Aerin put the mug back down and straightened, aware of the heat in her cheeks and the burning desire in her body. 'Thanks for what you did tonight. The charade and all. I think we managed to convince them we were the real deal.'

A ghost of a smile came and went on his mouth. 'You're welcome, Goldilocks.'

Drake mechanically cleared up their mugs and then made sure the fire screen was securely in place in front of the fireplace. The fire was still smouldering even though he hadn't put any more fuel on it. But so too, were the flames in his body smouldering like red-hot coals. He was in danger of crossing a line he swore he would never cross. And how ironic that it was in one of his safety houses. Maybe he was the one who should have the locked room and get Aerin to lock him in, so he couldn't be tempted to touch her again.

But he was already in a prison of sorts—the prison of his past.

He had shared more with Aerin than he had shared with anyone. The dark stuff kept leaking out of him as if holes had been bored into the steel of his armour and he didn't know how to plug them back up. He was grateful she hadn't pressed him for more details but he found the more he had revealed, the more he wanted to reveal. The tragic and largely avoidable circumstances of his past were something he carried with him every day of his life.

The survivor guilt was heavy and burdensome but his desire to make the world a better place for other people like his mother and sister drove him to work hard. Impossibly hard at times, but even knowing he had potentially saved some lives didn't undo the heartbreaking damage of the lives he had lost. The lives he wished he could have saved, would have saved if only he had known what his father was capable of. The lives of his mother and sister. The two people who had meant the world to him. Their lives taken brutally by his father, who would have taken his life too, if Drake had been home at the time.

But he hadn't been home and he had to live with the knowledge and guilt that came with that inescapable fact. *He had failed to protect his mother and sister.* It wasn't something he could ever forgive himself for, no matter how many shelters and charities he funded.

CHAPTER SIX

AERIN SLEPT DEEPLY for a couple of hours out of sheer exhaustion. But then she woke around dawn to the sound of Drake's muffled voice crying out in a long and anguished, 'No!'

She threw off the bedcovers and quickly pulled on her wrap to cover her nightgown and made her way to his bedroom further down the corridor. She tapped on the door. 'Drake? Are you okay?' There was no answer other than another groan, as if he was in some sort of anguished pain. Was he having some sort of medical event? She knew he occasionally had tension headaches in the past. But Tom had told her that, not Drake.

Aerin opened the door a crack and peered inside the dimly lit bedroom. She could make out his tall frame in the bed, the bedclothes in a tangle around his waist, revealing his flat stomach and toned abdomen. His upper body was naked, his chest sprinkled with dark hair, the same ink-black as his head. He was thrashing from side to side, his eyes tightly closed, his hands bunched into fists as he clutched at the sheets either side of his thighs. 'No, no, no, no!'

Aerin rushed over and, leaning over him, took him by the upper arms, giving him a gentle shake. 'Drake, wake up. You're having a nightmare.'

His eyes snapped wide open like one of those old-fashioned ventriloquist dolls. He blinked a couple of times and then let out a muttered curse and dragged himself up in a sitting position. He moved so quickly she had no choice but to remove her hands from his upper arms, but not before she'd noted how muscular and toned they were.

'Are you okay? I was so worried about you. I thought you might be having a migraine or something.'

Drake scraped his hand through his already tousled hair, her eyes drawn to the bulge of his biceps as he lifted his arm. 'I'm sorry for scaring you. I haven't had a nightmare in years. Ten at least.'

She was still sitting on the edge of his bed and had no desire to move away just yet. 'Maybe it was because of what we talked about in the car coming here last night. Your family being…' She couldn't bring herself to say the brutal word out loud.

Drake reached for her hand where it was resting on the bed next to his thigh. His fingers were warm and gentle around hers and a shiver scuttled down her spine. His expression was difficult to read in the muted light of a greyish dawn, but she could feel something in his touch that spoke volumes.

'I haven't talked to anyone about what happened

since I was a teenager. I hated being that kid. The kid whose father killed his own family.'

Aerin gasped. 'Oh, no…' His father killed his mother and sister? His own father? How on earth had he coped with such an awful event?

He gave her a grim look. 'He would have killed me too if I'd been home at the time, but I stayed at a mate's that night, drinking. Can you believe it? I was rip-roaring drunk at the age of fifteen and had no idea of what my father had planned to do.'

Aerin could feel tears pouring from her eyes and her heart was aching as if it were in a vice. 'Oh, you mustn't blame yourself. You were just a kid doing what a lot of boys that age do.'

His top lip curled in self-disgust. 'Yeah, well, not all of those kids do it because their fathers encouraged them to do it. My father liked me to have a beer or three with him. Then he got me to drink spirits. He told me it would make me loosen up a bit. Not be so uptight all the time. Little did I realise it was his plan to stop me from protecting my mother and sister.'

Some pennies were dropping rather loudly in Aerin's head. She glanced at his crooked nose and the scar on his left eyebrow. 'Is that how you got those? Your broken nose and scar?'

Drake let out a ragged sigh. 'I intervened one night when he was laying into my mother, but I wasn't strong enough to take him on. I should have just called the police, but he threatened to kill our dog if I did.' His throat moved up and down and he added in a tone loaded with sadness, 'He did that anyway a few weeks later. He knew how much I loved that damn dog.'

Aerin was openly crying now, broken sobs coming out no matter how hard she tried to stop them. 'I'm so sorry, so very sorry...'

Drake pulled her into his arms, holding her head against his chest, one of his hands gently stroking the back of her head. 'Hey, don't cry, Goldilocks.' His voice was soft and soothing. 'It was all a long time ago and I've managed to make a life for myself. What happened to my mother and sister should never have happened, but it did, and I could have prevented it if I had trusted my gut. But of course hindsight is a wonderful thing, isn't it?'

Aerin kept her head against his chest, her tears still falling for all he had suffered. 'Is he in prison now? Your father?'

'He's dead. It was a murder-suicide. I can only be thankful I wasn't the one to find them. That was a neighbour who ended up with PTSD.'

She lifted her head off his chest to look at him. 'Oh, Drake, it's just so awful to think of what you've been through. Does Tom know any of this? Or did you swear him to secrecy?'

'He doesn't know. I reinvented myself after the event, I felt compelled to. Cawthorn isn't even my real name. I changed my name by deed poll as soon as I was able to. I didn't want to spend the rest of my life being identified as the tragic kid who lost his entire family. I needed to move on and make my life count for something. To do something, anything, to change things for others like my mother and sister. But the figures on domestic violence are still way too high, not just in the UK but worldwide.'

'But at least you are doing something,' Aerin said. 'You're making a true difference in so many lives. The charity, the safety houses—it's such an honourable thing to do to use your own time and money to bring about change. There's a lot of talk about the issue of domestic violence but not enough action. Of course, any action you take now can never bring your mother and sister back but they would be so proud of you, I'm sure.'

One of Drake's hands was resting on the bed close to her hand. She wasn't sure whose hand moved first but suddenly his fingers and hers were entwined. Their gazes met and the air hummed with an electric energy.

'I think kissing you must've unlocked something in my psyche,' he said, slowly stroking his thumb over the fleshy part of her thumb. 'I still haven't figured out if that is a good thing or a bad thing.'

Aerin's eyes flicked to his mouth and her heart gave a little skip. 'Kissing you has unlocked something in me too.' It had awakened her to full-blooded human desire, the physical urge so strong and insistent she couldn't imagine having her first time with anyone else but him. He was the first man to kiss her. Why not ask him to be her first lover? It might help her overcome her cycle of perfectionistic procrastination. How else could she jump-start her life unless she took some decisive action? Don't wait for it to happen. *Make* it happen. That would be her new mantra.

A dark intensity shone in his eyes as they held hers. His thumb strokes on her hand were mesmerisingly slow and sensual, sending waves of incendiary heat throughout her body.

'This...chemistry we have is not something we have to act on,' Drake said in a husky tone.

'But what if I did want to act on it? Just until we get back to London?'

His thumb stopped stroking hers and a frown was etched on his forehead in twin pleats between his eyes. 'You're not talking sense, Aerin. Nothing of that nature can happen between us. You know it can't.'

'Because I'm a virgin?'

He drew in a deep breath and released it in a rush. 'That and because you're someone I can't just walk away from and never think of again.'

'No one has to know we've slept together. You're obviously good at keeping secrets, this one won't be hard to keep, surely?'

Drake suddenly pushed back the bedcovers and rolled out of the bed on the opposite side to where she was sitting. He stood and then strode over to the windows and pulled back the curtains with an almost savage movement of his hand. He stood with his back to her, staring at the view outside. The light that poured in was so pallid, it barely made any difference to the room. But it was enough light to see his physical perfection.

She found it hard to take her eyes off his tall and

athletic form, her gaze drawn by sheer magnetic force. Broad shoulders and a strong back tapering to a lean waist and slim hips, his only article of clothing a pair of black satin boxer shorts. The muscles of his long legs toned from hard exercise. An olive-toned tan covered his body and gave his skin a glow that made it all the more tempting for her to touch him.

Drake turned to look at her, his expression grave. 'We have a problem.'

Aerin was conscious of the heat flooding into her cheeks. She had made a spectacular fool of herself, coming across as gauche and unsophisticated, practically begging him to make love to her when he clearly wasn't interested. She rose from where she was perched on the edge of the bed with a sigh. 'Save me the lecture. I get it. You don't want to sleep with me. Sorry for embarrassing you by asking you.'

'I'm not embarrassed. But that's not the problem I'm talking about right now. Look.'

He pulled back the curtains a little further and she walked over to where he was standing and peered out of the windows. Snow had fallen overnight and it now covered everything in a white blanket as magical as a fairyland setting. The blue spruce pines were shrouded, some of the lower limbs bowing with the weight of snow, and the wide expanse of lawn was now a rectangle of white unmarked by any footprints, either animal or human.

'Oh, wow, snow!' Aerin said, unable to tone down the excitement of seeing it for the first time since last winter. 'Isn't it beautiful?'

Drake was standing right next to her, so close she could feel the brush of his upper arm against her left shoulder. 'Let me guess. Number Nine on your Mr Perfect checklist is *Must love snow*?'

Aerin turned to look up at him. He had a sardonic smile on his face that should have annoyed her but somehow didn't. She was getting to know and understand what was behind his mocking and cynical façade. 'Actually, I don't have a Number Nine or Ten. My list only goes to Eight.'

His gaze went to her mouth and it seemed to take him quite some effort to lift it again to meet her eyes. 'Aerin…' He swallowed deeply and continued, 'The car we drove up in is not an all-terrain vehicle.'

'So?'

'So, snow.'

Aerin frowned. 'You mean we can't leave? It's not safe on the roads?'

'Not until the snow melts a bit.' He glanced back out of the window. 'It looks like we might be in for another decent fall. See those clouds over there? I should've checked the weather app before I brought you here. And I should've booked a different vehicle.' The bitter self-recrimination in his voice was unmistakable.

'Because, clearly, being snowbound with me in a cottage in Scotland is your worst nightmare.' Aerin found it hard to remove the bitter edge to her own voice. Did he have to make her feel any more hideously embarrassed about herself? He'd probably had dozens of snowbound weekends with his long list of casual lovers, but he was baulking at the thought of one with her. Was she so undesirable? His kisses hadn't given her that impression at all, but rather the opposite.

'My worst nightmare happened twenty-one years ago, so no, being snowbound with you is not in the same category at all.'

Aerin bit down on her lower lip and cast him an apologetic glance. 'I'm sorry. My choice of words was a little insensitive.'

He lifted his hand to her face and glided one finger down from the top of her cheekbone to the base of her chin in a faineant movement that sent a shower of sparks down her spine. 'But it's still a problem.'

She ran the point of her tongue over her suddenly paper-dry lips. 'Why?' Her voice came out whisper soft.

His gaze drifted to her mouth and her heart rate sped up. His lazy finger left her face and traced the contour of her mouth, sending ticklish tingles through her flesh. 'Because I want to do this so damn much it hurts.' His mouth came down and covered hers in a gentle kiss that throbbed with reined in erotic energy.

Aerin instinctively moved closer to him, her hands sliding up his chest to then link around his neck. Drake gave a low deep groan and put one of his hands in the small of her back, pressing her to his hardening body. His tongue commanded entry to her mouth and she welcomed him in with a breathless sigh of pleasure. The playful duelling of his tongue with hers sent liquid heat to her core, making her legs tremble with growing need.

His other hand came down to rest on her hip, his touch electrifying even through the layers of her nightgown and wrap. His kiss deepened, became more passionate, more desperate. Never had she dreamed a kiss could incite such fiery lust in her body. Never had she imagined a man's lips and tongue could stir her senses into freefall. It was as though she had waited all her life for this moment—this passionate awakening of the senses that made her ache in her feminine core.

Drake lifted his mouth off hers but still kept her in his embrace. 'I want to touch you.' His voice was a deep, rough burr that sounded as if it were coming from Middle-earth itself.

'Then touch me.' Excitement thrummed in her blood, her heart hammered, her pulse raced, desire flaring between her legs in a tight throbbing ache.

His hand came up from her hip and gently brushed against her breast through the satin of her wrap and nightgown. It was a barely touching caress and yet it sent a laser strike of lust through her body. She pressed herself closer and his hand touched her breast again, this time cupping it in his hand. Aerin let out a gasp of pleasure, hardly believing it was possible that her breast could feel so different when touched by him instead of herself.

'Touch me skin on skin.'

'Are you sure?'

'I'm sure.' She hadn't been surer of anything in

her entire life. His touch was what she wanted. What she craved. It was as if she had been waiting all this time for this to happen—for Drake to be the one to introduce her to the wonderland of sensuality. She couldn't explain why she was so driven to allow him to be the first one to make love to her. It didn't make sense in the light of her checklist and careful plans for her life. But right now, it was the only thing she wanted. She was living in the moment in a way she had never done before. Not thinking too far ahead, just rolling with the tide of want that consumed her so totally.

Drake eased aside her nightgown and cupped her naked breast, his eyes gleaming. 'You're so perfect.'

Body issues were the bane of many young women's lives and while she was mostly happy with what genetics had handed her, there were some things she was self-conscious about. She had never been naked in front of a man before. She'd thought she would feel embarrassed, but she didn't. It seemed the most natural thing in the world to reveal her body to Drake, to have his eyes devour her form.

'I'm a bit on the small side...'

'Nonsense. You're just right. Not too big, not too small.' He stroked the pad of his thumb across her budded nipple and a tingle of delight went through her breast. Then he circled her nipple with one of his fingers, his touch light and explorative as if he was committing her shape to memory. His head came down and he caressed her breast with his lips and tongue, the tingling sensations flowing through her like a hot current.

Aerin could feel the proud ridge of his erection pressing against her, making her need for him all the more out of control. Who knew this alchemy could happen between two people? This ferocious need to be skin on skin, to touch and be touched, to desire and be desired. It was mysterious and magical and she wanted to experience all of it. Every step and stage of lust, the steps and stages she had only ever experienced in solo and in secret. To experience it with someone she admired and felt safe and comfortable with was surely the right thing to do at this point in her life. She could not turn thirty without having experienced making love with someone she desired.

Drake came back to kiss her on the lips once more, as if drawn there by a force beyond his control. His tongue thrust between her lips and it sent a shock wave of delight through her, the flickering movement of his tongue stoking a roaring fire in her loins. He lifted his mouth off hers and sent it on a blazing trail down the side of her neck, gently moving aside her nightgown as he went. He kissed and caressed her other breast, his lips and tongue working their magic on her naked flesh until she was all but purring with pleasure.

'You like that?'

'How could I not? You seem to know exactly what to do to make me want you all the more.' Aerin gave him a twisted smile. 'But then, you've had a lot of experience.'

Drake placed his hands on her hips, holding her to him but lightly enough to give her the freedom to move away if she wanted to. 'I admit I've lost count of how many lovers I've had, mostly because in the early days I used sex to blank out a lot of other stuff.' He let out a sigh and continued, 'I don't want to give you the impression I use women as sexual objects. Not these days, at least. I only sleep with women who want the same as me—casual and uncomplicated sex, which is why going any further with you is wrong on so many counts.'

'But how is it wrong if I want that too?'

'It's wrong because I can't give you more than a fling.'

This was probably not the time to point out to Drake that Lucas Rothwell and Jack Livingstone had said much the same words to Ruby and Harper and yet they were all happily together now. Dared she hope the same could happen to her? That Drake would gradually lower his guard and fall in love with her as Lucas and Jack had fallen for her friends?

Aerin placed her hands on the strong wall of his chest, looking up at him with clear focus. 'What if we were to forget about my checklist and the fact that you only ever do flings? What if we just went with the flow while we're stuck here?'

Drake's gaze drifted to her upturned mouth and his hands shifted from her hips to her waist. Then his narrowed gaze came back to hers. 'Is this a pity thing?'

Aerin closed her eyes in a slow blink to quell her frustration. Couldn't he see how much she wanted him? It wasn't about his tragic past but about *him*. The essential Drake she was finding so hard to resist. 'No, it's nothing to do with pity. Of course I feel sorry you've had such a shocking thing happen to you. But I want you for you. I want you to be my first lover. I don't want to get to the age of thirty and still be a virgin. I think you're the right person to give me that experience because I know and trust you. I'm not asking for anything other than a weekend fling.'

Drake released her from his light hold and put a slight distance between them. There was a battle playing out over his features, a tug-of-war between his body wanting to do as she suggested and his mind carefully weighing up the dangers. Muscles tensed in his jaw, shadows came and went in his gaze, the strong column of his throat rose and fell in a tight swallow. 'Are you sure you can keep your emotions out of it?' he asked, still frowning.

'I don't know because I've never slept with anyone before.' But weren't her emotions already in it now? Feelings she was trying to keep hidden. Feelings that had bloomed into life ever since his first kiss, like a spring bulb poking its head from beneath the ground, thawed by the warming rays of spring sunshine. 'How do you keep *your* emotions out of it?'

He gave a crooked smile that didn't make it to his eyes. His eyes were still troubled, the shadows lurking, the doubts circling, the yes and no debate ongoing. 'It's never been a problem before.'

Aerin closed the distance between them and lifted her hand to his unshaven jaw. 'But you're worried it might become one with me?' She stroked her fingers along the stubble-roughened skin, a light shiver coursing over her own flesh.

His strong hand encircled her wrist in a firm but gentle hold, his eyes locking on hers. 'It's a possibility that does concern me.'

Wasn't that something positive to cling to? That he was prepared to admit he could be in danger of falling for her? Didn't that show he had the potential to love even though he claimed he didn't? He lifted her wrist and turned it over to place a kiss to the sensitive skin on the underside. She shivered again, his electrifying touch sending livewires of need to her core.

'Because you don't want to hurt me or get hurt yourself?' she asked.

Drake planted another feather-light kiss to her wrist, the slight graze of his stubble against her skin sending a wave of incendiary heat and rolling fire through her blood. 'Some people don't care if they hurt others. But I do.'

He hadn't fully answered her question, though, about whether he was worried about getting hurt himself. Or had he already endured a lifetime's quota of hurt and pain? Losing his family in such a horrendous way was certainly a harrowing experience that would leave deep emotional scars.

Aerin ran her fingers through the thickness of his dark hair, her body so close to his she could feel her softer contours melting into his harder ones. Her breasts against his chest, her pelvis in the cradle of his hips, her thighs against his muscular ones...and the potent rise of his male body against her most sensitive flesh of all. 'If I wasn't a virgin, would you be feeling a little less reluctant, do you think?'

Drake slipped an arm around her back and brought her even closer, his bottomless brown eyes burning with lust. His other hand went to the back of her head, his fingers splaying through her hair, sending hot tingles down her spine. 'Physically, as you can probably tell, I'm not at all reluctant. But this is not going to be something we can forget ever happened. I'll always be your first lover, the first man who kissed you. And you'll be the first woman I've slept with who I can't simply delete from my phone and forget about. I don't want you to be embarrassed or uncomfortable when we cross paths in the future, either at one of your family's gatherings or professionally.'

'We've both adults, Drake. You're making it sound so terribly complicated. All I want is this weekend. Once it's over, we can pretend it never happened and move on with our lives.'

His eyes softened and he brushed a stray hair away from her face, a lopsided smile on his mouth. 'I have a feeling I'm not going to forget about it in a hurry.' He drew in a deep breath and released it in a not quite steady stream.

Aerin lifted her hand to his face and stroked his lean jaw. 'Nor me.'

His head came down and his mouth closed over hers in a searing kiss that sent a riot of sensations through her body. His tongue didn't ask for entry but demanded it, tangling with hers in a sexy combat that mimicked the intimacy they both craved. This was not a chaste kiss between old friends. This was not a kiss that could ever be forgotten. This was a kiss of urgency and explosive heat and longing. Drake's mouth continued its thrilling exploration of hers while his hands slipped beneath the opening of her wrap. She shivered as his hand shaped her, his caresses threatening to heat her blood to boiling.

Until he had touched her, she'd had no idea her breasts were so sensitive. She had not realised the intensity of feeling to have a man's hand cradle her shape while his thumb moved back and forth across her engorged nipple. But she wanted more than his hands on her breasts and, as if he had read her mind, he bent his head and took her nipple into the warm cave of his mouth. Aerin arched her spine as the tingling sensations shot through her, a groan of pleasure escaping her lips. 'That feels...so...so...good...'

Drake went to her other breast, exploring it in the same erotic detail, his lips and tongue wreaking havoc on her senses. But it wasn't enough. She wanted more. More skin-on-skin contact, more friction. More of the sensual heat his body promised as it surged against her.

Drake lifted his mouth from her breast and captured her mouth again in a kiss that was even more thrilling. His tongue played with hers in a game of catch-me-if-you-can and her heart pounded with excitement. His hands skimmed down the sides of her body, up and down in a caressing motion that made her skin lift in a delicate shiver. He peeled her

wrap away from her body, his mouth still clamped
to hers. But then he pulled back and, breathing heavily, slowly, ever so slowly peeled away her nightgown
until it fell in a pool of satin at her feet. His eyes roved
over her body, his gaze shining with lust as he took
in every inch of her naked form.

'You're so damn beautiful…' There was a note of
wonder in his tone as if he had never seen a woman
quite like her before. But then, maybe he hadn't. She
was hardly his usual type with her understated girl-
next-door looks.

Aerin glanced down at the shape of him tenting his
black boxer shorts. She was too shy to touch him but
ached to do so. He took her hand and held it against
his swollen flesh, allowing her to feel him through
the satin.

'Don't be afraid to touch me,' he said in a husky
tone.

Her fingers stroked the turgid length of him and,
with a boldness she'd had no idea she possessed, she
slipped her hand beneath the satin and touched him
skin on skin. He shuddered and groaned, his face
contorting with pleasure.

'I think you're going to be a quick learner,' he said
with a gleam in his eyes. Then he scooped her up in
his arms like a hero out of an old black and white
movie from the golden days of Hollywood and carried her to his bed…

Drake knew he could have put a stop to things right
then and there but for once in his life he couldn't ac-

cess his willpower. He wanted Aerin as he had wanted no other woman. He had weighed up the pros and cons of engaging in a weekend fling with her, he had carefully measured the risks and done his checks and balances. The rational part of his brain told him to keep his distance but another part of his brain—or maybe it wasn't his brain at all but his body alone—told him to have this secret weekend with her. To have what he had wanted from the moment he saw her across the street from his office. Their first kiss had only reinforced the want, the driving need, the urge he couldn't dampen down no matter how much he tried.

But was he worrying *too* much? Aerin was looking for the fairy tale, the perfect partner and he was certainly not that. She had already ruled him out with her eight-point checklist. She wouldn't allow herself to fall in love with anyone less than perfect, so why shouldn't he indulge her wish for a fling?

Drake laid her on his rumpled bed and stood above her for a long moment, hungrily taking in the slim curves of her body. She was so lithe and lissom, her skin a pale cream without a single blemish. Her golden blonde hair was tousled around her shoulders and he couldn't wait to bury his head in it and breathe in its flowery scent.

A worried look came into Aerin's eyes. 'Are you having second thoughts?'

He kneeled one knee on the bed beside her and leaned forward to cage her in with his arms. 'Are you?'

'No.' She lifted her hand to his nearest shoulder and stroked her fingers down the length of his arm in a touch as light as fairy footsteps. 'I want you.'

'You know this is madness, don't you? Us doing this.'

Her other hand trailed down his other arm, sending shivers up and down his spine. Her gaze was luminous at it met his, shining with the same need he knew shone in his. 'It would be madness if we both didn't agree on the terms.'

Drake planted a kiss on her lips, a long passionate kiss that sent his blood pounding all the more. He was hard and aching to possess her but he knew he would have to slow down and take things gently with her. She had cast some sort of spell over him; a magical spell that made it impossible for him to walk away and leave her well alone.

He straightened from the bed to step out of his boxer shorts. 'I have to get a condom.'

'Do you have any with you?'

'I always carry some in my wallet.'

She chewed at her lower lip for a moment, her eyes downcast. 'Of course...'

Drake picked up his wallet from where he had left it on the bedside table. But then he snapped its folds back together. 'It's too late to change your mind.'

'Why would I change my mind?'

He took in her pink cheeks and unblinking grey-blue gaze.

'Because I'm a playboy and you're a virgin.'

Her cheeks darkened another shade but her eyes remained steady on his. 'I'm not making any judgements on your lifestyle. You're not currently seeing anyone, so I don't see a problem.'

Drake could see a problem. His past was a problem that cast long shadows over his life. How he could be sure those dark shadows wouldn't somehow taint Aerin by being closer to him than anyone had got in years? He had told her things he had told no one. She had not pressed or pushed him to reveal his childhood trauma but he had opened up to her all the same. Why had he allowed her to get past the fortress he had built around his emotional centre? Wouldn't making love to her only bring her closer?

He would be her first lover.

That was not something he could dismiss from his mind like so many of his other lovers who had faded so easily into the background. He would carry the memory of this experience with Aerin for the rest of his life. And so would she of him. He would not be able to look at her without seeing her like this—naked, hungry for him, her chin reddened by his stubble. She would not be able to look at him and not recall this stolen moment of pleasure. What if he hurt her, even unintentionally? Could he live with that? Could he live with more guilt to lug around?

But maybe guilt was the price to pay for what he wanted right now.

Drake came back over to her and tilted her face up so her gaze meshed with his. His brushed his thumb across the reddened circle on her chin. 'I've given you beard rash.'

'Have you?'

He bent his head and lightly kissed her chin. 'I should shave before I make love to you.'

Her hand came up and stroked the rough stubble on his jaw. 'I like the feel of it, so raspy and prickly.'

Drake stroked her smooth cheek with a lazy finger. 'Your first time might be a little uncomfortable. I'll take it slowly and make sure you're well prepared.'

'Isn't that a bit of a myth? That all virgins feel discomfort or bleed? I read an article about it somewhere. Being forced to prove one's virginity is an outdated patriarchal practice that still happens in some developing countries. I've been physically active all my life so I might not feel a thing.'

He slipped his hands down to her waist, his smile wry. 'I'll definitely have to work on my technique if you don't feel a thing when we make love.'

Her cheeks were tinged with pink but her eyes were alight with anticipation. Her arms came up and looped around his neck, her breasts pressed against his chest, stirring his blood to a roaring, rushing river of fire. 'I thought I'd be nervous but I'm not with you. This feels like it's meant to be. Does that make sense?'

Drake brushed an imaginary wisp of hair off her face. 'It makes perfect sense,' he said, and, joining her on the bed, brought his mouth down to hers.

Because in a weird sort of way it did make sense.

They were snowbound, secluded, and attracted to each other. Why not enjoy this for what it was? A secret weekend fling that would be over before it got a chance to do any permanent damage.

CHAPTER SEVEN

AERIN SIGHED WITH deep pleasure as Drake's tongue tangled with hers in a sexy salsa. Her pulse rate soared, her lower body melting as the molten heat of desire flowed through her. Her hands explored him with increasing boldness, her fingers rolling over the tiny pebbles of his nipples and gliding over the toned muscles of his chest, the washboard ridges of his abdomen marking him as a man who enjoyed hard exercise.

She shuddered as his hand glided up her body to just below her breast. The warmth of his hand against her ribcage so close to the sensitive flesh of her breast drove her wild with anticipation. He brought his mouth to the upper curve of her breast, his tongue circling her pert nipple, her senses reeling at the expertise of his caress. He suckled on her gently, drawing her nipple into the warmth of his mouth, then slowly releasing it. He did the same to her other breast, sending shivers down her spine as his lips and tongue explored her contours in intimate detail.

He moved from her breasts to kiss a pathway to

her belly button. 'Relax for me.' His voice was deep and husky and his warm breath caressed the skin of her stomach.

She lay back and gripped the bedcovers either side of her body. 'I'm trying to…'

He glanced up at her, leaning his weight on one elbow. 'I won't do anything you don't want to do. Tell me to stop if you're not comfortable.'

Aerin let out a shuddering breath. 'Okay.'

Drake kissed her stomach again, then slowly worked his way down to the juncture of her thighs. Her female flesh was already swelling and twitching in excitement, pulses of lust firing through her like a current. He stroked her with his fingers, long slow strokes that sent her blood skyrocketing through her veins. The liquid heat intensified and the ache of need building in her core rose to an unbearable level.

Drake brought his mouth down to her most intimate flesh and the rhythmic strokes of his tongue sent a torrent of tingles through her body, concentrating in that one exquisite point—the heart of her femininity. The tension grew to a crescendo until she was finally catapulted into a spinning vortex that scattered her thoughts, leaving her without the ability to think, only to feel. And feel she did. Giant waves of pleasure unlike anything she had experienced when going solo. Showers of goosebumps peppered her body, she was dazed and limbless and out of her mind as the aftershocks rippled through her.

'Oh…' A breathless gasp escaped her lips and she

opened her eyes to find Drake looking at her indulgently.

'Good?'

Aerin let out a long blissful sigh, still trying to grasp how her body had responded to his intimate caresses. 'I'm not sure I have the words to describe it.'

Drake stroked a gentle hand down the flank of her thigh, sending another ripple of pleasure through her body. His eyes were impossibly dark, his pupils flared wide with lust. Her hand reached for him, stroking his potent length with shy fingers at first but she was emboldened by the expression on his face signalling his growing delight. He drew in a harsh breath and pulled her hand away.

'I need to put on a condom before we go any further.'

Aerin knew protection should always be a priority unless a couple was actively seeking to conceive. But something about Drake's tone reminded her that kids were something he never wanted in his life. She understood why, given the bleak circumstances of his own childhood, but it still made her sad that he had permanently ruled out one of the things most important to her. She could not imagine a future without a family. She had grown up in a loving home and had been sheltered and nurtured by parents who loved her and her brother as well as each other. *That* was what she wanted for her life.

Aerin leaned up on her elbows to watch him apply the condom. 'How many do you have stashed away in your wallet?'

He glanced at her with a twinkling look. 'Enough.'

'Three? Four? More?'

He came back over to her and pressed a long drugging kiss to her lips. He lifted his mouth off hers and looked deeply into her eyes. 'Enough to get us through the weekend.'

'What if the snow doesn't melt in time?'

His eyes flicked to her mouth and then back to her gaze, a shadow passing through his before he disguised it behind a playful smile. 'I'll have to get some airlifted in.'

Aerin's brows shot up in surprise. 'You can do that?'

He leaned down and kissed the tip of her nose. 'You bet I can.'

His mouth covered hers again and sent her pulses racing. His aroused body was pressing against her thigh and it ramped up her need for him all the more. To know it was her who had made him so turned on thrilled her. It gave her a sense of power she had never experienced before.

The kiss deepened, became more urgent, their limbs tangling with an erotic choreography as if they had made love in another lifetime. The alignment of their limbs for that ultimate moment of physical connection was simple and yet complex. Natural and yet strange. It was like learning the steps of a dance, one leg this way, the other that way, one arm here, the other there. Their chests close, their hips even closer. There was no shyness or hesitancy on Aerin's part. It felt completely normal to be in bed with Drake Cawthorn, his mouth clamped to hers, his hands caressing her breasts with exquisite tenderness. He made some guttural noises as her hands continued to explore him. Deep masculine sounds that spoke of a man who was keeping himself on a tight leash of self-control.

Drake dragged his mouth off hers, his breathing heavy. 'I want to be inside you, but I don't want to rush you.'

She lifted a hand to his hair, brushing it further back from his forehead. 'I'm ready for you. I want you.'

'Are you sure?'

'Of course I'm sure.' And she was. Right now, this was all she wanted. She refused to think about her checklist…about all the points on it Drake didn't tick. Wouldn't tick. Couldn't tick. Maybe she had been a bit too pedantic constructing a checklist in the first place. Maybe the Mr Perfect she longed for might never come along. She might have to learn to settle on something a little less than perfect even if it jarred with her perfectionistic outlook on life.

But nothing about Drake's lovemaking was less than perfect.

Her body sang arias under his touch. Her flesh tingled from head to foot and her senses did cartwheels of delight.

Drake gently probed her entrance, allowing her time to get used to him just being there. Close enough for her to feel the heft and weight of him without overwhelming her.

Aerin stroked his back and shoulders, loving the

feel of him against her, his bulk against her slim build a heady reminder of all that was different between them.

He slowly entered her, waiting for her to relax before he went any further. 'Are you okay with this?'

'Perfectly...' A shiver coursed over her as her intimate muscles began to stretch to take hold of him.

He began a slow rhythm that sent pleasure rippling through her body, the friction of male against female making her aware of her body in a way she had never been before. Nerves she'd had no idea were so intricately laced into her body were firing up, fizzing with life and sensual energy. Muscles that had been inactive for most of her life were now being subjected to a deeply pleasurable workout that had one sure goal. She could feel the anticipation of it beating in her blood. A tribal, primitive drumbeat that throbbed with increasing urgency.

'You feel so damn good,' Drake groaned against her mouth.

'So do you,' Aerin said, sweeping her tongue over his lower lip.

He thrust a little faster, a little deeper, his breathing as hectic as hers. A restless ache was building in her female flesh, a low dragging ache that was almost unbearable.

But as if Drake could read her silent pleas for more of that delicious friction, he slipped his hand between their bodies and sought the tightly budded heart of her arousal. The feminine bud of nerves that spread from that tightened point all throughout her pelvis. The stroking of his fingers against her slick wetness, with his own body tightly encased inside hers, sent her into a freefall of spinning, whirling, dizzying sensations. They ricocheted through her in giant shudders, making her lose her grasp on conscious thought. So *this* was mind-blowing sex. Sending her to a place almost beyond consciousness. Fireworks went off in her head, in her blood, the vivid colours bursting behind her squeezed-shut eyelids as she rode out the waves.

Then there was the slow wash of a wave of lassitude…like the tide finally quietening after a ferocious storm at sea.

But then, Aerin could feel another storm building, not in her flesh but in Drake's. His thrusts becoming more urgent, more desperate, his breathing laboured, as if his control were hanging by a gossamer thread. She could feel the exact moment he let go through the silkywalls of her feminine flesh. The pitching forward of his bulk, the ecstatic groan forced from him as powerfully as the life essence from his body. Something about that primal groan and those deep shudders of his sent a shiver across the floor of her belly like a breeze whispering over a lake. They were still joined intimately, their bodies in a tangle of limbs that made her feel safe and protected.

Drake's hand stroked the hair away from her face, his gaze searching. 'How are you feeling?' There was a chord of concern in the lower pitch of his voice, the same concern she could feel in his touch.

'I feel…wonderful. You didn't hurt me at all. It was amazing.' Aerin didn't have the words to truly express how he had made her feel. But would he want to hear them in any case? He was used to casual encounters that probably didn't include discussing how mind-blowing the sex was. She was supposed to be keeping her feelings out of this. Feelings were not a part of their weekend fling. Feelings were not a part of any of his encounters. They were not a part of his life…and yet she wondered if one day he would allow them to be. He had so much to offer. He was kind and gentle and far more sensitive than she had given him credit for in the past. Behind his cynical façade was a wounded man who cared deeply but was guarded about showing it.

Drake continued to look at her unwaveringly. 'No regrets?'

Her only regret was he was not interested in anything more than a weekend fling. Making love with him once or twice was not going to be enough. He had awakened a hunger in her that was not going to be so easily satisfied. It was tasting an exotic fruit for the first time and wanting more. 'Not so far.' She painted a smile on her face. 'You?'

He drew in a deep breath and released it on a rough-edged sigh. 'Only that this feels a little strange.'

'How so?'

He played with a wisp of her hair, winding it around his finger and letting it go again, the soft tug against her scalp sending a shiver rolling down her spine. 'Being with you like this.'

'No one has to know about it but us.'

A frown pulled at his brow. 'You won't even tell Ruby and Harper?'

Aerin ran the tip of her tongue over her lips. That was certainly going to be a little trickier to navigate than the reunion charade. That had worked on her school friends because she saw them so infrequently, but she worked closely with Harper and Ruby. They saw each other most days and even on weekends when they had a wedding. They knew her better than anyone. How was she going to conceal this from them? Could she conceal it or would it show on her person somehow?

Making love with Drake had been the most incredible experience of her life. She *felt* different, not just physically but—even more worryingly—emotionally. Everyone said you never forgot your first lover and there could be both good and bad reasons for that. But how much harder to forget when that first lover was so tender and attentive and made your pleasure and comfort paramount? How could she not fall a little bit in love with him?

'If you'd rather I didn't, then I won't. But I have to warn you they know me so well that they're likely to sense something's happened.'

Drake rolled away to dispose of the condom, then he came back to her, one of his hands capturing one of hers. His thumb stroked the back of her hand in a slow-moving caress that was soothing and yet hotly sensual at the same time. 'There's this saying I read somewhere, how you can ruin a perfectly good friendship by bringing sex into the equation.'

'But we weren't particularly friends in the first place, were we?'

He gave a half-smile. 'I guess not. You always seemed intent on avoiding me whenever you could. Tom even asked me a few months back if I'd done something to upset you.'

Aerin gave a shame-faced grimace. 'I was always so prejudiced against you. Your cynicism was so jarring up against my optimism and plan for lifelong love. I'm sorry I didn't take the time to get to know you better.'

Drake tucked a strand of her hair behind one of her ears, his touch so tender it made her heart squeeze as if it were in a vice. A flicker of something moved through his gaze like a passing thought leaving a long shadow in its wake. 'Are you sure I didn't hurt you when we made love?'

'I'm totally sure.'

His eyes drifted to her mouth and her pulse picked up its pace. 'I have this compulsive desire to kiss you again.'

Aerin linked her arms around his neck. She had a compulsion of her own—to feel his arms around her, to feel his body move within her, to feel the magic of his lovemaking all over again. 'Feel free.'

Drake rested his forehead on hers, his warm breath mingling with hers. 'Are you sure you wouldn't rather go outside and build a snowman or something?' There was a playful note in his voice.

Aerin toyed with the thick strands of his hair at the back of his head, her gaze mesmerised by the glint in his. 'Not right now. Or do you have a burning desire to make one before we even have breakfast?'

He smiled and a wave of heat coursed through her. 'I only have a burning desire for you.' And his mouth came down and proved it beyond a doubt.

Drake had lost count of the number of lovers he had had over the years, but he knew he would never forget this weekend with Aerin. How could he forget the sweet suppleness of her mouth? The soft shy touch of her hands on his naked skin? Her flowery fragrance that clung to his skin and dazzled his senses? The warm, wet, silky welcome of her body?

He was her first lover.

He couldn't get that sentence, that inescapable *fact* out of his mind. Nothing could ever be the same between them after this weekend. He was fooling himself to think it could. He had no intention of letting anyone know about their fling, but he was concerned others would find out, such as Aerin's friends. Or perhaps, her school friends would let something slip out on social media in spite of their promises not to. He didn't want their fling to be gossip fodder. He loathed sensationalised journalism. He had suffered enough of that when his father destroyed his family. Drake had seen headlines and stories no fifteen-year-old kid should ever see, especially when it was his family that was referenced there. It was one of the reasons he changed his surname. He couldn't bear the thought of anyone doing a search on him and reading about the worst event of his life.

But when he kissed Aerin, all of the dark shadows of his past melted away. She woke something in him that had been in a long cold hibernation. He could feel the tentative stirring in his chest, like the cramped limbs of a faceless creature slowly unfolding. He could feel the sense of freedom flowing through him, a sense of space he had not allowed himself in years.

The space to breathe.

The space to feel.

To *really* feel.

The soft but urgent press of Aerin's lips against his made his blood pound in his veins. The touch of her hands made every nerve beneath his skin come to throbbing life. Her taste was sweet and yet exotic, forbidden and yet addictive in a way he had no power to resist. Where was his damn willpower? The iron-strong willpower that had made him steer clear of intimate relationships where emotions clouded everything?

He had not intended to sleep with her this weekend. Of course the thought had crossed his mind but he hadn't allowed it to get too comfortable in there. But since making love with her, now other thoughts were not only crossing his mind but finding a seat to lounge in, order coffee and cake and stay put. Thoughts of not just one weekend with Aerin but a few weeks, a month or two, maybe more. Thoughts of what it would be like to be open to everyone about their relationship, instead of covering it up like a dirty little secret.

He didn't want to make Aerin feel he was ashamed

to be with her. He wasn't…but he was conflicted. It was as if there were suddenly two men inside him caught in a vicious tug of war. One wanted to keep safe inside the fortress, madly locking all the points of exit, while the other was sliding the bolts back, taking the fortress down brick by brick, nail by nail.

Drake was the man who didn't do relationships. He was the no strings, no rings, no promises guy who lived his life as a playboy. But kissing Aerin had changed him, transformed him like in one of those old fairy tales. The frog had turned into a prince who wanted to get out of the murky pond he'd been condemned to and live in the real world. The world of love and happiness and hope.

But did that world even exist? Especially for someone like him?

CHAPTER EIGHT

AERIN MUST HAVE drifted off to sleep after making love the second time, for when she woke, she saw Drake looking down at her with a contemplative look on his face. One of his hands was idly stroking the bare skin of her arm, a soft almost ticklish caress that sent shivers of delight down her spine.

She stretched her limbs and encountered one of his hairy legs. The sheer intimacy of lying in bed with him, let alone what had happened between them during their passionate lovemaking session, was mind-blowing. She was acutely, intensely, spine-tinglingly aware of him. The dark glitter in his eyes, the shape of his mouth that had given such pleasure out of her. The lean jaw with its generous regrowth of dark stubble, the strong column of his neck, his broad shoulders. Shoulders that had carried for too long a heavy burden from his past. A past he had spoken only to her about in such detail.

Did that mean he had a special place for her in his life? In his heart? Or was she being a fool to think he would ever lower his guard enough to fall in love? He made love to her so exquisitely it was impossible to imagine he didn't feel something for her. But then, she reminded herself, he was an experienced playboy. He had made love to dozens of women. She was just another in a long line of conquests.

And yet, she didn't see herself as a conquest. He had certainly never made her feel that way. Besides, she had been the one to instigate their intimacy. He had made her feel in control from the get-go. And yet her body had been out of control the moment he kissed her. She had no resistance to him, no immunity to the potency of his touch.

'Sleeping Beauty awakes,' Drake said with a teasing smile.

Aerin smiled back. 'Hey, thought I was Goldilocks?'

He released a little puff of air that was part laugh, part something else. 'Yes, well, you want everything just right.' He picked up a fistful of her hair and trailed it through his fingertips and added, 'And your hair is like spun gold.'

She rested her hand on his chest, right over the steady *thud-thud-thud* of his heart. 'I've always been a perfectionist—just ask my parents and Tom.' She gave a soft sigh and continued, 'I'm not sure it's doing me any favours, though. I mean, it's great for my work and all but not so good for my personal life. I think it's held me back. The fear of making a mistake has made me stall in some areas of my life.'

There was a long moment of silence. The only

sound was the rustling of the bedsheets when Drake moved one of his legs.

'Do you consider what happened between us this weekend a mistake?' There was a sombre quality to his voice, a slight rumble of uncertainty she hadn't heard in it before.

Aerin forced her gaze back to his. 'No. Do you?'

One side of his mouth came up in a rueful slant and his hand continued its slow stroke of her forearm. 'Yes and no.'

Her heart sank like a pricked balloon. Did he regret making love to her? Had she disappointed him in some way? Was he disgusted with himself for crossing the line he had sworn he would never cross? She disguised a nervous swallow. 'I'm sorry if I've made you feel compromised. You didn't have to make love to me. You could have said no.'

His gaze darkened and his hand came up to cup her cheek. 'Saying no to you wasn't as easy as I imagined it would be.' He leaned down and pressed a soft-as-air kiss to her lips. 'This is all it took—one kiss.'

Aerin stroked her hand along his lean jaw, gazing into his eyes, wondering if she was a fool for thinking he was falling for her. And wasn't she an even bigger fool for falling for him? She couldn't hide from the truth any longer. She had fallen in love with him the moment he kissed her. How was that even possible? But then, hadn't so many of her clients told her similar stories about their journey to happy ever after? Even her two best friends and business partners had experienced the sudden dart of Cupid's arrow. A first glance, a first touch, a first kiss, a first date—all or any of those things had happened to other people, including her own parents and older brother.

'It will seem strange not being able to kiss you when we get back to London. I mean, we never even pecked on the cheek before. You always seemed to keep your distance. Not like I can talk. I did too.'

Drake twirled a strand of her hair around his finger, sending shivers up and down her spine. 'We might have to keep our distance for a while, to let things go back to normal.'

Normal? Normal was not healthy for her, Aerin knew that now. 'I guess...' Her teeth sank into her lower lip, her thoughts in a tangle. Her checklist flashed up in her mind and she inwardly cringed at how naïve she had been to write that stuff down. Who could ever tick every box? And just because one or even two weren't ticked, did it mean all of the others that were didn't count for something?

Drake's features were set in grave lines. 'It'd be crazy to continue this back home. We couldn't hope to keep it a secret for long.'

Aerin forced a smile of agreement to her lips. 'Of course. That's what we agreed—just this weekend.'

A frown pulled at his intelligent forehead. 'There's one other thing we haven't considered.'

'What?'

'The snow.'

'Oh...'

Drake eased himself away from her and rose from the bed. She couldn't take her eyes off his naked form as he strode to the windows. Her hands had caressed almost every inch of his body. How could she go back to London and pretend this hadn't happened? Her body was so tinglingly aware of him. Of his every movement. His every glance in her direction. She would have her work cut out for her, disguising her reaction to him in future. Every nerve in her body tingled when he was near her. The sensual energy he stirred in her was not something she could so easily switch off.

Aerin slipped on her wrap and padded over to join him by the window. Not only had the snow not melted, more was falling in soft, silent flurries. 'It's so beautiful...' She couldn't disguise the sense of wonder in her voice.

Drake placed his hand on the small of her back. It was such a light touch and yet it sent a warm wave of longing straight to her core. He was still looking out at the view, his forehead creased in a frown. 'Yes, it is. Thank God it's not a blizzard, though.' He turned to face her, his hand moving from her lower back to settle on her hip. 'We might have to stay a couple of extra days. Is that going to be a problem for you and your work?'

Another couple of days...snowbound with Drake Cawthorn.

It was a problem, but not in the way he probably thought. It could snow for a month, two or three even and she would be happy here with him. Shut off from the rest of the world in their own little bubble of physical bliss.

'It's not a busy time for us just now, so it will be okay. I do have a wedding the weekend after next, though. But what about you?'

He gave a shrug of one broad shoulder. 'I'll get my secretary to reschedule my commitments.'

There was a beat or two of silence.

Drake glanced at her mouth and his hand on her hip gently nudged her closer to his body. A delicious shudder went through her as his other hand cupped the back of her head. 'I'm aware that if I hadn't brought you here away from the reunion hotel, you wouldn't be stuck here with me now.'

Aerin lifted her hand to his face and stroked the jagged scar on his left eyebrow with her finger. 'I don't feel stuck with you, in fact, quite the opposite. I feel free in a way I've never felt before.' Her finger came down to trace around his mouth. 'I didn't realise making love could be so...so amazing. I mean, I've talked to friends and so on, but I didn't realise the sheer power of it. The way it takes over your body and your mind and makes you feel so euphoric.' She lowered her hand to place it back on his chest. 'I'm glad I got to experience it first with you.'

Drake captured her hand and held it up to his mouth, within kissing reach of her fingertips, his eyes holding hers. 'I sensed you were uncomfortable pretending to be in love with me in front of your friends. I thought it'd be easier to be up here on our own.' His mouth twisted along rueful lines. 'But then I couldn't stop myself from wanting you.'

Oh, the irony.

Aerin had hated lying to her school friends, she had hated the thought of being caught out and found to be an imposter. But had she truly been pretending to be in love with Drake? Or had the real thing, the real emotion hit her the first time he kissed her? It certainly felt like it. Something had happened as soon as his mouth pressed against hers. Something she had no words to explain other than it was almost other-worldly. A magical sense of rightness that his mouth was the first to kiss hers.

Aerin leaned into his embrace, her free hand going up to play with his thick dark hair. 'I couldn't stop myself wanting you either. You're rather hard to resist when you kiss me so thoroughly.'

His eyes glinted and he drew her closer to the hot, hard heat of his body. 'Is that a hint to kiss you again?'

She gave him a coy smile. 'Only if you want to kiss me.'

He brought his mouth down to just above hers. 'I do.'

Some hours later, Drake was lingering over a second coffee in the kitchen while Aerin examined the contents of the pantry and fridge in order to plan dinner in a few hours' time. They had had a snatch-and-grab breakfast, which had been closer to lunchtime after they had made love.

Made love.

It was weird but he was finding it hard to think of having sex with Aerin as anything but making love. His many previous encounters were only ever about sex. The physical release of temporary passion. Satisfying to a point but not in any other way than physically. But with Aerin, he found it difficult to keep his emotions separate. Knowing he was her first lover was part of it. He was woke enough not to view a woman's virginity as a prize or trophy or even a gift on her part to bestow. But knowing he was her first, that she had chosen him, trusted him to make love to her, was an experience he knew he would not forget in a hurry.

'There's enough food here for a week or two at least,' Aerin said, closing the pantry door.

'Let's hope we don't have to be here that long.' Drake knew he should have chosen his words more carefully by the crestfallen look that came over her features. He put his cup down and went over to her, running his hand down the length of her spine. 'I'm sorry, I didn't mean it the way it sounded.'

Aerin lifted her gaze to his, a wounded look still shimmering in hers. 'It's okay…'

Drake cradled her face in both of his hands. 'It's not okay if you feel hurt by something careless I've said. I like being here with you. In fact, I wish we could stay a week or two.'

'You do?'

He planted a soft kiss to her lips, then lowered his hands from her face to take possession of her hands. 'But we both have work and other commitments. And people are going to wonder where we've got to.' He gave her hands a light squeeze. 'Have you told anyone where you are?'

'No, because we're not due back in London until later tonight. But I'll have to text Harper and Ruby to tell them I won't be back at work for a couple of days at least.'

'Will they put two and two together, do you think?'

'Knowing Ruby and Harper, yes.' A worried look came into her eyes. 'I don't want to lie to them. It was hard enough with my school friends but I'm not as close to them. Ruby and Harper are used to me carrying on about how cynical you are and how I always try to avoid you. I'm not sure I can be like that now that I know you better.'

Drake released her from his hold and went back to pick up his now cold coffee. But at least it was something to do with his hands. 'We have to go back to normal, or as normal as possible.' He put his cup down again on the table and scraped his hand through his hair. Emotions were bubbling inside him, but he was doing all he could to suppress them.

He would hurt her more if he extended their fling. He couldn't offer her any of the things she wanted for her life. But how were they ever going to go back to normal? By making love they had changed their relationship. *He* had changed their relationship and he couldn't change it back. He wanted her with an ache that was getting harder to manage each day. He was not used to the intensity of such feelings. He had never experienced anything quite like this before. In a weird way he was like Aerin—he wanted things he couldn't have. Fate had decided that for him. He was always going to be the tragic boy who lost his family through the despicable actions of his father.

He could not love again.

He would not love again.

He would not fail again.

How could he guarantee his love for someone would be enough to keep them safe?

'I guess you'll be glad to get back to your playboy life as soon as you can,' Aerin said with a hint of bitterness in her tone.

Drake wanted to tell her how, lately, he had started to hate his playboy life. He hated the shallow encounters, the short flings that didn't mean anything to either party other than physical release. He had been physically close with so many women but not one of them had unpicked the lock on his emotional fortress.

But Aerin with her kind and sweet nature had cast some sort of spell on him. A spell he could feel intensifying the longer he spent with her. He had found talking about his past painful for sure, but it had also released some bound-up darkness inside him. Freeing him in a way he had not been in years. Not totally free, but free enough for him to spread his cramped emotional limbs, to shake off the numbness, the deadness, to get the blood flowing again.

Drake came back to her and took her hands in his again. 'I will miss you, being with you like this. It's been…something special, something really special. I want you to know that.'

She swallowed and looked at him so openly and earnestly his heart spasmed. 'I'm sorry. I shouldn't have been snarky about your choice of lifestyle, it's just that I hate the thought of you missing out on what a real relationship feels like, one that is not transactional or temporary but a total commitment that lasts for ever.'

'I know you mean well, your whole working life and your personal one for that matter is about making people happy,' Drake said. 'But I've seen too many relationships fall apart, not always from lack of love, either. Sometimes it's a clash of values or the pressure of kids and illness or caring responsibilities or financial trouble. So many things can go wrong in even the best of relationships.'

Aerin gave him a sad smile. 'I know all of that, but you have closed yourself off from ever experiencing love. I don't know how you can do it, how it's even possible to be so locked down you can't feel normal feelings. It's not healthy, surely?'

Drake lifted her chin with his finger, locking his gaze on hers. 'Don't try and fix me, Goldilocks. I'm fine the way I am.' But there was a part of him that was starting to recognise he wasn't as fine as he had once thought. His playboy lifestyle had already begun to lose its shine even before Aerin turned up at his office to ask him to be a stand-in date.

He found his work fulfilling and time-consuming but coming home to any empty house each day was not something he looked forward to as much as he had before. Being with Aerin had shown him a new way of living. It was as if a locked door in his brain had been opened just a sliver, allowing light and healing into all his dark spaces. But how could he allow the thought of letting go of the past any traction? How could he possibly hope that his relationship with Aerin would be the perfect one she was looking for? He had faced horrendous failure at fifteen. He had spent the time since avoiding it. Entering into a permanent relationship with someone, even someone as lovely as Aerin, was only going to reinforce his deepest fear—failure. Failure to love and to protect.

A defiant light came into her grey-blue eyes. 'But are you fine? You must get lonely at times. You must want more out of your relationships than a quick fling.'

'Why must I?'

Aerin caught her lower lip between her teeth, her eyes shifting from his. 'Because…never mind.' She straightened her shoulders and reset her features into a rictus smile and turned back to the pantry. 'I'm going to rustle up some dinner for us. You made breakfast and lunch…it must be my turn to do something around here.'

Drake stepped closer and placed his hands on the tops of her slim shoulders. He felt her shudder under the gentle press of his hands and heard her soft sigh. He swept her hair over one of her shoulders and leaned down to kiss the sensitive skin just below her hairline on her neck. The flowery fragrance of her hair reminded him of a cottage garden in summer, her skin was like silk against his lips. He slowly turned her to face him, her luminous eyes meeting his. How would he ever look at her in the future without wanting her? How would he return to his old life of casual one-night stands and not think of her touch, her taste, her sweet fragrance that clung to his skin and sent his senses into overdrive?

He brushed his bent knuckles down the creamy slope of her cheek in a light-as-air touch. 'I'm not interested in food right now.'

A light shone in her eyes, a spark of heat similar to the one burning deep in his body, sending flames through his blood. 'What are you interested in?'

Drake brought his mouth down to within a short distance of hers. 'I could tell you or I could show you. You choose.'

'Show me.'

He closed the distance between their mouths and lost himself in the sweet addictive taste of her. His tongue stroked for entry and she opened to him and met him with a sexy dart of her own tongue. Heat exploded in his body, making him hot and hard and hungry for more. She pressed herself closer at the same time as he gathered her tightly in his arms. He loved the feel of her slight frame against him. He loved the anticipation of making love to her, the heady build-up of tension in his body so powerful it was unlike anything he had experienced before. Her hands crept up to wind around his neck, her fingers delving into his hair, sending shivers cascading down his spine in a river of heat.

Aerin made a soft, breathless sound and he deepened the kiss, their tongues dancing and duelling and mating each other into submission. A thrill ran through him at the boldness of her desire for him. No longer shy, she stroked her hand down to the rock-hard heat of his erection, almost sending him over the edge.

'I want you.' Her voice was soft but no less demanding and it delighted him that she was growing in sexual confidence.

'Ditto,' Drake said, sliding his hands underneath the jumper she was wearing. She wasn't wearing a bra, which gave him ready access to her breasts. He bent his head and caressed the tender flesh with his lips and tongue. She responded with little gasps and groans and pushed herself against him in a silent plea for more.

He slid his hands down to her waist, holding her against the throbbing pulse of his body. 'The kitchen isn't the most comfortable place to make love,' he said. 'Let's take this upstairs.'

'I'm not sure my legs are going to get me that far after that kiss.'

'That's easily fixed.' Drake swept her up in his arms and strode towards the door.

Aerin gave a playful squeal. 'What are you doing? You'll wreck your back carrying me all the way upstairs.'

'Don't worry, I work out.'

'I know you do.' She stroked one of her hands along the bunched muscles of his arm. 'Impressive.'

They got to the bedroom a short time later and while Drake was breathing heavily it had nothing to do with carrying Aerin. Or at least not because of her weight. It was the feel of her in his arms, the warm lithe body pressed against his, knowing she wanted him as much as he wanted her. He laid her down on the bed and stood looking at her for a moment. Her hair was splayed out over the pillows in a golden cloud, her eyes were shining with anticipation, her smile like a ray of sunshine. She was wearing a jumper and leggings and he soon peeled them off her body, before stripping off his own clothes.

He got a condom from his wallet and came down beside her on the bed. She reached for him without saying a word. But what else needed to be said? The mutual desire that crackled between them had not lessened but grown in intensity.

Aerin stroked her hands down his chest to his abdomen, slowly, slowly, slowly, ramping up the tension in his body to breaking point. Her touch wreaked havoc on his self-control. Red-hot pleasure shot through his body, luring him to the abyss where the dark magic of oblivion beckoned.

Drake had to stop her taking him over the edge because he wanted to ensure her pleasure first. He drew her hand away from his body and kissed his way down from her breasts to her belly, lingering over her feminine mound, breathing in the musky scent of her body that signalled her high arousal. He used his fingers to separate her folds, then tasted the honeyed dew of her desire with his tongue. She squirmed and whimpered as he increased the rhythm of his caresses, her body bucking and arching as she orgasmed. Her cries of release made him want her all the more. Her passion was so unfettered, so unrestrained it made him wonder if she would find the same freedom to express her sexuality with someone else.

Someone else...

Drake wished he could eradicate the thought from his mind. He didn't want to think about her with anyone else. He didn't want to think of her making love with some other guy who wouldn't make her pleasure a priority. A guy who might exploit her or pressure her into doing things she wasn't comfortable doing.

Aerin let out a long shuddering sigh and reached for him again. 'Can I try something on you?'

'What?'

She gave a sultry smile and wriggled down his body. 'I want to taste you like you tasted me.'

'You don't have to. I don't want you to do anything you're not comfortable doing.'

'But I am comfortable with you.'

And Drake was comfortable with her. Way too comfortable. To the point where he was wondering how he was going to manage without her going forward. He shuddered at the thought of her mouth and tongue on his most intimate flesh. How could he say no? 'Okay. But if you don't want to go the whole way, then don't.'

But she did and of course it was mind-blowing, earth-shattering and sent him into a tailspin from which he thought he might not ever recover...

CHAPTER NINE

LATER THAT NIGHT after dinner, Aerin took the opportunity to text Ruby and Harper about not being back in time for work as planned. Harper called her instead of texting a reply.

'What's going on?'

'Nothing. We just got caught out with the weather.'

'Who's we? Are the rest of your reunion friends there too?'

Aerin bit her lip. How could she lie to one of her closest friends? Especially Harper, who had been lied to throughout her childhood by the father who abandoned her even before she was born and then failed to come to her aid when her mother died. 'You can't tell anyone but I'm here with Drake. Alone. He took me to a lovely cottage in the country because the reunion hotel room was a bit cramped. It only had one bed and no sofa. But then a weather front came over and we got snowed in. We can't leave until it melts.'

Harper whistled through her teeth. 'Way to go, sister. Snowbound with your worst enemy.'

'He's not any such thing.' Aerin knew she sounded overly defensive but couldn't strip back her tone in time.

'Well, well, well,' Harper said. 'Looks like you two have kissed and made up.'

There was a beat or two of telling silence.

'And not only kissed, if I'm any judge,' Harper said.

'I'm not saying anything because I promised Drake I wouldn't. He doesn't want our…erm, involvement to be in the gossip pages. Nor do I want my family to know.'

'Hon, are you sure you're not getting in over your head? You're a babe in the woods when it comes to men like Drake Cawthorn.'

'I know what I'm doing.'

'So, what happens when you come back home? Will your secret involvement continue?'

'No, that's the agreement. We end it as soon as we get back to London.' Her heart ached at the thought of ending their relationship. How would she handle it?

Harper sighed. 'Oh, hon. I can sense heartbreak looming.'

'You were the one who suggested I ask him to come to the reunion with me,' Aerin pointed out.

'I know and that's why I'm worried about you now. You've got the softest heart and he has the hardest. How is that ever going to work out?'

It was Aerin's turn to sigh. 'Tell me something I don't already know.'

Two days later, although the snow was still thick on the ground, the sun was out and shining, making the countryside look all the more stunningly beautiful. London seemed a long way away and Aerin dreaded returning, knowing it would spell the end of this magical time with Drake.

Drake joined her outside and squinted against the blinding bright sun. He held his hand up to shield his eyes. 'The snow won't last long with a bit of sunshine.'

'No...'

He lowered his hand from his face and looked at her. 'This is the first time in a long time that I've taken time off work. I need to do it more often but there's always another client or a pressing court issue.'

Aerin looped her arm through his and he drew her closer to his side. 'You've always been a high achiever. Tom told me you left everyone in the shade at university.'

He gave a soft grunt. 'Yes, well, I had something to prove, I guess.' He gave her a grim smile and continued, 'I wanted my life to count for something to make up for the loss of my mother and sister. They didn't get to reach their potential, so I made sure I more than reached mine.'

Aerin leaned her head against his shoulder, wishing she could take away his pain but knowing it was impossible. How could anyone get over such a tragic loss? 'I'm sure they would be very proud of you.' She waited a beat and asked, 'What was your sister's name?'

'Natasha but I always called her Tash. My mother's name was Rosemary.'

There was a long silence before he spoke again.
'Thank you.'

'For?'

'For not asking what my father's name was. I hate remembering him in any capacity. His whole life was built
on lies and deception and double-dealing. My mother
was drawn in by his charm and only realised her mistake
when she gave birth to me. Everything changed after
that. He became even more controlling, and it only got
worse when Tash was born two years later. I did all I
could to protect them, but it wasn't enough. I can't tell
you how many times I begged my mother to go to the
police, but she was too frightened to do so. I think she
knew he would kill her if she left him. I didn't understand that dynamic as a kid but I do now.'

Aerin put her arms around his waist and held him
tightly. 'Oh, Drake, I can't bear the thought of all
you've suffered.'

His arms gathered her closer, his chin resting on
the top of her head. 'Enough talk of my awful past.
Do you know what I'd like to do right now?'

'Make love?'

He gave a short laugh. 'Not here in the snow. When
was the last time you made a snowman?'

'Years and years.'

'Shall we?'

Aerin smiled. 'I'd love to.'

Within minutes they had built a rather impres-
sive-looking snowman with black stones for eyes and
twigs for arms. Aerin stood back to look at their hand-
iwork. 'We need a carrot for his nose.'

'Hold that thought.' Drake went back to the house and came out soon after with a carrot. 'Here you go. One carrot as requested.'

Aerin placed the carrot on the snowman and stood back. 'I wonder how long before he melts?'

'Who knows?' There was a strange quality to Drake's voice, and when she glanced up at him he was looking at the snowman with a frown carved deep in his forehead.

Maybe he was thinking about his own frozen state. His locked-away heart that he refused to open to love. What would it take to melt the armour around him?

And was she the one to do it?

The sunshine did its job, so when Aerin and Drake woke the next morning, the roads were clear enough for travelling back to Edinburgh. Aerin was determined not to be teary or clingy when it came time to say goodbye. Within a few hours, they had landed back in London and Drake drove her to her flat. He had been silent for most of the journey, as had she.

Drake carried her luggage up to her flat and set it inside the door. He straightened and smiled but it didn't reach his eyes, which were shadowed and shuttered. 'I guess I'd better get going.'

'Would you like a cup of tea or something?' She could have bitten her tongue off for sounding so eager to keep him with her a little longer.

A flicker of something passed over his face. 'I'd better be on my way.' He hesitated for a long moment and then reached for her, holding her in a tight hug

against his tall frame. 'Take care of yourself, Goldilocks.' His voice was so husky it sounded as if he had
swallowed a handful of gravel.

A choking lump formed in her throat. 'I will.'

Drake slowly released her and looked at her upturned face for another beat or two. 'Keep sending
those clients my way, okay?'

Aerin forced a smile to her lips. 'I will.'

And then he was gone.

Drake let out a breath he had been holding for what felt
like years. So, that was it. Goodbye and thanks for the
memories. But it was different somehow. Different because he would be seeing her again, either at her parents'
or brother's house or through their work connections. He
would have to put the memories of their time together in
Scotland to one side. He must not think about her in that
way. He must not recall the gentle touch of her hands,
the sweet but explosive heat of her mouth. The warm
silky welcome of her body and the earth-shattering release that powered through them both.

He shuddered and strode to his car, hunching his
shoulders against the icy rain that had started. He had
never once broken his vow of sobriety. Never once had
he craved the taste of alcohol to numb his senses, to blank
out his mind. But right then, he wished he could find a
way to numb himself from the pain of saying goodbye.

'So, how was your trip?' Cathleen, his secretary,
asked the following morning.

'Fine.'

She leaned back in her chair and surveyed him with an assessing look. 'First holiday you've taken in years.'

'It wasn't a holiday.'

'What was it, then?'

It was the best time I've had in for ever. I feel like a different man. I feel freer than I've felt in years.

Disturbed by his torrent of thoughts, Drake masked his features and leafed through the sheaf of papers she had prepared for him on her desk. 'I was doing a favour for a friend.'

'Aerin Drysdale, right?'

He flicked faster through the paperwork, trying not to picture Aerin's naked body in bed beside him. Trying not to remember how it felt to hold her in his arms while she came apart in pleasure. Trying to remind himself that it was dumb of him to be thinking about her at all. Their fling was over. It had to be. 'I need to catch up on a bit of work for the next couple of days. I don't want to be interrupted unless it's an emergency.'

'Okay.'

He turned for his office further down the corridor and then stopped and looked back at Cathleen. 'Could you send Ms Drysdale some flowers?'

'What will I tell the florist to write on the card?'

Drake paused to think about it but couldn't come up with anything. 'Just get them to deliver them here and I'll drop them off myself after work.'

What are you doing? You can't last a day without seeing her?

He dismissed the voice of his conscience. He

wanted to check on her, to see her again, to reassure himself she was still okay with the end of their fling. He wasn't okay with it, though, and that was a problem, one he had not faced before. Would it be an option to extend their fling? To spend more time together? He weighed it up in his mind. Aerin knew he wasn't the for-ever type. She knew he wasn't the type of man who could or ever would tick all her boxes. So why not continue their fling for a little while longer?

Are you out of your mind? his conscience prodded him, with another warning, but he pushed it aside.

He was only dropping off a bunch of flowers, not going down on bended knee.

That was never going to happen.

Aerin heard Mutley barking in Mr McPhee's flat opposite. She had only seen her neighbour once since she'd got back and he hadn't looked well. She'd promised to check on him after work but he wasn't answering the doorbell. She went back to her flat to fetch the spare key he had insisted on giving her a couple of months ago. She was on her way back to open his door when she heard firm footsteps come up the stairwell. Her heart came to a shuddering halt when she saw it was Drake, carrying a huge bunch of flowers.

Under any other circumstances she would have smiled and given him a hug, but her worries about her neighbour took precedence. 'Drake, can you help me check on Mr McPhee? He's not answering the door and Mutley is barking. I'm worried something is wrong.'

'Sure.' He put the flowers inside her door and then

came over and took Mr McPhee's key from her. He opened the door effortlessly and Mutley came bounding out, yapping loudly and then running back and forth as if to say, *Follow me*.

'Mr McPhee? It's Aerin… Oh, no…' She had only got as far as the sitting room when she saw the old man's slumped figure on the sofa.

Drake moved past her and squatted down beside the sofa and took one of the old man's wrists to search for a pulse. 'Call an ambulance.' His air of command somehow helped her to keep calm, well, calmer than she would have been on her own.

The ambulance was there in under five minutes and the paramedics loaded Mr McPhee onto a stretcher. Aerin filled them in on what she knew about Mr McPhee's health and she was even able to bundle up his collection of medications that he kept in the kitchen.

'Are you his daughter and son-in-law?' one of the paramedics asked.

Aerin wasn't game enough to look at Drake. 'No, I'm his neighbour and Drake is…erm…just a friend.'

'Is there someone to take care of the dog?' the other paramedic said, clearly a dog lover who recognised the distress the poor old dog was feeling with his master semi-conscious on a stretcher.

'Yes, of course, I'll do that,' Aerin said without thinking it through in any detail.

The ambulance left and Aerin let out an exhausted breath. 'Oh, Drake, I'm so glad you showed up when you did. I'm not good at emergencies. I just panic and freeze.'

His arms came around her and held her close. 'You

did great. He'll be well taken care of and hopefully he'll be home soon.'

She swallowed and looked up at him. 'But what if he's not?'

Drake stroked her hair back off her face, a wry smile slanting his mouth. 'That big soft heart of yours is going to get you into trouble one day.'

It already has.

It would be so easy to say the words here and now. They were perched on the end of her tongue like a team of nervous divers, baulking at the distance they had to dive headfirst into. 'Seriously, though,' Aerin said, glancing at the woeful-looking dog at their feet. 'What am I going to do with Mutley? I work full-time and he's used to having Mr McPhee with him all day to take him out for his toilet breaks. If he barks too much, the neighbour will complain to the landlord.'

'What about a dog shelter? Or a boarding kennel?'

'No, he's too old for either of those, especially since he's always been with Mr McPhee.' She chewed at one of her fingernail cuticles, then added, 'I'd take him to my parents, but Mum's developed an allergy to dog hair.'

Mutley shuffled over and sat at Drake's feet and looked up at him imploringly, his tail sweeping the floor like a feather duster.

'He wants you to take him,' Aerin said.

Drake held up his hands like two stop signs. 'Oh, no, I'm no pet-sitter. I work long days and often stay away overnight when I'm—'

'Surely you could put your playboy life on hold

for a week or two? He'd settle better at your place because you have a garden.'

Drake set his mouth in an adamant line but then Mutley whined and wagged his tail again. 'Don't look at me like that.' He growled at the dog without malice.

Aerin laughed. 'He adores you. I think he senses you're a strong leader. Dogs need that, they get nervous if they're not given reliable leadership.'

Drake let out a long ragged-sounding breath. 'I knew it was a mistake coming to see you tonight.'

'Why did you?'

'I wanted to give you some flowers.'

'In person? Why not have them delivered?'

'This is why.' He took her by the upper arms and planted a lingering kiss on her lips.

Aerin melted into his embrace, relishing in the warmth and pent-up passion in his kiss, wanting him so badly it was a hollow ache deep inside.

Some breathless moments later, she eased back to look up at him. 'I'm not sure what's going on. You said our fling had to end once we came back to London.'

Drake stroked his thumb across her lower lip, his eyes hooded. 'It didn't feel right just dropping you off last night and carrying on as if the last few days never happened.'

Aerin tried to keep her hopes in check. What was he actually offering her? 'So, are you saying you want to continue our…involvement?' She was not fond of the term 'fling' when it came to what they had shared together. Those wonderful memories of being in his arms would be tainted if she referred to it as a fling.

Drake took her hands in his. 'I'm not ready to end it.' His voice had a rough edge and his eyes looked haunted.

'But you will end it.' It was a statement, not a question. A fact written on a tablet of stone that weighed down her heart with its cruel veracity. 'Not tonight, not next week but some time soon you will end it.'

'I can only offer you a fling.'

She squeezed her eyes shut on the word. 'Please don't call what we had together a fling. It was much more than that. You know it was.'

Drake squeezed her hands as if he never wanted to let her go. 'I want more time with you.'

'How much time?'

His throat rose and fell over a tight swallow. 'I don't know. I just want more time.'

Aerin knew she should insist on a clean break then and there but what if more time together actually helped him open up even more? He had shared with her so much, things he had not shared with anyone else, not even her older brother, who was his closest friend. Didn't that count for something? Didn't that suggest that *she* could be the key to opening his heart to love? Aerin let out a wobbly breath. 'Okay, but how are we going to keep our involvement a secret?'

A flash of relief lit his gaze and he drew her closer to his body, his arms wrapping around her. 'It's no one's business but ours what is going on between us. I'd like to keep it that way for as long as possible.'

Aerin didn't like to tell him she had more or less told Harper what was going on between them. Harper would have guessed in any case, so too Ruby, but still. 'So, how are we going to do it? I mean, are we going to meet in secret or—?'

'Can you come and stay at my place for a few days?' Drake asked. 'It will help Mutley settle in to have someone familiar there. It's closer to your work and far more private than a tenement flat.'

Aerin's eyes widened. 'Are you sure that's a good idea? I mean, do you ask many of your lovers to stay over?'

'Never, but you're different. Besides, it's only until Mr McPhee comes out of hospital. After that we can reassess.'

'How come you haven't had lovers stay over before?'

Drake's expression was shuttered. 'I've got used to living alone. I've been doing it since I was eighteen. I'm not the most convivial host but I would like you to stay.'

It wasn't a difficult choice, although it should have been given the sharp prods her conscience was giving her. Reminders about her plan for her life, the checklist she had so carefully written in order to find her Mr Perfect. Extending her temporary relationship with Drake Cawthorn was hardly going to help her achieve her goal. Not unless he morphed into the man of her dreams. But then, he already was the man of her dreams but he didn't want to be. He didn't want to be anyone's soulmate. He didn't want to love anyone with his whole heart. But the temptation to have more time with Drake, private time at his lovely home in Bloomsbury, was too much to resist.

He was too much to resist.

CHAPTER TEN

AN HOUR OR so later, Mutley was curled up asleep in his basket on Drake's sitting-room floor in front of the fireplace, snoring as if he belonged on a critical care chest ward. Drake was still wondering what the hell had come over him to agree to mind the scruffy mutt that looked like something out of an alien movie. But it just went to show how Aerin could get him to do almost anything.

Inviting her to stay with him was another thing that surprised him. He wasn't keen on visitors at the best of times. But then, Aerin was hardly a visitor. She was his current lover. For how long, he wasn't sure and that gave him a niggling sense of unease. He was usually very sure of when a fling was going to end, because he was the one who ended it.

But everything about his fling with Aerin was different.

Aerin was sitting on the sofa opposite him with a cup of hot chocolate cradled in her hands. Her slim legs were folded beneath her, her hair a golden cloud around her shoulders. 'Mutley looks quite at home.'

Drake gave a non-committal grunt and took a sip of his own hot drink before putting it on the table beside the sofa. He patted the cushion next to him. 'Why don't you come over here?'

Her eyes lit up and a shy smile curved her mouth. She put her drink down on the coffee table between the two sofas and came over to sit beside him. He laid one arm along the back of the sofa near her shoulders, his other hand picked up one of hers and he raised it to his mouth and kissed her bent knuckles. 'Have you heard how Mr McPhee is doing?'

'Not yet.' She sighed and glanced at her watch on her wrist. 'But I'm not his next of kin so they're hardly likely to tell me much. He has a son, but I don't think he's seen him in ages. I think he might live overseas. Do you think I should try and track him down?'

Drake played with the silky tresses of her hair. 'I can do that for you.'

'Oh, would you? I'd be so grateful. I have a big wedding this weekend and I'm starting to panic about it. I'm usually so organised but, with the reunion and our extended stay in Scotland, I have some serious catching up to do.'

He curled a strand of hair around his finger. 'Where's the wedding? Somewhere local?'

'Kent, on the most beautiful estate the bride's parents own. The service is at a local church. I hope the weather is kind to them, the bride and groom are such a lovely young couple. I want everything to be perfect for them.'

'It's a tricky time of year for a wedding, I would've

thought. Don't most people want a spring or summer wedding?'

'Yes, but the groom is dying of a brain tumour. There isn't time to wait for spring or summer. He might not make it to Christmas.'

Drake frowned. 'That's sad.'

'Yes, it is. But it's so wonderful to see how much they love each other. They truly are soulmates.' Her shoulders slumped on another sigh. 'I'm not sure how Yelena will cope without Viktor. He's her whole world and she is his.'

'It seems a risky business loving someone,' Drake said. 'You stand to lose them one way or the other.'

Aerin looked at him with her clear grey-blue gaze. 'Yes, but that's not a good enough reason to not love at all.'

He forced a smile and threaded his fingers through her hair again. 'Time for bed?'

'We'd better take Mutley out for a toilet break first.'

'I'll do that,' Drake said, rising from the sofa. 'You head on up.'

'Are you sure?'

'Absolutely.'

By the time Drake had taken the old dog out and waited for him to sniff the entire garden for the right place to take a leak, more than half an hour had gone by. Mutley finally waddled back in and went back to his bed in front of the fireplace. Drake offered him a treat, but the dog gave a rattling sigh and lowered his chin to the cushioned bed, giving him a doleful side-eye look.

Drake gave him a gentle scratch behind his ears.

'I know you miss him. But he'll be as good as new soon.'

The old dog blinked at him and then sighed again as if to say: *I don't believe in miracles.*

'Yeah, I hear you, buddy. I don't believe in them either.'

Aerin was in the process of unpacking her overnight bag, shaking out her work clothes for the next day, when Drake came in. 'Thank you for looking after Mutley,' she said. 'But what will we do tomorrow when we're both at work?'

'I've already organised a pet door to be installed. My housekeeper will be here too.'

'Oh, that's great. I can't really take him with me.'

'Yes, well, I'm not sure what the magistrate would say if I turned up with him, either. I guess I could pass him off as a therapy dog.'

Aerin smiled. 'I think he'd be brilliant at it. He's such a sweet old thing.'

Drake began to unbutton his business shirt. 'Do you want a shower before bed?'

'Are you having one?'

His eyes darkened to pitch. 'Want to join me?'

She walked over to him as if programmed like a robot to do everything he commanded. 'Sounds like fun.'

He gave a wolfish smile and peeled the clothes from her body, feasting on her naked form. Aerin stood proudly before him, thrilled at the way he found her so desirable. She set to work on his clothes, enjoying the sight of him fully aroused. He took her by the hand and led her to his luxurious bathroom. The shower was one of those open ones that was big enough for a crowd. He turned on the rainwater shower and once the water was the right temperature, they stepped under the spray.

Aerin tilted her head back, enjoying the water pressure but enjoying even more the pressure building in her body at Drake's closeness. Their wet bodies were locked together under the cascading water, the sensuality of it spine-tingling.

He kissed her firmly, passionately, desperately as if it had been years instead of hours since they last kissed. His hands glided down her wet body, stroking, caressing, stirring her senses into overdrive. He lowered his mouth to each of her breasts, then got on his knees and parted her intimate folds with his fingers, and then caressed her with his lips and tongue.

The orgasm hit her like a crashing wave, pulsing through her so violently she cried out and shook uncontrollably. Drake held her by the hips to stabilise her, the ripples and aftershocks still rumbling through her until finally they dissipated.

Drake straightened and pulled her close to his hardened form, his eyes gleaming in triumph. 'I love watching you come.'

Aerin was still trying to catch her breath. She placed her hands on his chest, stroking his rock-hard muscles and delighting in the heat and strength of him. She moved down his body as he had done to her, intent on subjecting him to the same intimate caress. She took him in her mouth and drew on him, confident now on how to pleasure him. He buckled at the knees and groaned but she kept going, emboldened by the way he was responding to her. He tensed and then spilled his essence, a low deep groan escaping from his lips and his whole body shuddering in the aftermath.

Aerin straightened and smiled at him. 'You sounded like you had a good time too.'

Drake gathered her close in a warm hug, his breathing still ragged. 'The best.'

Aerin was at work the following day with her friends Harper and Ruby. She'd had no choice but to tell them where she was currently staying because Ruby had suggested dropping by her flat that evening after work.

'You're staying with Drake Cawthorn?' Ruby's eyes almost bulged out of her head. 'But why?'

Aerin explained about Mr McPhee's stroke and Mutley needing a temporary home while Mr McPhee was in the rehabilitation centre. 'And I like being with Drake.'

'You're in love with him,' Harper said.

'Yes, I think I am.' Aerin sighed and continued, 'Strike that. I know I am.'

'How many boxes does he tick on your checklist?' Harper asked.

'Not many.'

'How many?' Ruby asked.

Aerin rose from her chair and paced the room. 'I think I made a mistake writing a checklist. I mean, how many people could tick every box? I know he's not perfect, but then nor am I. But I can't imagine life without him now. I love being with him.'

'Neither of us can tell you what to do,' Harper said. 'Ruby and I have been in your situation—in love with a man who we thought could never love us back. But I'm reluctant to say things will work out for you like they did for us because life doesn't always work out the way we want.'

'I know and I'm being careful.'

'But moving in with him?' Ruby said, frowning. 'What do your parents and brother think?'

'They don't know we're seeing each other. Anyway, I'm only staying with him until Mr McPhee comes home from rehab and can take Mutley back.'

Harper and Ruby exchanged worried looks.

'Please stop worrying about me,' Aerin said. 'I do enough of that myself. I know this is crazy. I know it but I can't help myself. I love Drake and I want to be with him.'

'Have you told him how you feel?' Harper asked.

'No.'

Ruby chewed at her lower lip. 'Are you going to at some point?'

'I don't know…maybe.'

'He'll probably end it before you get the chance,' Harper said. 'And that is going to hurt big time.'

'I know,' Aerin said on a heartfelt sigh.

Drake went on a stop-and-sniff-and-shuffle walk with Mutley after work. It was dark and cold and wet, but he had kind of got used to the old dog's company over the last week. But the thing he most looked forward to was when Aerin came in from work. He loved waking up next to her in the morning. He loved going to sleep with her in his arms at night. He loved sharing a meal with her and chatting about the days' events.

He loved…

He stopped as if he had slammed into an invisible wall. No. No. No. Love was not part of what he felt for Aerin. They were having a fling, an extended fling that was a little bit different from his usual ones. That didn't mean he was falling in love. He had no intention of falling in love with her or anyone. Ever.

Drake was only just back from walking the dog when his phone rang. He glanced at the screen and saw it was Aerin. He ignored the little jump of his heart, the tick of his blood, the thrum of excitement at hearing her voice. 'Hey, I thought you'd be home by now. Are you working late?'

'No, but I have to drop by my flat to pick up some things. I didn't bring much with me last week.'

'I'll swing by your office and take you.'

'Are you sure?'

'Of course. We can grab a bite of dinner somewhere afterwards.'

There was a little silence.

'Are you sure that's a good idea? Us being seen dining out in public?' Aerin asked. 'What if it gets back to my family?'

Drake was starting to realise the clandestine nature of their fling was a little compromising for someone as upfront and honest as Aerin. She loved her family dearly, so lying to them about her involvement with him must be hurting her. But then, her family weren't being completely honest with her either. Her brother Tom had met with him only the day before about seeking a divorce. It wasn't something Drake was at liberty to talk to Aerin about. She had such rose-coloured glasses on when it came to relationships. It would crush her to find her brother was leaving his wife. But to Drake, it was only further confirmation that most relationships were doomed to fail one way or the other.

'They'll have to find out sooner or later,' Drake said. 'We can't hide for ever.'

'But we're not going to be together for ever, are we?'

'No, but that doesn't mean we can't go out to dinner like a normal couple.' Drake was aware of the tension in his voice and tried to take a calming breath.

There was another beat or two of silence.

'Drake, don't bother to pick me up. I think I'll stay at my flat tonight. I need some time to think about things. I'll catch up with you tomorrow.'

A pain seized him in the chest. A panicked feeling as if he was losing control of a situation he had thought was well under control. 'If that's what you want.' It wasn't what he wanted at all but he was not going to beg her to change her mind.

'It's what I need right now.'

You're what I need right now. You're everything I need.

The words were inside his mouth, but he couldn't get them past the stiff line of his lips.

'Drake?'

'Yes.' His voice was cold as the rain dripping down the back of his coat collar.

'I thought you must have hung up on me.'

'I have to go,' Drake said. 'Mutley needs his dinner.' He ruthlessly clicked off his phone and shoved it in his pocket.

Aerin slipped her phone in her tote bag, distressed by the outcome of her conversation with Drake. But equally determined to spend a night at her flat to get her thoughts together, to get some perspective. Talking to Ruby and Harper had made her realise the trap she had fallen into. She was living in hope that Drake would fall in love with her. And yes, that had worked for her friends, but it didn't mean it would work for her. She had always been an optimist, glass-half-full type of person but she was starting to see how deluded she was in thinking everything would magically work out.

Sometimes, tragically, it didn't.

The doorbell rang later that night and Aerin's heart leapt in hope. Had Drake changed his mind? Had he regretted his abrupt end to their conversation? Had he come to apologise? To beg her to come back and stay with him tonight? But when she opened the door, it was her brother, Tom, standing there. 'Tom? What are you doing here?'

'Can we talk?'

Aerin stepped back to let him in. 'Of course.' She closed the door behind him. 'Are you okay?'

He drew in a breath and released it in a staggered stream. 'I saw Drake yesterday.'

'You did? He never mentioned anything about it.'

Tom frowned. 'When did you last see him?'

Aerin only then realised her gaffe. 'Oh, erm, I run into him from time to time, you know, referring clients to him and so on.' She could feel her cheeks heating and could barely look her brother in the eye. 'How are you? How is Saskia?'

Tom rubbed a hand down his face. 'We're getting a divorce.'

Aerin stared at him as if he had just told her he was an alien from outer space. 'What?'

He compressed his lips. 'That's why I met with Drake yesterday.'

'So, you're the one instigating a divorce? But why?'

'It's not working any more. Saskia is clearly unhappy.'

'But she's had, what, two or three miscarriages? How could you expect her to be happy? It doesn't mean she doesn't love you.'

Tom's shoulders drooped and two spots of red appeared high on his cheekbones. 'I made a stupid mistake.'

Aerin's stomach dropped like a novice diver pushed off the ten-metre diving board. 'Oh, no…'

'It was dumb and crazy and I still can't explain why I did it. I had a one-night stand with a woman I know from work. It meant nothing.'

'I never thought you would cheat on Saskia.' Anger and disappointment laced her tone in equal measure. For all of her life she had looked up to and idolised her older brother. And now she was finding he had clay feet after all. She had thought he had the perfect marriage A solid and for-ever marriage like her parents. The marriage she aspired to have one day. But now she was beginning to realise love wasn't always perfect. Was any relationship perfect?

'I'm sorry,' Tom said. 'I know how hard this is to hear but I wanted to tell you face to face.'

'Do Mum and Dad know?'

'Not yet. I'm going to see them this weekend. I'm not looking forward to it. I can only imagine what Dad will say. And Mum will be shattered. You know how much she loves Saskia.'

'How is Saskia?'

'Angry, hurt, disappointed.' He rubbed at his temple as if a tension headache was building.

'Has she agreed to the divorce?'

'Yes.'

'But she might change her mind. She needs time to heal, to forgive you. To learn to trust you again.'

Tom gave a rueful twist of his mouth that was nowhere near a smile. 'I'm not sure that's going to happen any time soon.'

'Do you still love her?'

He held her gaze for a moment or two then sighed and looked away. 'Of course I do. I just lost my way for a bit. The stress of losing all those babies and not being able to make it right for her did my head in. I've been a prize jerk. I didn't think I was the sort of man who would cheat on his wife. She deserves better.'

'Oh, Tom, I wish I could wave a magic wand and make everything right for you and Saskia, but I have my own issues to work through.' She licked her dry lips and continued, 'I've been seeing Drake.'

Tom's eyebrows shot up. 'Seeing him as in...?' He left the sentence hanging.

'I asked him to my school reunion in Scotland and we kind of drifted into a fling. We've been keeping it a secret.'

'You know it won't last. He won't allow it to.'

'I know and that's what I'm working through.'

'You're in love with him.'

Aerin screwed up her face. 'Is it that obvious?'

'Have you told him?'

'No. Do you think I should?'

Tom gave her a grim look. 'I'm hardly the one to be dishing out relationship advice.'

'But you know him so well.'

'No one knows Drake well,' Tom said. 'He's always been a bit of a closed-book type of guy.'

'Good luck with Mum and Dad. I'd come with you for moral support, but I have a wedding in Kent this weekend.'

'Thanks, but this is something I have to face on my own.'

Aerin closed the door to her brother a short time later and leaned back against it with a heavy sigh. It was like a bad dream to think of Tom and Saskia breaking up. She couldn't get her head around her brother's fall from grace. It was so unlike him and yet, who knew what anyone was capable of while under extreme stress?

CHAPTER ELEVEN

DRAKE HAD TO force himself not to text or call Aerin all day the next day. As someone who enjoyed periods of solitude to reflect on things, he was the last person who should be criticising her for wanting a bit of space. But he wanted her, and it was killing him to be left hanging, not knowing if she wanted to continue their fling or not.

But when he got back from his evening walk with Mutley, he found Aerin sitting on the step outside his house.

'Why haven't you used the key I gave you?' he asked.

She rose from the step and huddled further into her coat. 'I didn't feel comfortable letting myself in.' She bent down to pet Mutley, who, unlike him, was a lot less inhibited about showing how excited he was to see her. The silly old dog yapped and wagged its tail and panted as if it were going to have a heart attack in delight.

'Let's get out of this infernal cold,' Drake growled. 'Tell me why I live in London again?'

Aerin gave a soft laugh. 'It's hard not to think about a tropical island in the sun right now, that's for sure.'

Drake could think of no one he would enjoy being with on a tropical island more than her. Maybe that would solve the problem of keeping their fling a secret. They could take a holiday to some exotic far-away location where they could relax and soak up the sun.

He led the way inside his house, and Mutley immediately shook his wet fur, sending droplets of water all over the floor. 'How's Mr McPhee doing?'

'He's progressing well,' Aerin said, shrugging off her coat. 'He's using a walker, which he hates but he realises he needs it for balance.'

'It must be hard to get old and not be able to do the things you want to do.'

'Yes…'

Drake took her coat and hung it on the stand near the door. 'I'm sorry I ended our conversation so abruptly last night.'

'That's okay. I did kind of spring it on you about staying at my place instead of here. But just as well I did, as Tom dropped around unannounced.'

'Oh? How was he?'

'Why didn't you tell me you saw him the other day?'

Drake shrugged off his own coat and hung it next to hers. 'He saw me as a client, that's why. I don't break client confidentiality.'

'But surely you could have told me? I'm his sister and you and I are…are…in a relationship.'

Drake raised his scarred eyebrow. 'And here I was calling it a fling, silly me.' He knew his tone was mocking. He knew his expression was cynical, but he was cornered by her use of the term *relationship*. It was too…serious. Too confining. Too threatening.

Aerin pursed her lips, staring at him for a long moment without speaking. 'Is that all I am to you? Just another one of your casual lovers?'

'No, of course not.'

'Then tell me what you feel about me.'

Drake opened and closed his mouth, not sure he could find the words to describe how he felt about her. 'I care about you. You're a nice person to be around.'

'You care about me.' Her tone was jaded. 'Would you say you liked me?'

'Of course I like you.'

'What about love?'

His throat suddenly constricted. 'What about it?'

Her gaze was direct. 'Do you love me?'

Drake disguised a swallow, but it was as if he were choking on razorblades. 'Why are you asking me that? We agreed on a short-term fling. Love has nothing to do with two people enjoying a mutual attraction to each other.'

Her small chin came up to a defiant height. 'You won't say it, will you? You act like a man in love and yet you can't or won't say the words.'

Drake wanted to plug his ears like a wilful child and chant *la-la-la* so he didn't have to listen. 'And I suppose you're going to tell me you've fallen madly in love with me?'

Her eyes glittered. 'Would there be any point?'

'No.'

'Because those words frighten you. They make you uncomfortable. They make you feel vulnerable. But I'm going to say them anyway. I love you, Drake. I think I fell in love with you when you first kissed me. I didn't expect such a thing to happen. I certainly never saw you as my Mr Perfect. But I can't help feeling the way I do. I don't want to be in a fling with you. I want more than that.'

Drake raked a hand through his hair, his chest so tight he could barely draw in a breath. 'You're probably confusing good physical chemistry with something else.'

'I know my own heart. I know what I feel. Don't fob me off with it being infatuation or due to my lack of experience.'

'I'm not the settling-down type, I told you that from the get-go.'

'I know and I shouldn't have allowed things to progress the way they did but I couldn't help it. I wanted you and you wanted me and the rest, as they say, is history, or at least it is now.'

He frowned and narrowed his gaze. 'What do you mean?'

She gave him a sad smile and plucked her coat off the hook. 'It's time to say goodbye. I'm ending our relationship before any more damage is done. You're not ready for love. You have too much armour around your heart. And only you can remove it.'

Drake took a step towards her but then pulled himself into line. He had to let her go. He couldn't demand anything of her. He didn't have the right. He shoved his hands into his trouser pockets to keep them from reaching for her. 'You do realise we'll still have to see each other at times.' His voice sounded as frosty as the wintry air outside.

'I don't see why we have to.'

He pointed to the dog sitting at his feet. 'What about him?'

Aerin glanced at Mutley and then back at Drake. 'I'm sure you can deliver him to Mr McPhee some time without running into me. Text me and I'll make sure I'm not around if it makes you feel that uncomfortable.'

He thinned his lips into a cynical smile. 'So, you'd rather not see me? Fine. You won't.'

Aerin pressed her lips together. 'I think it's probably for the best. A clean break.'

She put her coat on and it took everything in him not to help her with it as he usually would. But he knew if his hands touched her again, he would not be able to let her go.

He held the door open for her instead. 'Can I give you a lift?' He wasn't that much of a bastard to let her find her way home alone.

'My car is up the street.'

'I'll walk you to it.'

'There's no need.'

'Indulge me.'

She gave a sigh of resignation. 'Okay.'

They walked along the street until they came to her car. Drake opened her driver's door for her and waited until she had clipped on her seat belt before closing it. He stepped back on the pavement and walked back to his house without even waving goodbye.

Aerin was in a final meeting with Ruby and Harper before the wedding in Kent that weekend, so told them of her decision to end things with Drake.

'Oh, hon,' Harper said, giving her a hug. 'I know how hurt and miserable you must be feeling. I wish I could say it will all work out in the end but that's not how life pans out sometimes.'

'It's so heartbreaking for you,' Ruby said, also enveloping her in a hug. 'But you've only been in a fling with him for a short time. Maybe he's not sure of his feelings yet.'

Aerin stepped out of Ruby's embrace and painted on a brave smile. 'Thanks for your support. It's hard but I'm determined to get through it. The hardest thing will be watching him go back to his playboy lifestyle. It's going to really sting to see him out and about with someone else.'

'Yes, of course that's going to be tough to face,' Harper said. 'But hopefully, you'll soon find your Mr Perfect and your time with Drake will be just a distant memory.'

Aerin had a feeling she would not forget about her time with Drake in a hurry. And she had an even

bigger feeling that her notion of a Mr Perfect waiting out there for her might be a fantasy she needed
to let go of and fast.

Drake called in to see Mr McPhee a few days later
at the rehabilitation centre. He had planned to bring
Mutley in with him for a visit but when he rang the
centre, they said it was against their policy to allow
pets in. He had only been in Mr McPhee's room a few
minutes when he realised the centre was not the place
he would send any of his relatives to—if he had any.
The old man was clearly miserable, and the meal that
was congealing on a tray was not fit for a stray dog,
let alone an elderly person who needed good nutri-
tion to get back on his feet.

'How are you doing?' Drake asked.

'Not so bad.' Mr McPhee tried to smile but couldn't
quite pull it off. 'How's my wee laddie, eh? Aerin told
me you're doing a grand job of taking care of him
for me.'

'It's no bother at all,' Drake said, realising with a
jolt it was true. He enjoyed the old mutt's company,
especially now that Aerin had ended their fling. And
the walks morning and evening, stop-start as they
were, did take his mind off things…a bit. 'But he
misses you. And I bet you're missing him.'

'I am…' Mr McPhee sighed and looked away.

'Has your son been in yet?' Drake had managed
to track down Mr McPhee's son, but he got the sense
the son was not all that interested in visiting his old
and frail father.

'Yes, but he can't get here for a wee bit. He's a busy man. Runs his own company in Spain.'

In his work as a lawyer, Drake had met too many relatives like Mr McPhee's son. People who were too busy to take any interest in their elderly relatives' welfare while they were still alive but who were the first to phone to ask when the estate was being finalised once they had passed away.

'Have you seen Aerin?' He was annoyed at himself for asking but he was so desperate for news of her. He was acting like a lovesick fool but he couldn't seem to help it.

'She came in yesterday on her way to a wedding in Kent, bless her.'

Drake licked his suddenly dry lips. What had Aerin told the old man about their relationship?

Mr McPhee must have sensed his discomfiture and said, 'She put me straight on your relationship, that you're just friends.'

Drake was worried they might not even be that now. 'I'm not what she's looking for.'

Mr McPhee eyeballed him. 'Why do you think that?'

'Has she talked about her checklist?'

'Och, aye, it's not a bad idea in today's world to know what you want and then go and look for it. My Maisie was the same, so organised and always knew what she wanted.' He gave a soft chuckle and then his gaze became wistful. 'I wasn't in with a chance at the beginning, to tell you the truth. I had a lot to learn but

I worked hard and won her over in the end. I learned that you don't find your soulmate, you become one.'

You don't find your soulmate, you become one.

The words were so profound, so wise and insightful, Drake wanted to jot them down in his notes folder in his phone so he wouldn't forget them. Maybe he had a lot to learn too. Maybe it was time for a bit of self-reflection about his attitude to relationships. He knew it stemmed from his tragic past. But how could he move past it?

'You must miss her terribly,' Drake said.

'Oh, I do,' the old man sighed. 'But I could have lost her so much earlier by not changing in order to win her over. I'd never told anyone I loved them until Maisie. Then I told her every day we were married, and those three words were the last words she heard before she took her last breath.'

I could have lost her so much earlier by not changing...

But Drake had lost Aerin. He had lost her by not recognising what he felt for her. The feelings that had grown from the moment he'd kissed her, but he had tried to squash, to ignore, to crush. Feelings that had sprouted and grown inside him regardless, nurtured by the sunshine of her smile, the healing magic of her touch. He'd been too afraid to speak his feelings out loud.

But he wasn't afraid now. The old man's wise words had triggered a realisation that he only had one life and what would that life look like without love? Without Aerin? A sad and lonely empty life. His father had destroyed Drake's family but why should he allow his father to destroy his ability to love? Not all love was toxic. Not all love failed. Not all love was perfect, but it was love, and he realised now he couldn't live without it. He could not escape the tragic end that came to his mother and sister, but he could escape the emotional prison his father's actions had placed him in.

Life was worth living to the full. Loving was part of being fully human. There was no guarantee he wouldn't end up sad and lonely as an elderly widower. He thought about the bravery of the young couple marrying this weekend in Kent, the courage of the young bride, Yelena, marrying her sweetheart, Viktor, even though he hadn't long to live. Drake was a fool to fail to grab life with both hands now and enjoy everything loving someone with your whole heart offered.

Drake put his hand on Mr McPhee's shoulder. 'I'm going to have you transferred to somewhere nicer than this. Somewhere you can have Mutley with you for part of the day. How does that sound?'

The old man's eyes watered. 'It sounds expensive. I don't have the money for anything like that. I'm fine here. Don't worry. I'll make do.'

Drake took one of the old man's craggy hands in both of his. 'I owe you for making me see what I couldn't see before. I love Aerin like you loved your Maisie. I'm going to tell her now, even though I'll be gatecrashing a wedding to do it.'

Mr McPhee beamed. 'That's my lad, you go for it. I'll be cheering for you all the way.'

Aerin stood at the back of the church as the young bride and groom exchanged their vows. It was sad and poignant and happy at the same time. The groom was in a wheelchair, too frail to walk, but the bride stood proudly beside him and promised to love him in sickness and health, till death do us part. Harper was doing the photography and Aerin could see her every now and again brushing at her eyes before she took the next shot. Her assistant running the video was also having trouble holding back tears. Jack was in the back pew, bouncing Marli on his knee, not far from where Aerin was sitting. Ruby and Lucas were further along, holding hands, the love they felt for each other plain for all to see.

It wasn't often that the wedding planner and caterer and photographer's partners were invited to their clients' wedding, but Yelena and Viktor had insisted on them being there. Of course Aerin didn't have a partner, and it was particularly sad to be sitting, once more, on her own. Maybe it would have been better if she had been brave enough to attend her school reunion on her own and then she wouldn't have this gnawing pain of emptiness and loss.

But then she wouldn't have experienced the magic of falling in love with Drake.

Aerin heard someone come in the church behind her pew, where she was seated on the end of the row.

And then a familiar deep voice asked in a gentle whisper, 'Is there room for me next to you?'

Aerin glanced up in shock to see Drake standing there. Her heart banged in her chest as loudly as the church bells had done outside earlier. What was he doing here? Dared she hope he had come to see her? No, she dared not hope. She had learned her lesson by now. She had to be sensible and level-headed about Drake Cawthorn.

'Of course.' She shuffled along, her pulse suddenly racing. 'I thought you weren't a fan of weddings?' she said softly so no one else could hear. A musical piece was being played by the wedding couple's friend, so it offered a quick moment to find out why he was here.

Drake gave a mock shudder and smiled at her. 'I'll have to get used to them.'

'Why's that?'

'Because how else will I marry you?'

Aerin stared at him with wide eyes, her heart skipping, her mouth dropping open. 'Are you...*proposing*?' She said the word as if it was the most unthinkable thing he would ever bring himself to do. Because, for the last few days, that was exactly what she had accepted. He didn't love her. He didn't want her to be with him for ever.

His dark eyes twinkled and he leaned closer to speak against her ear. 'I love you and I want you to be my wife. I couldn't wait until later to ask you. I'm sorry about gatecrashing the wedding but I couldn't waste another minute without you.'

Aerin was overjoyed, but she was forced to restrain herself due to the wedding service, which was resuming now the musical performance was coming to a close. So many feelings bubbled up inside her she could barely keep still. She was about as restless as little Marli, who was babbling and bouncing on her daddy's knee further along the row. 'I love you too. So very much. And yes, I will marry you.'

Drake pressed a brief kiss to her lips and then took her left hand and laid it on his thigh. He stroked her bare ring finger, his touch gentle, almost reverent. 'I've come without a ring. I thought we could choose one together.'

'I think that would be a lovely thing to do.'

'I also wrote a poem on my way here, given that was, what, number six or seven on your checklist?'

Aerin tried but failed to suppress a giggle, but no one seemed to notice. 'Number seven. Six is: *must have a pet or want one.*'

'Does Mutley count? I've grown quite fond of him, even if he leaves hair everywhere and farts a lot.'

Aerin smiled. 'So, what's your poem?'

'Roses are red, violets are blue, I want you in my life, as my loving wife, so please say "I do".'

'I do.'

The wedding service finally ended and Drake took Aerin's hand and led her outside to the watery sunshine. 'You've made me the happiest of men. I didn't think I could ever be happy again, not after what happened when I was fifteen. But you've made me want more out of my life. I can't live in fear of loss any more. Everybody has to face it at some point. Look at this brave young couple. They'll have to face it sooner than most and yet they've just demonstrated their love for each other.'

'Oh, Drake…' Aerin hugged him so tightly she was sure she would either break her arms or crack his ribs. 'I love you so much. I was so shocked to see you come into the church. I thought I must be dreaming. It's like all my wishes and dreams have come true.'

He brought her left hand up to his lips and kissed the back of her hand. 'My darling Aerin, I'm not Mr Perfect but I'll work on it so I can become him.'

'You're just right as you are.'

He grinned. 'Said like a true Goldilocks.'

EPILOGUE

Christmas, one year later

DRAKE PUT THE last present under the Christmas tree at Aerin's family's house in Buckinghamshire. It was a huge tree, beautifully decorated with baubles and tinsel, and twinkling LED lights. The whole family was gathered, and he was now a bona fide part of that family. It gave him a true sense of belonging he had never felt before. Or maybe it was because he was happy in himself, happy with the man he had become rather than the man he had been. How could he have lived in that emotionless prison for all that time? He would still be in it if not for his beautiful Aerin.

Aerin came up beside him and looped her arm through one of his. 'Isn't it wonderful that Mr McPhee could join us?' Her eyes shone with happiness. 'He's over there chatting to my dad with a whisky in his hand. And Mutley has made himself quite at home near the fire.'

Drake glanced at the old dog, lying on his side, snoring contentedly in front of the roaring fire in the hearth. He had become increasingly close to Hamish McPhee over the past year. Hamish had become the father figure he had longed for all his life, a reliable, well-regulated elder who was wise in his counsel and fun to be around as well. 'I'm glad they both made it this far. I had my doubts there for a while.'

'You saved them both by moving Mr McPhee to the private rehab centre. He never looked back after that. He's even walking without the walker now.'

Drake was pleased with the old man's progress, but he was also pleased with his own. He had had to be rehabilitated into recognising and articulating his feelings. And he had worked at not being so worried about loss. He was preparing for the loss of both Mutley and Mr McPhee, knowing there were some miracles you could not pull off. But young Viktor, the groom from the wedding at Kent last year, was still miraculously with his adoring wife Yelena. A new treatment had become available—hideously expensive, but Drake was happy to donate to such a good cause and it had worked so far. It had bought them some time, and that was surely another thing to celebrate at this time of year.

There had been another happy ending in that Tom and Saskia had decided to work at their relationship rather than to press on with the divorce. They were now back together and expecting a baby in the spring.

Speaking of babies, Harper and Jack were expecting another baby, a boy this time, due in a matter of days. Their other celebration was the success of Jack's first watercolour exhibition, which was a sell-out. Jack had put his dream of being an artist on hold when his father died, in order to take over the running of the family hotel business. But it was with Harper's love and encouragement that he finally got to pursue his love of painting.

Ruby and Lucas had exciting news too—they were expecting a baby. So far the gender was still a secret but Drake knew they would be fabulous parents. It was an experience he was looking forward to in the not so distant future. He had never wanted to be a father until he fell in love with Aerin. She would be the most wonderful mother and he looked forward to raising a family with her. He was confident that their little family would feel secure in his love and protection, unlike the example his own father had set.

Drake took Aerin's left hand where not only a beautiful diamond ring sat but a wedding ring as well. They had married before her thirtieth birthday in January and it had been a fabulous celebration. Only a wedding planner with Aerin's skill set could have organised a fabulous wedding so quickly. It was a day he would never forget as long as he lived. Seeing her walk up the aisle towards him had been the most amazing experience. One that made his heart overflow with love and hope for a long and happy future together.

'Happy, my love?' he asked.

'So happy my heart feels like it is going to burst.'

Drake drew her closer, his own heart feeling so full it was taking up all the room in his chest. 'I wrote you another poem. Want to hear it?'

Her eyes danced. 'Yes, please.'

'I love you as the ocean loves the shore, I love you as the wind loves the autumn leaves, I love you as far and wide as the sky, I love the life we have together, the future as yet unknown. But I love that we can face any weather or any season because we are each other's own.'

'Oh, darling that was perfect!'

'Perfect, eh?' Drake grinned. 'That's what you are, my love. Perfect in every possible way.'

* * * * *

COMING SOON!

We really hope you enjoyed reading this book.
If you're looking for more romance, be sure to
head to the shops when new books are
available on

Thursday 2ⁿᵈ February

To see which titles are coming soon, please visit
millsandboon.co.uk/nextmonth

MILLS & BOON

MILLS & BOON®

Coming next month

THE HOUSEKEEPER'S INVITATION TO ITALY
Cathy Williams

"I'm not following you. Where is he going to move to? London? Leonard has always told me how much he hates London."

"Not that he's actually been there more than a handful of times," Alessio returned drily. "But no. London wasn't what I had in mind."

"Then where?"

"I have a place at Lake Garda in northern Italy. It's close enough to get there on my private jet in a matter of hours so the trip shouldn't be too taxing for him."

"Oh, right. Okay."

"If we plan on leaving in roughly a week's time, it will give me sufficient time to get the ball rolling with the company so that I can install some of my own people to tie up all the loose ends. I'll also have enough time for my PA to source the best crew available to get this job done here and of course, there will have to be time spent packing away anything valuable that needs to be protected. I suggest several of the more robust rooms in the West Wing would be suitable for that."

"Wait, hang on just a minute! We…?"

Continue reading
THE HOUSEKEEPER'S INVITATION TO ITALY
Cathy Williams

Available next month
www.millsandboon.co.uk

MILLS & BOON

THE HEART OF ROMANCE

A ROMANCE FOR EVERY READER

MODERN

Prepare to be swept off your feet by sophisticated, sexy and seductive heroes, in some of the world's most glamourous and romantic locations, where power and passion collide.

HISTORICAL

Escape with historical heroes from time gone by. Whether your passion is for wicked Regency Rakes, muscled Vikings or rugged Highlanders, awake the romance of the past.

MEDICAL

Set your pulse racing with dedicated, delectable doctors in the high-pressure world of medicine, where emotions run high and passion, comfort and love are the best medicine.

True Love

Celebrate true love with tender stories of heartfelt romance, from the rush of falling in love to the joy a new baby can bring, and a focus on the emotional heart of a relationship.

Desire

Indulge in secrets and scandal, intense drama and plenty of sizzling hot action with powerful and passionate heroes who have it all: wealth, status, good looks…everything but the right woman.

HEROES

Experience all the excitement of a gripping thriller, with an intense romance at its heart. Resourceful, true-to-life women and strong, fearless m face danger and desire - a killer combination!

To see which titles are coming soon, please visit

millsandboon.co.uk/nextmonth

LET'S TALK
Romance

For exclusive extracts, competitions
and special offers, find us online:

- facebook.com/millsandboon
- @MillsandBoon
- @MillsandBoonUK

Get in touch on 01413 063232

For all the latest titles coming soon, visit
millsandboon.co.uk/nextmonth

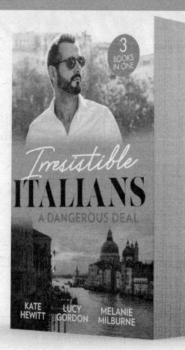